JELA KREČIČ ŽIŽEK (b. 1979) is a Slovene journalist, columnist and philosopher. She writes for *Delo*, the largest national newspaper in Slovenia, where she notably published an exclusive interview with Julian Assange in 2013. Her philosophical research focuses on films, television series, the star system and aesthetics, and she has contributed to several studies on these topics. She has co-edited a couple of anthologies, one on contemporary television series and another on Ernst Lubitsch. An anthology of writings about Lubitsch, *Lubitsch Can't Wait*, was published in English in 2014. *Ni Druge* (*None Like Her*), her literary début, was well received critically when published in Slovenia in 2015 and now appears in English for the first time.

OLIVIA HELLEWELL is a literary translator from Slovene and a doctoral researcher at the University of Nottingham. She was awarded the Rado L. Lenček prize in 2013 by the Society for Slovene Studies for her essay on translating the poetry of Dane Zajc. Her current Ph.D. research explores the sociocultural functions of translated literature in Slovenia since 1991. She has previously translated a selection of short stories, poems and literary extracts including the prize-winning 'Dry Season' by Gabriela Babnik for the European Commission's European Union Prize for Literature. *None Like Her* marks her full-length literary translation debut.

OTHER TITLES IN
THE WORLD SERIES
SLOVENIAN SEASON

Evald Flisar, *Three Loves, One Death* (translated by David Limon)
Dušan Šarotar, *Panorama* (translated by Rawley Grau)

PETER OWEN WORLD SERIES

'*The world is a book, and those who do not travel read only one page*,' wrote St Augustine. Journey with us to explore outstanding contemporary literature translated into English for the first time. Read a single book in each season – which will focus on a different country or region every time – or try all three and experience the range and diversity to be found in contemporary literature from across the globe.

Read the world – three books at a time

3 works of literature in
2 seasons each year from
1 country each season

For information on forthcoming seasons go to www.peterowen.com.

NONE LIKE HER

Jela Krečič

NONE LIKE HER

Translated from the Slovene by Olivia Hellewell

PETER OWEN
WORLD SERIES

WORLD SERIES SEASON 1: SLOVENIA

THE WORLD SERIES IS A JOINT INITIATIVE BETWEEN
PETER OWEN PUBLISHERS AND ISTROS BOOKS

Peter Owen Publishers/Istros Books
81 Ridge Road, London N8 9NP, UK

Peter Owen and Istros Books are distributed in the USA and Canada by
Independent Publishers Group/Trafalgar Square
814 North Franklin Street, Chicago, IL 60610, USA

Originally published in Slovene as *Ni druge* by Beletrina Academic Press
First English language edition published by Peter Owen/Istros Books 2016
(in collaboration with Beletrina Academic Press)

Paperback ISBN   978-0-7206-1911-9
Epub ISBN   978-0-7206-1915-7
Mobipocket ISBN   978-0-7206-1916-4
PDF ISBN   978-0-7206-1917-1

A catalogue record for this book is available from the British Library.

This book is part of the EU co-funded project 'Stories that Can Change the World'
in partnership with Beletrina Academic Press | www.beletrina.si

**Co-funded by the
Creative Europe Programme
of the European Union**

The European Commission support for the production of this publication does not constitute an
endorsement of the contents which reflects the views only of the authors, and the Commission cannot be
held responsible for any use which may be made of the information contained therein.

To Asja, for the sparkling soul,
Dubrovnik and highlighters

CONTENTS

A NOTE ON SLOVENE PRONUNCIATION

č	ch (as in church)	Nebotičnik (Nebo-teech-nik)
š	sh (as in dish)	Urša (Ursha), Gašper (Gashper)
ž	zh (as in pleasure)	Matjaž (Mat-yazh), Žale (Zha-le)
j	y (as in yellow or boy)	Jela (Ye-la), Jernej (Yer-nay)

NONE LIKE HER

'What do you know!' Matjaž retorted, looking at Aleksander reproachfully.

Matjaž, who had already lit his tenth cigarette in a row, received a blank look from his friend, who was taking in their surroundings on the Petkovšek Embankment. Once again it was packed with hordes of people, who in late August had checked back into the capital, into their small, enchanting city and their favourite bars after their holidays. Sitting around on Petkovšek Embankment was the easiest way to meet up with friends, to have a beer, and to tell stories about what had happened by the sea. If memories of these escapes to more beautiful places had already faded, they grumbled about the government, parliament, the courts, the president, or, if they had drunk enough, their work, wives and children.

Matjaž and Aleksander didn't talk to each other about their holidays, and they didn't discuss the worrying political situation, or the crisis, or how the EU had become detached from its citizens. They didn't catch up on the escapades in which they had found themselves over the past three days, since they had last seen each other in this very same place. They didn't talk about work and they didn't even ask how each other's parents were. No, they talked about the same issue that had been on the agenda every day and night for the past two months, since Matjaž had broken up with Sara. While Aleksander, despite now being a married man, was able to appreciate the crowds of girls – some younger, some older – parading past them along Petkovšek, Matjaž was seized by one single image and one single thought.

'I don't have a clue, I admit it. But how many more times?' Aleksander replied.

Matjaž was silent for a moment. 'Why is she so withdrawn around me?' he asked sulkily.

'I think she just doesn't want to hurt your feelings.'

'I don't understand – the fact that she doesn't want to meet up for a coffee is what hurts me the most.'

'She doesn't want to give you false hope. I think she still loves you, at least that's what she said.'

'When did she say that?' he asked anxiously.

'I don't know when, Matjaž,' sighed Aleksander, already tired of this same repetitive back-and-forth with his right-hand man.

'But what else did she say?' he continued restlessly.

'Oh, how many times! Nothing, that's what she said, just that she wants you to be happy.'

'Happy?' Matjaž looked like he was ready for a fight.

'Yes, happy,' nodded Aleksander, as if it were a neutral statement.

'Stupid cow! What does she mean by that, happy? I'd be happy if she was still here, with me.'

'Well, that's clearly the problem,' Aleksander replied, nervously running his fingers through his thick hair.

'Of course that's the problem.' Matjaž looked straight at him, agitated. 'If she were here, I wouldn't need to be arguing with you.'

'She can't talk to you when you're like this – that's the problem.'

'Like what?'

Aleksander considered his words before releasing them with the smoke of his cigarette, 'If you could find someone and be happy with them, like she is with Jaka . . .'

Matjaž lowered his head and fell silent momentarily. He didn't want to hear that she was happy with Jaka. He absolutely never wanted to hear that, and it was of no interest to him whatsoever.

'The Jaka thing is just a fling,' he insisted. 'I hope you realize that.' He raised his gaze towards Aleksander, who closed his eyes wearily.

'Matjaž, this is exactly the problem. You won't accept the present – well, the ongoing situation – which I agree is a difficult one. And she knows that you don't just want to go for coffee with her, you want a lot more . . .'

'A lot more. What is a lot more? A few sentences maybe, a smile of some sort, maybe a little hug,' Matjaž admitted repentantly. 'After ten years am I asking too much, if I want a little hug?'

'A fair amount of time has passed now; not a lot, I admit, but a fair amount. What would you do after that little hug?'

'I'd promise her that I'm a completely different man . . .' blurted Matjaž, full of hope.

'Which you're not . . .'

'No, OK, but I'd assure her that I'm still the same man that she fell in love with.'

'Which is the same man she clearly fell out of love with,' said Aleksander firmly.

'Don't be so harsh!' Matjaž cried.

'I'm sorry, I really don't like to see you suffering, but I think the time has come for you to move on. Maybe then she'll go for a coffee with you.'

'Did she say that to you?'

'No, of course she didn't say that, but it makes sense – only when you move forwards can you then go back,' Aleksander said reasonably.

'It doesn't make sense to me yet.'

'But you know how it is,' he said, concentrating again. 'Until you have a girlfriend of your own, until enough time has passed, there will be no grounds for a comfortable conversation.'

'Why would the conversation have to be comfortable?' Matjaž persisted. 'I like her when she's uncomfortable, too.'

'It's not about that! Until you move on, she'll always be asking herself whether you have some kind of hidden agenda, or she'll be scared that she's giving you false hope.'

'False hope is better than no hope at all! I'd sleep soundly with false hope,' protested Matjaž once more.

'It's not going to work. You're not yet separate enough to be together. That's just how it is.'

Aleksander's words gave Matjaž something to think about. If he found a new girlfriend, and stayed with her for long enough, Sara would be more relaxed around him. And that might pave the way for them to uncover their old closeness, directness and completely unique sense of humour. How he missed that humour; the new words and phrases that spring up organically between a couple and only have meaning for the two of them. Maybe if they could get back to that she would realize what she was missing. And if she was going around saying that she still loved him, that meant she was still thinking about him and probably even missed him.

Enough time had passed, a huge amount of time, more than a month – even more; two months. Quite some time. He wasn't going to wait any more. He had dedicated vast amounts of time to passing the time, had spent far too much time waiting for time to do its proverbial healing. He had given time to all of that time without any visible results. He was still sleeping badly, still thinking about her, and the thought of their break-up still turned his stomach. There was no more time. Time had run out. He had to find a way to her, and if that meant spending time with another girl then so be it. He'd better get to work. It couldn't be too hard. They always say there's plenty more fish in the sea, and Sara was always telling him how handsome and funny he was – something that was not entirely negligible in today's world. Girls like that: an attractive guy with a fiery sense of humour.

The decision did him good; his eyes lit up, and when he looked in the mirror the next morning, for once he didn't shake his head miserably. Quite the opposite: he gave himself a nod, and if he didn't know better he would swear he saw the beginnings of a smile in the corners of his mouth. A new time, a new girlfriend – it was a brilliant idea!

SAŠA

Since Matjaž and Sara had broken up, the only thing Matjaž could remember was that he had forgotten a lot. The working day was one big haze for him; voices without meaning, faces without names. He would hear himself answering questions and greeting known yet unfamiliar faces, doing a few things, but he quickly forgot about all of it. It wasn't just the alcohol, although that wasn't something he particularly resisted at the time. He had a feeling that he couldn't break through into what appeared to be life. And the more the bars filled with people in the evenings, the more the streets bustled, the more the summer lifted spirits and settled itself inside of people, the more he felt like a foreigner among the crowd, a walking corpse in the midst of a city euphoric with happiness.

He had forgotten about the time he'd spent with Jernej; watching him clear glasses at the Billiard House, pouring customers' drinks and taking their money, giving them their change and a smile in return. The mechanical repetition of the barman's movements, and those of the people on the thirsty side of the bar, had cleared his thoughts so thoroughly that he forgot even himself.

From his walks with Suzana and her dog along the bank of the Ljubljanica river he remembered the treetops, imprinted like sophisticated graphics on a fresh blue sky, the scorched grass, the coloured façades and an occasional polished antique car. Suzana held forth with her impassioned meditation on the plight of young contract workers at the national television station; his only contribution was an occasional murmur of agreement. She gently punched him on the shoulder a few times when she realized that he wasn't listening to her, or that he was indifferent towards her commitment, and he responded with forlorn laughter.

This reaction made her even more despondent and she cried, 'Oh man, listen to me! I don't know how to deal with people in distress, you know? I just don't have the knack. Why can't you just insult me like you usually do, or at least just . . . get lost? See, I don't even dare swear in front of you any more! Why don't you just go hang yourself?'

Matjaž sidestepped this awkwardness with inexpressive laughter, made the excuse that he had to go and get some milk or something, and quickly went home. He felt as if she was relieved when they said goodbye.

At first he couldn't talk about Sara, even with Aleksander. He went for lunch at Aleksander and Karla's house and just stared with bewilderment into his bowl, wondering what exactly goes on at a chemical level when a tomato is cooked and how other ingredients, like garlic and pepper, react to it. Before long, his best friend managed to tease out of him a word or two about Sara and about how he was feeling at the moment. Matjaž gradually felt his pain become just about palpable, deep in his guts. Once he started to talk about Sara, he couldn't stop. But this didn't diminish the pain in any way; it kept growing with every thought of her, every fleeting association of their life together. She persisted, he couldn't forget her, and the pain did not want to forget him.

But the Friday that followed Matjaž's latest conversation with Aleksander was different. Matjaž no longer felt so indifferent towards all of his forgetting; it even seemed amusing to him. Up until then his pain had taken away his appetite for silliness, for exploring what was left of himself after his break-up with Sara. What words, what inappropriate remarks, what kinds of sarcasm and ridiculous things would come out of his mouth if a crowd of party-hungry people were to encourage him? What would his response be like to a call from one of those people – or rather, from one of those girls?

He arrived at Orto Bar with Aleksander in a fairly good mood already, and promptly lost his friend in the crowd and forgot about him immediately. He danced around a little and then battled his way towards the bar, smiling at people in a state of pleasant obsolescence. 'Excuse me, sorry, oops,' he said as he pushed into people, standing on their toes and elbowing them as he thrust past. He let out the odd 'Move that fat arse, you stupid cow!' but fortunately the music was loud enough for his words not to really bother anybody. When he finally reached his goal, he encountered a second problem: not one barman noticed him. He waved, shouted, insulted the bar's service, but amid the crowd of other visibly thirsty individuals and the music that was blasting out, Matjaž's efforts were all to no avail. Well, almost to no avail. His gesticulations and insults were noticed by a girl, slight, with a soft look about her, leaning against the bar next to him.

'What are you staring at?' Matjaž barked at her.

'I'm staring at you because I like you,' a soft voice whispered into his ear, a voice to which he would never have attributed a message so bold and direct.

He finally pulled himself together.

'What are you drinking?'

'Vodka and orange.'

'Disgusting, but your call.' He looked back towards the barman, who now completely by chance caught his eye. He called out, 'Mate, mate, we're thirsty over here!' She'll have a vodka and orange, and a beer for me.'

'A large one?'

'Is there any other sort?' he laughed. He turned around and, with little subtlety, checked out the girl beside him, from head (short fair hair, thick make-up) to toe (clad in high heels). Her outfit was short and low-cut enough for him to make a more in-depth appraisal, too. Her appearance was not repulsive to him, but upon critical examination of her qualities he furrowed his brow.

'Why are you so horrible?' she asked as she sipped her vodka and orange.

'So that I can entertain girls like you, Mrs.'

'Don't call me Mrs.'

'Why not?'

'Because I like to think of myself as more of a Miss.'

'Fine, Mrs Miss.'

The girl looked away and smiled. 'How about you call me Saša?'

'Steady on. I'm a gentle, bashful young man,' he said, looking into his freshly acquired beer as if he were deliberating something. Then he took her by the hand and led her outside, spilling their drinks in the process, and headed over to the best-lit table. When they sat down, he asked, with a barely discernible hint of irony in his voice, 'Should we not start with something a bit more straightforward, with questions that allow us to progress on to the more demanding stuff?' He looked at her imploringly and wrinkled his forehead. 'Hang on, I'll think of a nice neutral topic . . .'

'Choose something that isn't too demanding, I'm really ignorant,' she said, going along with his game.

'Yeah, and it has to be the kind of thing that doesn't lead to conflict . . .' he deliberated.

'Just no politics, please,' she let out.

'Oh no, you're not apolitical, are you?' he tested.

'No, I just don't like politics, it doesn't interest me at all,' she affirmed ignorantly.

'Good, as long as you're not right wing,' he said, trying to rouse her anyway. He was unsuccessful. She laughed, raised her right hand and beckoned with it slightly, saying, 'No, I just write with my right hand.'

'So we can't argue about politics, even if you'd wanted to,' he reflected.

'No, definitely not, and not about art either. I don't have a clue about it. I don't have anything to say, even about the more commercial stuff. I still mix up my De Niro and Pacino, and they're meant to be classics!' she shrugged.

'Me neither, at this moment in time,' he replied, racking his brains for some interesting, unproblematic topic. 'In that case we're left with the environment,' he suggested, with hope in his eyes.

'No, I don't like nature,' she swiftly rejected.

'Me neither,' he remembered suddenly.

'I'll do as much light polluting as I like,' she added frankly.

'That makes two of us!' he said, quickly becoming enthusiastic about the idea. The two of them fell silent for a while, both absorbed in their own thoughts. She looked at him cautiously, and with a smile in the corners of her mouth she said, 'We could talk about sex.' She blushed as she said it, but it was too dim outside for anyone else to notice. Alarmed, Matjaž looked at her and said 'No no, too early for sex. We need something more subtle for our first meeting.'

'What about the weather?' suggested Saša.

'Of course, the weather, why didn't I think of that before!' Matjaž was impressed. 'And what do you think of the weather today?'

'Not bad. It could be a little bit warmer,' she replied, stroking her bare legs.

'You see, look how well we get along!' cheered Matjaž.

'Are the evenings too cold for you now, too?' continued Saša.

'No, this is ideal for me, but I'm entirely receptive to other opinions.'

'In that case I can add that I love the heat, the real crazy summer heat. I even like the summer humidity,' she continued bravely.

'Really? Come on, that seems like a rather extreme position to take,' Matjaž said, alarmed.

'Didn't you say you were open to all kinds of weather?' Saša looked at him confrontationally.

'If I'm completely honest, I'd be open to the odd drop of rain right now,' he remarked modestly.

'A drop of rain here and there never hurt anyone,' she smiled sweetly.

'That's just as well. If I put you under an umbrella, could you withstand a proper, full-on downpour too?'

'I wouldn't go as far as a downpour, the most I can stand under an umbrella is a light drizzle.'

'Drizzle's one thing, but does that mean I can't interest you in a summer storm?' Matjaž asked, testing the boundaries.

'Outside or at home?' Saša enquired.

'Wherever.'

'OK, I'll take the storm, if I'm safe and sheltered indoors. Can I take you, on the other hand, to a beautiful beach on the Dalmatian coast, midday on a lovely hot sunny day?'

'You can, if you set me up with some sort of pine forest there.'

'OK, there's always space for at least a pine tree.'

'What are your feelings on snow?' he enquired.

'No, I don't get on with snow at all,' she said decisively.

'What? You don't allow it even for a snowman?'

'All right then. One snowman, somewhere around Krvavec,' she allowed.

'I guess that means sleet won't make it through either, then,' Matjaž suggested tentatively.

'No, none. Anything remotely connected to ice does not do it for me.' She sighed matter-of-factly and took a sip of her drink.

'Not even a bit of frost around Christmas?' he asked, trying his luck.

'A centimetre of snow can fall at Christmas,' she allowed.

'I thought you said that you didn't get on well with snow?'

'I don't, but for Christmas I'm giving you a centimetre of snow,' she smiled.

'Thank you kindly. May I offer you a pleasant summer's breeze in return?'

'Be more specific. To me, wind is fundamentally unnecessary.'

'Gosh, if our weather reporters could hear you being so picky about the weather. It isn't here to be questioned, it just *is*.'

'But they'll never find out about our dream weather,' she said simply. Her point seemed an important one to Matjaž.

'Would you be happy about the wind if it was thirty-eight or forty degrees outside? Can there at least be a small breeze in the evening?'

'There can, but only enough to blow away any potential clouds.'

'Fog doesn't stand a chance then with you, then?'

'No, only if I'm looking at it from afar, from a small sunlit hill.'

'Not from Triglav?'

'Nah, I'm not a bit fan of summits.' She shrugged her lovely shoulders.

'Me neither.' They smiled and shook hands. She had a small but strong palm.

'Anticyclones are the only things that get you going, clearly,' Matjaž surmised.

'Oh, no, I'm not anti-anything. I'm very positive; as long as the cyclones go where they're wanted.'

'Like to Africa?' he asked.

'I've no idea where they need them, just as long as they don't come here.' She lowered her head in embarrassment and took a small sip, as if she were being interrogated.

'Agreed.' He thought for a while, as if trying to put two and two together, and decided that he needed further clarification. 'If I've got this right, even spring isn't quite right for you.'

'No. I think spring is really hypocritical. The afternoon can be warm, but in the evening you catch a chill,' she explained.

'I get you. What about the grey area that is May?'

'You should know by now that I don't like grey areas. I'm sorry, but to me the blossoming in May is just nature tarting around.' She pulled a face.

'No need to apologize, I'd just like to clear these things up. So for you life begins in June then.'

'Basically, yes. When the days get long enough, I'm somehow longer, too. I mean, more lively.'

'September?'

'Maybe, if I'm by the sea – far enough south, obviously. By then it's already a bit . . .' She faltered.

'Wow, you're a demanding girl. I'd rather not ask about October.'

'By then I'm slowly starting to prepare for hibernation,' she said, rubbing her hands together.

'Well, we've arrived at something!' Matjaž was happy.

'At what?' She looked at him, surprised.

'At a weather forecast.'

'Yes, but what kind?'

'Imagine: outside there's your thirty-five degrees, it's evening. You've cheered up entirely, I'm slowly dying and you take pity on me.'

'No, sorry, I don't take pity on you at all. My great-grandmother said to never take pity on a man.'

'OK, well if we're including your great-grandmother in this forecast, you can just decide that you're going to put me in a slightly better mood.'

'Are you in a bad mood?' Saša worried.

'Not really, but at thirty-five degrees in the evening I'm not at my strongest, if you know what I mean,' he concluded.

'So how do I put you in a better frame of mind, then?'

'Like this . . . you take me to an air-conditioned dance floor –'

'Oh no, I don't want air-conditioning!' she protested.

'Seriously? You won't cool things down a little bit, even for dancing?' Matjaž finished his beer.

'OK, if you want – but only a little bit. Only down to thirty degrees.'

'Thanks!' he grinned.

'And once we're on this air-conditioned dance floor?' she enquired.

'Then,' he continued, as carefully as if he were trying to salvage peace negotiations in the Middle East, 'then you spin me around, nice and slowly, and you softly wrap your arms around my shoulders, as if I were that gentle breeze that you never knew you needed until now.'

Such a weather forecast clearly appealed to Saša. She embraced him gently and placed a delicate kiss on his cheek, which slowly shifted into a longer, sunnier, almost sultry kiss on the mouth. The movement of her body made Matjaž think that anatomy might be as interesting and appealing a subject as meteorology.

When Matjaž awoke the next morning, his memory of the previous evening was not good. His hand hoped to reach for a glass of water, but instead ran into a body. 'Oops,' he thought. He looked at what he'd poked, rubbed his eyes and said out loud, 'Oops!' The girl opened her eyes and gave him a big smile.

'Kara, Lara, Anja . . .' His head was spinning.

'Good morning,' she said.

'And who are you?' He looked at her confusedly, failing to remember who this girl in his bed was, with the tousled hair and smudged lipstick.

Saša laughed. 'I'm a mirage.'

'I really have to stop drinking so much,' mumbled Matjaž.

'Why?' she asked him, still smiling.

Matjaž liked her response. 'That is not a bad answer, Mrs.' Saša blushed, smiled and snuggled up to him like a kid to a mummy goat. It was at this point that it became clear to Matjaž that he did not want her in his bed.

'What are we going to do today, Matjaž?' asked Saša, full of joy.

'Who told you my name?'

'You did.'

He closed his eyes. 'I have to start being more careful about who I tell my secrets to.'

'I'm sure you're not a secret,' she said, stroking his shoulder.

'Just ask my parents!' He looked at her seriously and ran his fingers through his hair.

'So, what are we doing today?' Saša chirped happily.

'Nothing.'

'Great, that's my favourite thing to do!'

'No, no, Mrs –' Matjaž began with a hoarse voice.

'Miss!' she interrupted him.

'So, Miss, my dear, you haven't understood. We're not going to be doing anything today, do you understand?'

'Yeah, we can both laze around,' she laughed enthusiastically.

'No, no, no. You can do nothing wherever you please, but just leave me in peace.'

'Yeah, what are you doing then?'

'That is none of your business.'

'But how can it be none of my business?' Saša retorted angrily. 'After all the fronts, seasons and dancing in testing climates that we went through yesterday, I deserve some kind of forecast for today!'

Her words slightly confused Matjaž. He had only a fleeting notion that the fronts were something weather-related, and that the weather was related to everything else that he couldn't remember.

'The forecast is like this, Miss: take yourself away on that gust of wind that brought you here.'

'I wasn't brought here by any gust of wind, are you crazy? You brought me here!'

'Mrs Miss, I'm sure that yesterday evening, or night, was unforgettable, but now I have to try to forget about it!'

'But I don't understand!' persisted Saša. 'Yesterday we got engaged in the most perfect weather!'

For a moment Matjaž considered this, then quickly continued, 'No, you see, it's exactly those kinds of things that I have to try to forget!'

'No, why would you do that? This ring, here, that you made from a ring pull and put on me, it shows that we promised ourselves to one another, and I don't intend to take it off just like that!' Saša cried desperately.

'What am I supposed to say? You can keep the ring if you like, but there won't be a wedding!'

'You're a . . . you're a . . . you're a scumbag!' she stuttered, trying to articulate her rage.

'Spot on – and a drunken scumbag at that. Now let's go! Chop chop!'

The young Saša got angrily out of bed. From the doorway, where she stood a minute later, she shouted curtly, 'And that centimetre of snow that I gave you for Christmas? I'm taking it back!'

'How did it end with the pretty blonde?' Aleksander asked Matjaž the next evening, the two men sat outside the same Petkovšek bar once again. Aleksander couldn't help but notice how the previous evening his friend had completely forgotten about him in the midst of female company.

'In bed and with an engagement,' said Matjaž, keeping it short.

'Aah!' Aleksander was impressed. 'Well done, well done. The only thing I'd say is that you might be rushing into things a bit, mate. But the girl is cute and well, pretty gifted, so I'll be the last one to judge.'

'There's no need for celebration. The engagement's off, and she's no longer in my bed.'

'But why? I don't get it!' Aleksander protested. 'How can you turn down an opportunity of such beautiful proportions?'

'I think we'd have to know each other a bit better before getting engaged,' Matjaž said soberly.

'I agree, but maybe you could have held on to her for . . . well, you know, and then weighed up whether her personality suited you.'

'I guarantee you that there was no personality there, and I am not that superficial,' Matjaž replied convincingly, reaching for his beer.

It was then that Karla arrived and sat down at their table. She gave a perfunctory kiss to her husband and turned enthusiastically towards Matjaž.

'What are you smiling at?' Matjaž asked her.

'I heard you had a wild night with a stunning blonde. So? How is she?'

'She's not.'

'What do you mean? Aleksander said that you confessed she was the woman of your dreams.'

Matjaž scratched his head, not recalling that exchange with his friend. He replied calmly, 'As I said to Saša, never trust the beer when it speaks from a man's mouth.'

'How long are you going to hide behind that beer mask?' she snapped, getting angry.

'Karla', he turned towards her and said sincerely, 'I think we both know that it is not a mask.'

'That's an easy way out,' she retorted, a little more calmly.

'Really? You think so? Why don't you try manoeuvring a girl, full of alcohol, into your bed and then driving her out again when you wake up. That is hard work!'

'You know exactly what I'm talking about,' she said impatiently. 'You're not prepared to commit!'

'Believe me, it's at the top of my agenda, but I'm not going to marry every stunning Saša that comes my way just because she can stand the summer heat.'

BRIGITA

He met Brigita on All Saints' Day. In the evening he had set out for the graveyard with his camera, looking for interesting subjects. As he lost himself among the numerous graves, the crowds slowly made their way back to the land of the living and the tranquillity of peaceful candles descended over Žale. It was then he caught sight of a girl on a bench under a tree. She was dressed in a long black leather coat, with a hat covering what seemed in the candlelight to be a heap of unruly red hair. She occasionally wound a strand of it around her finger, bringing it up towards her lips as if chewing it nervously. He noticed the cover of the book in which she was engrossed: Marx's *Capital*. It seemed a bit out of place and heavy-going to him, but he decided it was worth a photo. It could make an amusing shot, he thought to himself. He was far enough away for her to not immediately notice his activities.

As he focused on her face, he saw that he liked it. It was pale, distinguished by her severe, uneasy expression and stern features but softened by her lips. And, if he was not mistaken, by her big blue eyes too, although with the enormous amount of black eyeshadow all over them he couldn't be quite sure of the colour. Her lower lip was punctured with a piercing, a decoration repeated once more on her eyebrow. A red-haired version of Larsson's *Girl with a Dragon Tattoo*, he thought to himself, only in this case the probable tattoos were covered by her clothes. He took some time framing his close-up of this unusual beauty, but his photographic subject kept her gaze – quite an angry gaze – fixed elsewhere. Suddenly the girl stood up and shouted, 'Hey! Hey! What are you doing? What are you playing at, you pervert?'

Matjaž turned and marched away, but she caught up with him and firmly grabbed hold of his jacket.

'Well, what are you doing? Go on, delete it!'

'No, no, look, the photos are symbolic, they're for the Marx . . . you can't see you at all,' he excused himself, clumsily.

'And who are you taking those for?'

'For a newspaper.'

'Why?'

'For *Delo*.'

'I got that, I'm asking for your motive.'

'It's All Saints' Day.'

'And?'

'And we're commemorating it in the newspaper.'

'What a load of crap!' After a short pause, she continued, 'I don't care anyway, delete it. I don't want to be dragged through the papers.'

'But it's not about you, it's about Marx and the dead. That's much more interesting.' Matjaž replied, becoming somewhat more confident.

'How funny that my life makes a useful representation of death, but still no thanks. My Žale is my own, and my Marx in Žale is mine alone, too.' She was determined.

Matjaž realized that she would be a tough nut to crack. He took his camera, pressed a few buttons and gave it to her. 'Look how beautiful you are.'

The girl glanced at the photos and snorted, 'Oh piss off, will you, with your "beautiful". Delete them all!'

'But I'm convinced this is the best photo from Žale that anyone has taken today, probably ever!' Matjaž pleaded helplessly.

'Listen, moron. Once again – I am not going to be your poster girl for All Saints' Day, get it?'

'Why not? Don't you like the dead?'

'Fine, let's put it this way: given that the only people I like are those in a deceased state, I do not want to be in a newspaper for the living.'

'I'm no promoter of the afterlife, but at the same time I don't see any evidence to suggest that your deceased don't read *Delo*.'

That made her smile. They agreed to compromise between the living and the dead, and chose an image where her face was indistinguishable but where Marx could be seen clearly beside a grave.

Such reconciliations must be celebrated. And where better than the Billiard House, a haven for persecuted smokers, the living dead of this world. Matjaž quickly learned that the girl's name was Brigita and that she studied economics.

She had applied to the Faculty of Economics to study the framework of this – in her words – quasi-science, so she could find a way of implementing Marx's ideas within the world of modern economics.

While she went into more detail about her attempt to resurrect Marx within contemporary economic dogma, Matjaž devoted himself to her physique. He noticed that she had small palms with thin fingers, which returned again and again to the red hair that she wound around her fingers and released only when she reached for her tobacco to roll a cigarette. As she went on talking intently he admired her lips – not too full, but rounded enough for her words to sound out brightly, for him to find her convictions convincing and her enthusiasm authentic. He was frustrated that he was unable to better detect the fullness of her figure beneath her long black jumper, but after seeing her legs in tight black jeans as she took off her leather jacket, he was convinced that her body would not disappoint.

'You are so not listening to me,' she accused, finally becoming aware of his shallow thoughts.

'Of course I'm not. I'm far more interested in you, alive, than in Marx, dead.'

'That is the stupidest thing I've ever heard! Just because an author is dead doesn't mean that their theory isn't alive.' At this point she set out on a fairly long excursus through the basic principles of Marxism, evidencing how they were entirely relevant and useful even today by invoking concrete examples from several countries. She was particularly concerned about data on how the gap between rich and poor had expanded over the past three years, and about the privileged 'one per cent' who were already the talk of the town. Matjaž couldn't concentrate on the theory, and instead preferred to surrender himself to the alluring appearance of the quick-tempered beauty. When she had concluded her Marxist monologue, which at the end turned into a modern manifesto and a call for the unification of all precarious workers across the world, she realized that Matjaž had not been following at all and once again lost her temper.

'No, don't get me wrong,' apologized Matjaž. 'I'm a Marxist, too, it's just that – as opposed to you – I'm interested in real-life Marxist practices.' Brigita looked at him sceptically from beneath her arched eyebrows; it was clear that she did not like what her conversation partner was getting at. Still, Matjaž could not resist adding, with a teasing smile, 'I'd be interested, for example, in finding out what it's like, in practice, to kiss a girl with a pierced lip?'

'How much does that interest you?' the redhead asked calmly.

'Oh, a lot,' Matjaž replied, looking at her seductively.

'It does, does it?' she raised her voice. 'Well, you're not going to be learning about Marxist practices with me,' she shouted angrily, and stormed out.

Matjaž called out after her, saying that he was prepared to make do with just the theory, but she wasn't listening to him any more.

Luckily, not long afterwards his circle of friends appeared at the Billiard House: Aleksander, Karla and Jernej.

'Woah-ho ho, what are you doing here? Not at the graveyard?' joked Aleksander, reaching his arms out towards his friend.

'Ah, if only I were . . .' began Matjaž, as his friends pulled up their chairs.

'Why?' Aleksander worried, fearing that his friend was once again pining for his ex-girlfriend and feeling sorry for himself.

'Ah, I met a very, very beautiful girl.' Matjaž looked down.

'And?' Karla asked curiously.

'Yeah, I then promptly drove her away – see, this is her half-drunk beer right here.' Matjaž turned his head away, not best pleased with himself.

'How?' Karla was still interested.

'I told her that Marxism interested me in practice,' he replied remorsefully.

'And what the hell is that supposed to mean?' insisted Karla, raising her voice.

'Long story,' replied Matjaž.

'Finding a new woman isn't going that well for you, is it?' Jernej chimed in, bursting out laughing. Matjaž frowned at him.

'It's because he doesn't really want to get over Sara,' Karla said bluntly.

'No, I quite liked this one, I actually quite liked her,' Matjaž said quietly.

'Really?' Now Karla became serious, too.

'Yeah . . . she was so unusual, so untamed. I'm not used to those ones,' he said, starting to pour his heart out. But he was interrupted by Aleksander's burst of laughter, which his friend could barely control for long enough to splutter, 'But you're not used to any of them!'

'Thanks, man. Really, thanks. Your support is invaluable. But it doesn't matter now anyway, because she's gone. She ran away, actually . . .'

'You're exaggerating, mate!' insisted Jernej, unhappy with the seriousness of the debate. He'd come out for a beer at the end of the day, and just wanted to exchange some light, easy platitudes.

'I agree,' said Karla, surprised. 'You like her because she left. Now you can feel sorry for yourself again and complain about your cruel fate. Get lost!'

'I swear, I'd do it all again to have one more chance with her!' Matjaž said, trying to placate Karla. He wasn't sure why she was suddenly so concerned with his private life anyway.

'Don't speak too soon, the chance could come round again before you know it,' she replied prophetically.

Karla wasn't wrong. But neither did Matjaž flee in the face of this new challenge. He ran into Brigita a few days later in a bar, Respect, as she sat in the company of kindred girls and guys with badly styled clothes and hair. Matjaž peered at her between the heads of his own friends, the same line-up as at the Billiard House except that this time their friends Katja and Suzana had also joined the drinking session. Just like the rest of the group, in ten years neither of them had been able to move beyond these unproductive Friday night gatherings with the same group of friends, not even by escaping into some sort of calamitous romantic relationship.

Matjaž couldn't follow the conversation that was going on around him, and it didn't interest him anyway. He was very familiar with Katja's excessive complaining about her demanding job in PR, and it was as boring to him that evening as it had been on every Friday before then. He didn't have anything to add to Suzana's weekly political analysis this time, either, although he had to at least give her credit for her rich use of language. Her unbridled sharpness and occasional vulgarity were two things that had helped him through times of need after losing Sara. The fact that she was unable to find stable employment, and that her future was cobbled together with occasional French and English translation work for national television, did him good after the break-up. On the other hand, the late nights he spent with her then had threatened his own job; it was with Suzana that he learned to wait for sunrise at Metelkova more times than he would have liked.

He couldn't expect much from the remaining three, with whom he'd been at the Billiard House two days previously. He knew them inside out; knew what they were thinking, what they were drinking, how soon they'd order another round, what they were going to ask and how they would answer, which jokes they'd repeat and how, when and at whom they'd laugh. He was a little fed up of this same company, of the obligatory drinking repertoire, with the obligatory progression to Metelkova – regardless of the time of year, the weather and the mood of the group. He felt the only enjoyable part of the evening was his view of the lively Brigita, who knew how to relax among her friends.

'What's up with you today?' Katja asked Matjaž. 'Why so pensive?'

'I'm not pensive, I'm just admiring the prettiest girl in this place,' he said, looking at Katja seriously. That threw her a bit; she blushed, stroked her short black hair and smiled. 'Who's this beauty, then?'

'Brigita,' Matjaž retorted.

'Who?' blurted Katja, clearly a little taken aback that it wasn't her after all.

'Where? Where's Brigita?' Karla called out noisily, seizing upon the only interesting point of the wholly predictable, barely survivable evening.

'She's sat at that hipster table.' Matjaž signalled subtly with his head.

'Those aren't hipsters', Karla said knowingly, 'they're more like metalheads. There aren't that many of them these days, but it's a completely different scene to the hipsters . . .' She added that she knows young people quite well, as she's quite heavily involved with that target group at work, so she has to stay up to date.

No one wanted to point out that Karla herself fell into this category that she so studiously researched at work. Even Suzana, her best and most critical friend, put her head in her hands helplessly upon hearing that sentence.

In the meantime Karla had inspected Brigita closely, and nodded her agreement. 'She really is very beautiful.'

That sentence caught Aleksander's attention, and he took his own much less subtle look at Matjaž's chosen one. 'Wow!' he exclaimed.

Brigita could avoid the stares of Matjaž's friends no longer. Matjaž looked at her apologetically and waved cutely, only for her to look away and immediately return her attention to her friends.

'I don't think she's anything special at all,' said Katja.

'That's jealousy talking,' Suzana retorted, silencing her harshly. 'I think Matjaž falls for really good-looking girls.'

'Shame about her dress sense,' persisted Katja.

'That's exactly what I like, that she doesn't know that she's beautiful. Like it doesn't even occur to her,' Jernej said, surprising everyone with his analysis.

Up to this point no one was aware that he'd even noticed the girl, and they looked at him quizzically. 'What?' he responded. 'It's true.'

'And what are you going to do?' Karla turned to Matjaž.

'I'm not sure yet. I'm thinking about it,' he replied, as he lit another cigarette. 'Go over there and apologize to her,' Karla suggested.

'No, too risky – over there she's surrounded by her own, and she could easily pin him down,' said Suzana, thinking strategically.

'It's true, you have to ambush her,' Aleksander added. 'Like when she goes to the bathroom. Intercept her there and then pour your heart out.'

'But wait until she's done her thing, otherwise she might get irritable,' said Jernej, sharing his urological expertise.

Matjaž followed Brigita to the toilets and waited for her to come out.

'Hello there!' he said when she appeared.

'What are you doing here?' she asked curtly.

'I'm waiting for you,' said Matjaž, not mincing his words.

'I'm not sure what good that will do.' She started to walk away.

'Don't be so stuck up!'

That stopped her in her tracks. 'Do you think you're going to soften me up by insulting me?'

'Do you think you're going to soften me up with your icy ignorance?' Matjaž replied, resorting to the absurd.

'I think you're quite soft enough already,' she said, a smile appearing on her face none the less.

Matjaž, encouraged by this friendly expression, continued, 'Well then, can I ask you something?' He felt like a teenager.

'You can try,' Brigita replied, feigning indifference. 'As long as you're not going to ask about my piercings again.'

'No, I'm sorry about last time. I realize now that it was unbecoming to talk about your piercings on the first date.'

'As it would be on the second.'

'So we're agreed?' Matjaž cheered up. 'When and where your shout.'

Once again Brigita had to smile at his resourcefulness. 'OK, fine. I'll give you my email so we can arrange the details.'

'Wouldn't you rather give me your phone number?'

'Phone numbers are given on the third date. Only if the second goes well, of course . . .'

Matjaž felt pretty solid after being offered those few titbits. He returned to his friends in high spirits, taking more of an active role in the conversation but never forgetting to look round at the prettiest girl there by far. After a few beers, he chose to go home to bed, rather than feeling obligated to go along and wait for sunrise in Metelkova.

He and Brigita met a few days later in Prešeren Square, so that they could decide where to head next from there. It was a cold, dry Wednesday evening in November. She suggested that they go to the Tea House, but Matjaž confessed that a confrontation with her called for something substantially more soothing than chamomile. When she explained to him that this place did also have stronger concoctions he gave in, although he had to admit to himself and to her that he was getting old.

The change of usual location made him slightly anxious. On the way to the tea place he laid out an entire theory about how difficult it was for people to find their own crowd, but that compared to the challenge of finding your ideal local it was actually nothing. It wasn't just about the place – there were so many of those – but also the chemistry, and therefore how the clientele as a whole respected the relationship with waiting staff. In turn, the staff had to know each customer's every wish before it had even been expressed, quietly allow themselves to be insulted, and not resent it when rowdy groups of friends didn't clear out straight away late at night despite being asked many times.

He then explained to Brigita how his group once found themselves facing a trial when one part of the group (if we're being precise, Suzana's group of friends) wanted to change their 'summer residence' of Bar Petkovšek for somewhere new. After their encouragement they started to meet in Trnovo. He occasionally went there, too, surrendering to that tactless and ill-thought-out coercion, but never understood why someone should change their habits just because a few girls and boys think that there's some promise of adventure at the other end of town. For that same reason he stopped going to Trnfest. There was a considerable array of young women there, but the sacrifice of standing in a crowd and jostling towards a hard-earned beer, not to mention waiting for the toilet, had become too much for him over the years.

Matjaž's declaration clearly made an impression on Brigita as she suggested, when they had reached their destination, that maybe it would be better if they turned back towards Pekovšek, so as not to leave Matjaž with any more scars upon open wounds on what was only their second date. He was grateful for this suggestion, as in the tea place he would have felt like, well, an alcoholic in a tea place. The two of them walked back along the river towards Matjaž's preferred drinking spot.

On the way, Brigita reflected on her various stop-off points around the city. She would often end up at Maček in the evenings, if she'd had a productive enough day in the library. She headed there with friends that she had made while studying in the library. In truth they were a fairly uninspiring bunch of economists and lawyers, who were handy for recommendations of bizarre YouTube videos or new television series. In terms of films her taste differed from theirs quite considerably, while other matters of art didn't interest them in the slightest. Despite being aware of how art clings to capitalist trends and is disconnected from the working masses, Brigita was nevertheless a lover of bourgeois novels and the abstract works of Malevich, as well as a few modern artists such as Duchamp and Rothko. She also enjoyed the classics – in litera- ture she gravitated towards Dostoyevsky, and architecturally things such as the Robba Fountain made her happy, even if it was a copy. Likewise Plečnik's Triple Bridge, including the magnificent flourish of markets, seemed to her like a nice place to go for a walk.

On Saturdays she liked to meet at the square with friends. She was still living at home with her parents, who had no interest whatsoever in going into town for those kinds of rituals. They were intensely religious members of the Murgle *petite bourgeoisie*. She added quickly that she didn't like talking about her family, as their conservatism and stupidity caused her too much trauma. Her sister Sonja was the exception: she was like 'a breath of fresh air', but she had moved out and now lived and worked at the other end of Ljubljana, so wasn't around to help her out . . .

Over a beer at Petkovšek their chat became more relaxed. Matjaž was inter- ested in who her friends were, if they weren't the law and economics misfits from the library. 'Is it that scruffy lot that I saw in Respect?'

'Which scruffy lot? Just because they don't shop in Hugo Boss it doesn't mean that they don't have style,' Brigita protested.

'OK, they have style, but shit style . . .'

'I dress the same way,' she reminded him.

'Well . . . you make it work,' said Matjaž, saving himself.

In the end she explained that they were friends of hers from primary and secondary school. For years they had been getting together every Friday. Most of them studied at the Arts Faculty and they all shared similar politics. Well, a few of them fancied themselves as anarchists and they were the ones with whom she argued the most. To her, anarchism served the ideals of neoliberalism very well, as eradicating the state and abolishing regulations would make for an even freer flow of capital. She argued with her friends about this topic nearly every time they saw each other. But despite that they were still very fond of each other. Brigita admitted that she rarely had such disagreements with people – apart from perhaps her sister – as she did with those miserable Kropotkinites. She said a few more words on the subject, about how a few of them had starting going out with each other. She pondered that maybe that's not unusual, if people spend so much time together. 'The world's not as big as it often seems, especially if you're looking to be close to someone.'

Matjaž was strangely moved by that sentence, but she, not having noticed, carried on deliberating. Time and proximity could bring about feelings that were never there before, she added, as if in a dream. Of course, Matjaž was interested to know if she had ever formed such attachments with people who were clearly her closest friends, but Brigita clarified that she had never got close to any of the guys. They had given her clear signals at various concerts in Rog, and they'd also made hints at club nights in Gala Hala, but every time it came to that dangerous proximity, she felt like something was too much or not enough; too familiar and too strange at the same time.

Even though they got on well and had a good time that evening, neither Matjaž nor Brigita had felt the need to share their most intimate thoughts with each other. However, by the time they were eventually kicked out of Petkovšek, they both wanted to invest further in their new closeness. Brigita took Matjaž's hand and said, 'So . . .'

'So, what?' Matjaž looked at her fondly.

'Maybe it's time we do something about my piercing, as it intrigues you so much.'

'Really, like what?' Matjaž smiled and let the red-haired girl press her lips against his. The kiss was slow and he liked it. He liked it so much that he invited Brigita back for a glass of whisky.

'As much as I like the idea, I think we ought to go for a few more beers before we jump ahead to the whisky.'

'Aha', Matjaž said, somewhat disappointed, 'but only if you bring your piercing with you.'

'I rarely take it out!' she consoled him.

'You're torturing me,' he groaned, as he imagined her naked with her intimate jewels. She smiled at him nicely. 'And there's something else you still owe me, too!'

'What's that?'

'Your phone number.'

'No, that'll come next time,' she said, so assuredly that Matjaž didn't push it.

He set off home without even realizing that all night he hadn't given a single thought to his ten-year relationship with Sara.

'You're in love,' Aleksander affirmed. He looked searchingly at his best friend's face as he put some crisps into a bowl.

'I'm not in love; I'm intrigued,' Matjaž replied, making himself comfortable on his sofa, in front of the television. The football experts in the studio were already opining on the Spanish league, on the strongest and most expensive players, on goals at home and away, on the advantages of both of these, on the significance of home turf and the right tactics for the away team. The ball being round was also an important factor, or, rather, it was all about the leather being spherical. Even better, they expressed that irrefutable, although unwritten, rule of football: that you never lose a game if the opponent doesn't score.

'Because she didn't want to go for a whisky?' Aleksander asked, refocusing his attention.

'Because she's got style, because she does things her way.' Matjaž chose his words carefully.

'You're such a player, jeez,' jibed Aleksander. 'Of course you're intrigued, but are you interested in the girl or just her 'decorations', as you stupidly call them?'

'Not sure about that yet. I get the impression that she's quite a challenge.'

'What woman isn't?'

'I know, but at my age a man has to think long and hard before he decides whether a young woman is worth all of that effort.'

'I can see already that your efforts won't bear any fruit!'

'No, no, my friend, don't be so pessimistic . . . it'll soon become clear where we're at. We're meeting up on Friday, and then, if it goes as well as last time, I get her phone number . . .'

'You mean she hasn't given it to you yet? How do you communicate then?'

'Gmail.'

'She really has set the pace.'

'Yes, and it's *andante*,' quipped Matjaž.

'No wonder you're intrigued. But I'm still worried about what happens when you finally get her phone number.'

'She promised me that maybe then she'll come over for a whisky.'

'Please tell me that whisky means . . .' Aleksander sighed, impatiently.

'Yes, it does,' smiled Matjaž.

'Fucking *andante*. Now even I'm nervous.'

'No need to be. I have a very, very good feeling about Brigita,' he said, reassuring his friend.

'I wouldn't get too carried away with those feelings of yours. Just remember your poker-playing days.'

'Oh that!' Matjaž waved his arm dismissively. 'We're both still here, alive and well.'

To that Aleksander gave only a knowing cough, reached for the crisps and his beer, and turned up the volume on the television. What was one girl in comparison with *El Clásico* between Barcelona and Real?

For their next date, Matjaž went with Brigita to the Kolosej cinema. The film was crap, but it gave Brigita the perfect cue to discuss all the problems with Hollywood. There was a time when they still made good films there, even under the pressure to make profits, but they just didn't know how to any more. Matjaž told her that she sounded like his grandma, to which she answered that his grandma was clearly a very intelligent young lady. Matjaž replied that he couldn't agree with that; sure, maybe she was young, but she had certainly never been a lady. Brigita persevered: OK, she was just intelligent then, but Matjaž protested that time, too. He replied diplomatically to Brigita's question as to whether he agreed with what she had said about Hollywood, saying that the Kolosej never did its films any favours: it was smelly, dirty, scruffy and anyone could see that it might collapse like a house of cards at any moment.

He suggested that they go and console themselves at a similarly smelly, dirty and scruffy place – McDonald's. To his surprise, Brigita happily agreed, as if the bad film had given her an appetite. When he asked whether she was bothered by the capitalist reputation of this mega-corporation, she replied that at least the issues with it were obvious and out in the open.

So they sat for some time over two small cheeseburgers and a large fries, musing over this and that. They set themselves the task of finding crucial lapses in the McDonald's experience and devised ways in which to redeem them. They both agreed, for example, that the fries needed to be cooked in seriously hot oil, and to be taken out and served straight away; otherwise they lost their crispiness. Brigita felt that the taste of the ketchup was too artificial, but that was where they fell out; Matjaž believed the very essence of McDonald's was its artificiality – it was naturally fake. It became apparent that each of them would save this company in completely different ways (of course, the fact that the company was doing fine without their interventions didn't bother either of them). Brigita would take a naturalizing approach, using the best-quality ingredients possible, whereas Matjaž would go for an even greater use of chemicals and replace the already artificial foundations of the food with even faker ones. Brigita analysed his theory with suspicion, while Matjaž only smiled at her apologetically.

When they'd had enough of saving the culinary world, they arrived at Brigita's favourite topic: art in the context of its historical conditions. She told him about how during the fifties the CIA had supported American modern artists, including her beloved Pollock, as part of their Cold War strategy to expand the USA's influence in the world. She spiced up the story with a fact about how the American intelligence agency swayed between Pollock and her other favourite, Rothko, but in the end settled upon Pollock because he was more established and behaved like a cowboy. Matjaž expressed his regret that the secret service had not taken an interest in his own photography. It bothered Brigita slightly that he didn't care if his art were used in order to further specific political propaganda. Matjaž replied that an artist did not always have the luxury of being able to adhere to her Marxist ideals. When he saw Brigita's somewhat disheartened expression, he said, 'You know I only say things like that to wind you up.'

'I know, yes. But I don't see what's so funny about it.'

'I think that comes from your tendency towards antagonism,' he tried to explain gently.

'I'm sorry?'

'You know, when you draw attention to all this antagonism in the world, I'm longing be some kind of antagonist for you.'

'Sorry, what?' She was not going to be convinced.

'Isn't it kind of beautiful, if the two of us are one big antagonism together? And then we create some kind of beautiful dialectical love?' Matjaž said, entangling himself.

'I don't know, maybe it's beautiful, but at the same time it's seriously tiresome.'

'I did think that you were definitely too young for all this antagonism.'

She looked at him seriously. 'How can you be so indifferent? Do you have any idea what they did to Haiti?'

'Something bad?' he smiled.

'Yes, they stifled one of the most authentic revolutions of the nineteenth century. Then, in true colonial style, the French still demanded debt repayments when there had been freedom and independence there for years, as if they still hadn't taken enough from that subjugated country.' She paused briefly, then added, 'Antagonism really is tiring with you! You're so uneducated.'

'Well, then enlighten me,' he implored her.

'Didn't you say I was too young?' she said to provoke him.

'Oh believe me, you can't be younger than I am, and as you correctly identify I'm in serious need of an education.'

'Don't take the piss!'

'Why not?'

'Because I'm very sensitive,' she added, this time without a jokey or impatient tone. A glance at this strange and vulnerable warrior softened Matjaž, making him stop in the middle of the car park to kiss her.

'Oh, not here, not in public . . .' She pulled away and looked at the floor, blushing.

'Do you mean to say that you're ready for that whisky now?'

'Not just yet,' she smiled. 'You have, however, despite your shameless provocation, earned my phone number.'

*

'I don't understand what all of this antagonism between the two of you is all about, at all,' Aleksander smirked as he hung out the washing.

'Antagonism is what happens when you are here keeping house while Karla is out getting wasted with her workmates. That is antagonism between the sexes.'

'I know, because all of my joints are hurting after changing the sheets today,' moaned Aleksander.

'That's it, aching joints are also a form of antagonism,' smiled Matjaž.

'And what do you do about it?'

'How should I know, I hardly ever do housework. Ask your wife. She's got to do something for you, too.'

'Don't be unfair, you know full well that she sometimes helps me with the cooking,' said Aleksander, sticking up for Karla.

'Let's get back to my problem.'

'Antagonism, right.'

'In any case, I don't understand why she shrinks away like that. It comes to the point where we get close, and then she pulls away.'

'We used to call that being shy,' theorized Aleksander.

'Stop joking about it. Does it seem normal to you that she doesn't want to drink whisky, even after the third date?'

'Nothing about you two seems normal to me. How could it, when you go looking for girls in graveyards?' Aleksander replied, becoming slightly irritated.

'You know full well that I wasn't looking for her. I just found her there.'

'Same thing. I don't know why you're worrying about it, though. You got her phone number, and in my book that means that she's opened the door.'

'Opened the whisky, you mean?'

'Fifth time lucky, or will it be sixth?' he said to himself as he got ready for his next date with Brigita. They met at the café at the Ethnographic Museum, where smokers had the honour of outside heaters and blankets and were protected from the wind by a plastic shelter.

This time she seemed more nicely dressed and made-up, which confirmed his suspicions that this would be the evening for stiff drinks. They started, of course, with something more innocent – a beer – and dedicated some conversation to this light beverage.

'Last year, when I had terrible gastritis, I felt awful all the time – even though I was drinking tea, eating carefully and not smoking, not to mention taking all those tablets – and beer saved me.'

'I know, when you're hungover and –'

'No, seriously,' she interrupted him. 'It was the first time in half a year that I felt a sense of huge relief. The fog cleared, the darkness lifted –'

'Are you sure that it actually lifted?' he observed doubtfully, looking at her pretty but very black outfit.

'You never take me seriously!' she complained.

'Rubbish. At this moment there's nothing I take more seriously than you.'

'Really?' she asked softly.

He nodded, preoccupied trying to look as it he were thinking seriously. He knew it was the only way he would earn a bit of sweetness. Then he steadied his palms and softly stroked her hair as he kissed her.

When their lips softly parted, they fell silent for a while and then lit their cigarettes at almost exactly the same moment.

'We never talk about love,' observed Brigita, without any kind of explicit undertone.

'I completely disagree. Last time we talked about food, today about beer . . . You talk to me about Marx. As far as I'm concerned, love is the only thing we talk about,' he remarked playfully.

'No, I don't mean that kind of love. You never ask me about my past,' Brigita said.

'If there's anything you'd like to talk to me about, I offer you all the ears I have,' he replied encouragingly.

'But then I don't ask you either', she added, as if anticipating his answer, 'because I've got a feeling you don't want to talk about it.'

'Just ask!'

'OK, what happened with your ex-girlfriend?'

The question threw Matjaž but he very quickly returned a smile. 'I don't want to talk about that.'

'You see . . . you're impossible!'

'I'm sorry,' he began seriously. 'I just don't understand what the fact that I once had a girl that I loved has to do with the two of us. It's in the past, where I no longer am; neither is she, and that's how it should be,' he said with self-assurance.

'I know I'm taking this too far, but it's always seemed to me that love isn't just when you love someone now and in the past, but also onwards and for ever. In that sense love is eternal – because you love somebody past and future, before you're even together.'

'Young lady, you seem to be talking as if you are on the brink of love yourself,' he said, wanting to somehow ease the gravity of her words.

'But that's exactly what I'm doubting, because neither of us have any interest in falling for our past selves, only from now onwards.'

'Maybe we just want to start from zero,' he said cautiously.

'It's impossible to start from zero,' she replied irritably.

'And you're supposed to be some kind of revolutionary!'

'Revolution's got nothing to do with it,' she said, looking down.

'Of course it has, revolution counts its own time, a new time for love!' Matjaž finished grandiosely.

They drank and smoked a bit more, and told each other childhood stories. Matjaž found out, among other things, that Brigita was a very clumsy child who by some miracle had never sustained a serious injury, while her older and much daintier sister was a frequent visitor to A&E. The funniest thing was that Brigita was jealous of the plaster cast that her sister got for her broken arm – it seemed so chic and fancy to her to have a plaster cast on which children could leave drawings and messages such as 'Ana was here'. Brigita learned that Matjaž was a very calm little boy, endlessly stuck in books and with no wish to play with other children his age – so much so that his parents took him to see a psychiatrist when he was seven years old. It was the psychiatrist who established that the boy was very bright and had fairly stupid parents, although he didn't tell them that in quite so many words. He promised them that puberty would do its work, and it really did – and some more. It contributed to such changes in Matjaž that for a time his secondary-school-educated parents started seeing councillors and psychiatrists themselves.

'And? How did it all work out?'

'As you see now. I grew into a quite handsome and exceedingly honourable young man.' Brigita burst out laughing. 'And your parents?' she enquired.

'They didn't come off so well. They separated, and each one regularly sees a therapist.'

'Do you know what?' she asked, as she lit a cigarette decisively.

'What?' he looked at her dreamily.

'I'm thinking that today I'd go for . . . for a whisky. But I'm not sure –'

'O, revolution!' he interrupted her, with an over-enthusiastic smile. 'I'm not sure if whisky helps with gastritis, but if you don't have gastritis it definitely can't hurt.'

The improvised quip clearly worked. They quickly settled the bill and headed to Matjaž's place.

They hadn't even touched the whisky when they started kissing more clumsily and Matjaž began to stroke Brigita all over her body. As he did, she started flinching and smiling.

'What is it?'

'Nothing, I'm just ticklish,' she said, embarrassed.

Matjaž tried again, this time more passionately and enthusiastically. It was clear that Brigita had surrendered herself to his caresses, but the giggles kept escaping from her. Despite this, Matjaž had somehow succeeded in removing her long jumper so she was now just in her bra. As he went to undo it, she pulled back with a start. He looked at her questioningly, and when no words came out of her mouth he said softly, 'Maybe we should chat a bit more.'

She nodded ashamedly, and they sat silently drinking whisky. It seemed to Matjaž that time was dragging on and that he'd no longer be steaming ahead on his previously imagined trajectory. After a few difficult minutes of silence Brigita said, 'I thought it would work . . . you know, because I like you. And because you're one of the rare good guys and silly and funny . . .'

'But,' Matjaž came to her aid, looking at her, shaken.

'But I think I'm a lesbian,' she sighed, covering her face with her hands.

He looked at her calmly. 'No big deal, I don't have anything against lesbians.'

'I know, it's just with men . . . I just can't.'

'What a coincidence! Nor me!' he said, trying to ease the situation.

She laughed. They drank whisky. Matjaž asked her if she thought that she'd ever be able to try whisky with him again. She replied that she could try, but that it probably wouldn't change anything.

'But what about all those conversations that we haven't got caught up in yet?' he asked her.

'We can always squabble, Matjaž . . .' she said, looking at him with a clear, sad expression that unsettled him. 'But I got the impression that you only accept what women have to say on the proviso that the words will at some point dry up and be replaced by something else . . . and I understand that.'

'You are quite correct in saying that,' Matjaž said, deep in thought. He looked away. Then he didn't know what to say. He thought that he saw tears in her eyes, but before he could wipe away the first she quickly got dressed and murmured a goodbye.

'A lesbian?' Aleksander was confounded when he met up with Matjaž in the near-deserted Sunday billiard hall.

'Yes, a pure-blooded lesbian,' confirmed Matjaž, tilting his glass.

'Maybe she just didn't like you, but didn't want to admit it,' Aleksander tried to console him.

'Yeah true, it hurts a lot less if you just tell a guy you're a lesbian,' Matjaž said ironically.

'OK, well what's the answer then? Are you sure you didn't do anything to put her off?' Aleksander was absorbed in thought.

'Are you trying to say that she became a lesbian because of me? Thanks very much. That's just what every man on the trail of new love needs to hear,' he replied sarcastically.

'Well, nothing unusual can be ruled out as far as you're concerned,' Aleksander began to apologize.

'I was under the impression that that might sometimes be to my advantage, especially with this last one.'

Aleksander thought for a moment, and said, 'I wouldn't bet on that.'

'And you tell me this now, when she's already a lesbian!' Matjaž said, getting offended.

'Maybe she'll get tired of it at some point,' suggested Aleksander in a conciliatory tone.

'Well, I don't intend to hang around waiting in the meantime,' he said with a roguish smile.

POKER QUEENS ON NEW YEAR'S EVE

Katja

How was it possible to cram fifty people into thirty square metres? That was the question occupying Matjaž's mind on New Year's Eve. At a small kitchen table he sat observing the guests at Suzana's New Year's Eve party, who were showing visible signs of enthusiasm over the fact that one unit of time was coming to an end and another was beginning – as if this carried some deeper existential meaning besides a banal certitude of the calendar year. As if there were something magic in the figure 00:00, which proclaimed the last day of December – or rather the first day of January.

He knew a few people at the party; some of them even used to be his close friends, once upon a time. Of those he was seeing for the first time, he wondered whether Suzana really knew them, or if she had generously invited them over while in one of her enraptured states at Metelkova, and now pretended to remember the first-class dialogue over beers that had bound them for life.

He was smoking his cigarette, and just at the moment when he could easily have become melancholic, as the shy snowflakes began to scatter outside and he remembered the previous New Year's Eve spent at home with Sara watching all of the *Die Hard* films, Katja sat down beside him. For a few seconds they stared together into the night, which was perforated with increasingly aggressive snowflakes. Then the round-faced young woman with short dark hair and dark eyes could hold her tongue no more. 'What are you thinking about?'

'What's it to you?' blurted Matjaž, as if she'd awoken him from a pleasant dream.

'All right, sorry!' she said, looking at the floor and making Matjaž feel a bit sorry for her. 'I thought we were friends.'

'We are, hence why I can snap back at you so politely,' he said, trying to comfort her. A minute later he was already regretting his compassion. She started lecturing him on friendship, on years of building relationships, on the meaning of those years and of the people who stand by you even when you're at your lowest point.

Her monologue concluded even more melodramatically, 'Friends are important, Matjaž. You don't realize that. Why are you pushing me away when I'm trying so desperately to help you?'

He looked at her in astonishment and, gathering all the honesty he could, said, 'My dear friend, on no account must you make such an effort, OK? Maybe it's time you accept that it's a lost cause.'

'How can you say something like that? I'll never give up on you!' she said emphatically, clearly oblivious to his indifference.

'Oh my God,' muttered Matjaž, to himself more than anyone else. He then looked deeply into her eyes. 'Katja, I'll do anything, really, I'll be nice, kind, but please just don't try to help me!'

Katja burst out laughing, thinking he was trying to be funny. Before she had a chance to say that he could never stop her enduring friendship and kindness, he excused himself to go and get another beer. 'But the beer you've got is still full!'

'OK, well then I'll get a beer for you . . .' he replied.

'But I don't drink beer,' she called after him, but he pretended not to hear.

He was surprised to catch sight of Gašper on the balcony. They'd been friends at secondary school, best friends actually, and together they had got up to all sorts of possible and impossible mischief. It was with Gašper's help that Matjaž had driven his parents to seek psychiatric help, with him that he tried weed for the first time and they both nearly choked. Together they discovered the bars on Poljanska Street, next to their school, and tallied up an inexcusable number of hours watching and teasing girls. From the girls' reactions they judged who was witty or convincing enough in their anger to earn a place in their gang, and in this way they accumulated a varied group of boys and girls – among whom were Sara and Katja. Their gang of friends focused on the 'research of life' – as they called their lack of interest in the curriculum – and Gašper and Matjaž dictated what kinds of stupidity took place during break times, and in more intensive forms over the weekend.

They went skiing together during the holidays, and sometimes to the seaside, too. They'd pretend to be studying together while they were actually playing Nintendo. Even ten years ago they were completely inseparable; in the first year of uni they'd meet for a beer after lectures in Žmavc – until it turned out, of course, that attending university was a completely superfluous chore amid the rest of student life. Every day the two of them would dissect the insignificant details of their everyday lives – in good health or ill, alone or in a group, when they felt like it and even when they didn't. Occasionally this conversation would be peppered with analyses of socio-political situations at home and abroad – if only to show how far they had come after only a few months of studying. In doing so they failed to notice how they still made fun of girls, just like at school, and how they still enjoyed putting them to the test – to see if they were resilient enough, had a good enough sense of humour, or were at least quick-tempered enough for them to be worth engaging with in further dialogue.

They shared the same taste in clothes, watches, games and films. Back then they even shared girls most of the time; they would realize time and time again that their friendship was worth more than long legs and cleavage. Matjaž couldn't exactly remember when all of that came to an end. When career goals became a priority over an afternoon beer, when girls became more important than playing games, and when their taste in films started to differ so markedly that they stopped going to the cinema together. As always – just like with the Beatles, he thought – women were to blame. Although he conceded, for the first time, the women who rouse that masculine core are indeed more valuable than the Beatles.

'How are you doing, Gašper?' Matjaž greeted him eventually, when he'd awoken from his flashback.

'Whatever mate, you're no friend of mine,' he snapped, taking a deep drag of marijuana into his lungs. 'You haven't called me in about a hundred years.

That's not friendship, you get me? Friends call each other, call each other at least once week, mate, they don't wait until New Year to tap you on the shoulder.'

'What about you, mate, don't you have a phone?' Matjaž snapped back at him.

'You know what I'm talking about . . .' said Gašper, in a more conciliatory tone.

'I'm not sure if you know, but I've been really down and out for quite a while,' Matjaž said, realizing that Gašper's silence during his most difficult time had obviously hurt him.

'Yeah, well then, especially mate, especially then!' his friend smirked.

'You mean I could always easily slot myself in somewhere during your lunch break or at the end of the working day, just before you have to run off to put your daughter to bed at seven?'

'You've no idea what it means to be a mate!' said Gašper, blowing smoke into the cold night.

'Not least how much time and energy it takes to work in the best, biggest, most prestigious law firm in Ljubljana,' Matjaž added with obvious sarcasm.

Gašper didn't notice his friend's jibe at first, and just affirmed, 'Exactly mate, exactly!' A second later he registered it and continued defensively, 'But I'll tell you something. They're really sound. It's a lot of work and all, and at the start I still had to study like mad to keep up with the work, but when they see that you're a hard worker and they know that clients like you, then they also know how to reward you. That's how it is, mate. Honest work for honest money.'

'Hmm, aren't you specialists in tax avoidance for the rich, in how to transfer assets abroad . . .'

'Where did you hear that?' Gašper asked indignantly. 'We simply take care of foreign investments.'

'And of course that involves the investment of capital in foreign banks – for example, Swiss banks.'

'Oh no, no mate. We don't work with Europe at all any more, it's too – risky,' his friend corrected him.

'Well, the main thing is it's an honest salary,' Matjaž said ironically, already somewhat weary of the stoned Gašper and baffled about what happened to the person with whom he shared the most formative years of his life.

'Honest, honest!' he heard him say again, after he'd set off towards the throng of partygoers.

*

When he got back to the small kitchen table Katja was still sitting there. She was propping up her head with her hands and looked rather down.

'What's up with you, girl, does nobody like you?' Matjaž said jokingly, but his words had the opposite effect to the one he'd expected; she began to cry, to sob in fact. He looked around for help – someone like Suzana who could take control and calm her down – but at that moment she was dancing with some curly-haired hipster and was oblivious to her surroundings, so he had to help his friend himself. He tenderly gave Katja a hug.

'Hey, come on, it's not so bad. I'm here!' he said, patting her clumsily on the shoulder.

'Yeah, but you've come back without the beer you promised,' she complained.

'Oh I see, there's too much blood in your alcohol. I'll take care of that immediately,' he said, and swiftly took a beer out of the fridge for her. His eagerness to be a good friend calmed her down somewhat. She wiped her tears away and blew her nose, then opened her beer and sipped it in silence.

'Is that better now?' Matjaž asked her.

'Yes, it is,' she said quietly. Completely out of character, Matjaž thought.

Again they fell silent, but then Katja starting talking, now in her usual piercing voice, 'Matjaž, you have no idea how cruel you are, especially to those who love you.'

'Oh I know that all right, don't worry,' he laughed wickedly.

'But it hurts people!' she said, now looking up at him with her sad expression.

In a reconciliatory tone he said, 'Katja, my dear friend, we have known each other long enough to know that the only reason we're friends is because neither of us has ever had to change and we can carry on being harsh towards one another when we feel like it.'

'But I don't know if that's good for me,' she said, sniffling.

'I can understand if my coarseness is a bit much for you, but I'm not demanding that you love me or put up with me,' Matjaž kept on.

Katja was deep in thought. Tears came to her eyes once again but she held them back. She looked up and the pain in her expression almost melted him. 'I know, maybe that's what hurts. But not just that . . . ever since you broke up with that . . . that . . . cow, who clearly had no idea what she had, it seems you've become even more ruthless. That you're even more shameless and arrogant and on the path to self-destruction.'

'But maybe Sara was just a period in the middle of my ruthlessness, maybe that's just how I am, maybe that's all that's in me.'

'I won't accept that!' Katja raised her voice.

'Why not? Because life seems a little less meaningless to you if you can tame the beast, if you can make his pain go away? That's nice, Katja, I'll give you that. It's entirely nice and kind, but also totally misguided. If I say that I don't need someone to save me, I'm being entirely serious, without any kind of self-pity. Everyone has their own way of dealing with things when they find themselves in chaos, either internally or externally. First and foremost I do not want to become the pet project of some woman hopelessly searching for a sense of order and meaning in her life.'

Even he was surprised at the words that came out of his mouth, which he washed down with beer as they were still reverberating in mid-air. Katja pondered, and then said, 'But I just can't accept that the world is meaningless, like you say, and that there is no meaning to human existence. Everyone is here for a reason!' Clearly she was unsettled by Matjaž's spontaneous ontological outburst.

'I don't think this is the right environment for a teleological debate, although admittedly I'm not sure I'd be capable of leading one even in the right environment.' With this last statement he laughed a little, but Katja looked at him seriously. He had to continue, 'I can't pretend to be disillusioned by my recognition of the emptiness and meaningless of life, of my existence or yours – you know me too well for that. But there's also a big, fat lie in all the gloating over the meaninglessness of everything – that I admit, too. I just think that people should be honest about what they are. And in my case there is no point pretending; I know that most of the time, and in most of the things that I do, with most of the fleeting relationships I have, I am completely nothing. Don't look at me so suspiciously. Just because you're doubting me doesn't make it any less true. It's a huge relief, because things and people can't disappoint me, because I know what I am – or rather, what I'm not.'

Katja gave him a piercing look. He could see the surprise in her gaze; she wasn't used to such long sentences coming from him. In fact, she only ever remembered him making one-line jokes.

'But you didn't feel like shit with her, with her you felt like you were something more,' she eventually said.

'No, I wouldn't say that. It was more that with her, in us, I, uh, how to say this, I escaped myself. I don't know if this makes sense but I was happy that

I was completely submerged in a relationship and not alone with myself so much,' Matjaž said, once again surprising himself on this New Year's Eve. He wiped his sweaty forehead. 'Now please, can we leave this? Look what you've done to me. Soon I'll be starting to suspect that I'm not a complete idiot after all. And that would be fatal for my self-confidence!'

He was trying to be funny, but Katja had once again started to cry. 'I'm just such a nobody! My existence is so stupid, so meaningless, so pointless. And I can't handle it that nobody likes me! I can't go on like this any more!' Now Matjaž was surprised. Such a genuine, totally honest Katja wasn't recognizable to him. To him she was just a chatty airhead, incapable of any kind of self-reflection, full of handy but utterly meaningless clichés for every occasion. Looking at her reddened cheeks and smudged mascara, something stirred in him. He stepped towards her and hugged her tightly. At first she resisted, but then relented. Just at that point Suzana, no doubt ironically but also with the intention of offending most of her rock- and metal-loving guests, put on Bon Jovi's 'Always'. Matjaž, who wouldn't normally pretend that he knew the way to a woman's heart, at that moment felt his humanitarian calling. He took Katja by the hand and led her to the cramped and improvised dance floor. Her head was lowered, but she didn't resist. At first they were both awkward and reserved. Then they laughed at their clumsy moves. 'You never did know how to dance,' she laughed at him.

'Don't tempt me, I can stop at any time!'

She pulled him towards her and held him in an embrace. 'No, this dance is mine!' She did it so decisively that he indulged her, shrugged his shoulders as if to say OK, as you wish, and the two of them continued in their clumsiness. At first they made fun of each other and their own ineptitude, but at some point they gave in to their ridiculous movements, their unskilled bodies, and made the dance floor their own, letting themselves go. They received quite a few disapproving looks, especially as they flew all over the place into other dancers, but Matjaž simply responded to their irritation by sticking out his tongue. He couldn't have reacted to their annoyance any differently, because in that totally inept physical shifting of two untalented people, a very tender moment of friendship emerged.

Saša

The dance was clearly therapeutic for Katja, as afterwards she could be seen chatting with strangers with her old enthusiasm and appetite for life. He noticed with some concern that it was only eleven and the present company was already getting out of control. This was certainly not helped by the drinking game being led by Suzana and five friends. Nor did it help that the others had turned the music up even louder and were increasingly losing it. He looked around, familiar faces everywhere, people euphoric from alcohol and God knows what else. Gašper was chatting with some curly redheaded women that Matjaž didn't recognize. She had a pretty freckled face hiding beneath her lively mane. What a shame, he thought to himself, that this beauty had fallen into the clutches of such an idiot, even if only for one night. Maybe redheads go for each other. Until this point he'd never considered them a minority, probably feeling uncomfortable in their own skin – especially if their ginger hair was accompanied by pale skin, freckles and perhaps yellowed teeth, too.

When he stepped on to the balcony for a bit of fresh air, his thoughts wandered to Aleksander. He was slightly angry at him for taking Karla to the seaside on New Year's Eve. He hoped that it was colder there than it was in Ljubljana, that the wind was blowing a gale, that the heating wasn't working, that there was no hot water and that they were drinking tea all evening just to keep warm. Aleksander's text had tried to convince him of the opposite, that they were having a nice time in their small apartment in Rovinj as they could smoke there, and what shame it was that he didn't go with them but no doubt he will meet some babe on NYE if Suzana's hospitality meant anything in this world . . . What a shame, Matjaž thought ironically, that he wasn't down in Istria being a third wheel. He replied saying that there were several babes at the party, but that he was in no mood for the chase and he was dedicating the evening to humanitarian activity. That sentence was sure to confuse Aleksander. It was Katja he had in mind, although he didn't know that his humanitarian activity was not yet over for the evening.

Saša stepped on to the balcony.

'All alone, are we?' she asked, offering an ambiguous smile.

'What?' said Matjaž, as if she'd awoken him from a trance. 'Where did you come from? I thought you'd be somewhere warm,' he said, almost with relief, after he eventually recognized the familiar face now framed by a light-coloured bob. It took him just a few seconds to remember Orto Bar, the embarrassing morning with engagement rings made out of ring pulls, and the minor quarrel between the newly engaged couple about weather forecasts, all right before they eventually split up.

'You only just remembered, you scoundrel . . .' She looked at him scornfully, and without waiting for a response she carried on, comfortably enough. 'What do I know? At first we were out and about, then Šeki – my *boyfriend* (she said this with particular emphasis) – got Suzana's invite and we decided to spend the evening with company,' Saša said, almost with pride.

'Šeki, I see! Didn't take you long to forget about your fiancée, did it . . .' Matjaž retorted, throwing in a little ironic scorn.

'Me? You were the one who cruelly dashed all of my hopes, all my appreciation for the seasons!' Saša exclaimed. Šeki, who had clearly noticed the animated movements of his charming girlfriend, moved towards them. Matjaž was afraid that the skinny guy with long dreads and squinted eyes was going to burst into a fit of jealousy, but as he approached them he just offered out his limp hand and introduced himself. Then they stood in silence for several long seconds.

'Nice hair,' Matjaž said finally, bothered somewhat by the awkward silence.

'Thanks,' Šeki said, gently tugging at one of his dreads.

'Do they take a lot of looking after?' Matjaž asked, trying to make conversation with this new acquaintance.

'Not at all!' Saša joined in, explaining. 'That's the idea, that you don't wash them.'

'For a long, long time,' added Šeki proudly.

'You don't wash them for a really, really long time and they just somehow fuse together. Well, maybe you help them along a bit so they're evenly spaced around your head . . .' Saša explained with great enthusiasm.

'You don't help them along at all, what are you on about! Patience, super-human patience, mate – that's the secret.' Šeki became animated, obviously proud of the long-term effort that he'd invested in his distinguished hairstyle.

'Sorry, babe, you know what I meant,' replied Saša with a fearful respect, blushing.

'Pft.' Šeki waved his hand, as if teaching idiots about the cleanliness of hair was just too much for him, and walked over to some other people.

'Congratulations, you seem like a very happy couple,' Matjaž said to Saša, once again with a hint of scepticism, as she looked over towards her boyfriend miserably.

'I know what you're doing. I know what you're trying to do. You're sharp and sarcastic, because you're desperate yourself, you're down and out and you can't bear to see others happy! But everything's great with Šeki, really good, get it? Never been better, for your information!' Saša said, getting angry and leaving the balcony. Matjaž watched and saw that she couldn't hold back her tears before she got to the bathroom. What an evening, he thought to himself. An evening when he'd driven girls to tears and was then almost sorry for his own unkindness.

He smoked and looked around at what was going on inside. Saša came back from the bathroom red-faced and looking upset. She looked around for Šeki and noticed that he was talking with a guy. Matjaž realized that Gašper and Šeki had clearly found some common ground in terms of weed – at least that's how it looked, as the two of them showed each other small bags with green contents and talked at great length. He imagined them discussing the origin of this noble grass, its source and quality. Saša went up to the two guys and tenderly put her arms around Šeki's waist, but he ignored her. When she tried to include herself in the conversation he avoided her at first, turning his back on her as if he hadn't noticed her. It confused her. Anger and tears welled up in her eyes; she was on the verge of running straight back to the bathroom. Matjaž put out his half-smoked cigarette, let out a deep breath, shook his head and stepped in from the balcony. He stood in front of Saša and said, loud enough for Šeki, Gašper and everyone else to hear, 'Oh there you are! Where did you go, I was looking for you!' He yelled so loudly that he almost drowned out the music. Saša looked at him, trembling, and finally said in a low voice, 'Stop messing about Matjaž, I'm really not in the mood!' Matjaž took her by the arm to a small inconspicuous sofa where there was just about enough room for two behinds.

'Are you crazy? Are you completely messed up?' she berated him, with fear in her voice.

'So what if you've got a boyfriend,' he continued loudly, as if he hadn't heard her. 'He doesn't deserve you!' Matjaž kept looking over towards Šeki, to see if he had noticed his efforts.

Confused by Matjaž's behaviour, Saša said, 'I'll be the one to decide who deserves me and who doesn't – or, more importantly, what I deserve myself. And I'm convinced that I don't deserve you on New Year's Eve.' She started to get up, but he pulled her back down forcefully.

He moved in towards her face, making her think that he was going to kiss her, but just whispered, 'Listen, your Šeki is no good, believe me. I've spent enough time with myself to know what it means to be a bad guy. If you keep letting him walk all over you, he's just going to hurt you even more. My advice? Leave him!'

'But I love him!' The words surged out of her almost too loudly. That somewhat complicates the situation, thought Matjaž.

'OK, well, on the other hand, if you act a bit more hard to get and look more open to respectable options around you, then he might start to squirm. Do you understand?'

Saša had calmed down now and was nodding obediently. Then she bowed her head, as if lost in her thoughts. Matjaž gently touched her chin, lifting her head, and said, 'Speak, woman!'

'I know you're right,' she started slowly. 'This is my problem. When I fall in love, I immediately give my all. I don't have any reserves – as you well know. And then one by one, everyone starts acting towards me like . . . well, you know, how you did. And with you I had a feeling that we could have a great future,' she added.

'OK, now I see that intuition isn't your best friend either,' he replied concernedly.

'Don't make fun of me, I'm aware that I have no control over my own feelings.'

'OK, but tell me. How did you end up with him? True, you're not exactly a rocket scientist yourself, but to me, he seems a bit . . . simple.'

'But he's not! He's not thick. Šeki reads a lot, and he writes, too,' she protested. 'He's going to go to uni. To study philosophy and sociology. Sometimes he writes poetry. When he was still in love with me, he wrote poems for me. So beautiful, you know! I know one of them by heart. I can recite it to you . . .'

'Woah no, not that, please. I've suffered enough this evening.'

'Fine.' Saša lowered her head, sniffling like a little mouse. 'Anyway, on the inside he's really kind and warm. It's only in a group that he acts like a closet intellectual. To me it's weird, but I try to respect him.'

'And what's wrong with that?'

'What's wrong is that I think he's losing interest in me. I just don't interest him enough any more. I'm too dumb.'

'Don't be so hard on yourself. You still have a nice figure, which you dress up extremely well.' Matjaž failed to console her as he gazed at her long legs in fishnet tights, barely covered by a short red dress.

'But as we both well know, men get tired of women's bodies if there's nothing else to offer. So I started reading. That Deluze, or whatever you call him, who Šeki loves so much, and that Fullcoat, or however you pronounce it . . . but I don't understand anything! It's all Greek to me. Then I read some poetry and I ran into a similar problem. I'm stupid, and men treat me that way.'

'Enough now. I'm not going to listen to you putting yourself down like this. Do you think that Šeki understands Deleuze and Foucault? Do you think he gets it all? There's a lot of bluffing going on there, probably all of it. Maybe Šeki does write nice poems, but so what! Maybe he likes to read, but so what! If he knew anything at all, and especially if he understood anything at all, he'd know how to look after his girl. Don't ever be taken in by male superiority – there are usually small, frightened souls hiding behind that arrogance.'

'But what does that make me, if I can't even impress one of those losers?' Saša complained, in a moment of realization. She looked at Matjaž, distressed.

'Well, you're a young girl who hasn't had much luck in her choice of partners. Don't beat yourself up over it. You'll find someone yet, you just need to show a little more self-confidence. You're a great girl and there aren't many of those around.'

'But I want Šeki!' whined Saša.

'You want Šeki now, but maybe by tomorrow some Fleki will have popped up.'

'You're so cynical! What if this love is meant to be?' she appealed.

'Look, I'm really not a cynic. I just know how many stupid things a woman will do out of the need for someone to love her. She quickly confuses happiness over the fact that someone finally likes her for her own genuine admiration for that person. Just think about how quickly you got engaged to a complete idiot like me.'

Saša thought for a moment, then she smiled and said in a conciliatory tone, 'You're not a total idiot.'

'Thanks very much,' Matjaž laughed, and the two of them took each other's hands. At that moment Šeki started walking towards them, looking jealously towards Matjaž.

'If you're interested in hairstyles, you can come and have a quiet word with me,' he began curtly.

'Oh no, mate, Saša and I are talking about love,' Matjaž said, turning towards him nonchalantly.

'About love?' Šeki raised his voice, and was clearly unaccustomed to such bold tones coming from his own mouth.

'Yeah, you know, about when a man falls in love with a woman, and when a woman falls in love with a man,' Matjaž answered, just as relaxed as before, casting glances at Saša.

'It wasn't quite like that,' a frightened Saša interrupted. Šeki signalled with his hand that it was now his turn to speak.

'Listen, poor curly boy, I'm the only one that talks to my girl about love. Is that clear? There's a whole range of birds here for you to talk about love with, and I'll keep right out of your way –'

'But we were just talking!' interrupted Matjaž.

'Just talking!' Šeki let out a breath and snorted in disgust. 'Talking – as if love exists beyond words!' He was offended by Matjaž's ignorance. 'Come on, darling, let the two of us go and have a little debate about love ourselves now.' He offered his hand out to Saša, pulled her towards him, hugged her and took her away. As the two of them walked away, Saša looked back towards Matjaž, smiled at him and winked.

Maria

When Matjaž went to the bathroom, after having done his Good Samaritan deed, he felt a woman's hand give his palm a firm squeeze. He turned around to see the beautiful redhead, who had the smiling face of someone who has the impression that they know you. His mind filled with scenes from Metelkova in summer, autumn scenes from the Billiard House and Orto Bar, scenes from Respect, scenes from work. Then from secondary school and, just in case, from primary school, as far back as his memory served him. He sifted through memories of summer holidays, winter festivities, camping madness, and then in the end he even tried to envision all of the neighbours and acquaintances from travelling he'd known in his lifetime. All without success. Meanwhile they were already hugging like friends and exchanging small talk.

Before Matjaž could even speak, the beautiful girl was already jabbering away in full swing. It hadn't been five minutes and he had found out that she was studying in the USA – at Duke, to be precise. With that she smiled significantly and drew breath, 'Ivy League and all that.' She was very happy there. She'd decided to study comparative literature – *complit*, as they called it. It was really expensive to study there, but she'd got a scholarship. Those experiences were priceless; she really recommended studying abroad – if possible, of course. The professors were a lot more serious there than they were here, they were available to students all the time; for them it was about really educating their students. The downside was that it was a lot of work, but it was satisfying. And in comparison to what she'd experienced here, the professors really dedicated themselves to your work. Oh yes, she'd already said that, ha ha. At Duke the professors marked you harshly, of course, which could be damaging to your ego – 'We're not all native speakers, are we?' – but, she continued, that actually helped when you were young, to shape you as a thinker, as a figure, as a person; the kind of person, a human, that really lived within society. 'Do you see what I mean?'

Before Matjaž got the opportunity to explain that there had been a misunderstanding and they didn't in fact know each other, she beat him to it once again. She'd give anything to be able to stay in the USA, for postgrad study too, maybe even get a Ph.D. there, and Professor Jenkins – or was it Professor Jameson? She always got those two mixed up, ha ha – who she really got on with said to her that maybe then he could even supervise her. But for her to be able to afford that she'd need a job. 'I don't know what exactly, maybe I could do some tutoring . . .' She thought for a moment. At this point Matjaž wanted to run away, but he didn't manage it. Her small, dainty hand held on to his shoulder and she was now starting to feel quite heavy. The redhead then threw in how she would have to, if she applied to do a Ph.D. with Professor Jenkins – 'or is it Jameson, oh dear, I've clearly drunk too much, ha ha' – publish something, in some serious journal, or even better a book, but a book was no mean feat, especially over there, although not just there, the competition was immense. Thousands of young doctoral graduates were just waiting for their opportunity. Yeah, sometimes she loses confidence in herself, but Professor Jenkins (or Jameson?) was so helpful, supportive. But again, you just couldn't imagine how many intelligent, really intelligent and talented people tried to make it, and who was she – especially being a foreigner — to really succeed. 'But Professor Jenkins, Jameson, oh, it doesn't matter . . .' The more she spoke, the less attractive she seemed to Matjaž. He saw pretentiousness in her curls, stupidity in her freckles, vanity in her smile, and in her gestures – argh!

'Who even are you?' he interrupted her in the middle of her prattle.

'Stop messing with me, Zoran!'

'Interesting. I'm not Zoran,' he said coldly.

The girl burst out laughing at the top of her voice, 'That is so typical of you – you see that I'm not wearing my glasses, and straight away you're taking the piss.'

'Glasses?' Matjaž was surprised.

'Very good, Zoki, very good. Only how can you be sure that I don't have my contacts in?' she smiled at him, as if she couldn't be fooled so easily.

'Because you seem to think I'm Zoki,' he replied calmly.

'Ha ha, very funny. Well if you're not Zoki, then why did you listen to me for such a long time?'

'I was just asking myself the same question,' he let slip.

'Well, get you, all superior!' she said, becoming irritated. 'You know so many people, so many acquaintances, so many pretty birds, so much of all that, that of course you can't remember Maria among it all.'

'Nice to meet you, Maria,' he said, extending his hand. He then headed to the bathroom, but her beseeching voice intercepted him.

'It's Matjaž, isn't it? There's no need to leave now, when we're just getting to know each other.'

'When then, if not right now?' he asked, without a trace of guilt on his face, and once again he tried to step aside. Her hand became more determined.

'If I thought you were Zoki it means you must really look like him and that's why I like the look of you so much. Stay here,' she said suggestively, her blue eyes sparkling. Fine, thought Matjaž. This would be the last good deed of the day – he'd give this annoying girl one more chance. At the end of the day she was a very pretty redhead, and if he was being honest with himself it seemed that he owed it not just to himself, but to the whole of mankind, to test out a few stereotypes about this ginger species.

'So then, Maria,' he said. She laughed, took him by the hand and led him to the kitchen, which was now the quietest corner in this flat of celebrations. They sat at the table and were silent for a while. Matjaž went first. 'So it seems your future looks pretty promising now,' he said, saying the first thing that came into his head and regretting it immediately.

'Well, we'll see. You know how it is with these things,' she said, acted modest.

'What else are you into, apart from studying?' he quickly threw in, and he shuddered under his own unbelievable lack of soul.

'Travelling!'

'Oh, travelling,' he sighed wearily. He looked up towards the ceiling, and asked for Maria not to start explaining about all of the places she'd ever been to. But as he was looking pleadingly upwards, she'd already set off on her travels. First they visited India, which impressed her not only with its exoticism and cuisine but also with its friendly people who were in touch, so in touch, with life, with the land, with nature. Then they went on a small tour of the Asian continent, first to the south, to the islands of Indonesia. In Thailand they enjoyed the excellent food and shook off stereotypes about excessive prostitution. That's just Thailand, prostitution is a part of their culture, what can you do – who were they to judge another culture, Maria mused. With that, Matjaž looked up to the ceiling once more, looking for a sign of hope. Then followed Vietnam, Cambodia, where the people were a little more reserved, a bit more rigid, maybe . . . Or could that have been her distorted perception, as it was right there she was poisoned and got diarrhoea. It happened in a village. She lay there helpless for several days, while the villagers brought the shaman to her. And a miracle. Then she recovered, and the journey to Japan didn't take too much out of her. But she was not going to be lost for words about Japan. It was clean, beautiful, and organized . . . with a subtlety towards everything that was beautiful. Their gardens were simply divine and who couldn't admire the beauty of bonsai trees?

'People who force trees stay small are just torturing them,' Matjaž remarked, but Maria wasn't listening to him.

They worked through Europe quite quickly, just long enough for Maria to study French in Paris and German in Berlin, and then in Barcelona – she already knew Spanish from secondary school ('It's so worth it, investing in languages – it's invaluable!') – to go on a course to become a tour guide in South America. And they were on their way again. Peru, Chile, Uruguay and Paraguay, Argentina and to Colombia, Brazil and finally Mexico. Maria couldn't speak highly enough of South America, where the countries and people differed so much, but were at the same time so similar. They were the lands of open hearts, temperamental men and extremely white teeth. The infinite passion that flowed from their food and music just belonged in South America. Every night was full of life and joy. 'You've only got to think about tango. Can you dance the tango?' She didn't wait for his reply. Obviously she'd learned to dance the tango in Buenos Aires, she could show him – it wasn't actually that difficult, even for beginners, the basic step was really simple. How many great, friendly people she had met at tango lessons, how many beautiful, forthright men had seduced her on the dance floor – with such fire, with such charm. Oh, Buenos Aires!

Matjaž started to sweat in torment. He feared these travels would never end. He feared North America, Canada, he feared Australia. He wanted to go back home, he wanted to go back, back, back to Suzana's flat, to the New Year's Eve party. Any moment now it would be midnight, and he still had two entire continents to discover and – heaven forbid – Central America. For a minute he thought that Maria was getting restless, that in her travelling stupor she was going to jump from one of the earth's poles to the other. He could see no way out. For now they were staying in Mexico. 'I simply just adore Mexico,' he heard her tell him, dreamily. 'Little villages with friendly people – it was unforgettable. Spectacular nature, I could have started writing a novel there. Really, it's a completely different world to the big cities there. They're dreadful places, you know. Did you know, that by number of kidnappings, ninety per cent of which end in rape, Mexico ranks highest in the world?'

'Interesting,' smiled Matjaž.

'If I think about the danger I was in some nights – on some significant enough road in Ciudad de Mexico, right by one of the main roads, what do you call it now . . .' She thought for a second.

Matjaž came to her rescue. 'Did they mug you?'

'Yes they did, yeah,' she said, with hurt in her voice.

'Did they rape you?'

'No,' she shook her head.

'Some people, hey,' he said seriously. Then he stood up and left, so he didn't have to wait for the appalled look on her face.

Suzana

Midnight was behind them and Matjaž was visibly relieved. He wrote a nice text to Aleksander, saying he hoped that he and Karla would be able to meet up with their best, most handsome friend as much as possible. 'We don't know anyone like that,' Aleksander replied.

He thought to himself – this year will be my year. Last year was not his year. Not from any angle could last year be considered his year, and he was happy to see the back of it. But this year would in many ways be mostly the same . . . he'd try to smoke as many cigarettes as he felt like and drink even more beer, he thought. It shouldn't be too hard now. He'd meet many more stupid girls, and if they happened to be very persistent and dedicated, who knows . . . Maybe he'd be taking Sara for a coffee once more. That's it! This year he'd take Sara for a coffee. Perhaps, if everything went well, for a beer, too, and maybe, no, he mustn't get his hopes up, maybe even to dinner. That would be nice: a dinner, although not necessarily a proper dinner, they could just go for a *burek*, or a sandwich, a salad, olives, peanuts . . . whatever. He shuddered at that thought and looked around. The drinking-game team was still very lively, although somewhat diminished, and the clear winner in terms of alcohol consumption was Suzana. Saša was kissing Šeki in the corner, who meanwhile had his eye on a girl who was flicking through an environmental magazine. Well, that relationship wouldn't last long.

Katja, Gašper and a few others were rolling a fresh joint and eagerly debating bars in Ljubljana – how Bar Žmavc was now ruined because of all the unruly teenagers, how much better Daktari was, how Metelkova had had its day and the only reason it was still going was because it was open until the early hours of the morning. Although only if you were lucky, of course, as Katja pointed out.

Matjaž looked at his phone. The New Year messages were flooding in, even from those people whose numbers he'd lost long ago. Suzana came over to him and gave him a kiss on the cheek. She had clearly grown tired of her little crowd; either that or they were all exhausted. She was no longer paying attention to the volume or the quality of the music; she'd left the playlist in the hands of anyone who felt like winding up the nervous guests and the neighbours, who were surely ready to complain at any moment. After all, just because it was New Year's Eve did not mean the whingers and whiners on duty had any reason to stop now.

'Anything interesting?' asked Suzana, when she noticed that Matjaž had his phone in his hand.

'Loads of people writing something along the lines of "Happy New Year" ... Is today some sort of special day? Maybe you know something about this?'

Suzana smiled, looked at him through squinted eyes, offered out her hand, and with a suggestive smile said, 'Come and dance with me. This is our song.'

Matjaž heard the opening chords of 'November Rain', looked at Suzana and said, 'Since when did we have our own song? And if we do, who in God's name decided on 'November Rain'?'

'Ah you're such a pedant. From now on, this will be our song.'

'Why are you punishing me like this? What did I do to you? Or do you have no musical shame?' Before he could finish his insult, she was already dragging him to a small space in among the other dancers and winding herself around him. He tried to help her with this but was unsuccessful; she had placed her soft hands around his neck and started to sway her hips, which had some interesting effects upon Matjaž. He looked around, then said to himself, sod it, and let go. They danced and danced, spun around. Suzana looked at him adoringly and said something that to Matjaž sounded like, 'Can't you see how good we are together?' Fortunately the music sufficiently stifled the romantic charge of her words, and there was still enough alcohol at the party to ensure that one of them would forget such declarations, which were always something of a threat to the preservation of friendship.

When Matjaž next opened his eyes, still standing in Suzana's embrace and pressed against her swaying hips, it was six in the morning and most people had gone. Some random was dozing on the sofa and Katja had fallen asleep in the bath. Gašper was just heading home.

'Mate!' he called out, launching his body on to him in a hug. 'So good to see you again! We must, really must, do it again soon. I'll give you a call tomorrow, we'll go for coffee!' He was full of enthusiasm.

Matjaž just smiled and nodded. 'Course, mate!'

Suzana was more hot-tempered. 'No, stay a bit longer . . .'

'Suzana, I'm tired, I can't . . . the kids and all that, you know how it is,' he said as he opened the door and quickly ran down the steps. Suzana and Matjaž watched him leave, closed the door and sat down on the dusty carpet.

'What now?' Matjaž asked.

'We're going to sleep.'

'To sleep?'

'Yes, I'm sure you're familiar with that human habit. You get undressed, lie on a bed in a horizontal position, cover yourself with a duvet, close your eyes and then – yayyy – you're already away!'

'But . . .'

'No buts. Just come.'

She took hold of his hand and led him to her small bedroom. She undressed him carefully, making sure that he was thoroughly covered with kisses. 'This is how to start a New Year,' he thought to himself, but aloud he said, 'This is not going to end well.'

Suzana continued her indiscreet activity. Things became heated and Matjaž began to return her kisses. He laid her down on the bed and, with all the tenderness available to a man after hours of drinking, he entered her. Freely she gave herself to him, and he moved into her willing vagina. He closed his eyes and enjoyed the repetitive rhythm of sex. He had never imagined that Suzana's body could bring him so much pleasure. She had always been a friend, always just . . . He surrendered himself to the love-making, and at certain points it felt as if he were falling into a trance with the repeating movements of pleasure. Until, that is, he was stuck by a resounding 'Snnnhhhhrrrr' that had not come from him. He opened his eyes, looked beneath him and saw Suzana, who was peacefully snoring with a smile on her face.

'With friends like these . . .' he thought to himself, and decided that not even Aleksander would get to hear about this episode.

STELA

It was one of those evenings where everything came together: when the waitresses at the Billiard House were friendly, when Jernej told new jokes, when Aleksander preferred to gossip rather than discuss politics and Karla didn't pull him up on it, when the beer slipped easily down your throat and every cigarette agreed with you. It was what Matjaž called a good Friday. Such Fridays always like to turn into early Saturdays. So when the Billiard House closed, the most dedicated of the night-time enthusiasts had to do something about which they wouldn't be so enthusiastic the next day. Call it a last cry of youth, hope, faith in destiny or even just alcoholism, but they had to go on. And so they went: Jernej, Aleksander, Matjaž and Karla, to Metelkova. At this time of year, in January, there were not exactly a lot of familiar faces. Even Suzana had decided to spend the evening at home with Katja and a few friends, where it was warm. Matjaž dreaded the thought of such a claustrophobic evening, the sort much preferred by women, where they share their feelings with no scruples at all and slag off men.

No, the youth were reigning over Metelkova at this time. The same youth who believed Friday evening was the definitive entrance to a parallel universe, where school and parents faded into the background and where they started to live their own lives, with people their own age. They drank how they wanted, they loved who they wanted and they debated new trends they'd seen on social media. They complained about how quick adults were to write them off as the generation that lived and existed only online without aspiring to anything else, while they nevertheless felt – and were aware of feeling – its presence everywhere, constantly, including within all of their thoughts. Yet for these unfortunate inhabitants of Metelkova, for whom fate had dealt the humiliation of currently existing in the interspace between being young and being adult, they had to at some point say goodbye to those rare moments of freedom and take the last bus, or an early taxi, to join their family – who didn't even notice from the look of their faces on Saturday morning that they had arrived home a little more experienced in word and deed the night before.

If the age of mortals was determined by the time they left Metelkova, that night Aleksander would have been a typical teenager, too. He was ordered by Karla to go bed, right away, as he really was no longer even a shadow of his former self. On the other hand, Matjaž and Jernej decided that as definite shadows of their former selves they were grown up enough – or childish enough – to hang around in Metelkova. They roamed around practically everywhere that was still open within the maze-like complex, and with each new unit of alcohol in the different bars – Jalli Jalli, Gromka, Mariča – they got the feeling that somehow they hadn't quite found what they were searching for. This probably had something to do with the fact that they had nothing left to say to each other and they saw each other as a unwelcome reminder of where an otherwise solid Friday night out could lead.

Jernej eventually decided that he would find the meaning of his existence at home, asleep. Yet Matjaž was somehow still unwilling to accept that the evening was drawing to a close, and he decided to persevere. As such, without knowing how or why, he ended up in another one of Metelkova's bars. It didn't take long for him to work out, although he was tipsy and far too optimistic, that the atmosphere in this place had livened up. His drink was good. The music was loud, full of dynamic energy – just the sort he needed right now to keep him awake . . . As he took a brief glance around the room, he was happy to see that the club was incredibly diverse. Students, old tramps, roguish youths with chiselled bodies, pretty girls on the lookout, and full-blooded mature women getting annoyed at any old thing – a long queue at the bar, let's say – but that's just one of many unpleasant consequences of women knowing what they want.

If he tried really hard to focus through the overcrowded space of dancing bodies he could just catch sight of a very attractive young woman with dark skin and black wavy hair, a delicate figure and a pretty smile. He watched her, he watched her for quite a while; and for once, all of a sudden, luck was on his side. Even in his semi-conscious state he didn't have to approach her – she just walked straight up to him and said, 'Stela'.

'Stela, as in *A Streetcar Named Desire*. Nice,' he said with a stutter, as he felt the firm touch of her hand. She didn't hear his remark over the loud music; either that, or she just pretended not to. She was wearing a skin-tight red dress that, even though it concealed her cleavage, was much more generous in its long split up to the thigh, which revealed lovely smooth legs. Her face seemed unusually large, but then again every aspect of her was tall and elongated. This pretty girl with big, brown, searching eyes smiled at him, and all broke loose within him.

The words 'So what are you doing here?' came out of his mouth.

'Celebrating,' she replied with a secretive smile.

'Oh, happy birthday! How many springs, autumns, summers do you have behind you?'

'Oh it's not my b'day. I'm celebrating Friday,' she said, coyly stroking her hair.

'Is it a special Friday?' He had to make an effort to concentrate.

'Every Friday's special for those who work, and then new faces and new challenges await them here.' With that she blushed and looked down.

'Friday!' Matjaž said, almost shrieking. 'It's true, Friday really is a big cause for celebration. I'd say I'm one of its most devout worshippers and admirers, so congratulations once again!'

They clinked glasses, he with his pint of Laško and she with her cocktail of unknown extraction. Matjaž felt the urge to make some grandiose statement about Friday, to celebrate the fact that it stands at the end of the week, therefore before the weekend. Then he thought he'd rather celebrate the fact that Friday gets so many young, lively people out on the ground, making Ljubljana almost seem like a capital city. All that eagerness to think exhausted him, then he remembered that it was Saturday, the papers were printed, the market was practically open already . . . he lost his train of thought, and Stela was still looking at him expectantly. When he made no sound, she eventually said, 'And what's your name?' He decided that he wasn't going to judge her personality on her rather unusual voice. This time he was going to focus on what was important, get to the heart of it. So he took a chance on a more challenging, provocative answer, which would demand an unambiguous, meaningful reaction.

'What would you like me to be called?' he smiled, teasing.

'Wow, some people have brought too much testosterone into this place,' she jibed, casting him a well-meaning smile.

'Why? Are you looking for some?' Matjaž laughed gormlessly.

'Why? Are you offering some?' She looked at him defiantly from beneath her eyebrows.

'Maybe. What are you offering in return?' he asked, pretending to be secretive and leaning clumsily at the bar.

'Something similar. It depends if you're going to tell me what your name is.' She winked at him. And he was confused.

'What has that go to do with testosterone?' he enquired.

'You wouldn't believe!' she jibed in her high-pitched voice, which wasn't entirely repulsive to Matjaž.

'Fine, my name is Elvis, Elvis Presley,' he finally said.

Stela shook her head, dissatisfied. He furrowed his brows, racked his brains and gave in to associations. 'Buddy Holly,' he tried, but a look of reluctance settled on her face.

'Bond, James Bond,' he tried a reliable name once again, but she just coolly shook her head, now clearly unimpressed with his lack of imagination. He thought for a while and then fired back again:

'Bill Gates!' He hoped that money would count for something with this girl, but she merely responded with an appalled 'Eugh!' Which he thought was adorable.

'Bill Clinton,' he tried, convinced that she wouldn't be able to resist an American president, but she wearily rolled her eyes. He sensed he was losing her attention.

He shrugged his shoulders, once again falling into his own confused thoughts, and then half out of desperation said, 'Louis Armstrong.'

That name was the key to her demanding heart. She said, not without elegance, 'I've never been able to resist a black man.'

'And why would you resist?' He looked deep into her eyes and spun her around.

Matjaž didn't really know how they had ended up on a lone bench in Metelkova. But he was glad that Stela didn't want to waste time chatting. He was quite tired from the long night out and he feared that excessive deliberation would drain his motivation for action – or motivAction, as the life coach Smiljan Mori had once beautifully coined. So they familiarized themselves with one another through kisses, gentle caresses and more. Perhaps because of this fervent passion, neither of them noticed that it was actually incredibly cold and that there was not a living soul around. At some point Matjaž realized that he was capable of exposing a world of wild and passionate love in this girl. Her occasional gasps of 'Louis, Louis!' and her deep breathing seemed like some of the most feverish Matjaž had experienced with recent women of note. He invited her home. They didn't have much to say on the way there, but he did notice that she stroked his hair while they were walking, and every now and again said, 'Oh, what beautiful curls!' At the time he wasn't too concerned that Stela probably wasn't marriage material; he just knew that he found her relaxed naïvety and her genuine youthfulness completely disarming.

When they arrived back at his place, they poured themselves a glass of wine each and sat on the sofa. All the while her long legs and slender, exceedingly slender, elegant ankles maintained their connection with his feet. Her pretty head looked around the flat and she complimented the rug, the odd neglected bunch of flowers, the pictures and the soft lighting. Perhaps out of discretion, she didn't note the dust on any of these objects. Meanwhile the gentle caressing of each other's extremities soon led to another frantic embrace, so frantic that it made Matjaž think, in his still-foggy head, that he had never been kissed so forcefully, so decisively, by any girl. He started to stroke her hair, and then when she started to kiss him even more ardently, almost aggressively, his grip became stronger too. He pulled her hair, making her head tilt back. She unbuttoned his trousers and had already seized his masculine asset with her hand – she did it so meticulously and so attentively at the same time that he started to shudder with desire. How long it had been since he had surrendered himself like this, surrendered to these measures so completely that he heard his own gasps of pleasure. Stela aroused him with her motions, and when she touched his pride with her lips he thought he was going to explode. In a rush of passion he grasped her hair sharply, forcefully, roughly, and she released a piercing shriek. As the shriek faded away, he saw a bouquet lying in his hands . . . not a bouquet – a wig! Matjaž shrieked himself and looked at his bald-headed lover. Stela, Stela . . . He was momentarily paralysed by his realization. Then, a few seconds later, he said stoically, 'Well, so here we are.'

'Where?' a masculine voice asked him.

'Well, there, where else,' said Matjaž, now slightly confused again.

'But what has changed? I'm still me,' said his lover who never was.

'That's debateable,' said Matjaž, and sat beside her.

'Oh, you men . . . you only judge on appearances, that's your problem!' said Stela, becoming rather feminine once more.

'And you women, I mean, men – whatever – it's all a performance to you!'

'That's not true!' said Stela hysterically, with tears welling up in her eyes.

'It is true!' Matjaž said, with the same hysteria.

'But you should have known, you were in a club called Tiffany!' she protested.

Matjaž clutched at his hair. 'Oops, I clearly missed that fact. But anyway, normal girls go there too,' added Matjaž.

'But I'm not a normal girl,' she sighed, clasping her hands in torment.

'Me neither, and therein lies the problem!' said Matjaž, attempting to compete with Stela's strange logic.

'And what's wrong with that, are you really that macho?' She looked at him, hurt.

'Oh, no, no, no. I'm not having that! Just because I like fanny, no woman – or man – is going to make me out to be a misogynist.'

'But are you as rude to fannies as you are to me?'

'Even ruder!' Matjaž blurted out resolutely.

'Well, then you're even more of a misogynist!' Stela lost her temper.

'Yes, that's probably true,' he said, lost in thought.

'Well, I'm not actually offended now that I know you're a misogynist. You just prefer fannies,' Stela said, wiping away her tears.

'A pity,' Matjaž said quietly.

'Why is it a pity?' Her big, bright eyes turned towards him.

'Because you're pretty, because you have really good legs, a woman's legs.'

'I know, right?' giggled Stela, stroking her face as if wanting to emphasize her other features, and stroking her slender extremities, too, just in case. 'And what now?' she asked him, a little bit frightened.

'Hmm, I don't know, when I come face to face with a woman like this, I mean, with you . . .'

'With a penis,' interrupted Stela, with a playful look on her face.

'Erm, no,' Matjaž laughed. 'There'll be none of that – of the two penises thing.'

'Ah,' said Stela, wiping away her tears with a hanky when they started to roll down her cheeks again. 'Well then, I'd better go,' she said, a little offended, and started to gather her things, including her wig.

*

Matjaž was overcome by a feeling that he was not entirely used to. He felt sorry for Stela. Really sorry. With her bald, shaved head, her long eyelashes that combined with the tears on her cheeks to leave black traces of mascara on her flawless complexion, and oh, those soft ankles at the end of those skilful legs. And that was without even thinking about those lovely heels.

'Well, maybe we can watch a few episodes of *Seinfeld* together, then go to sleep – but without any kind of you-know-what.'

A wide grin flooded over her face. 'That would be great. I'm knackered, though, completely knackered . . . I don't know if I . . .'

'Pst!' said Matjaž. 'Drop any ideas of romance!'

Stela simply nodded, knowingly.

'But when you wake up', and here Matjaž's tone was almost fatherly, 'you have to go home. OK?'

'OK,' she confirmed obediently. She went quiet for a while, as if battling with her thoughts, and then eventually asked, 'Can we be friends on Facebook?'

'Ahem,' Matjaž coughed. 'Firstly I should say that no woman has made me feel like you did tonight, not for a very long time. But wouldn't it be more romantic, more in keeping with all the passion of this evening, if we parted without the need for letters and Facebook contacts? And you know what, "*We'll always have Tiffany!*"'

It didn't take long for this conclusion to satisfy Stela; she felt as if she were in a movie. They both stretched out on the sofa to watch the television. Their eyes slowly began to close as they watched, and with their arms around each other they fell asleep.

'What? You slept with a man?' shrieked Aleksander, who could not get his head around the idea. There was not a single soul in Bar Činkole. Even the barman had sneaked off somewhere, so on that Sunday afternoon it was just the two of them sat there, around a welcome heater, with a coffee.

'No, we just slept. Together,' Matjaž said frankly.

'And after that?' Aleksander persisted, still overwhelmed.

'Ah, after that. Why can't women be more like Stela? She went to the shop, prepared breakfast with croissants, orange juice and coffee and everything. She even brought me the papers; *Delo* and *Dnevnik* for me, and a copy of *The Lady* for herself. Isn't she a gem?' Matjaž smiled at the thought of his morning. 'We ate croissants and read. We chatted a bit about the papers. I read her the editorial in the Saturday supplement, she filled me in on celebrity gossip – did you know that Scarlett had a baby? Or is it that she's going to have another – I forgot, but anyway, it's not important.' The sour look on Aleksander's face signalled that not only was the celebrity gossip too much for him, he refused to accept that it was of interest to his best friend either. He wiped his perspiring forehead, and Matjaž carried on, 'We talked about cosmetic surgery. Stela thinks about it, she's completely obsessed with it, but I warned her against it because she really doesn't need it. You should see her skin, those animated eyes. Surgery – as if!' Matjaž waved his hand in a manner that was unusual for him.

'What about a sex change?'

'No, she's not thinking about that,' Matjaž continued enthusiastically. 'She's heard some gruesome stories, about how hormone therapy somehow fails or affects your libido. And she's proud of her libido, she told me, it would be hard for her to separate herself from it. I have to say that I'm completely with her on that one.'

'Oh, Jesus!' came a shrill exhalation from Aleksander. 'Why are you talking about her as if she's a girl? She's a he!'

'I don't know, Aleksander – he, or she, is a woman and a half, I'm telling you!' said Matjaž, as if unaware of his friend's agitation.

'Yeah, she's a woman, and then there's another half there. You know what I don't get, is how come you've got so much compassion and patience for this guy. I don't have anything against gays, I don't have anything against heterosexuals, nor anything against men or women or anyone in between, as long as people decide what they are once and for all and stop mixing up worlds like this!' Aleksander shouted, flying off the handle.

'You really are conservative, aren't you!' exclaimed Matjaž as he wound a curl around his finger, as if he'd been taken over by the movements of his beloved from the previous evening.

'So, how did you leave it?' Aleksander asked, somewhat resigned.

'When we'd finished eating and we'd chatted a bit about the celebrity gossip and all that, she left.' Matjaž said, looking at his friend melancholically.

'And she didn't force you into anything, or cry, or anything like that?'

'No, she left with her head held high.'

'She didn't want your number or anything?' Aleksander still went on.

'No, last night she wanted to add me on Facebook, but I said maybe it was best if we kept the evening as a nice memory – like in *Casablanca*,' Matjaž said dreamily. 'Maybe that was a mistake, maybe we could be Facebook friends, but I don't even know her, I mean his, real name,' he said worriedly. As if in despair, he cried out into the winter's day, 'Stela, Stelaaaaa!'

Aleksander quickly glanced around to see if anyone was listening or looking at them, and gestured to the barman that his friend was a bit confused. 'Calm yourself down, mate, you've had a nice evening without any post-coital agonies . . .' he finally said.

'Well, that's because there wasn't any coitus . . .' Matjaž corrected him.

'Anyway. There wasn't the usual agony after an intimate evening, night and breakfast. You do know it doesn't get any better than that?' Aleksander said, almost sounding envious.

'Exactly! Maybe we're going after the completely wrong sex,' Matjaž added, ever so slightly embittered.

MINI

The first few warmer days of spring coaxed out to Metelkova even those who had stayed at home through the cold, who had run away to go skiing or visited cultural exhibitions. After midnight, while a large proportion of the city slept, people gathered there, convinced that at that hour life was only just beginning. One of those people was, of course, Matjaž. As he thought about how he had always been prepared to go one step further in his quest for a good time, he remembered how Sara used to tease him about being a party animal. Paradoxically, this had now taken on a meaning of its own, as the appearance of a full and carefree life would hopefully now lead him down a path back to her.

By his side was Jernej, known for his preference for drinking rather than talking; however much of a welcome and refreshing trait this was, in comparison with other members of his social circle, Matjaž felt at certain points that he'd actually quite like to be able to show off the finer points of his intellect, charm and humour, his sharp cynicism, on a Friday evening. At first he followed the debate between some of Jernej's friends from afar, about how Metelkova had lost its subversive nature, and how the beer was getting more and more expensive although the place was as unkempt as ever. Some girl added that Metelkova operated exactly like a typical capitalist organization under the banner of 'alternative', then some metalhead picked up where she left off, saying, 'The same dicks as the rest of them, just disguised in slightly scruffier packaging'. After him came some smaller, chubbier metalhead, swearing and complaining that the bar staff and bouncers there were arrogant snobs; and then some scrawny girl went even further and said that people in Metelkova were stupid because they didn't notice any of it. Matjaž got bored and left the group, asking, 'So why are you all here, then?'

He cast his eye over the girls at Metelkova, and with his slightly blurred vision and a fresh dose of beer he discovered what seemed to him a promising female population. Then Katja thwarted his plans. The polite 'How are you?' was followed by a monologue: how good she was feeling since the weather had picked up, how she was a better person now – something they had also noticed at work, how she'd started a new weight-loss treatment – its secret was that you just ate greens for a week. Of course it was disgusting – green soup for breakfast was the worst form of torture, but that was the price you paid for being a woman. And it really was hard being a woman, much harder than being a man. As far as she was concerned, the emancipation hadn't really got started yet; for her it would only be complete when men started putting on make-up before leaving for Metelkova on a Friday night, in order to impress the girls. She admitted that, naturally, she herself had become a slave to fashion and beauty trends, but people had to understand that we exist within a certain context, and therefore have to acknowledge the context in which we live – like it or not.

Matjaž wanted to excuse himself and go literally anywhere else, but Katja drew herself in closer. 'Anyway, I think I've fallen in love,' she said. Before Matjaž could ask who the lucky young man was, she was already describing him. He was a new intern at work, whom she was now supervising. He was really clumsy and weedy but he laughed at all of her jokes, brought her coffee even if she hadn't asked for it, and he sometimes baked on a Sunday and brought the cakes into work on Monday. He didn't know how to dress appropriately for company events; he wore his graduation suit way too often, for the most everyday occasions. He wasn't very talkative, but then his eyes said a lot – 'if you know what I mean,' she said, staring deeply into Matjaž's eyes. He nodded as if to say he understood, and congratulated her on the new catch. Well, for the moment nothing concrete had happened, she corrected him, although the last time they were at a dinner they'd organized for some company, it did seem like he had softly stroked her hand. But she wasn't born yesterday, and she knew what these little gestures meant. Matjaž nodded obediently and looked around to see which one of his euphoric friends would be the least painful to say hello to. 'Never lose hope!' he heard her say, full of commiseration. Matjaž didn't really understand the commiseration, and pulled a face. This made her laugh – she'd be so much prettier, he thought, if she didn't talk so much. Then she said, as if he were in need of further punishment,

'But we can agree that if we haven't found anyone in a few years' time, the two of us can just get married.' Matjaž choked, and by the time he'd caught his breath he'd already started walking away and simply waved her goodbye.

He sat down next to Suzana, who tonight was celebrating in the company of Mini, a journalist from one of those here-today-gone-tomorrow online news portals.

'How are you?' Suzana greeted him, smiling from ear to ear.

'Uf, just choking slightly,' he coughed.

'Ha, you were too thirsty for beer,' grinned Suzana.

'I'd say it was more that a certain sentence proved rather difficult to digest,' he corrected her.

'And which sentence would that be?'

'Oh it doesn't matter . . . the main thing is that I'm safe now.' He looked back just in case, and was pleased to see that Katja had found a new Metelkova victim.

'This is Mini,' Suzana said, introducing the friend who was sat beside her.

The two of them shook hands, and Matjaž could not resist blurting out something stupid. 'Is it hard, being Mini?'

'No, why?' wondered the reasonably attractive young woman with pale skin, thick black hair and a fringe.

'Well, I bet all the boys at school wanted to race and play with Mini, then as you got older I bet there was a queue of boys wanting a ride,' Matjaž explained, in all sincerity.

She laughed. 'That's the first time I've heard that one.'

'It definitely won't be the last,' he said directly.

'Why?' asked the young woman, surprised.

'Because your parents clearly didn't love you,' he continued, already tiring of it.

'You're mean,' she said, pretending to be upset.

Meanwhile, Suzana had caught sight of some people whom she hadn't seen 'for centuries', and marched over to them. She always bumped into people she knew – and people she didn't, too – whom she hadn't seen 'for centuries'. Matjaž didn't envy her social obligations, he was happy that he could carry on winding up the pretty girl. When he'd eased off the jokes, Mini asked him what it was like being a photographer.

'How do you mean?' he asked her.

'Do you enjoy your job?' she asked him, seriously.

'Of course I do, otherwise I wouldn't do it,' he answered her.

'So you only do things that you enjoy?' Mini asked, trying to be provocative.

'Exactly. Don't you?'

'No,' she replied sparingly.

'Why not?

'Because life's a serious thing sometimes,' she said with particular pathos, like a person whose life experiences – perhaps several years living in Darfur – had already taught them a thing or two.

'Aah,' Matjaž said, pretending to be enlightened. 'Life really is a big word not to be joked about.'

'I didn't say that,' opposed Mini. She had correctly detected a pinch of sarcasm in his statement, and it offended her.

'Of course not,' Matjaž replied, persisting with his ironic tone. 'And you're absolutely right. Life is sometimes a seriously serious thing, which demands one sacrifice after another from mankind, even causing wrinkled foreheads and raised eyebrows. In Africa they're hungry, in South East Asia they're victims of tsunamis, there are earthquakes in Haiti and political prisoners in China. Life really is just one big hardship.'

'Don't judge people for caring about others!' she snapped at him angrily.

Matjaž looked tiredly into her big blue eyes and shook his head. 'No, darling, you think about others in order to feel better about yourself.' With that he stood up and left. He had soon purposefully forgotten about the conversation and instead focused his attention on other people – like Maki and Simon from his secondary school, who were trying to roll a spliff. While doing so they discussed the one thing that really stumped them about weed: they understood how it was grown, they could imagine how it was distributed, too, but who was it that produced those little papers that they were wrapping it in? Where were those trees grown? How was paper actually made? The Chinese had invented paper way back . . . what was the difference between making these little papers for rolling, and paper for writing? Would it be possible to print books on tobacco paper? Maki and Simon developed whole theories on this, even questioning whether or not the Bible could be printed on the little papers – in the end they agreed that it probably could be, but you would have to print on just one side, because the papers were so transparent you wouldn't be able to read it if the print were on both sides. But who even read the Bible these days, anyway . . . When they got stuck into the issue of filters and how they were made, Matjaž realized that he had to say goodbye and find more stimulating company. 'Why are you leaving, mate?' Maki called after him. 'Do you know if you need gas to make filters?'

Matjaž decided to ignore the question. Luckily, Suzana came up to him at just that moment and asked discreetly, 'Why did you walk away from Mini?'

'Yeah, I had other social obligations.'

'I know, but Mini really likes you.'

'Really?' He was astonished. 'Sometimes it really surprises me, how much humiliation women will put up with – it's almost worthy of admiration.'

'Would you please stop making generalizations? Although she's clearly pretty crazy, because she's asked me to give you her phone number,' she said, pressing a piece of paper with a phone number on it into his hand.

'And what should I do with this?'

'I'm not sure what you do with a phone number,' she replied curtly. 'Make a note of it or give her a call sometime? Mini's a great girl!' Suzana said, convincingly.

'Mini is above all an incredibly stupid girl,' Matjaž corrected her.

'So what!' retorted Suzana, as if to say that those two things weren't mutually exclusive.

Matjaž thought for a moment and said, 'OK fine, but then what? I'm here because I'm clever, she's here because she likes to listen to clever people.'

'She's unbelievably stupid!' he said to Aleksander over the phone.

'But she's pretty, you say? Is she pretty in an average way or really pretty, more sexy, more classic? Describe her to me . . .' his friend said excitedly.

'Erm, I'm not sure about those sorts of details. I'd say that there's an elegance about her, and she has a nice face. More of a classic beauty. Not enough to be truly beautiful. You know what I mean: symmetrical face, a strong nose, not crooked, big bright eyes and fairly full lips and a decent smile.'

'What about her figure?'

'Not sure about that. She was sitting down, so I couldn't judge. But given how self-obsessed she is, I'd imagine that she's quite slim, likes to work out, probably runs, eats nuts and raw vegetables, so her figure must be in pretty good shape,' Matjaž ruminated.

'Hm, but is she really young, though?' Aleksander enquired.

'Yeah, she's about twenty-five. At least as far as her body is concerned; in terms of her head, I dread to think!'

'Leave her head to one side for now. What's important is that she's young, after that it hardly matters what she's like and how much she works out . . .' he said expertly.

'That's the plan, yeah, to forget about what's on the inside and focus on the exterior. If only she wouldn't talk so much,' he said, deep in thought.

'You're right, the only reason men manage to retain more dignity is because they don't usually prattle on like women do,' said Aleksander. 'In any case, I look forward to the update.'

'You'll get one.'

'Where are you taking her?'

'To the Spanish restaurant.'

'Ooh, close to home – smart, smart!' sniggered his friend, and then they quickly said goodbye.

And so they went, Mini and Matjaž, for a late lunch on Sunday. Before the wine had even arrived at the table, Matjaž found out that Mini was a humanitarian; in the sense that she respected the work of Brangelina, who set a good example with their actions, and in today's world setting an example was important. In her free time she liked to watch *House*, even though she found Dr House a bit arrogant; she liked the series *Castle* even better because she found it relaxing. She didn't watch the news because it stressed her out, she didn't read *The Lady* because it was a stupid magazine; instead, she bought *The Economist*, because it was like a window on the world. Mini took a slight breath so that they could order the main course, but soon enough picked up where she had left off.

She didn't believe in female emancipation because she thought it had turned men into wimps; she wanted a real man, the kind who knew how to look after his woman, who knew how to enthral, captivate, charm and protect her above all others. On the other hand, it didn't seem right to her that women earned less; she herself was underpaid as a freelance journalist. But what could we do, that's the way of the world, shameless and cruel, which is why a bit of good humour and positive energy doesn't go amiss. That was why she was very mindful of the colour of her clothes. 'You wouldn't believe how the colours you wear influence your mood and the moods of those around you. It's crazy, honestly!' she said, pointing to her current choice – red.

'I can see you're somewhat alarmed, yeah,' Matjaž said dully, and signalled to the waiter to bring him another glass of wine. Mini, not noticing the weary look on her date's face, carried on.

Obviously, she didn't believe in horoscopes, she continued while chewing on her salad, but sometimes she read them and sometimes they were actually true. Just this Friday she had read that if Libra coincided with the moon 'or what was it again?' she could meet someone with whom she would have a long future. She gave him a knowing look, and Matjaž could hardly keep himself from spitting out his mouthful of *bife de chorizo*. Instead, he looked up again to the ceiling for help. Mini ignored his sigh and overlooked his expression, to try and keep things in line with her horoscope prediction, and went on. She'd like to get married, but not just yet. Again she looked at Matjaž with intent, and he could only cough. She'd like to have children, just two (because she'd still like to have other things in life), but not just yet. She directed yet another provocative look at Matjaž, who in turn looked towards the waiter. She was still young, she continued, she was twenty-six and you have to think carefully about such serious matters before you make any decisions. Because it's a cruel world and – as she knew from personal experience – acts of kindness are rarely met with gratitude. She smiled at him. 'Don't you think?'

As evening drew nearer, Matjaž's head began to spin from Mini's vast number of predictions and analyses of the past and future – of men and women, good and bad, thoughts and words, and from environmental awareness to the rights of sexual and racial minorities. After this barrage he was so tired of the woman that he couldn't even bring himself to say goodbye politely, although he had promised himself that this time he wouldn't break away with his usual savagery. When they left the restaurant he just said, tiredly, 'Well, see you!'

'Are we saying goodbye so quickly? Was it something I said?' she reacted playfully.

'No, no, it's not you, I'm the problem. For a start, I don't recycle and I don't believe in recycling. Secondly, I'm reluctant to wear bright colours, and even less to think about food in terms of colour. I hate yoga, I don't like Brangelina, humanitarians or not, and above all I can't stand horoscopes. And, most importantly, I would like to have children immediately and get married right away, but these things must be considered seriously so that fateful mistakes aren't made. All the more so in this cruel world, where the only thing we can rely on is a partner and their unconditional love.'

'But I can be unconditional,' Mini said pleadingly, while tears of humiliation began to gather in the corners of her eyes.

Matjaž smiled. 'I don't doubt that. As I said, there's a whole list of reasons.'

'I don't understand women like that,' said Karla as she lit a cigarette. Their balcony was ideal for lazy Sundays with friends. She added contemplatively, 'Why do they need to put the world to rights over just one lunch?'

'It's true, they could at least keep something back until the second time around,' Aleksander agreed, as he mixed a gin and tonic.

'The main reason the world's in crisis, I think, is because it's constantly being saved over one lunch or another,' she continued, thinking aloud.

'Or over drinks in the evening,' her husband added.

Matjaž just stared resignedly into the distance and sipped his drink. He'd now calmed down after the lunch debacle and was enjoying the mild spring evening.

'You're miles away . . .' said Aleksander, who was a little worried about his friend after hearing about his afternoon with Mini; even he still dreaded meeting another woman like that.

'No, no, you're not going to get any more cruel comments from me. I'm just surrendering myself to your nice balcony, the nice evening, and I'm not going to think about anything else. At least nothing serious,' he said calmly.

'Maybe you're right,' said Karla. 'Let's leave the world to chance and put our troubles to one side, for today at least!'

'And which troubles are bothering you, may I ask?' Aleksander said sharply.

'I'm married to you,' she smiled at him mischievously. Matjaž gave her a nod, but Aleksander decided he wasn't going to rise to their remarks.

Smiling, they raised their glasses so that the chink sounded softly out into the night. 'To the world!'

THE JOURNEY TO JAJCE

Melita

On the way to Zagreb he was thinking about how he ought to be a bit more careful about late-night decisions made over fine liquor. If he had been a little bit more on guard, a bit more discerning, today he would not have been one of twenty or so passengers – of a predominantly pensioner persuasion – on a coach from Ljubljana to Jajce, Bosnia. He could have quite easily carried on until the end of May in Ljubljana, gone out for the odd beer, hung out with Jernej and his Metelkova crowd down by the river down at Trnovo, where they'd try to forget that their teenage years were never coming back. Although then they did sometimes miraculously come back, just through the sounds of familiar songs: Radiohead's 'Creep', the Beatles' 'In My Life', the Rolling Stones' 'Time Is on My Side' and so on. Yesterday, when Aleksander's father had suggested that Matjaž accompany him on an excursion, it had seemed like a once-in-a-lifetime opportunity. Now he was regretting it. To put it briefly, devotees of the former Yugoslavia, Tito's Yugoslavia, were travelling to the place where it all began. These things often happen: one minute you've come over to help move a fridge, and the next thing you know you're on the road to Jajce.

Everything could have turned out fine, as well, if only Dušan's enthusiasm, his stories of his time in the Yugoslav army (as though it were the most romantic and comedic of adventures) and his doses of authentic Serbian *dunja*, had petered out in his sleep. But no, in all the excitement he just had to go and call his boss to convince her that a report on a journey like this, to celebrate the anniversary of Tito's birthday on the 25th May, would be one of the most-read articles in internet newspaper history. Of course he did convince her, and in truth it wasn't that difficult because for some unknown reason his words carried weight with her. Now he was disappointed that he didn't have a more competent editor who would realize that trips like this did not warrant expenses in a time of austerity. Where are the financial cuts and the frugal editors when you need them?

He looked over to his right, where Dušan was now sitting and snoring. He should have known, as soon as Aleksander emphatically declined his father's invitation, as soon as he saw the look of despair on Aleksander's mum's face – she had already heard the old stories of socialist Yugoslavia five hundred or so times. He should have known better. He realized now that those raised eyebrows were a warning sign, telling him that on no account should he go – or else he'd regret it.

But Dušan had been so convincing, slipping into Serbo-Croat as he spoke, 'Listen, Matjaž my boy, this will be a great trip. You can relax a bit, after slaving away at work so much. And fantastic company, too. Well, if they – what's their names – Albert and his wife, they might bother you a bit with all their knowledge of the Partisan resistance, but you'll love the rest of the gang. I'm telling you, *povem ti*, just great people, but you'll learn something, too, you can tell the kids what it was all like.' When he had noticed that Matjaž wasn't particularly interested in Yugonostalgia, he quickly added, 'And you know how they like to eat over there! Sausages, *čevapčiči*, little pies, they're out of this world, really authentic. And oh my God, the quince brandy they have! You wouldn't believe it, gah! But no, you're not made of strong enough stuff for that; you don't have the right constitution, you're not hard enough – are you, my dear Slovene?'

Aleksander had clutched his head at this point. This is how his dad would get Matjaž – no one was going to tell him that he didn't have the constitution for *dunja*. He'd been working on his constitution for *dunja* his whole life.

And so, Matjaž thought, here he was – thanks to his own wretched alcoholic pride. Just to prove to this retired lover of Partisan war films, of the five-pointed star and 'brotherhood and unity', that he was hard. Matjaž took a sharp intake of breath as a robust man with thick, dark hair and a round, friendly face tapped him on the shoulder across the bus's central aisle.

'I've not seen you here before, young man.'

'No, this is my first time,' he smiled reservedly.

'Bravo! There's no need to fear the future with young people like you!' his fellow traveller nodded, satisfied.

Matjaž was just able to hold his tongue in time before asking how exactly his departure for Jajce inspired hope in the future. Some future! Maybe his journey to Jajce would pave the way for precarious employment opportunities in the public sector, or lower unemployment and put an end to rising levels of poverty. But Matjaž felt that the man to whom he was speaking didn't deserve his bitterness; he only had himself to blame for letting Dušan bring him along on this adventure.

'Albert,' said the man, as if he'd read his mind, and offered his hand.

'Matjaž.'

'Do you know, Matjaž, this is my fortieth trip here.'

'Wow, congratulations, that's an anniversary, that's dedication!'

Albert went quiet for a moment and, looking out of the window, said, 'Yes, it really is . . .'

Matjaž thought that Albert was going to say something else, but he merely carried on staring out of the window, lost in his thoughts. Matjaž decided that there would be plenty more opportunities for conversation, so he leaned back and closed his eyes, and pretended to be asleep.

The relative silence, which was only disturbed by the hushed voices of some women sat behind him and the humming of the bus, caused Matjaž to fall asleep for real. He was awoken by a strong hand shaking him. 'Matjaž, wake up! Can you hear me, son?' Dušan explained that they'd stopped in Zagreb to have a bite to eat and do what people usually do when they make a stop. Matjaž soon discovered that 'Zagreb' was in fact only a metaphor for a petrol station located somewhere on the motorway.

Dušan and Matjaž sat down at one of the tables in the café there, both a little tired after their sleep. It was nine o'clock. They ordered coffee and a snack. When Albert and another older couple walked past, Dušan called after them, 'Albert, you going to sit down and have a coffee?'

'Thanks, Dušan, but we're heading to the shop to get a few things for the journey,' he replied. When they disappeared out of sight, Dušan discreetly turned to Matjaž and said in Serbian, 'Albert is a legend here, you know, a proper legend. He's been coming on this trip for forty years.'

'I know, he told me.'

'I don't know where his wife is, though,' said Dušan, to himself more than anything. 'The two of them always travelled together. Maybe she's not well.'

Matjaž also learned that Albert was over seventy years old, retired, and once worked at the Ministry for Transport. He was a good official, stressed Dušan – whatever that may mean, Matjaž thought to himself – or perhaps just a really good person. He had three children, one of whom had been gravely ill and died of leukaemia aged five. Those must be terrible times for a family, Dušan went on, but through that tragedy they united, so much so that the other two children still called their parents every day, visited them regularly and cooked for them often.

Now Albert had grandchildren, three, if Dušan was not mistaken, and he was really happy; he and his wife looked after them often. Last year they showed their photos to the entire bus, telling everyone what the children had been up to, which words they already knew, how the eldest was already singing songs and his brother danced to nursery rhymes. Matjaž was grateful that Albert didn't feel the need to show his family photos this year, or to repeat his grandchildren's first syllables and tell stories of how adorable they were when they threw everything that came their way on to the floor. Matjaž didn't find children cute, sweet and utterly adorable. No, he saw a pure evil in them, one that sucked parents dry.

'What about the others, do you know them?' Matjaž asked eventually.

'A few, a bit. There are fewer of us every year. Some have already passed away, for others health won't allow it any more, some just don't feel like it.'

'I see,' said Matjaž. 'So who else apart from Albert do you still know?'

'Well, of the young ones I think the tour guide is the same as last year, then there's you, and Anica and Lojze, the nice couple from just outside Ljubljana. They were both so intensely, passionately involved with the Communist Party, and it was really painful for them when war broke out here in the Balkans. Martin and Milica are funny, though. They're both Catholic, never joined the Party, but then when everything collapsed they slowly, really slowly, started to realize that it was better before, and they became interested. They're both doctors. When the Party was still in power they wanted democracy and the West, but later they started studying and now they're more on our side.'

Matjaž nodded and shortly afterwards Dušan continued in his mix of Serbian, Croatian and Slovene, 'There was one other young woman – I mean, not terribly young, about forty-five – stunning, the beautiful Nada, who usually came with her husband and daughter. I thought I saw her, but without her husband . . .'

They had something to eat and finished their coffees in silence, and then like two obedient schoolboys they reported back to the bus exactly fifteen minutes later. A few women were late and ran up to the bus, out of breath. 'Oh, so sorry!' and 'Sorry, excuse us!' They lugged numerous bags from the service station with them, as if it were the last service station on civilized earth, with only savage wilderness ahead. Matjaž didn't pay much attention to these women until he caught sight of a pair who didn't fit the bill of the average expedition member.

First a middle-aged woman, very well presented and wearing a fairly short skirt, walked past him without batting an eyelid. Behind her, he caught sight of a girl who was really young and very pretty – incredibly pretty, thought Matjaž. She wore headphones and her eyes were fixed to the floor. It was clear that travelling around the old Yugoslavia (yes, Tito's Yugoslavia was already old) was not her thing, and that she'd had entirely different plans for this long weekend. Maybe some kind of 'spring break', as they now called it, where young people organized a get-away to somewhere on the Adriatic coast and tried to drink as much alcohol as possible and then do boring, stupid things. She can't be more than sixteen, he thought to himself.

'See, now, she's really young. She can't be more than seventeen, can she?' Dušan laughed, clearly unable to take his eyes off the young beauty. 'I remember her mum from before, she came here with her husband. Nice couple, the pair of them, but now . . . who knows, who knows?'

At the front of the bus a young guy appeared, standing behind the driver, and spoke into the microphone, 'Ladies and gentlemen, delegates on the journey to Jajce, ho, ho!'

'That's Peter. He's the guide. He's been travelling with us for a few years. He's a good lad, you'll like him, everyone does. He's just a bit pushy sometimes,' Dušan explained to his travelling companion. Matjaž nodded and listened to the tour guide.

'Here we are, together again on the same journey. There we are. It will be a while until the next stop now, unless there's a real emergency . . .' He chuckled to himself. Matjaž, meanwhile, shuddered at the thought of this man – this relatively tall, pale, fair-haired young man of around thirty-five – thinking that he was funny. 'So, dear ladies, dear gents – or should I say, comrades . . . our next stop is Bosnia, where we'll stop somewhere for lunch as soon as we're over the border.' Someone on the bus shouted something to the guide. Matjaž didn't understand what they had said, but of course Peter understood it immediately. 'Ah yes, brilliant, Anica. The restaurant is booked, so no one will be suffering from hunger and thirst, and the price is – as always – included in your package deal, which you've already paid for, ha ha ha.'

Matjaž rolled his eyes and looked to Dušan for confirmation of his feelings, but he only said, laughing to himself, 'This Peter's so happy.' Matjaž had just decided to leaf through his copies of *Mladina* and *Global*, when he heard the familiar tone of a text message. It was Aleksander, of course.

'How's the Liberation Front? Is freedom on the horizon yet?'

Matjaž smiled and replied, 'The war is only just beginning!'

'If you don't behave, I'll tell my Dad on you!' came Aleksander's quick rejoinder. Matjaž didn't bother to reply; he knew that the exchange could easily carry on until his return to Ljubljana and beyond.

'Is that your lady?' Albert asked Matjaž from across the aisle, using the polite form of address and nodding towards the mobile phone with a friendly smile.

'Ah, no, I don't have a girlfriend. And please, let's be on first-name terms – we're all brotherhood and unity here after all, aren't we?'

Albert laughed, 'Of course, of course.' They were quiet for a moment, then Albert began, 'When my wife, Theodora, and I started courting, I always addressed her formally – that's what I called her back then. When we got married, she slowly became Thea. It was normal back then.'

Matjaž just nodded. He didn't know how to answer, it seemed silly to him.

'Maybe it seems silly these days', Albert began, as if he'd overheard Matjaž's thoughts yet again, 'but actually there was something respectful about it, a kind of honesty and affirmation, which the suitor – in this case me, ha ha – could use to prove that he was genuine, that he really liked a girl and that he really wanted to ask her to dance.'

'Hey up Albert, where's your Thea this year?' Dušan butted in, with the best of intentions, having obviously overheard their conversation. Albert fell silent and swept his hand over his eyes. The question had obviously upset him.

'What is it, Albert? Is she not well? Tell us, don't bottle it up.' Albert shook his head and looked as if he could hardly hold back the tears. Dušan clearly did not believe that people in pain ought to be left in peace, and sat down next to him in the empty seat.

Matjaž wanted to respect Albert's grief, and he turned away, although he could still hear their conversation. Albert explained that other friends on the bus already knew; Anica, Martin and Milica. He went quiet again, took a breath and then smiled softly, as if to apologize for having put it off for so long. When he began to speak again, he explained the basics very briefly. Around Christmas his Thea had started to feel extremely unwell. Her doctor made her see several specialists and straight away the diagnosis was cancer. The final stages. Within a month she had bid them farewell. 'She bid us farewell,' was the phrase Albert that used, and it struck Matjaž right in the guts.

Tears ran down Albert's cheeks, and he wiped them away with his palms. Dušan began to comfort him. He was good at that. 'Oh Albert, how was I to know? I'm so sorry. She was such a good wife, your Thea, I'll never forget how she prepared *potica* for everyone on every trip . . .'

Matjaž couldn't listen to him any more; he looked at his phone and thought about what it would be like to love the same woman for fifty years, maybe more. Thea and Albert had been a couple for so long and, as far as he had heard and sensed, they were a good, maybe even happy, couple. How did such happy, solid couples come to be in those days? Were they like that because courting began with polite forms of address, and when you accepted a polite invitation to dance it took on a deeper meaning, it became more existential? Matjaž knew what it was for love to be existential, but so far for him existential love had been tied to the fact that it did not last. Existential love was possible, but it passed. The day had come for his Sara to bid him farewell.

At around one o'clock they arrived in Gradiška, one of those numerous non-descript towns of former Yugoslavia that always seemed to Matjaž like forgotten corners of the earth, where the present was a fleeting reminder that the past was not so glamorous after all, and where there was no future to be seen on the horizon either. Actually it seemed to him as if the whole of Bosnia operated as one such cut-off piece of the world, a piece of the world that time had forgotten. However, in the restaurant, which was attached to some neglected motel, he felt completely fine. The waiters were even joking with him; they enjoyed exchanging tasteless jokes with each other, and in the spirit of hospitality they gave out shots of rakia for free. He sat with Albert and Dušan and two couples, who he soon found out belonged to that old family of AVNOJ veterans – veterans of the Anti-Fascist Council for the National Liberation of Yugoslavia. That was what they called themselves anyway, even though the majority of them had been born after the Second World War.

Matjaž kept quiet for most of the time, following events around the table. Anica and Lojze seemed like one of those couples that you couldn't ever really imagine getting together. Which is to say that she was a rather polished lady, who clearly put a lot of effort into her appearance even though she had – as he gleaned from the conversation – worked as an accountant in some small company her whole life. He, on the other hand, was a typical small-town guy: a little bit chunky, his ample figure hiding beneath clothes that were too tight for him. And whereas his wife spoke less frequently, Lojze was constantly brooding over things; whether it concerned NASA's space programme or the sale of the Mercator supermarket chain, he knew plenty about many subjects and was happy to share his knowledge with others. It was clear that he'd never been able to achieve his full potential in his career as a food inspector. This unlikely couple had two children, with whom they didn't exactly have a lot of contact; at least that was his impression, given how little Anica and Lojze had said about them – only mentioning that they were fine after Martin and Milica enquired after the family.

It was entirely clear to Matjaž why Martin and Milica, a kind-hearted couple, were together. In fact, he felt it would have been strange if these two people, similar even in appearance – both rotund and rosy-cheeked with short red hair – were not together. Both of them were quick to reveal everything new in the life of their only child Reza and their granddaughter Ivana to their AVNOJ friends. Naturally the group gave a lot of time to Albert, too; the reserved Anica even took his hand and softly asked after his health.

As soon as the second round of beers arrived at the table, conversations became less formal and more jovial. They gossiped about this year's expedition group. Milica thought Peter was looking a little older and more tired; Lojze said that he was missing a woman in his life, but Anica corrected him and said it was probably a man that he was missing more than anything. Lojze didn't understand that comment, just as he probably didn't understand the majority of the things that his wife said. Then they came to the subject of Nada. Dušan was surprised not to see her gentleman friend this year, and Milica was able to provide him with an answer. Her husband had moved out and married a much younger woman, who was already carrying his child. Everyone began shaking their heads. Albert muttered something to the effect of 'Poor woman!' to which Milica immediately also added, 'Poor child!' to which Martin went one further, saying, 'That's no child any more!' Dušan had to agree that the young Melita had turned into a real stunner, who was surely going to break a lot of men's hearts. 'Until she reaches her mother's age, then someone will break her heart,' Anica said wisely, surprising the group with her contribution. 'Well, she's still got sufficient time before then to completely ruin some guy's life,' remarked Matjaž, as if in defence of the young girl. The present company smiled at his attempt to be gentlemanly, and Dušan patted him heartily on the back for having slotted into the group so well.

There wasn't much news on the other passengers. A few of them seemed familiar from last year, and there were even a few new faces on the excursion. 'There are also these two friends . . .' remarked Milica, and it now became clear that she would be providing the majority of the hot gossip. 'They sit behind us on the bus. They're young, maybe a bit older than our Matjaž here. Patrik, that's the skinny bald guy, is recently divorced and pretty devastated. And his friend Matevž isn't really helping. He talks constantly about magnetic forces going back and forth, and about molecules sometimes coming together and then repelling each other . . . something like that. I gathered from Patrik's reply that Matevž is a physics teacher, which explains a lot.' She nodded at her own conclusions.

At that point a laughing Peter came up to the table. 'Hello, dear friends, nice to see you all here again. Can I sit down for a moment?' The group nodded although he had already sat down among them. He offered his hand to everyone, and he and Matjaž exchanged official introductions. After that he began, 'How are you, how are you all doing?' He looked at Albert with pity, took his hand and gave him a sympathetic wink. Albert just returned a hazy smile. 'Listen up, the plan is after we've eaten we go back to the bus, then we head off on to Jajce. There we'll be staying at the Hotel Turist, as before. We'll meet up again for dinner at the hotel. OK?' Everyone nodded their heads enthusiastically. 'Now, the rooms. I'm afraid one of you will have to be in a room by yourself . . .' He looked around as if trying to work out who would make the noble sacrifice.

Matjaž quickly made the most of this opportunity. 'Well if nobody else minds, that'd be OK with me.'

'Albert & Dušan, would you two be all right in the same room?' asked Peter, like an over-protective parent who wants to treat all of his children equally. This confirmed Matjaž's first impression of Mr Tourguide: that he really did not like him. Albert and Dušan nodded their heads. Peter continued, 'See, my friend, it'll be nice, we'll have a great time . . . Not like oldies, but just like back at school.' He patted Albert on the back, and received only a sullen smile in return.

Anica spoke up, 'What about after that?'

'After?' queried Peter.

'What's the plan for tomorrow and the day after?'

'Oh of course, of course. How could I forget! Well, first thing tomorrow we'll start off around Jajce and finish the tour at the scene of the crime . . .' (As he said this he laughed conspiratorially, as if visiting the National Liberation War memorial was highly illegal.) 'Then the afternoon is free for you to do your own thing, or rest – basically whatever you like. Then in the evening one of our fellow passengers has prepared a little surprise for us all. His cousin Elvis and his family have invited us to a picnic. Elvis is a butcher by trade, and he lives in a villa with a splendid big garden, so there'll be plenty of space. This encounter with some authentic Jajce community and their generosity is already included in the price, so everything is sorted.' When he'd finished, he was left with a smile imprinted on his face, which Matjaž read as a mix of self-satisfaction and an old habit of feeling like he had to make everyone happy.

'And we leave on . . .' Anica asked, wanting to know every single detail of her journey.

'On Thursday,' exhaled Peter quickly, as if he had to satisfy his passengers as soon as possible. He took a breath and carried on. 'So yes, Thursday, not too early as it will probably have been a wild night with Elvis' – he giggled and winked at Anica – 'we'll head back to Ljubljana, probably around ten. Full of memories and experiences.' Matjaž could only think that he added that last cliché to apologize for talking and probably for his own existence, too.

'Any other questions?' he asked with a pristine smile. The table shook their heads like obedient school children, Peter stood up and added, 'Well, it'll be time for us to be on our way soon!' With a smile full of teeth, he left.

*

Matjaž didn't fancy dinner. He was sick of travelling, sick of the laughing Peter, and was even starting to tire of Dušan's ability to talk non-stop and comment on places that they drove past, getting Matjaž to take photos of them because it was, after all, a historical region and a historical excursion. When he failed to convince the photographer that there were photo opportunities everywhere, he brought out stories of Second World War battles, interpreting strategic Partisan decisions on one side and those of the Nazis on the other. He had ideas about how events at the Battle of the Neretva could have been better executed, and at the Drina, and so on. Even if Matjaž changed the topic for a moment to ask after Aleksander, his wife and family, Dušan immediately found a way back to the Balkan front. No, Matjaž concluded, he could not survive one more meal with these people.

He considered going into town and finding something to eat there, but in truth he didn't really fancy it. They said it was only about five minutes' walk to the centre, but Matjaž didn't wish to uncover the charms of this historical place by himself. And besides, all towns were the same at night anyway. He looked at his phone and discovered that Aleksander had sent him a provocative text message, asking how it was going. He replied to this provocation with 'I'm balls-deep in the Balkans.'

He was getting irritated that he couldn't decide what to do with himself, whether he wanted to be alone in his room or whether he'd prefer company, when he heard voices on the neighbouring balcony. It was a mother and daughter, and Matjaž immediately deduced it must be Nada and Melita. He stepped on to his own small balcony so that he could overhear more easily.

'You're not wearing that, is that clear? You're too young, and even if you weren't it would still be inappropriate.'

'You don't have a clue what people dress like these days,' he heard the girl's voice reply.

'You're not going to tell me that people today dress like prostitutes, wearing clothes that clearly only serve one purpose.'

'What purpose?'

'You know exactly what I mean. The one that you are too young for.'

'You wanna take a look at what you're wearing! That clearly only serves one purpose, too.'

The girl had clearly pushed her mother way too far. 'Silence! Enough of your backchat. You're not going to dinner dressed like that!'

'Fine, I won't go to dinner then!'

The mother lowered her voice a notch and said, 'Suit yourself.'

'Fine!' yelled the unruly teenager, as her mother closed the door behind her.

Then the balcony doors opened and made Matjaž jump. Melita was similarly startled when she saw him sitting there.

'Nice dress,' Matjaž blurted out, when he saw the far-too-short mini-dress for himself, paired with laddered tights that exposed her attractive, slender legs. A piece of fishnet clothing, which she'd put on over a skin-tight top, once again revealed more than it concealed.

'I'm glad you like it,' she said bitterly, pulling her top down as if doing so would lessen her exposure. She lit herself a cigarette. They smoked in silence for several long seconds and looked out into the moderately clear sky, which was surrendering to the darkness with every passing moment.

'So, how's things?' Matjaž asked, trying to initiate contact, but Melita didn't feel like answering his clichéd question. Desperately, he tried to rescue the situation. 'I'm Matjaž.'

'Melita,' she said quietly, but in a more reconciliatory tone. She even looked at him briefly, before once again showing him her beautiful profile. She puffed skilfully on her cigarette and went on, 'They still treat me like a child all the time, like a little girl even, as if I have no say in anything. Of course I wanted to stay at home; it'd be a break, three days of freedom, but she dragged me here! Here! What am I supposed to do here with you pensioners . . .'

'Ahem,' coughed Matjaž.

'I mean, with you oldies . . .' Melita tried to take back what she'd said.

'A-hem!' Matjaž coughed even more forcefully.

'You know what I mean, you, the generation of '68.'

'I know, it's pointless,' he eventually said. 'Carry on . . .'

'Don't get me wrong, it's not as if I haven't been with men as old as you. I've been with a lot with different guys already, quite a few of them, but she still treats me like a little girl. If only she knew!'

'She almost certainly does know, but she pretends that she doesn't. That way she can preserve her illusion of you. You can't resent your parents for simply not wanting to know.'

'What she really wants is to preserve the illusion of herself, to pretend that she's still young and that she has a young daughter who doesn't think about sex under any circumstances.' Melita blew out a deep breath of cigarette smoke and continued, 'AVNOJ means so much to her, and my dad always brought her here, so obviously I won't go home and leave her here. But, really, she came here to hit on guys the same age as her – or even older.' With that she looked at Matjaž, unimpressed.

'And when you try to do the same, she won't let you,' he said, quite at ease.

'Exactly,' she agreed feistily. Immediately afterwards she burst out, 'No hang on, what are you trying to say, dumbass?'

'Well, sorry, but women never wear clothes like that just for themselves.' He nodded towards her dress.

'That's not true!' yelled Melita childishly.

'And then they furiously deny it, of course,' smiled Matjaž.

'Chauvinist pig! Why can't a woman look nice and be desirable just for herself, or just because she is confident enough and comfortable with who she is.'

'I'm not saying that she shouldn't, I'm not saying that she can't, but normally she isn't. Like with you, you didn't wear that out of respect for yourself, I'm convinced. If nothing else you wore it for your mum, just to provoke her!'

'Seriously?' She feigned indignation, and in her defiance her woman's face revealed the girl within once again. 'I can't believe I'm even talking to such a moron.'

'Of course you are, because then at least I can admire you,' Matjaž calmly replied, his statement confusing Melita for a moment.

'Oh it's like that, is it . . . So why didn't you say so?' she remarked, lowering her voice.

'I didn't say anything of the sort, it's just you who has a bit of a guilty conscience because you're still bothered by your mum's criticism, even though it's exactly what you wanted,' Matjaž said, almost monotone, and waited with interest to see how the girl would react.

'Fuck it!' she said, and left the balcony. Matjaž stayed on his and stared into the darkness. 'Jajce is beautiful in the dark,' he thought to himself. He lit another cigarette so that he could decide once and for all whether he was going to go to dinner or not. His own indecision was getting on his nerves. Just then the door of the neighbouring balcony opened once again and Melita appeared in a somewhat more conservative outfit, so she looked more like her own age.

'Is that better?' she asked with a hint of sarcasm.

'The previous version was better on so many levels, but if I'm honest you're almost prettier than before in this variation.'

'Thank you,' she said softly. 'Let's go to dinner. I'm starving.' Now she had confused him, and he didn't know what to say.

'I don't know what to say,' he replied.

'Say "Yes, of course!"' she smiled at him.

In the restaurant of the incredibly run-down hotel the two of them sat at Nada's table, where she was kept company by Peter and two other elderly women who Matjaž hadn't noticed yet. 'Oh how nice, you came then,' Nada turned towards her daughter and softly stroked her long curly hair. Now in the light, Matjaž realized that Nada really was dressed rather provocatively in a tight dress, but he had to admit that she looked pretty good in it. If she used a little less make-up to cover up her wrinkles, she'd look much younger. The thought darted through his mind that so many older women made the mistake of applying too much make-up, and he immediately had another thought that maybe he could be some kind of style consultant and make-up artist for women of a certain age. He would explain to them how Photoshop is much more easy-going on the skin than make-up is.

They introduced themselves. He also met Uršula and Ludovika, the best and oldest of friends, who like Albert and Dušan had both been coming to Jajce their whole life, for some forty years. 'As schoolgirls we both made fun of it. When both of us became mothers we'd still talk sarcastically about the ritual,' explained Uršula.

Ludovika added, 'It was a time for escape, for just the two of us.'

'And as much as neither of us were ever party members', Uršula said, picking up the story's thread once again, 'over the years we came to view it with a certain respect.' She took her friend by the hand.

'And you came here even after everything had collapsed – I mean, during the war here?' Matjaž queried, somehow not grasping how Jajce had become a metaphor for female emancipation and some sort of respect as well.

'During the war we didn't come here, no,' answered Ludovika.

'But straight away, as soon as it was possible, we came back,' Uršula continued.

'I see, I see', began Matjaž, 'but what I was getting at was that the war exposed how Yugoslavia as a project was nevertheless misguided, that right from its very inception something was seriously wrong.'

'What are you talking about, boy?' came the voice of a slightly plump gentleman from the table behind them, whom Matjaž later discovered was called Svetozar. He had fought with the Partisans when he was still supposed to be a child, an experience that had clearly not impaired his excellent hearing. 'Are you aware of how many people sacrificed themselves for freedom, how many people died, were injured, how many orphans were left after the war? And now you're saying that everything was misguided from the start. Peter, I thought that only people who understood our cause came here!' Svetozar said, turning to the organizer. Matjaž was just about to speak when from across the table Dušan stepped in, clearly under the impression that he was responsible for his co-passenger and everything that he said. 'Zare, Zare, please, don't listen to him. He's still young, he doesn't understand.'

'Well, he should be quiet then!' snapped Svetozar, and he turned back to his table.

It was quiet at Matjaž's table for a few moments. It was Ludovika who broke the awkward silence, when she turned to Matjaž and said quietly, 'Me and Uršula never took this trip as something so political.'

'Yes,' her companion immediately stepped in. 'For us it was more of a personal ritual.'

Ludovika spoke up again. 'A metaphor for youth. A metaphor for the good old days!'

'Yes, the good old days.' Nada gave a heavy sigh and raised her glass. They toasted the good old days, and Peter's face, which previously had gone white from the potential conflict, was now showing a glistening smile.

From this point everything ran without a hitch. Ludovika – or Vika, as everyone started calling her, following Uršula's example – was thrilled to discover that Matjaž was a photographer. Her late husband had loved to take pictures and now her grandson loved to as well. 'He's really talented,' she said.

'Mischievous, but talented,' Uršula had to utter.

'Better that he's creative rather than suspiciously quiet, like your Anabela!' Vika protested.

'At least Anabela doesn't wet the bed!' Her friend gave as good as she got.

'Girls, girls!' intervened Peter with a smile. 'Let's not fight over grandchildren now.'

'Exactly – quiet or noisy, children are trouble!' said Matjaž. Vika smiled and admitted that wine always brought out her lively temperament.

Uršula returned her smile and lovingly patted her hand. 'You know, little Vid really does take some nice pictures!' Once again they were the best of friends. Nada dedicated most of the evening to Peter. Matjaž couldn't hear them, but it was obvious that some sort of alliance was forming between them – if not more. This was the conclusion he reached after seeing how Nada enjoyed smiling and shrieking with laughter, how she ever-so-accidently brushed against him and how, as if that wasn't enough, she spent the entire evening leaned towards him, whispering and then laughing again. Her mother's coquettish behaviour with a much younger man clearly put Melita in a bad mood; once she had satisfied her healthy appetite and was no longer required to reply to the two elderly women, she furiously rolled her eyes.

When the meal had officially come to an end, staff dragged a synthesizer, a guitar and a tamboura on to the improvised stage and started to play. It seemed to Matjaž to be a spontaneous reaction from the spirited Bosnian population, but he couldn't be sure as the singers were actually reasonably in tune. They served up a series of Yugo-rock numbers, in a slightly more rudimentary format than the originals but this clearly didn't bother those gathered around the ten tables, who soon started jumping up.

'Look, Milica and Martin are already on their feet,' said Matjaž, commenting on the dance-floor situation. Melita laughed when she saw that the pair had decided to dance the polka to the rock ballad *Ružica si bila*. 'You see that chap? That's Lojze, and now he's trying to persuade his wife Anica . . . Is she going to accept?' Matjaž paused for a moment. 'Will she give herself up, will she let her husband, who she's been with for a hundred years, get her on her feet one more time?' He took to the role of commentator with greater enthusiasm.

Melita sprang to his assistance. 'No, it looks like Anica is tired, fed up maybe. No, now it's clear that Anica is not going to dance.'

Lojze turned around and approached another woman, whom Matjaž and Melita didn't recognize, took a fairly awkward bow and gained her consent. 'And how will Anica react to the new situation?' asked Melita, searching for Matjaž's nod of approval. When she received it, she continued, 'As is typical in such situations, she's going to reach for the classic solution, by which I mean I can see the table well enough to confirm that Anica has just poured herself another glass of wine.'

'We can be sure it won't be the last . . .' added Matjaž, making Melita laugh. 'And now she's smiling,' he commented. 'Dušan and Albert have made her laugh – what did they just say to her? Did they just accuse the modest and pretty Anica of alcoholism, or sabotage even?' He earned another laugh from Melita. 'Meanwhile Lojze is dancing, he's dancing well . . .' he added.

'Excuse me, Matjaž, I'm sensing activity on Anica's table again,' his co-commentator interrupted.

'So there is.' He focused on the new action. 'Dušan's standing up. Does this mean that he's going to try and get Anica on her feet himself? Let's wait a minute to see which direction this goes. Melita, I'm afraid it's not looking likely. No, Dušan is heading this way, towards our commentary box. Will he manage to ask anyone to dance?'

Dušan was actually walking towards their table, but he just gave them a friendly wave and then wound past them. 'Nothing's going to happen. No action for Dušan, it seems, he just went to powder his nose,' said Melita, taking the initiative. In the meantime, something unbelievable happened. Anica and Albert appeared on the dance floor.

'I can't believe it. We've got two new performers on the stage,' began Matjaž. 'On the dance floor', corrected Melita, 'although the basic information still holds.'

Matjaž continued. 'Here we have our two old friends, very interesting performers, Anica and Albert. But how long will they last together?' he wondered.

'And why on earth are those two together? Why did Anica give herself up to Albert, when she didn't want to dance with her own husband?' asked Melita, stepping up the tension.

'Perhaps out of sympathy . . .' Matjaž said, in his normal voice.

'Out of sympathy?' Melita looked at him questioningly, no longer with her commentator's accent. They put down their imaginary microphones for a moment.

'Yeah, Albert lost his wife this year,' he told her, being serious again. Melita looked towards Albert with empathy.

'They were very attached to one another,' Matjaž added. 'They were a couple for fifty years.'

'Fifty years,' repeated Melita, absorbed in thought.

'Can you imagine that? I can't. I really can't, and I'm quite a bit older than you.'

'Don't you believe in true love?' Melita asked him, with a naïve and romantic enthusiasm.

'I don't know,' he replied. 'I think I do, I just don't believe that it can last so long. And then of course that makes you wonder if it was ever true love at all.'

'I always thought that my parents would be together for ever,' she sighed with a slight sadness. 'They were a good match, I think. We used to have fun together . . .'

'That's what I mean, something always goes wrong,' Matjaž added sadly.

'Not always,' Melita smiled, and pointed towards Milica and Martin, who were eagerly spinning each other around as if they were a small tornado set to wipe the remaining couples from the dance floor.

The two self-proclaimed commentators had just picked up their imaginary microphones again, in order to now accompany Peter and Nada to the dance floor, when Patrik and Matevž appeared at their table, both looking very awkward. Patrik turned to Melita and asked her, in a very gentlemanly manner, if she would like to dance. Melita's face showed signs of panic, and in desperation she turned to Matjaž and stuttered, as if she were straight out of *Pride and Prejudice*, 'I'd love to, erm, dance, but I've already promised the next dance to Matjaž.' He assumed his new role immediately and nodded politely, and Patrik and Matevž literally froze.

Matjaž looked at the two frightened young men and could not resist the temptation. He said politely, 'I think that those two ladies are still available, though', and nodded towards Uršula and Ludovika. Not having noticed the touch of malice in his suggestion, Patrik and Matevž blushed, and then headed off to do what was right. They led the two elderly ladies to the dance floor.

Soon no one remained seated. Matjaž spun Melita around. Nada placed herself in the capable hands of Peter, who had decided to show his dancing pedigree to the entire community of Hotel Turist, Jajce. Patrik danced unconvincingly with Vika, while Uršula commandeered Matevž with a fair amount of success. Finally Anica ended up in the arms of Lojze, while Dušan took over with the lively Milica.

At around midnight Melita and Matjaž sat themselves down in the safety of the darkness beneath the old linden tree, away from the remaining company, and smoked cheerfully. Looking at the dancing lunatics, with an average age of around sixty, she smiled and said, 'You are the only normal person on this trip.' She butted his shoulder with her head.

'It's that bad, I know, right!' he smiled, and she smiled back at him playfully.

'So how come you don't have a girlfriend?'

'How do you know that I don't have one?'

'You wouldn't have been so determined about true love not lasting for ever if you did' she said, proud that she had accurately connected her observations.

'But how do you know that I'm not just a cynic who doubts and undermines everything, even when in a relationship?' He looked at her provocatively.

She averted the overly complicated question. 'As if cynics don't believe in love!'

Matjaž looked at her with distrust. He didn't have a response, so he asked her, 'Why don't you have a boyfriend?'

'How do you know that I don't have one?' She looked at him from beneath her eyebrows.

'Because women who are happily in love don't need to dress so desperately provocatively, like you first wanted to for our gathering this evening,' he replied.

'Mate, what do you know!' she spat back at him scathingly. 'Girls always try everything to impress, or at least the cool ones do anyway. Also, you're being unintentionally offensive now, you know.'

'Don't you dare insult me; my offence is always intentional. What did I say?'

'You suggested, perhaps without realizing, that I didn't really want to impress anyone by dressing like this, or even worse that I'm not impressive at all.'

'Guilty!' Matjaž clutched his head. 'It was completely involuntarily and unintentional. But on the other hand, it didn't seem especially necessary to point out that you're very pretty.'

'Why do men always think that they don't need to tell women they're pretty?'

'As far as I'm concerned, you pretty women are already well aware of it and know how to exploit your charms, so why would I encourage narcissism?' he insisted.

'Now I understand why you're hot, I mean why you've not, got a girlfriend.' The two of them laughed at her slip of the tongue.

'I don't actually know why women love to hear it so much. Do you collect compliments like trophies to show the grandkids?'

'No, it's simpler than that. It's just nice to hear. It's a code so that we know you like us,' Melita said, trying to explain things more clearly.

'I understand, but all too often female beauty is a veil concealing the horror underneath,' Matjaž said, testing her.

'And so veiling things is something that only women do, is it?' she remarked, and again searched for his response with her eyes.

Matjaž ran his hands through his hair, as though he were thinking about it, and finally said, 'Wouldn't you rather a guy told you that you were intelligent, that you were kind?'

'No,' she replied dryly.

'Elaborate!' Matjaž was enjoying the role of mentor.

'What? Oh, I need to explain it to you, do I? If a guy says to me that I'm fucking clever, he's just friend-zoned me, get it? It's like the equivalent of saying that my Ugg boots don't suit me or that he's gay.'

'Does your mum know that you talk like that?' Matjaž goaded her with his moralizing tone; her slang, and especially her tone, reminded him just of how much younger than him she was.

'Let me elabo . . . raborate. Basically, saying "You're pretty!" actually means, in translation, that a woman is attractive, like, that the man wants to fuck her.' She looked at him for confirmation of whether she was clear, and when she received it she continued, 'But not just that, when a person invests in their beauty, in their appearance, that orderliness then settles inside, and even if you're not really beautiful you act that way around others and then you start to like yourself, too. Get it?'

'And so earlier you thought that short skirt and fishnet top would top up your inner beauty?' he stung her again.

'I don't believe in inner beauty,' she said provocatively.

'Neither do I' he replied, and he caught her expression of pride when she realized that she had been a good match for him. He couldn't resist kissing her. She didn't pull back.

He'd already had his hands all over her body even before they ended up in his room, and she was a quite a match for him in the art of groping, too. He laid her on the bed and started to caress her. 'What was it like, your first time?' she asked him.

'What, is this your first time? Didn't you say that . . .'

She burst out laughing. 'Of course I did, it's not my first, not even second or third, I just wanted to see your reaction,' she said and quickly clasped her arms around him, as if she was scared that he'd now run away. Matjaž realized that in matters of love and affection Melita expected an even shorter duration than he did. It was he who then took the lead in kissing her, until she started talking again. 'Do you know, for a photographer you don't take very many photographs?'

Without removing his lips from her body, he replied, 'There aren't that many things worthy of a photograph in this world.'

'What about people?'

'Would you like me to photograph you?'

She burst out laughing again. 'Of course not, I just suddenly thought that I know absolutely nothing about you.'

'Would you like me to stop?' He finally let her go from his arms.

'No way,' she said, again slightly in fear, clutching him tightly. They slipped back into a sumptuous embrace. When Matjaž placed his lips on her neck for the second time, she started talking again. 'Did you take pictures of your ex?'

He was now completely confused. 'Sorry?'

'Your ex, did you ever take pictures of her?'

'Rarely,' he said, and turned over on to his back, away from her.

'Don't turn away,' she said gently, scared that she had finally repelled him. 'We'll get to that, I'd just like to talk a bit more,' she said pleadingly.

'I hardly ever photographed her,' he said, turning back to face her.

'Why? Was she not worth a photograph?' asked the naked Melita, taking his hand.

'No, it wasn't that,' he said, lost in thought, starting to stroke her.

'At first it was the opposite. It seemed like taking a photo of her wouldn't do her justice.'

'Do you mean that she wouldn't have liked how she looked?'

'Oh, no, she really encouraged me to take photos. She really liked my pictures. More than that, there were many times when she wanted me to take her picture.' He smiled at the memory. 'She wanted me to take a photo of her every year in the same place, so that in our old age we could put on an exhibition of her portraits entitled "Free Fall".' He laughed, and Melita did too, although when she heard about such closeness between two people she wished for a moment that she could also have that with somebody for once.

'But what then?'

'What when?'

'Why didn't you want to photograph her?'

'Like I said, I didn't want to betray her image. It seemed like I just couldn't get it down properly, couldn't capture it. A photo would have been an injustice.'

'Interesting.'

'Why?'

'You don't want to photograph most people because they're uninteresting, but you didn't want to photograph her because she was too beautiful?'

'I never thought I'd need her photograph, I thought we'd always be together,' he said bitterly.

'What, would you rather have loads of pictures of her, so that now you're not together any more you could maliciously delete them?'

'I wouldn't delete them,' he said honestly.

'Will you do me a favour?'

'What?'

'Take a photo of me!'

'Sorry, what?'

'Yeah, right now, beside you, take a photo of me!'

'I don't want to. The light is bad, you won't look as nice as you could.'

'One photo, Matjaž, please.'

Without really understanding what Melita really wanted, or knowing what would come of it, he took out his camera and started to photograph his naked lover. Through the lens she seemed almost prettier than before; so young and soft and with a kind of indefinable determination on her face – almost no longer the girl that he had heard on the balcony earlier, but a woman who was chasing something.

'What now?' he asked her.

'Show me,' she smiled. 'Nice,' she admired her images. 'Now delete them.'

'What? But they're good pictures, they're not bad at all, a lot better than I thought . . .'

'Nah, just delete them. I'm not going to be one of these nostalgic women like my mum, who looks back wistfully at old pictures of herself.'

'Then at least leave me to be nostalgic, so I can look at these pictures of you wistfully when I'm an old man . . .' Matjaž said, almost in a panic.

Melita burst out laughing. 'No, just delete them, they won't do you any good either.'

'No, I won't!' said a desperate Matjaž.

'Things come and go! It's no tragedy if those go,' she said enigmatically, almost as if she were a grown-up who had skilfully manoeuvred the scene in order to finally ensnare her lover.

He looked at her sternly, trying to understand what she wanted him to say, whether it was some kind of perverse game where she was going to accuse him of abuse. Melita's face gave nothing away except a trace of victory for having taken the initiative in this situation. He deleted the photographs, shrugged his shoulders and smiled. Melita turned off the light and snuggled up to him. Then they slowly glided into tender lovemaking.

When he woke up, she was no longer there. He was pleased that there was a new day on the horizon, that the day was sunny and that his hangover was not too awful. Before going down for breakfast, he took a shower and shaved. He liked what he saw in the mirror, and he gave himself a seductive wink.

Nada

At breakfast he caught sight of the smiling and incredibly attractive Melita, who was joined at the table by Patrik and Matevž. Those two were also looking rather different compared to the night before, seeming much more relaxed and talkative. He realized that most people had already had breakfast, as apart from the full table in front of him there was only one other occupied table, full of people that he didn't recognize. Matjaž went over to the table of familiar faces and greeted them, smiling.

'Well good morning!' Melita beckoned him over seductively. The young guys offered their hands, realizing that they still hadn't introduced themselves.

'May I sit down?' asked Matjaž.

'Of course,' said Patrik kindly.

'We're actually just leaving, though,' Matevž said dryly.

Matjaž looked at Melita questioningly. She shrugged her shoulders and, slightly embarrassed, smiled at him and said, 'Before we leave we're going to quickly pop to town for postcards and stamps.'

'Oh really, are you going to write to Daddy?' Matjaž asked coldly. The smile disappeared from her face.

'When are we leaving?' Matjaž asked the remaining two members of the group, not looking back at his fickle lover.

'In just over half an hour, if I'm not mistaken,' answered Matevž, again in a monotone voice.

The anxious Patrik looked at his buddy. 'So we really had better get going.'

Matjaž was left alone with his bread, butter and marmalade, the brew that they rather uncritically called coffee, and an apple. Nada sat down next to him, rather conspicuously. She smelled like a rose garden and was dressed in a white tunic, which served as a means of revealing her rather impressive cleavage.

'Oh, good morning' he greeted her.

'Listen, do you happen to have seen . . .'

'Yeah, she just left with the two guys to get a postcard for her dad,' he interrupted.

'No, I know where Melita is. Have you seen Peter anywhere?'

'No I haven't seen anyone, apart from Melita and the guys.'

Nada stood up. 'Well I'm going to dash off, then, I need to ask him something urgently . . .' Matjaž couldn't bear to think what could be so critical at this hour. He decided that he was not going to over-think her daughter's inappropriate behaviour, but he had to admit that the tempestuous Melita had succeeded somewhat in eating away at his self-confidence.

On the way to the AVNOJ museum, where the group were to pay their respects to the fallen Partisans and the whole awe-inspiring history, he bore witness to a controversy that arose between Dušan and Albert, accompanied by another pair of pensioners who had no real enthusiasm for discussion and just nodded here and there – first to one side, then at the other.

Matjaž, not well versed in the matters of the National Liberation War himself, joined in with interest although he barely understood the situation.

'How can you question the second AVNOJ assembly? This is where the foundations of equal rights for each of the six republics were put in place – its independence, even Slovene independence,' said Albert passionately.

'But that's just it – tell me, where did that get us, dear Albert? If Yugoslavia had been more centralized and less nationalistic, it never would have met its demise.'

'It would have happened even sooner, all the disparities between republics would have appeared even sooner,' persisted his hot-blooded companion.

'I don't think so myself, I think it would have been better.'

'But will you accept that the second assembly was presided over by intellectuals from all over Yugoslavia, such as Josip Vidmar, Edvard Kocbek . . . ?'

'So what?' Dušan reacted childishly.

'That is what earned AVNOJ additional legitimacy; it was founded on intellect, on reflection. If nothing else, it was a reflection of the political reality at that time, in particular the way in which we broke away from the old Yugoslavia, a prison of nations.'

'It doesn't matter, let's leave it there,' Dušan said, calming down.

When they arrived in front of the museum, Matjaž distanced himself from his group and went with his camera to look around. He was moved by the crowds who had gathered there. They came from all over, from different republics and generations, with flags, with their *titkovkas* – the green Partisan caps, with pictures of Tito, with banners reading 'Death to fascism, freedom to the people!' and 'Brotherhood and Unity!' and 'Tito – The Party!' People were shaking hands; some even hugged each other. They sang Partisan songs. It seemed to him that the groups from Slovenia were the loudest and most organized. He even appreciated the choir, and of course documented them immediately. He had no idea before now that these weren't the only crazy Slovenes who came here, and that detachments from the Štajerska, Primorska and even Dolenjska regions were here, too. At one point he felt as if he had found himself in an alternate universe of friendly, smiling people who had surrendered themselves to communal ritual with no trouble at all, with a shared love of some old, fallen country.

He was taken aback when a group of women in neckerchiefs came towards him, offered him a carnation and mumbled something; nor did he know how to best to respond when some men, wearing unfamiliar uniforms, wanted to shake his hand, and even less so when a group of young Pioneer scouts asked him to join in with their traditional dance. He captured those happy faces through the lens, as if this would allow him to understand them better. To him it all seemed stupid, absurd – as if people came here to visit their own past, or worse, to recreate a history that was never experienced in such a nice, relaxed environment, as they tried to make out now. He looked around, back and forth, to see whether he could catch a glimpse of Melita, but he didn't see her. He looked for other members of his expedition, too, but in vain.

He thought, maybe Yugoslavia now remained entirely within this construction of an entity that never existed, and had become only the missing link between the strangers that came here. In a similar way, the museum interior seemed like a piece of history that had been relocated, intact, to the present, to this reality where it coexisted perfectly with a kind of promise of peace provided by nice ideas and courageous acts of the past – except by now these were disfigured, fratricidal acts of the not-so-distant past.

He was happy to find his fellow travellers in a nearby bar having a coffee break. Some had been impressed by the event countless times before. Albert and Dušan, who after seeing the exhibition had obviously been able to smooth over their disagreement, were revisiting their experiences of the museum's most inspiring artefacts. More earthly thoughts ran through the minds of other members of the group: Milica was explaining to Anica about a special

OAP discount at Spar, which was a much better value supermarket than Mercator. Martin and Lojze just listened without much interest, first to the male and then to the female debates. The table livened up somewhat when Nada joined them. 'Ah phew, I was worried that I was going to be left in Jajce for ever. I can't find my daughter, I can't find her anywhere, and Peter isn't anywhere to be seen either.'

'It seems that Peter became thoroughly acquainted with rakia yesterday,' Lojze winked at Nada.

'That's right, this morning he had big black rings under his eyes and he could barely wave when we said hello,' announced Milica.

'Well, that really is worrying!' smiled Albert. Matjaž wouldn't have had him down as the sarcastic type.

Not long afterwards, Milica and Anica said their goodbyes. They wanted to take a short walk, as the doctor had ordered. Thus the men remained alone with Nada, who had treated herself to a sandwich and a shot of rakia. 'This occasion calls for a tasty drink...' she said, as if excusing herself.

'And even without an occasion, we can easily create one for a drink as tasty as that.' Matjaž couldn't resist. Luckily all of the men laughed and Nada only gave him a stern look, like a teacher who might punish her student but in actual fact has already forgiven him.

Nada succeeded in persuading the men to also have a drink themselves, which soon put the group in a much livelier frame of mind. They were no longer concerned with AVNOJ, battles, victims, Liberation Day, but instead only with trivialities – from the love lives of Slovene politicians ('That Urška really is a beautiful woman' the men agreed) to the promotion of Prince William in the Royal Court (Duchess Kate is very attractive, established the men, and little Prince George is so cute, Nada had to add).

'And how about you?' Lojze looked at her enquiringly.

'I'm sorry?' she smiled with her mouth full, embarrassed.

'How are you finding things without the husband, what's his name again?'

'Oh Lojze, I can't tell you how good I've been feeling since we went our separate ways. It's only now that I see how totally trapped I was in that marriage,' sighed Nada, and it was clear from all the men's faces, except Albert's, that they too were thinking of their marriages as cages.

'I've really started to discover myself,' she summarized. 'Now I'm finally doing things that I couldn't do before, things that I had no idea I even wanted to do.'

'Such as what?' Matjaž asked innocently.

'Doing cultural things, for example. I've always loved culture. As a young girl I regularly went to productions at the national theatre, Drama, but then after giving birth and getting married I completely neglected that.'

'And you've started going to the Drama again?' asked Matjaž, involving himself.

'Exactly, to Drama, and other places . . .' said Nada resolutely. Matjaž only just resisted the temptation to ask her for theatre recommendations.

'But enough about me. Tell me, Dušan, how are you? Are you still waiting on that grandchild?'

'Jesus, don't remind me! Ah, that son of mine is such a slacker. He and his Karla still don't feel ready. They're still waiting, as if it will become easier with time.'

'No, nothing easier about it,' agreed Martin. 'It gets so much harder.'

'And doesn't your genetic material get weaker every year as well?' attested Lojze, the self-proclaimed DNA expert.

Albert turned to the photographer. 'What about you, Matjaž, when are you going to have a kid?'

'Not just now, it seems,' he replied.

'Why not, Matjaž?' Dušan looked at him with a scolding expression.

'Well, they say that having a womb helps these things, and if you don't have one of those it helps to have some sort of woman,' he explained with a sad look on his face.

'You're not trying to tell me that a handsome young gentleman such as yourself doesn't have a girlfriend?' Nada leaned towards him seductively.

'Would you like to have him for yourself, or what?' Dušan burst into laughter, and the rest of the group with him.

'And why ever not?' Nada winked at Matjaž, who pulled a wry face in return. She presumably wouldn't have winked at him had she suspected what had happened with her daughter the night before.

'And what about that beautiful daughter of yours, Nada?' enquired Dušan.

'Who knows,' she sighed worriedly. 'Young people at that age are impossible to tame,' she said, excusing her ignorance as she checked her phone to see whether it held some sort of answer as to her daughter's whereabouts.

'Yeah, it's true, I saw her walking around Jajce arm in arm with two boys,' said Lojze purposefully. 'I was having coffee with Anica and we saw her. She appeared to be cavorting rather a lot,' he added.

Nada looked at him sternly, so much so that he immediately added, 'But only as young people usually cavort on a nice spring day. And Patrik and Matevž really are very young.'

'And well behaved,' added Matjaž, not without irony.

Towards the evening Matjaž wanted to be alone. He decided that he'd go and have a look around Jajce for himself. After half an hour he was fairly certain that there was nothing to explore. 'How's it going with the combabes?' chirped a text from Aleksander. He was grateful to him for not having ended such an obviously cocky message with a smiley face. Combabes. What should he write? 'I'm sickle of them!' he typed, and pressed send. He did not expect the evening ahead to provide any relief.

Elvis had quite a large estate some ten kilometres outside of Jajce. At its heart was a villa, which reflected the owner's healthy financial situation and unfortunate lack of taste. He had, for example, decorated the entire house in a bright apricot colour, covered the interior with a reddish marble and, naturally, crammed the enormous space full of rustic furniture adorned with garish patterned velvet. There were numerous statues, with a particular focus on lions, adorning the baroque entrance, arranged around the garden, suspended in the water fountains and, of course, populating the interior. Elvis did not actually show everyone around the house; the majority of people decided to remain in the safety of the garden. Matjaž discovered all of this through his own initiative, when he went to look for a toilet that was slightly more private than the bathroom of the small, overpopulated cabin that stood by the pool.

Yes, Elvis's enormous garden included a cabin, which was actually a house in itself and quite a luxurious house at that, and a pool – similarly luxurious and utterly tasteless. He also had a wife, Azra, and some children. There were allegedly more, but on this occasion it was only Selma and Damir who kept the Slovene Yugophiles entertained. They were both around twenty years of age, twenty-two perhaps, and quite pleasing to look at – exotic beauties, actually, with black curls and dark eyes. During the awkward introductory pleasantries Matjaž discovered that Selma was named after the very popular rock ballad, and that it was not something of which she was proud. She would have much preferred the inspiration behind her name to have been Salma Hayek – that's how she explained her name whenever she travelled. Although anyone capable of basic arithmetic would surely know that Salma Hayek wasn't anywhere near Hollywood in time for the naming of this Bosnian Selma.

Elvis's pigs, which were probably crammed into one of the neighbouring properties, clearly brought in a lot of money. Martin was nevertheless convinced that there had to be a mafia-style story behind all of this, although he didn't voice this too loudly as they were there as guests after all. Besides, it didn't seem overly important to question why they had been blessed with such luxury – bordering on wantonness – on what had been presented as a fairly modest excursion.

Albert was more concerned about the fact that Elvis was raising pigs willy-nilly in a Muslim region. But Peter comforted him, saying that he mainly sold his pigs to the West where it wasn't a sin. In the end the guests forgave Elvis of all potential sins as he told them with pride about the part he played in Yugoslav history, in the Partisan resistance, and that he was also a descendant of those who took part in the liberation of Jajce and in one way or another, whether as soldiers or even as cooks or pot washers, took part in the second AVNOJ assembly.

On the large terrace by the pool, Elvis prepared tables set with tablecloths and flowers for his guests. Matjaž couldn't fathom why anyone would make so much effort for a cousin and a handful of strangers who were travelling with him. Dušan was convinced that Elvis was bored of this country, that he wanted news from abroad – as if he lived in the Middle Ages and had to wait for passing traders to bring him news from the wider world.

Later it turned out that maybe Dušan wasn't too far wrong. Well, in terms of the Middle Ages of course he was, but as far as Elvis was concerned he was right. This greying, tall-grown Bosnian welcomed everyone as one of his own, engaged in conversation with every single one, asked who, where, what and why, how 'the Slovenes' were, how the EU was. When the polite expedition members returned the question and asked how things were going in Bosnia, he just shrugged his shoulders and said, 'Well, it's still going!' When he'd had a bit more to drink, he elaborated a little further: yes, the situation was difficult, tensions were running high, the financial outlook was catastrophic, but on the other hand Bosnians have always been the best at knowing how to survive in the face of turmoil – as Meša Selimović would say, 'Man is always at a loss.'

Matjaž thought this observation seemed a little inappropriate, especially given that it came from someone who had never had first-hand experience of surviving that turmoil – his children even less so, at least as far as he could tell from the spoiled Selma and the boisterous Damir. The former sneered at the Slovene guests here and there, or appeared visibly bored when listening to their stories. If she had only a small expression of disdain on her face, this was a peculiar compliment to whoever had tried to amuse her. Her brother, on the other hand, artfully recruited the non-smoking Slovenes to the joys of smoking, and politely lit cigarettes for them.

Regardless of whether you agreed with the political stance of Elvis the great butcher, it was impossible to overlook his genuine desire to give the flock of Slovene guests the best possible celebration. Here there was an abundance of food, dominated of course by meat, especially pork, but he was not short of other delicacies either: from various types of little pies to salads and bean stews. The wine was flowing, too, as well as good, homemade rakia aplenty. It wasn't entirely clear who had created this feast. Azra only took credit for one lot of baklava, and her vivacious, casual and tidy appearance was not that of someone who had spent the past two days in front of a stove.

When the evening reached the point where everyone was acquainted and had steeled themselves with food and drink, Matjaž ended up at a table with Patrik, Matevž and Nada. He hadn't had anything more to do with Melita, who was now giving Peter generous amounts of company. He rather stoically resigned himself to the situation, whatever that even was.

'Actually I'm discovering that women only start to realize what they want from sex somewhere around their forties,' Nada said, breaking the silence within the small group of youngsters for no specific reason.

'Forty-five, even', Matjaž mischievously thought aloud.

Patrik and Matevž were about to run off when Nada, overlooking that comment, continued, 'It's the age when a woman achieves a kind of confidence, when she's already made something of her life and doesn't have to worry about the kind of impression she makes on the male sex. It's all about emancipation from men, actually. And that can only happen after many years, when experiences have already uncovered all the weaknesses of your sex but at the same time have made you realize the strength of womanhood.' In a daze, she occasionally caressed her cleavage and looked suggestively at all three men.

'That's no doubt true,' began the shy Patrik. 'Only I wouldn't know too much about that; my wife left me when she was thirty-four, saying she was a lesbian . . .' Matjaž felt sorry for Patrik and thought about how to reply sympathetically, and whether he ought to admit that a girl had once left him for the other team, too. But Nada beat him to it.

'She obviously set out on a path of self-discovery very early.'

'But, in her case, she at least put herself on that path,' snapped Matjaž. Patrik looked at him questioningly, and Nada's face became serious.

'What are you trying to say?' she asked seriously.

Matjaž, who at that point regretted having spoken so freely, tried to ease the situation and said gently, 'Nothing, nothing, I just meant that some women explore on their own initiative, while others need a little encouragement.' The moment he uttered those words, he realized that he had made the situation even worse. Nada, obviously picking up on the unkind implication, stood up and left the table. Matevž followed her, and Matjaž noticed him hugging her and starting to comfort her. Then they both disappeared to the other end of the garden.

'Rascal!' roared Patrik, looking at his new friend. That was the first almost-rude word that had come out of his mouth on the whole trip, and probably ever. Matjaž looked at him enquiringly.

'I told him to at least let me have Nada!' he hissed.

'Everyone needs at least a little tenderness,' Matjaž tried to comfort him, not being sarcastic.

Patrik thought to himself and, true to his reputation for kindness, said, 'You're right. Matevž has also been through hell with his Breda.'

'Really?' asked Matjaž, interested mainly in what Patrik considered to be hell.

'The year they tried to conceive, they went from one doctor to the next, did goodness knows how many expensive tests – Matevž paid for everything of course – only for her to run off with his best friend, who then immediately knocked her up.'

Patrik placed emphasis on those last words, to show his disapproval of Matevž's ex.

'But weren't you that friend?' Matjaž joked.

Patrik didn't get the joke at first and got very angry. 'Of course not, do you think that we'd then go together . . .' At that point he realized that Matjaž was grinning at him, and burst out laughing himself. 'Matjaž, you son of a bitch!' And they raised their glasses.

Not long afterwards Uršula, Vika and Milica came and sat with them.

'Why the long faces, boys?' asked Uršula chattily, immediately after the ladies had sat down at the table – without asking, naturally. Each of them had a glass of red and they were in quite a good mood.

'We don't have them,' said Patrik unconvincingly.

'All right, where have your friend – and your new lady friend, if I may call her that – gone then?' Vika burst out into a friendly laugh.

'Ah, everyone's left me!' Patrik shook his head.

'And where's the pretty Melita?' enquired Milica, who was clearly bothered by the fact that Uršula and Vika were more up to date with happenings than she was.

'She's around somewhere. Perfect Peter invited her to sit at his table and she went over there,' grumbled Patrik.

'And after you'd been out on the rampage all day together, too!' Uršula patted him in consolation.

'We weren't on the rampage at all, we just walked around, went for a coffee and something to eat, looked at the river . . .' Patrik corrected her.

'Well, maybe there's your problem – your Melita needs a lot more male attention,' Vika smiled playfully, but Patrik didn't really understand what she meant by that. 'Oh look, now Damir's gone and sat beside her,' she added with a hint of glee.

Soon the dancing began. Elvis had clearly thought of everything and had procured a real musical troupe of eight men with various instruments, who knew how to sing traditional *sevdalinke* and classic rock and pop numbers, too. The ladies jumped to their feet, so Matjaž excused himself and fled to go for a walk before the dancing euphoria set in.

Elvis's garden offered several small, alluring hiding places. Matjaž investigated all of the charms concealed by the greenery, and soon discovered that many people had already gone on the same investigative mission and were sitting down on the benches. He finally found a place to sit for himself, which the gods – hallelujah! – had laid out for him beneath an enormous treetop that had been left unlit. Solitude suited Matjaž; it allowed his soul to unwind a little.

He realized above all just how tired and listless he was. The mass of new faces, the group of Yugoslav enthusiasts, the images of history, had all left him completely drained. He didn't have the strength to think about his past, let alone about the future. The night with Melita now seemed like an old, dusty postcard. When he got a text from Aleksander, asking him for more concrete information about everyone on the trip, he decided that he didn't have the strength to explain. Images of the women who had made their mark on him in the last six months, including the beautiful Melita, were blurred and he didn't try to bring any of them into focus. He was content with them sinking into oblivion, and happy that with the help of Elvis's rakia he could once again forget even himself.

'Is it something about this country, or what? I stopped smoking ten years ago but here it's impossible to resist tobacco,' Matjaž heard the voice of Matevž, coming out of nowhere, over his shoulder. All of a sudden he appeared under the tree, puffing passionately on his roll-up. Matjaž wondered how the hell he'd ended up here, and then figured that maybe he had needed a quiet corner, too.

'I can't resist it in Ljubljana either,' remarked Matjaž.

'True, true,' considered Matevž, and with that took a deep drag of tobacco. 'But there's something about this place, something . . .'

Out of courtesy Matjaž agreed, although he thought that this place would be an awful lot better without these haughty Slovenes.

'Did you start to get bored of the company?' Matjaž asked politely.

'Well, they all love that Yugo music, even Nada got really excited over it, but me, I don't get that nostalgia, that feeling that settles in every new generation and makes them sing 'Stavi ruke na moja ramena' like it's the latest fashion trend.'

'I'm not convinced that this is about nostalgia,' considered Matjaž.

'What's it all about, then?' Matevž looked at him challengingly.

'Maybe Yugoslavia's only function was that in some strange way, in spite of everything, it enabled the creation of so much eclectic and quality popular music,' he replied.

'So now even you're going to sing this band's praises without thinking about it,' Matevž looked at him sharply.

'No, not at all. I don't have a personal affinity towards them, but I can understand how you can listen to Azra or Bijelo dugme just because you like the music – just like you can listen to the Beatles, the Rolling Stones or Pink Floyd. It's got nothing to do with longing for Yugoslavia. Maybe you listen to 'Jesen u meni' just because it reminds you of your first school dance. You wouldn't say that respect for classic Western rock is about British nostalgia, would you?' Matjaž addressed the question to himself as much as Matevž.

'You know what, if you can't see that there's still a kind of pathos lingering in these songs, a kind of longing for the good old days that never really were . . .' Matevž said, more calmly.

Matjaž did not feel like debating Yugoslav bands any more, and so the two of them smoked a cigarette in silence.

Eventually Matevž began again. 'Have you noticed that everyone here only thinks about sex? A holiday about memories and comradeship is just an excuse. It's actually a holiday of completely new memories and a completely new kind of comradeship,' moralized Matevž.

Matjaž laughed. 'No, I hadn't noticed, but it sounds to me like you didn't get the ration you were hoping for.'

'You don't mince your words, do you? I think even the married couples haven't had what they were hoping for,' he chuckled.

As if that sentence somehow brought the two men together, over the next hour they chatted about women, relationships, travels, and became sociably drunk. Feeling at ease, Matevž said, 'I do think you overdid it at lunchtime, though.'

'What do you mean?' asked Matjaž, having already forgotten about anything that might have happened over lunch.

'You offended her,' the bloke replied.

'A little honesty doesn't hurt,' Matjaž said, almost angrily.

'I'm not sure if that's true. It is not enough that her husband left her? Do we have to then take away the dignity of her new-found freedom? Sometimes it's better to at least make it look as if you agree.' Matjaž couldn't really argue with that, so he kept quiet.

'But you comforted her earlier, though, didn't you?' Matjaž made a dig at him.

'A little, maybe. I wouldn't quite say that she likes me, but she likes the feeling that men are still interested in her.'

'And how did you lose her?'

'Oh at some point she started dancing with Elvis, and it was clear that the southern temperament does something for her. He obviously flattered her. Pair that with all this property, the man was most likely irresistible,' Matevž explained, without any bitterness. 'What's up with your Melita?'

'I don't know, you tell me. I thought she actually liked me, but it seems a similar thing happened – that what she liked about me the most was that I liked her. After that she obviously needed to be liked by someone else.'

'Sometimes feeling lost is clearly the same when you're young as it is when you're older,' Matevž observed wisely.

'Or there's no big difference between mothers and daughters,' Matjaž added.

'But then who would blame them?' Matevž blew out his cigarette smoke. 'The world can be so cold and lonely sometimes. Why shouldn't they have trophies of their own, too?'

Matjaž was enjoying his chat with Matevž, who, once he'd relaxed over a beer and a cigarette, acted like a wise old priest with an insight into the wounds of the human soul and no need to judge people, who could easily put himself and his own needs aside. The two men drank, smoked, looked at the stars and were quiet for a long time.

They eventually heard a young female voice shouting 'Come, come!' Both stood up immediately, thinking that the Slovenes had started a fire, but it was just Selma with an urgent request for them to come to the dance floor, where there was a desperate lack of men. Matevž decided to comply with the charming Selma, even though Matjaž would have put money on her actually having come for him. But it was better for him this way; he didn't need any additional complications with young women. One per trip is quite enough, he said to himself, and he raised his glass.

An hour or so later the poor Bosnian's garden looked considerably different to how it had done when Matjaž had left it earlier. Everyone was on their feet, they were dancing on the tables, some were jumping into the pool and shrieking – as if this throng of middle-aged people had realized that this was their last opportunity to go crazy, to let go, before they eventually reconciled themselves with the fact that one day they would die. The orgy-like atmosphere was already palpable as married men circled around Nada and Melita, while Matevž kissed Selma in the shadows, not so discreetly. The host, too, had decided to show the largest and oldest of the women what hospitality really meant, and was spinning her around wildly. Matjaž, who for observational purposes had chosen quite a faraway table for himself, was soon approached by one of the women who he hadn't really noticed before. Out of breath, she panted, 'It's not very nice, you sat here, when there are so many girls wanting a dance.' She led him to the dance floor. He looked around, but try as he might he couldn't see a single girl who compared to Melita. She, meanwhile, was having no problem finding suitors to dance with. Thus he politely explained to the woman that he had sprained his ankle and unfortunately he wouldn't be able to satisfy the lovely dancers. At the end of the day he was wanting for nothing, sat there at the candlelit table. He was cheered by the thought that by the next day he'd be home, safe in the hands of Aleksander or even the whole crowd. Just as he was enjoying the thought of Petkovšek Embankment in late May, he was startled by Nada's voice.

'May I join you?'

'Of course,' Matjaž said.

'You know, you're a really good guy,' she said. 'I know you're not mean,' she added, uninhibited.

'How can you be so sure?' He was almost disappointed that she wasn't ascribing even the slightest bit of malice to him.

'I can tell that you're suffering, too, deep down inside,' she said sympathetically, looking at him with her dark eyes, still beautiful. He knew that those kind words were going to cost him something.

'And if I tell you that I'm not in any such deep pain, except perhaps just a little that stems from the fact that I've found myself on this goddamn trip with all of you? What will you say then?' he asked, provoking her.

'I'll nod, as if I understand, although obviously I won't believe you,' she replied, the corners of her mouth outlining a secretive smile.

'Of course you won't. Women have to make victims out of men so that then they can save them!' Matjaž blurted out.

'Who says I want to save you?' She looked at him alluringly.

'What will you do with me, then?' He now saw Nada as a woman who knew exactly how the dramaturgy of games between the sexes played out, and it pleasantly unnerved him.

'I'll torment you,' she said suggestively. It didn't so much excite Matjaž as rouse his curiosity. And so Nada – on this warm evening in this ample, remote corner of land belonging to a friendly Bosnian who was partying with a crowd of wild Slovenes – got a chance to torment Matjaž. Only in order to do so, she had to use all of her feminine charms and the skills of a seasoned lover.

The palm of her hand seemed to love savouring the surface of this man; it seemed to know how to reconcile itself with his reflexes. Whereas with Melita he had to seek out the path to joining their two bodies himself, now it was Nada who was leading the game. She discreetly removed his clothes, and set her body forth in a slow, consistent snake-like motion. Every time she made contact with his skin it roused all of his senses, which were increasingly heightened by her movements – or, more accurately, by her flowing hips, by her impressive cleavage that now, after this natural progression into love-making, offered itself up to him for exploration. He was surprised by how well she knew the game of two bodies; not a single breath, touch or impression of her body was ever out of place or too much. He was fixated by how she aroused him almost to the point of pain, but then alleviated the tension with a soft, almost maternal kiss. All of her measured sensuality, which occasionally overflowed into a passionate kiss or a cry of delight, invited and drew him in further and further by the second. As if she were conducting an orchestra, she linked his excitement into an artful rhythm; at first still slow enough for each new movement, every new touch – still so gentle – to be all the more arousing, until it eventually became unbearable and demanded his reaction – his wild, uninhibited finale.

The next day, the atmosphere on the bus was completely different to that of the previous evening. All the passengers seemed downcast, traces of shame on their faces – as if the evening before they had all taken part in a collective misdeed that now bound them all with an invisible thread, and they could not speak of what they had done to anyone, not even among themselves. That was how Matjaž saw his fellow sufferers, as he boarded the bus with the last few. It had been true, he thought; an entirely unique type of memories and comradeship.

He identified the disgraced souls through his sunglasses. Pale Patrik and Matevž, also hidden by sunglasses, were looking out of the window. They nodded at him, but neither of them felt the need to strike up a conversation. Milica was resting her head on her Martin, who was also dozing off. Lojze and Anica were completely the opposite: Lojze was resting his head on his wife's shoulder, while she was acting as if she'd never even met this foreigner and dreamily gazed in another direction. Melita and Nada were almost a perfect picture of mother and daughter – their pretty heads leaning on one another, making them look like one organism with two heads, both drifting off to sleep. Even Vika and Uršula, always in the mood for chitchat, this morning sat quietly in their seats, flicking through *Gloria* and *Story*, not taking any notice of their surroundings.

Matjaž sat down to the right of Albert and Dušan. Dušan was already snoring by the window; Albert, meanwhile, was writing something in a notebook. When he saw Matjaž he said, 'Well, we're off.'

'We are indeed,' Matjaž said, confirming the obvious.

'It was nice,' continued Albert, and wrote some more in his book.

'Nice, yeah,' said Matjaž.

'So will you come on another trip with us?' the widower asked him expectantly.

'Without a doubt,' Matjaž quickly replied, knowing that he'd had enough of memories and comradeship, death to fascism and freedom to the people, to last him a lifetime.

Aleksander was thrilled. 'Mother and daughter!' The two of them were sat outside Bar Petkovšek, just as Matjaž had so longed to do; he could finally touch down on home soil and put aside those vivid memories from Bosnia.

'Mate, but that's crazy! That's every man's dream, that's it!' Aleksander continued in envy.

'Come on, it was nothing special,' remarked Matjaž, not feigning modesty.

'Nothing special, there's something wrong with you. One trip, two women, and relatives at that! Nothing special. You know what's really nothing special? Spring cleaning. Yep, that's nothing special, and, what's more, it's so completely not special that it pushes even happy couples like Karla and I right to the brink,' Aleksander complained crossly, ruffling his mane of dark hair.

'Really? Where is Karla? I kind of hoped that she'd come to say hi.'

'Where is she? She's taking a break from a lot of serious TV-watching,' his friend answered, still angry. They gazed up at the dense canopy of treetops, then Aleksander looked to Matjaž pleadingly.

'So, take pity on me and tell me, how was it?'

'You know that I am a gentleman, one hundred per cent, and I never reveal details about my ladies.'

'Oh, come on!' his friend complained.

Matjaž looked at him patronizingly, played with his cigarette lighter, and after some consideration said, 'I can only tell you that there was a clear difference, but not so much for me to say that one was better than the other.'

'What the hell is that supposed to mean?'

'It simply means that it can be nice to tame a youth, and it's also nice when you're the youth being tamed . . .'

'I don't believe it. That's all you're going to give away? That first you were the hunter and the second time the prey?'

'If you want to put it like that,' he said, remaining enigmatic.

'I don't want to put it like anything, I want lurid details!' raged Aleksander, which quietly amused Matjaž.

'Ha, well then I suggest you become an AVNOJ delegate and get a good close look at that Jajce for yourself!'

KAT AND
THE THREE HORSEMEN
OF THE APOCALYPSE

Aleksander, Karla and Matjaž had agreed to meet at the usual time in the usual place on this particular Friday. Matjaž was inspecting the spring–summer collection of Ljubljana girls, and did not appear dissatisfied. He was enjoying his beer, surrounded by people who were likewise sipping beer and chatting. He, too, was about to throw himself into the conversation at any moment, enriching it with his own nonsense. He, too, was going to phase one beer into a second and then a third, suddenly making the defined edges of the world and his own words slightly more rounded. Thought – if you could even call it that – was going to gain its own kind of independence, its own kind of freedom, so that it didn't take into account the feelings of those who expressed it or of those to whom it was expressed. No guilty consciences, only the prospect of a Saturday spent sleeping, after which the previous evening always – well, maybe not quite always – seemed like an episode of a beloved sitcom.

That was, of course, provided that Aleksander and Karla came out to play . . . actually, that they even turned up, it occurred to him. He looked at his watch. They were already fifteen minutes late. He pulled a face, and was already reaching for his phone to enquire how much longer he was going to be left alone with his thoughts – which when left to their own devices never garnered anything intelligent – when in the distance he caught sight of a long-legged girl with long chestnut hair, coming towards him. Convinced that she was going to sit down at the neighbouring table, he continued to look for Aleksander's name in his contacts. But the pretty girl came and stood at his table.

'Matjaž?'

'Can I help you?'

'I'm Kat.'

'I'm more of a dog man myself.'

'Nice to meet you,' she laughed with a cheerful smile full of slightly curved teeth. Matjaž was convinced it could have cleared a cloudy sky. 'My name is Kat.'

'Oh, I see. Matjaž,' he said, placing his hand into the one she had offered. Confused, he looked around and signalled for her to sit down.

'I know,' she said confidently.

'And who carelessly gave that secret away?' smirked Matjaž.

'Karla!'

'That, that . . . that traitor! She'll pay for this,' Matjaž said, pretending to be aggrieved, once he realized how his friends had tricked him. 'And you're supposed to be just right for me?'

'No, I heard the opposite version. You're supposed to be just right for me.'

'What a careless lie!' Matjaž declared.

'Well, OK, there's nothing for me here then,' she said, feigning a sad voice and starting to leave.

'Well, hey, if you've already made this long journey to disappointment, then you've certainly earned it,' Matjaž stopped her, almost too enthusiastically.

'Pint of Laško, please!' she said to the waitress who appeared at the table.

After that, they began to chat almost as if they were friends. Kat was an architect, and worked as an intern at some small but up-and-coming studio, the name of which Matjaž forgot immediately, of course. He was surprised by how sensible she seemed. He felt relieved that for once while out for a drink with a girl he wasn't saving the world, solving hunger in Somalia, global warming, the aftermath of tsunamis, the illegal war in Iraq or one of the many conflicts in the Middle East – and let's not even mention Haiti. Kat lived in a rented flat on Trubarjeva Street, liked to drink beer, didn't like working out, liked to dance and didn't like eating bio-eco-organic food. She liked to sleep in and she didn't like going to bed early. So work was a bit of a pain for her and it encroached upon her natural rhythms. She looked forward to parties and she hated her working hours, even though her work was creative. Her hands were the most productive part of her body, she said.

'But I think that's the same for everyone,' countered Matjaž, demonstrating how he took photographs.

'Yeah, but most people look at their hands as useless weapons that just translate orders from the brain; I can see real artists in mine,' she said. 'I often feel like the hand dictates the creative tempo, and that the vision of what's being created develops through it . . . A hand can sometimes go beyond that point where the brain comes to a halt.'

Matjaž nodded. He was a little disappointed not to have any cynical remarks to make. Then he noticed her lips, which became even more appealing as she was speaking. Her artistic hands tossed her hair skilfully over her shoulder, just enough to reveal her neck, which looked long, soft and smooth. The thought of how happy he would be to shower it with kisses crossed his mind. As she rolled a cigarette he noticed how slight and rather long her fingers were – they had a gentle echo of long legs about them, and an almost shy but self-assured gait. She talked to him openly about her family – about her mum, who had found some esoteric god who was in all of us, naturally, and to whom you just had to open all the chakras inside you.

'When I said to my mum that she ought to try opening the chakra in her brain, she flew off the handle. We didn't speak for two days – can you imagine?' she smiled.

Matjaž returned her smile, and felt an unstoppable urge to stroke her graceful fingers. Instead, he simply asked, 'And how have your dad's chakras taken to her god?'

'There's a slight issue there, you see – she didn't have any chakras at all until my dad found a younger chakra – or should I say, chick,' she clarified.

'I thought as much. Although isn't that a rather anti-feminist message? If you say a woman has to replace a man with a god when he leaves her, that's like saying the man was like a god to her before . . .'

'Maybe you're right. She seemed completely at ease without any such authority before that. I hope that I'm able to remain atheist myself.' She smiled slightly.

'And you don't resent your dad?' he smiled back.

'Oh of course I resent him, just not for that. Besides, you can't really resent your parents.'

'Why not? They brought you into this stupid world,' complained Matjaž.

'I know, I know, but what I'm trying to get at is that it's too easy to blame our parents for this stupid world. Yes, they were stupid and the world is stupid, but even more stupid is the person who tries to use that to justify their own miserable existence.'

'What is it that you resent your dad for?' Matjaž asked, returning to her story.

'I don't know. It was always the little things, white lies – like why he couldn't come to my piano recital, for example,' she explained.

'And why couldn't he?' Matjaž was intrigued.

'He'd say that he had to stay at work, but I knew that he'd gone for a beer with his friends,' she said. 'He thought that little girls couldn't smell alcohol on people, but they can.' There was a trace of bitterness in her voice.

'And how did he react when you told him?'

'I never did. I played my mum's game, always overlooking those kinds of things. It was as if she was so grateful for the relative comfort of our life, and those ten days' holiday where we'd have a lovely time, that she'd indulge him in those kinds of little deceptions,' Kat explained.

'Until he deceived her in a big way . . .' Matjaž said.

'Yeah. It's funny in a way. He stopped drinking because he suddenly discovered the meaning of life in the Saturday organic market and his preparations for some marathon or other – his new wife's god comes in the form of running. Maybe it would have been better if Mum had stood up to him, if just once she'd got angry. But it's pointless thinking about it now,' she said softly.

Just then Matjaž caught sight of some people he knew approaching their table, the *nouveau riche* louts, and swore to himself. He could just feel that they were going to brutally tear down the fragile atmosphere of trust that he and Kat had built. He would have tried to hide, but he saw they'd already noticed him. He didn't have time to warn her, either. Now it was what it was.

'How's it going, Matjaž?' asked a tall guy called Andraž, whose legs were barely keeping him upright.

'It's going. How about you guys?' he asked reservedly, addressing him formally.

'Jure here's just had a kid. We're celebrating.' He hiccupped.

'Congratulations, Jure,' Matjaž said, turning to another suit who was more wasted than the first two, and who took this as an invitation to join the table before he'd even introduced himself properly.

Jure sat down and began to ponder. 'Childbirth, childbirth, it's such a miracle. One minute it's inside, the next it's out. In – out, in – out, know what

I mean?' He emphasized this profound insight with gestures, then continued. 'Father, son, grandson. And the circle is complete,' he said in a deep, thoughtful voice. Then, as if he'd awoken from a trance, 'What are you two drinking?' They ordered another round. The company of the three young guys was now firmly established, and they offered a very perfunctory introduction to Matjaž's companion. Marko, Jure and Andraž were presented to Kat like an anthology of the Slovene legal profession.

'What have you done with Gašper, then?' Matjaž tried to carve out a civilized conversation. He considered Gašper to be one of these guys, who had never wanted for anything in life and now that they'd gained good jobs – often on the merit of their ambitious fathers – never would.

'Gašper, Gašper, yeah, his wife doesn't let him out, mate,' laughed Jure. 'You know, 'cos he's got a . . . Well, a kid of his own now, too. And these days women don't want to look after kids by themselves any more, they expect the man to be part of that, that, you know, the upbringing and education.'

'Seriously, unbelievable!' Kat spoke up, clearly disgusted at this pack of arrogant young guys.

'Sorry, sorry, love. I didn't know that we had members of, you know, the other sex among us,' the new father apologized clumsily.

The circle of drunkards laughed, including Matjaž, for which he was rewarded with a weary expression from Kat.

'So. How's work?' asked Matjaž, trying again to make the conversation more civilized.

'Mate, it's work. Work's good. You know how it is. If you put in this much effort and spend that many years at school, if you work hard every day, then you've earned the right to a comfortable life,' said Marko, summarizing the circle of life.

'Is that right,' said Matjaž, not wanting to argue.

Noticing his embarrassment, Kat turned to the new father and asked, 'What's your son's name?'

'Yeah, not a son, no, I mean, it's a daughter. Where'd you get that from? What are you on about?' Jure asked rudely.

'Oh, sorry – before you were talking about generations and you mentioned a grandson . . .' replied Kat in an apologetic tone.

'That was a metaphor,' said Andraž, coming to his friend's rescue. Kat was convinced that Andraž had no idea what a metaphor was.

'I see, for human reproduction in general,' she remarked ironically, although no one but Matjaž really picked up on it.

'That's it. Reproduction. I've been trying to think of that word all day. Did you hear that, mate? Reproduction!' Jure shouted, brandishing his glass. It threatened to spill all over either him or the unsuspecting patrons sat at nearby tables.

'So what's the name of this offspring of yours, then? Matjaž persisted, with basic good manners.

'Offspring – you see, mate, all the beautiful words we have for reproduction,' said Marko, adding his two cents to the conversation and laughing. The next moment he had dragged his backside over to the riverbank, where he not-so-discreetly emptied the contents of his stomach.

'Listen, mate, you got anything white?' Andraž piped up, not showing too much concern for his friend.

'Sorry?' asked Matjaž, acting as if he had no idea what Andraž was talking about.

'Cocaine!' Kat explained anxiously, rolling her eyes.

'That's the one, mate. We're getting fucked up today! You got anything? Can you sort us out?' asked Jure.

Matjaž smirked as if to say, of course not, where'd he get the idea that he would know anything about that.

The look on Kat's face clearly showed her incredulity. 'What is wrong with you, man? You've got a baby at home!'

'A baby girl,' Matjaž quietly reminded her, in the hope that he might pacify his partner for the evening.

'You've got a baby girl, and you're completely off your face, and you want to do coke as well!' she raged.

'Psssst,' Marko dismissed her, returning to the table visibly revived although still shaky.

'Seriously, though, children are a big deal. You're a parent now, Jesus – act like a parent!' Kat said resolutely.

Jure held his head in his hands and came over extremely concerned, serious, full of self-reproach. The group stared at him for a few long seconds, until he straightened himself up, smiled and said, 'No, I'm gonna be a good dad, but just not today. Today I'm gonna celebrate like a happy kid, so tomorrow I'll be a good dad. I gained a son today, anything's allowed!' He raised his glass.

'A daughter,' Andraž corrected him, but Jure was already happily sipping his beer.

Kat sighed irritably and anxiously lit a cigarette. Matjaž gave her a reassuring look and shrugged his shoulders as if to say 'such is life.' She folded her arms, looked away and huffed angrily.

'What's his name, then?' Matjaž asked Marko, although it seemed that throughout the course of the evening he must've found out several times already.

'You know already, mate. His name is . . . what you always takin' the piss out me for?' grinned the father. 'Her name is Julija. Nice, right? You know the song . . .' He started to sing the Aleksander Mežek hit. His mates joined in and earned themselves some surprised glances and looks of disgust from the bar's unsuspecting customers.

Mežek was clearly the straw that broke the camel's back for Kat, who picked up her handbag and started to leave.

'What about . . . ?' Matjaž was confused.

'No, everything's fine, I just have to, I have to get out of here,' she said.

'Congratulations on Julija,' she said to Jure, unconvincingly. Then she walked away, not waiting for the slow responses of 'Ciao love!'

Matjaž stood up and went after her. When they were a far enough distance from the new dad and his colleagues, he asked her, 'What's the problem, I thought we . . .'

'We did, but I can't stand those kind of situations!' Kat said, irritated again.

'Then let's go somewhere else. They're not good friends of mine, my friends are totally different . . .' he started to try and convince her.

She interrupted him. 'No, after that debacle I can't. Those people are totally . . . they're animals.'

'Your mum's into that New Age stuff, but I didn't walk away,' Matjaž laughed.

'Yeah, but you can't really get rid of your mum,' she smiled sourly.

'You can't get rid of your friends either!' said Matjaž, getting a little cross.

'If they're like that you can!' she exclaimed, pointing towards the table of singing drinkers.

Her superiority started to get on Matjaž's nerves. 'Yep, that's what they're like, awful. Most people are awful, in case you hadn't noticed. But at least those idiots don't mean any harm . . .'

'What about that child!' Kat almost shrieked.

Matjaž shook his head. 'Jeez, everything will be fine with the child – or rather, everything will be wrong, just like it was for all of us. One happy father's drunken evening doesn't make him a monster.'

'Well, anyway. I just don't think it's acceptable!' she persisted.

'I don't know, maybe I am too tolerant of people like that who love to party, but in any case your reaction seems a lot worse than their alleged crimes. You're patronizing, moralizing!' Matjaž snapped.

'Sorry, but that's too much. Perhaps I'm over-sensitive. Well, not perhaps, I am quite sensitive, but it's hard to accept scenes like that. That blatant sexism, chauvinism – that poor baby! It's especially difficult to accept you, when I see you among them,' she sighed, tired and disappointed.

Matjaž sensed that he'd lost Kat for good, but just at that moment in time it didn't bother him. He looked at her coldly. 'If you can't stay with me when I'm with them, there's nothing I can do to help you. We'll see what you're like when you have your first child!' he said firmly and turned away.

'That's it, mate, you're ours for the evening!' Marko hugged him when he returned to the table.

'Well, I'm clearly not hers,' Matjaž laughed, somewhat bitterly.

'Oh, dear God, when will this end!' Karla moaned.

'It's not the end of the world, Karla,' said Matjaž, patting her on the shoulder. They were sitting in one of the ubiquitous Mercator supermarket cafés after some urgent Sunday shopping.

'Not for you, no, but Kat still hasn't got over it,' she said sharply.

'What am I supposed to do about it? You two hatched this plan, now you've got to deal with it,' Matjaž protested.

'But mate, what went wrong, really?' asked Aleksander, who up until this point had seemed indifferent.

'Everything was great until my mates arrived,' Matjaž started to explain.

'Which mates?'

'Those crazy lawyers, Gašper's lot, you've both met them.'

'Oof,' sighed Karla. 'Then no wonder everything went tits up.' She lit herself a cigarette.

'Come on, they're not that bad,' Matjaž tried to defend them. 'Right?' He looked at Aleksander.

'You know what, my friend, if you ask me it's almost like they're on a different planet,' he said, siding with his wife.

Matjaž didn't understand. 'But why? I don't see it.'

'They wear expensive suits but they still can't choose ties to go with them,' began Karla in a weary voice, although not without enjoyment in her utter disdain. 'They buy expensive cars that they can't drive in the snow. They order expensive dishes that they don't like, they drink expensive wine just because it's expensive. They marry blondes just so they can show them off to their friends and business partners. They speak a language that only they understand among themselves. I don't know how to put it; it often seems as if they don't have brains, as if they're programmed in a completely different way.'

'But they've studied, they're successful lawyers!' Matjaž protested.

'Precisely,' said Aleksander. 'They're from another planet!'

RONJA

'Ah, it's a work thing, can't get out of it,' said Matjaž, talking on the phone while trying to set off. 'My boss has invited me, I don't know why,' he went on. A glance behind, a glance forward, a little more wheel-turning. He'd already been on the phone to Aleksander for at least fifteen minutes, since he'd packed up everything for this unusual trip. 'Tim Bilding. How should I know? I'll tell you when I get back.'

Somehow he managed to pull out on to the road. 'Aleksander, stop. No, I'm not interested!' he shouted, listening restlessly to his friend. He then remembered that he'd left something essential at home. Naturally, Aleksander was still talking. Matjaž parked up again and closed the door, still on the phone. 'No, there's no . . . Because I just know. I've already seen them. No, Urša's too tall for me . . . just way too tall. And too healthy . . . No, you know, veggie, teas, baby carrots, all that cleansing of internal energies, of chi, chakra, gonga, I don't know. She's always nurturing her spirituality, while mine, as you know, is stagnating. Walking up the steps, his friend's persuasion was too much. 'Gabi, are you crazy? She's a religious nut . . . No, not a good-looking Catholic waiting for her first major transgression.'

Aleksander was evolving his theory about the Catholic susceptibility to pleasure as Matjaž unlocked the door, stepped into his flat and glanced around. 'I don't know about Liza, I don't fancy her. Too much of a cynic, it's all wrong.' He searched around, walking quickly from one room to another like a headless chicken. 'No, she's definitely cute and skinny enough, and all that short black curly hair, but she's always taking issue with something.' He still hadn't found his bag. 'Gah, stop it now, Sandra's got a boyfriend . . . No, I don't fancy testing how strong that union . . . Of course she's cute. Blonde, yes. No, there'll be no more blondes after Saša . . . I'm not trying to test out every type of woman here . . . Obviously you would, but now you're married someone else has to sample everything for you.'

He finally spotted his camera bag, put it on his shoulder, locked up the flat and quickly ran to his car. 'Ronja? My friend Ronja? Ronja, who's just had a baby?' He unlocked the car. 'Young mums, you say . . . their hormones. Yes that's what I want, maternal hormones. Like I don't have enough hormones of my own.' He was driving again now. 'What is it with you? I'd rather sell my mother into slavery than have to go to Ksenja's summer house . . . Yes, I'd rather go out with you than to that hen house . . . No, Ksenja is not an option . . . Because she's my boss . . . I don't know, maybe forty . . . with some rich guy . . . One child . . . Not exactly a beauty, but she's a very well-presented woman, but forget it, you hear me, forget it . . . I don't believe she has a sense of humour . . . Intelligent? Since when has any woman been intelligent? Ha ha ha.'

He was battling against the traffic, which he was finding more difficult to manage than usual thanks to Aleksander's nagging. 'Just four other guys,' he sighed, worn out. 'Why would I tell you about them, you're not gay . . .' He finally managed to get through the crossing. 'Why do you want to know the bigger picture? I'm not going to tell you about men whose names I barely know.' As he drove his answers became increasingly impatient. 'Yes, Roko's the one you liked when we went for a beer about a hundred years ago. Yes, hard-working, good guy, quiet. It true, quiet people are like gold dust . . . Which is why I'd be really grateful if we could leave . . . I don't know Aleksander, honestly, I don't know. Tadej is just an average ambitious young guy who gels his hair . . . How should I know if he's gay? Jeez, seriously now, your tongue is going to get me fined . . . Kristjan . . . That one would sell his mum, family, girlfriend, basically everything, for the chance of a career . . . Yeah, he's quite handsome – why? You're not normal. No, I'm not going to play guessing games with you about which girl would rather go with him than me . . . I think that's it . . .' He was driving anxiously now, as once again he was running late. 'Oh true, you're right, there's Andrej too . . . I have no idea why you know my colleagues better than I do – maybe because you're crazy? Jesus! Enough! Yes, Andrej is that lunatic programmer who smokes weed and then eats beansprouts. That's it, yin and yang, that's his philosophy . . . No, I don't know if it works. Try it!'

Matjaž was still driving, slightly resignedly. He began to wonder if this conversation would ever end. 'Why are you bringing up Urša again? When have I ever mentioned anything about her? Just because her dad's a pilot it doesn't mean . . . I know you like planes. But a girl is not her dad, even less so an aeroplane, you know,' he said wearily. 'She's available to everyone because she makes herself available . . . yeah, available to men. No, look, I'd prefer a woman who thinks for herself . . . well, at work she draws, I mean, she designs graphs . . . Jeez, I'm not saying it directly implies that she doesn't know how to think, but this Urša in particular doesn't know . . .' Matjaž drove anxiously around Ljubljana, cursing everyone who lived beyond Bežigrad. 'I'm not every man . . . Well, OK, I am every man, but a special everyman . . . OK, that everyman who would like to feel like a special everyman – you happy now . . .? You're going to start with that now, are you? Fine, I don't have any particular criteria, but Urša is pushing it . . . I'm just going to pick her up now . . .'

At last he pulled into Bratovševa Square. 'Seriously, enough now. Do you want her phone number so you can get in touch with her dad and ask him to take you for a little ride . . .' He looked down the street, trying to catch sight of the pilot's daughter. 'No, I won't . . . I have no idea if she understands the concept of buoyancy in air. Even I think flying is witchcraft . . . Yeah, every one of those one hundred thousand flights a day is a total miracle . . . Jeez, don't start talking flight theory with me, please . . .' Matjaž gave only a perfunctory ear to the principles of aviation. 'OK so buoyancy is the scientific explanation for how planes fly, but then it's still a small miracle every time . . . No, I'm not a mystic. I really have to go now, she's here waiting for me . . .' He drove up to Urša, who was waving at him eagerly. Matjaž waved back absentmindedly, still agonizing over how to end the conversation. 'Aleksander, I promise you I won't have a good time.' Meanwhile Urša had got into the car, and she gave Matjaž a friendly tap. 'No I'm not putting her on the phone, are you crazy? Seriously, bye now . . . Yes, I'll miss you too!'

'Was that your jealous sweetheart?' Urša asked, with a provocative look on her face.

'You probably could say that, yes,' he replied. He turned the car around and barely noticed that Urša had gone quiet.

'So, where now?' he asked her.

'How should I know?' she replied quite bluntly.

'Aren't you and Sandra friends?'

'Not really,' she replied coldly.

'Well, where does she live?' Unease had taken hold of Matjaž.

'I have no idea . . .'

'Have you got her number?'

'Yes, of course.'

It took a lot of effort for him to keep his cool. 'Could you call her then, please, and ask where we should pick her up?'

Urša called her. 'Aha, aha, aha, OK, we'll be there in . . . how long will it take to get to Tabor?' she turned to Matjaž.

'Are you having a laugh? You can't be serious. I just came from that direction. You lot are so unorganized!' Matjaž fumed.

'Well, how long? She's asking.'

'Tell her to start tottering down now,' Matjaž replied coldly, already determined that he'd never be designated driver ever again.

Urša relayed the message and listened to Sandra's response. 'No, she wants you to be more specific,' she said, summarizing her colleague's words.

'Five minutes.'

The process began again. Urša passed on Sandra's message to the driver once more, 'That's not going to work, she needs at least ten.'

'Ten!' Matjaž was becoming angry. 'But we agreed on a time!'

Once again Urša relayed her colleague's situation, 'She's got to dry her hair!'

'Her hair can dry on the way,' the driver said firmly.

Urša listened carefully, first to one then to the other, and then said, 'No it can't, because it's incredibly unruly.'

'If she's not down in ten minutes, we're going without her and then she'll have well-behaved hair in Ljubljana!' Matjaž concluded.

After keeping them waiting for fifteen minutes, the neatly preened Sandra got into the car and warmly greeted her fellow passengers.

Urša smiled in return, while Matjaž offered only a stern look.

'Oh yeah, Liza just rang me to ask if we could pick her up because her car's packed in,' Sandra said.

'Where does this Liza live?' asked Matjaž, trying to suppress his anger.

'In Vič, near where the Faculty of Physics is, or whichever faculty it is,' explained the new passenger.

'It's a good job she lives in Vič!' Matjaž grumbled, to himself more than anyone.

'Why?' asked Sandra.

'Because it's on the way to the motorway,' whispered Urša, by now acquainted with the driver's psychological state.

Soon yet another person had squeezed into the car. Liza greeted everyone, but Matjaž was never sure if she was genuine or not so he didn't get too involved with her.

'What a nightmare,' she began. 'It was still working yesterday but now that's it, finito. If you hadn't have come for me I'd probably have missed the party of the year,' she said in a voice that, again, barely concealed ironic undertones.

'You're welcome,' Matjaž retorted.

'What's wrong with him?' Liza enquired.

'He's got womanitis,' smiled Sandra. Urša smiled, too, and Liza just rolled her eyes wearily.

'Which poor devil is on duty today, then?' asked Sandra.

'Tadej,' Urša replied.

'Yeah, but how's he going to be on duty?' said Liza, involving herself in the conversation.

'How do you mean?' Urša asked naïvely.

'He agreed with Ksenja that he'd be at the editorial office until eight, then he's coming to hers and he'll add any extra news online – I overheard their conversation today,' Liza explained.

'That crafty fox!' smiled Sandra.

'Why? I think it's nice that he wants to celebrate with his colleagues,' said Urša.

'And the rest!' Liza shouted.

'You're clearly still very new here,' surmised Sandra.

'I've been here for half a year already!' protested Urša, looking scornfully at the other two.

'Well, exactly,' said Liza cynically.

'What Liza is trying to say,' Sandra translated, 'is that if you'd been with us longer you would know, firstly, that in doing this Tadej is pandering to the boss, as he'll cover two work duties at once, and secondly, that if anything comes up he'll immediately find one of us to do his work for him.'

'He won't find me!' claimed Urša. 'I'm getting drunk today.'

'Really?' Sandra looked at her.

'On what? Beetroot juice?' smiled Liza.

'No, on pure unadulterated alcohol. I'll be in line for a detox tomorrow, though,' replied the raw-vegetable fanatic in all seriousness.

'I don't doubt it,' Matjaž heard Liza mutter to herself from behind him.

*

They drove in silence for a while. Matjaž was enjoying the Van Morrison on his playlist, when Urša started up again.

'What's Kristjan like, then? Sometimes it seems like he's a bit of a show-off, and I find him the most difficult out of everyone.'

'He really is good, diligent, hard-working,' Sandra answered.

'And ambitious,' Liza couldn't resist commenting.

'What's wrong with ambitions, Liza? As if we're not ambitious,' Sandra protested.

'Yes, of course we are. We really are the ideal workforce, prepared to sacrifice the best years of our lives for our great calling, our journalistic calling. To sacrifice ourselves for pocket money, and then be satisfied when Ksenja gives us a pat on the back – even more so when she promises to put our names on the longlist for assignments.'

'So what makes Kristjan stand out, then?' Urša asked with interest.

'Kristjan steps up. He brings ideas, he works hard and writes well, and he's also got a sense for technology . . .' Sandra replied.

'And he's not ashamed to make a point of it, and he's not ashamed to go back and forth to Ksenja, or whoever's in charge, to do a little, or a lot, of ass-kissing.' Liza added once again.

'Is that right?' Urša pondered. Somewhat worriedly she said, 'I didn't realize until recently that none of you were actually permanently employed, that you were all freelance.'

'Well, not all of us are in that boat,' said Liza pointedly.

'I knew it,' Matjaž said, breaking his long silence. 'I knew this car would turn into a site of class war. That's right, dear Urša, your driver for today has a permanent job, but don't think that doesn't mean he can't complain about work, about his colleagues and his boss. Yep, isn't life unfair!'

'She didn't mean it like that,' said Sandra, trying to ease the situation.

'Of course she did, and in her own way she's right. But I'm not going to apologize to you all for having gained a permanent post before the crisis, after many long years of part-time work!' protested the man among the women.

'No one's asking you to!' Sandra spoke up again.

'But you could bear in mind, however, whenever you assign us a job or criticize what we've done, that we're not as well paid as you are,' Liza piped up again.

'Are you serious?' Matjaž got angry.

'Of course. It's not ethical – it's not fair!' spouted Urša.

'This debate stops right now, you cackling hens!' Matjaž lost his temper and barely kept track of what was happening on the motorway. 'Have you any idea how pitiful my salary is? Or how many things I do without even telling you – I just correct your stupid mistakes. Urša, you did that table for Andrej about Slovene holidays, which took you a whole month. I mean, come on. Liza, what was with that long video and the piece on the toilets of Ljubljana bars or whatever it was? And Sandra – how many times have I done the *Goodnight Melody* feature and similar shit instead of you? If it's a class war you're after, look for it somewhere else, not with badly paid colleagues who slave away with you, help you and – if we're being damn straight – save your names in front of the boss . . .' He let out a deep sigh. 'You've obviously forgotten about all the times I've spoken to her and that dumbass deputy about your situation.'

His speech obviously had an impact, as even Liza kept quiet. After a long silence, she said, 'Fine, that wasn't right. I'm a bit tense. I've got PMS. We shouldn't take it out on you,' she said.

'Liza apologizing,' mumbled Sandra, 'that's a first.'

'What I want to know is, when do you women ever not have PMS?' said Matjaž, diverting the conversation.

The question caused serious uproar in the car. Above all it was Urša who had an awful lot to say on the dilemmas of the female sex. Sandra also joined her, primarily pointing out what women have to go through with their hair, legs, hands and nails, as well as the face with its eyes, eyebrows, cheekbones and lips, and their woman's skin, too, an incredibly sensitive organ. And of course then there was the *diferentia specia* – menstruation. No man could possibly imagine what menstruation signified; there were so many inconveniences that came with it – and the pain, Urša said. To that Matjaž remarked that there was one thing worse than menstruation itself – and that was putting up with a menstrual woman. This raised a few laughs, and then Urša reached an important conclusion. 'I think there's one battle that's even more important than the class war – the battle of the sexes!'

'Yes, and my next beer will be the most well-earned drink of my life,' Matjaž swore.

'That's exactly what I'm talking about!' Urša attested. 'As soon as a woman says anything about the disadvantages of her gender, a man is already dying for a beer.'

'That's one of the world's hidden truths,' laughed Sandra.

'And even truer is that while one sex complains and the other drinks beer, someone in the middle is making a profit,' said Liza, summing up the situation. At that point they exited the motorway. 'Well, my dear feminists, I've done my bit, I've driven you as far as their explanation went, then they said one of you knows this area.'

'What?' Sandra was surprised.

'How should I know where Ksenja's summer house is? Someone was boasting about how they knew exactly how to get there,' he said.

'But how should we know?' Sandra flapped.

'I ought to know,' Urša admitted apologetically.

'But?' the driver enquired gently.

'Well, I'd have known if we'd gone via the old road, but I've never come this way before,' she apologized.

'I'll call her,' Liza announced. Meanwhile Matjaž pulled over and lit a cigarette, from which he took a drag so strong it was as if they were on the brink of a third world war. When Liza had finished talking, she said, 'I've got it!'

It turned out that Liza didn't quite have it, at least not straight away. A few kilometres there and back, a bit of driving around in circles, a few additional calls to Ksenja, Tadej, Kristjan and Andrej, a few small disagreements between Liza and Matjaž, some bickering between Sandra and Liza, a desperate call to Gabi and then to Rok, one stop to ask for directions locally, some tears from Urša and half a packet of Matjaž's cigarettes later, they were eventually on the right track to Ksenja's village and house.

Gabi and Ksenja were waiting for them in front of a large new-build with a sheltered veranda, which – apart from the rather large swimming pool – attempted to blend in with the architecture of the region. Both smiled at the sight of the four pitiful passengers who stepped out of the car.

'How wonderful that it's still possible to get lost in the Karst!' Ksenja burst out laughing. Matjaž scowled at her.

Ksenja and Gabi poured them all a welcome drink, some sort of homemade wine, a nice gesture about which nobody complained. 'So how did you get so lost, then? Gabi and Ronja have been here since six, and even Tadej beat you to it.'

'The Karst is very complex, Ksenja, very complex,' Sandra reminded her.

'Yeah, almost as complex as women,' hissed Matjaž, who chose to join a group of colleagues on the veranda while his fellow passengers started relating to their superior the story of one of the toughest journeys in the world.

'What happened, Matjaž, did you not have enough women in the car to help you navigate?' Kristjan grinned.

'Why didn't you leave it to Urša to summon the spirits so that they could tell you where to go?' Tadej teased him. Matjaž gave each of them a dirty look and snorted.

'Give the man a break,' said Roko, passing Matjaž a beer. The guys chinked glasses.

'All I'm going to say is that I'll drink to men, even if they do take the piss out of their fellow sufferers too much sometimes!' said Matjaž, raising his glass.

'Oh really, have you forgotten about your old work colleagues already?' asked a voice from the darkness.

'Ronja!' Matjaž cried, and hugged her immediately. 'How's it going, pal? I heard something finally fell out of you!'

'It's true, it fell out a good six months ago and we call it Igor.' She smiled at him sweetly.

'Wouldn't you rather have called it – I mean, just off the top of my head – Matjaž?'

'It's a nice name, it's just that I don't know any decent guys called Matjaž,' his friend replied seriously.

'Good, well at least it hasn't sucked your sense of humour from you.' He smiled kind-heartedly and sat next to her at the less crowded end of the table.

'I really hope not,' she replied.

'So you'll survive?'

'Right now I wouldn't quite count on it, but I'm getting there,' she promised.

'So, if you do survive, when are you coming back?'

'In a couple of months.'

'Oof, you played that one well. And women say they're exploited,' he teased her again.

'Careful now, I'm sleep deprived and grumpy,' she warned. Again they raised their glasses to one another and quenched their raging thirst. The late June evening was almost breathtaking. The sun hadn't quite set, and in the last remaining light of the evening the everyday sounds of nature were dying down and coming alive again in the form of insects, owls and whatever else it was that inhabited the cypress trees and the nearby oak.

Soon all members of the group were sitting around the table and making polite conversation. Matjaž was smoking and thinking about how perfectly content he was just sat right there. He had always been relaxed around Ronja. They had known each other since secondary school and, although they'd never spent vast amounts of time together, a quiet sort of mutual understanding had been developing between them ever since they were young. They knew how to coexist exceptionally well, whether it be at work or at this kind of social gathering, even though they didn't usually say much to one another. In the last few months Matjaž had almost stopped doing silence altogether, and now he realized that he missed it. He was also pleased to see Ronja's bright face, which had gained a sort of sharpness, a depth, that made her seem even more attractive to him than before.

'Now it's your turn,' said Ronja.

'My turn for what?' Matjaž looked at her, confused.

'For you to tell me something. I haven't seen you in at least a year.'

'What do you want to know?' he asked obligingly.

'You're so annoying!' She punched him on the arm. 'How are things with Sara, for example? Are you going to finally make a respectable woman of her, are you going to ruin your lives with children?'

Ronja understood Matjaž's expression upon hearing that sentence, and was visibly moved. 'I'm sorry, I didn't know.' She patted him on the shoulder.

'It's OK, it was a year ago now,' he said quietly, looking around to see if anyone was listening.

'A year,' Ronja said, to herself more than anything.

'Yeah, one year,' confirmed Matjaž, with rather a gloomy face. He surprised even himself at how bothered he was in the present by the question that Ronja had taken from the past, from a time when he and Sara had still been a couple. He swept his hand over his face and said, 'No, I'm OK, you know, for a minute there you just stirred up time – and maybe reality, too – so I just got confused.'

'I get that,' she answered. 'So what happened?'

'She found someone else.'

'Really?' Ronja asked. 'It rarely happens just like that, out of nowhere. You were such a good, close couple for so many years, after all.'

'I know what you want. You want me to bad-mouth myself, say how I fucked it up . . . I'm not saying that I don't take my share of the blame, a large share.' He fell silent and tried to speak more clearly – for his own sake, too. 'Above all I just never felt like we ought to be settling down, that anything ought to change. Our lifestyle had always come first; children were never at the forefront. Suddenly our aims had become opposites. And good-looking women, God knows, you always know how to procure a replacement, he said, barely disguising his bitterness.

'Maybe that's true, but only when we feel that you've given up on us, probably for good and probably many times before, she replied matter-of-factly.

'And don't forget about when we've disappointed you many a time, too, Matjaž said, half remorsefully, half sarcastically.

'Love isn't permanent and everlasting, Matjaž, Ronja sighed. 'Maybe it is, if it's totally abstract and allows us to hold on to our expectations, not be launched into a concrete relationship, into the life of a couple, into our innermost feelings. Concrete love has boundaries. Mine are being put to the test at the moment, too. Somewhere, disappointments big and small, sufferings big and small, they build up, even if the woman tries to forget about them. Then at some point you look back and you don't see any spectacular wounds, no big explosions; you just feel as if the love has gone, or maybe the fundamental part of it, at least – the part that had been prepared to put that man above all others.

'Are you OK, Ronja?' Matjaž looked at her worriedly, as it seemed that she was speaking from experience.

'Yeah, yeah, of course, said Ronja, as if coming out of a trance. She smiled and apologized. 'I'm not going to bore you with the details. All I'll say is that children are a test for every couple.'

'See, now you understand why I was never too keen on those little people, he laughed. Her expression softened, too.

'We'd better leave your slow rate of maturing to one side, she continued. 'I'd rather you told me whether there's a new Miss Matjaž on the scene.'

'No, Miss Matjaž is still hiding and it doesn't seem like she wants to come out.'

'They never do, until all of a sudden they're right there, she concluded.

'I think I'm past that now, Matjaž remarked knowingly.

'Of course you are, Ronja backed him up, unconvincingly.

'Don't take the piss, or I'm going to say something mean about Igor.'

'Go for it, I'll join in; you cannot imagine how shameless that child is, she added cheekily.

Gabi, who had just sat down, heard that last sentence and became wound up. 'How can you say such a thing about your own child, who's still only tiny and can't defend himself at all?'

'Because he's shameless,' Matjaž explained to her.

'But little children don't know anything, they don't do it on purpose!' Gabi protested.

'Neither do I,' Ronja said, trying to calm her down.

'Yes, but children sense these vibrations, they sense it all, and if you talk about them like that they'll, they'll . . . When I have children, I'm only going to say the nicest of things to them,' Gabi continued stubbornly.

'Of course you are,' Ronja said to her patronizingly.

'Gabi, you'll be taking back those words in no time at all,' Ksenja spoke up as she brought a dish full of *čevapčiči* to the table. 'Here we are, the fruits of Roko's labour are here! *Bon appétit!*' Gabi didn't dare to question the pitfalls of motherhood in front of her boss, and was not bold enough to claim that she was going to be the best young mum in the world.

'They're amazing, Roko!' called Gabi with her mouth full, and everyone loudly agreed.

'Have you all got everything?' asked Ksenja. They nodded. 'Well, then allow me to make one small toast.' She stopped for a moment and said solemnly, 'My dear colleagues! It's a great honour to work with you, to collaborate with you, to hear your ideas and develop them with you from one day to the next.' Matjaž and Ronja gave each other a knowing look. 'And to show how much I value each and every one of you and our collective, I invited you here and I'd like to say thank you to each of you, all together, above all for coming here! Enjoy yourselves, make yourselves at home – I think, if I've understood correctly, you've sorted out the bedrooms. Thank you, and cheers!' The group clapped, slightly embarrassed. Matjaž could have sworn that he saw Liza rolling her eyes during Ksenja's speech. After that awkward moment, and a sufficient amount of beer, the guests began to relax.

In this relaxed context, Gabi and Andrej began to bicker about whether or not the snooze function on a phone was actually useful or not. 'There is nothing sweeter than being awake, but knowing that you still have a few more minutes to sleep,' said Andrej, explaining the beauty of the mobile function. But the uncompromising Gabi resisted, 'No, that goes entirely against the teachings of Christianity – an alarm clock is there to wake you. You have to bite the bullet and admit to yourself: it's time to get up!'

'Explain to me just one thing, please, Gabi,' Kristjan intervened. 'What has that logic got to do with Christianity? It seems more Spartan to me.'

'Christianity is conscious of what commitments and responsibilities are!'

'Just like Spartanism,' Kristjan persisted.

'It's about a sense of asceticism,' Gabi tried to explain.

'Oh, we're at asceticism already? But, again, denial is absolutely not unique to the Christian faith.'

'Fine, then let's leave religion to one side and say only that the snooze function is for wimps!' Gabi said animatedly, for the whole table to hear.

'Excuse me?' an outraged Liza overheard.

'Nothing. Gabi and I are just debating the phenomenon of the snooze function,' Andrej explained to her.

'And you're prepared to derive and explain entire personalities based on the way that someone wakes up?' Liza asked sternly.

'You're all typical snoozers, no sense of accountability to anyone!' Gabi burst out.

'But at the end of the day we all get up at the same time,' Andrej said, attempting to pacify her, while Liza merely snorted and carried on talking to her co-workers.

The girls had set upon on another burning issue, 'I don't know, when I got my first Mercator bag – the big reusable one you get so you don't have to buy more carrier bags – I was over the moon,' Sandra said.

'I know what you mean,' Urša interrupted. 'They're so handy. Especially because you can carry them on your shoulder.'

'Anyway,' resumed Sandra, 'for that and many other reasons . . .'

'Because they're so roomy!' Urša couldn't resist, making Ksenja laugh and Liza look up to the sky resignedly.

'If I may add,' Sandra said, already slightly impatiently, 'at first they seemed a great idea and everyone looked after their own bag and wouldn't lend it to anyone for love nor money. But then something strange started to happen. Those kinds of bags started to multiply and now everyone's got loads of them and can't wait to "accidently" leave one at a friend's house when they take over a six-pack of beer.'

'It's true,' Liza agreed. 'Even if you inadvertently leave one of those bags with someone, they give it back to you. And that seemingly friendly gesture belies a growing resentment towards the Mercator carrier bag.'

'I think the problem is that all supermarket chains have these bags now,' explained Urša. The girls looked at her in confusion, willing her to explain. 'The bags have multiplied! Something that started out in the name of the environment is now flooding it,' she concluded smartly, and the others had to agree.

'And then there's a whole cycle of guilt,' Liza continued. 'If you forget one of these bags you feel guilty, because then you buy one of the non-degradable ones. If you go to Spar with a Mercator bag you automatically feel guilty, as if there's going to be a group of cashiers thinking that you're not a faithful customer and treating you differently to the regular clients. And, of course, it's the same if you take a Spar bag to Lidl.'

'Yes, although the red Mercator one really is very obvious,' said Ksenja, involving herself in the debate. Naturally, no one disagreed with her statement.

'You can't win with carrier bags, that's the point,' Sandra summed up the problem.

'It's so typical, though, isn't it – something that is meant to solve an eco crisis just creates another one. Weren't we quite happy with normal carrier bags, which we could then use for rubbish or whatever?' Liza reflected nostalgically.

'Do you know what, that's not a bad topic at all,' Ksenja declared at the end.

'Sorry?' Urša asked, startled.

'For our newspaper. We could research how many of these bags there are, how they're flooding Slovenia and how no one really knows what to do with them. They're accumulating in households and at some point we're going to have to get rid of them.'

The members of the editorial office fell silent at once. If they'd known that their complaints about ineffective eco schemes would have landed them with new work, they'd rather have talked about the weather.

Kristjan, who had been keeping one ear tuned to what the group including his superior was doing and saying, finally chipped in, 'I can get started on that. I'd build on what Liza was talking about, about general ecological culpability, and go even further. We've got all this sorting of rubbish, where each individual is now responsible for the environment, and if you don't sort it correctly, you're practically responsible for the downfall of humanity.'

'Are you saying that you don't sort your rubbish, either?' Gabi asked, getting wound up again.

'It's not about that, Gabi!' Kristjan tried to explain to her.

'So what is it about, then? If everyone in their small habitat saw to their own sorting, there would be so much less pollution on a global scale.'

'Not technically, no,' Andrej spoke up, although he was busy with a game of poker started by Ronja, Matjaž and Tadej. 'There's the same amount of rubbish as before, if not more, now that it's sorted.'

'Yeah, but if it's sorted, it's easier to recycle,' Gabi argued.

'I don't know. The sorting also happened before – and someone was paid for it, too.' Andrej persisted.

'Exactly, and now we pay them a higher collection fee to sort it ourselves,' added Kristjan.

'I'm not having anyone tell me that the collective effort is null and void, that it doesn't count for anything,' Gabi said, not wanting to back down.

'Yeah, but at the end you ask yourself, what are we doing? If every mortal starts sorting rubbish, what does it mean for factories, factory waste, industrial waste? How much does that sorting actually make a difference in relation to global traffic –'

'You're all typical cynics!' Gabi despaired.

'Does it not seem like a handy government weapon to you?' Kristjan asked, not wanting to leave it alone.

'Leave me alone!' Gabi cried hysterically.

Ksenja tried to calm her. 'Gabi, don't get angry just because someone doesn't agree with you.' But the angry Christian just folded her arms and looked ahead angrily.

'Finish what you were saying, Kristjan, I'm intrigued,' Ksenja encouraged him.

'It's very simple, really. The government is no longer here to help the individual, it's no longer a safety net, or a pillar, it's just a load of cops keeping watch over whether people are taking enough responsibility for their health, their education and now the environment, too – because of course, for every mistake in each one of those sectors, they can issue heavy fines,' Tadej told everyone, passionately.

'Yeah, in Ljubljana the fine for not sorting your rubbish is 800 euros,' Liza added.

'Interesting,' Ksenja remarked, thinking to herself. 'Yeah, this would make a good story,' she went on.

Sandra, who was beginning to tire of the serious conversation, turned to Andrej. 'Did you bring your guitar with you?'

'Everything for you, beautiful,' he smiled, showing her his instrument.

'What are you waiting for?' Urša asked eagerly, and focused on her beer. Andrej left his game of poker to the three keen players at the end of the table, and took up his instrument. Ksenja sat him at the head of the table and sat herself next to Gabi, who stopped sulking at the first sound of the guitar. Andrej's repertoire was limited to Slovene sixties pop classics, old Yugoslav bands and classic rock. The girls were really enjoying his playing and sang along, and even Ksenja was impressed. It didn't take long for Tadej to invite Urša to dance, and she started writhing strangely around him. Matjaž, who noticed the soulful undulation of her arms and hips out of the corner of his eye, could have sworn that this mystical movement was an indiscreet romantic advance. But Tadej didn't stray from his classic repertoire of waltz and polka, so together the two of them formed an interesting dance experiment, which amused Liza the most.

But even Liza did not remain immune to the sound of the guitar, to the songs. As she put it, they took her back to her youth. She and Sandra occupied a large share of the veranda, inventing technical dance moves with abandon. Soon even Ksenja joined the other dancers. Likewise, Kristjan didn't hold back for long, skilfully spinning his editor around. Commenting on the situation, to himself more than anything, Roko said, 'Alcohol is a remedy.'

'Then have a drink and dance with me,' Gabi winked at him. Roko looked at her, frightened, and tilted his glass back. Obviously Gabi didn't care. She took the glass out of his hand and led him to where the others were dancing. The image of this dancing couple left most of the guests feeling perturbed. The rather rotund Gabi performed fitful, skilful leaps and turns around her dance partner; repeatedly she went down on her knees and then suddenly jumped, just to confuse him even more. All of this was carried out with her own sense of rhythm, if that's what you could call it. Eventually Matjaž picked up on Ronja's pleading glances, indicating that she wanted to join the rest of the hooligans.

'Don't you think it's unbearable, how collective euphoria is infecting everyone here?' Matjaž asked, trying to avoid his dancing duties.

'It won't work, my friend, those words won't save you from the collective madness this time,' she smiled. So Matjaž had to dance, too.

'But why doesn't Andrej have to dance!' he complained.

Ronja replied, 'Because Andrej is playing for us all!'

A sarcastic response was waiting on the tip of his tongue, but Ronja had him in such a firm hold that he was out of breath. As Andrej went from the lively 'classics' of Plavi orkestar into 'April u Beogradu', Ronja followed the example of some of the other couples and put her head on Matjaž's shoulder, clinging on to him so they swayed softly together.

His heart ached as he gently held Ronja in an embrace. It was nice to feel a warm female body . . . but it wasn't just about the body; he'd had plenty of bodies, maybe too many. It was intimacy he missed. Music entered the ears, became the joint rhythm of two bodies, and two minds could travel wherever they liked. That's why you were there together, to gift to each other all that space to dream. This is what peace is, he thought – when you're together so you can sail off in your own direction. But, of course, no peace is eternal. No sooner had he relaxed into Ronja's embrace than Gabi was barging in between them; Roko had left to relax by his barbecue again.

Gabi took Matjaž by the hands; she threw him back and forth, expecting him to perform moves under her instruction, but he just tried helplessly to convince his body not to succumb to gravity and the various forces she imposed upon him. After this dizzying dance routine Andrej decided to take a short break, and Matjaž followed suit with a loud cry of approval amid the others' disappointed voices.

They sat down, swiftly refreshed themselves with a drop of fine wine and started to sing the praises of Andrej and his treasure trove of hidden talents. Gabi put together a rambling toast: 'Not only does he maintain our work equipment and always respond to our calls for assistance, but he can strum a guitar beautifully as well.'

'And sing!' shouted Sandra, clearly already quite merry.

After that Roko brought more food to the table, which he knowledgeably called sweetmeats. Ksenja explained the source of this meat and listed all of its health benefits, like a true food expert. Her explanation was so full of passion and scientific conviction that she even convinced Urša the sworn vegetarian to try some, as well as Liza, who had recently been flirting with vegetables more than ever. When they'd finished the meat, Ksenja suggested a very special something to help them digest it. It turned out that her homemade herbal liquor was a source of goodness and eternal youth, so nobody resisted and they each took a sip as if it were the elixir of life.

It was unlikely that the number of extra minutes of life gained on account of the herbal liquor's wholesome ingredients would ever be scientifically proven, but it clearly had a pleasing effect on everyone's spirits at least. They chatted away cheerfully about everything imaginable, with pink cheeks and smiling faces. Matjaž had a strategic spot that allowed him to overhear the various debates developing around the table after the dose of 'medicine'. The conversations to his right were the deeper ones. Ksenja and Kristjan were ruminating on Al Jazeera. 'You know what!' said the slightly boisterous Ksenja, 'if an Arab or someone from Saudi Arabia were to offer to buy us and wanted to create a reputable media, if they were in favour of professional journalism, I'd say, 'Why not?'' Kristjan lightly pursed his lips before he nodded, even though as a scrupulous agent of free speech he had doubts about Saudi Arabia and Qatar (the human rights, the corrupt élite and so on) and wondered how much autonomy that kind of ownership could allow.

Ksenja reiterated her argument, but Matjaž decided he'd rather follow the conversation that Urša had started from the other side of the table by saying, 'Humans are not natural!'

'Yeah, after this many drinks it's very difficult to act natural,' Tadej burst out laughing.

'No!' explained Urša. 'Drunk or sober, athletic or a fatty – humans aren't natural.'

'I don't understand,' Gabi piped up. She was sitting next to Urša – and there was nothing natural about that either.

'There are studies that look at the body in a more holistic, more complete way,' Urša said, trying to be clear. 'According to their findings, the greatest human fallacy is that we can stand and distribute our weight on two legs.'

'Why?' Tadej asked.

'Because it's not natural,' said Urša, repeating her original argument.

'But why isn't it natural?'

'I don't know why, evolution or some such – when humans stand on two legs, they're living with the impression that their weight is correctly distributed but it's not, we're still crooked. The problem is that this impression that we're natural is the thing that harms the body the most.'

'Seriously?' Gabi was now worried.

'Seriously,' Urša replied earnestly.

'So what's the solution, then?' Tadej said, turning to her.

'The solution is that we bear our weight on one leg or the other, but never on both at the same time,' Urša explained expertly.

'And then we're natural?' asked Gabi.

'No, of course we're not, but at least then we're not pretending that we are,' Urša informed her.

Her two interlocutors nodded thoughtfully, but Matjaž couldn't resist the temptation, 'What's so bad about the conviction that we're natural?'

'Because it means we're curving our spines, and our extremities suffer the consequences – problems with our back and lower back, rheumatism. All of that can be avoided if you accept that you're not natural, and if you distribute your weight from one side of the body to another accordingly.'

Silence fell. 'There are exercises,' Urša added, as if this further proved her argument.

'I don't doubt it,' Matjaž remarked quietly, to himself more than anyone. And then he said aloud, 'I'm just interested to know how the human race has survived for the last ten thousand years with the erroneous assumption that it's natural.'

'It has survived', Gabi replied sagely, 'but the real question is, in what way has it survived?'

Matjaž didn't feel that there was anything else to add to such an argument, so he fell silent, while Urša demonstrated to Tadej and Gabi the exercises that would help humans to drive out the conviction that they were natural.

Sandra, who quite readily accepted the new workout that would bring balance to the human race, eventually said, half joking, 'But there is, of course, another theory.' Everyone with the exception of Ksenja and Kristjan, who were still dissecting the possibility of a free press in the Arab world, looked at her inquisitively. 'Has anyone seen the series *Louie*?' she began. Liza was the only one who nodded, although it was clear that she didn't know what the series had to with humans being crooked.

'Well, in one episode the main character – Louie – hurts his back', Sandra summarized, 'and he goes to a very old doctor. Louie complains that he's twisted something. The funny thing is that it happens while he's buying a vibrator. But that's actually beside the point. The doctor listens to him without interest, and looks away at his sandwich as if to say "What am I supposed to do about it?" And then the doctor gives his spiel. He explains that the problem lies entirely in the fact that a human stands on two legs. At one time we actually walked on all fours and the entire human physiology, with the spine and the arrangement of our internal organs, was based on this. And after more than ten thousand years, the doctor explains, the structure of the human body has still not adjusted to standing on two legs, which is why it causes back pain.'

'And?' Gabi asked.

'So, the doctor gives Louie two options,' Sandra continued. 'He can either go back to standing on all fours or he can just wait for the pain to go away. He also adds that he didn't go to medical school just to deal with nonsense like lower back pain, and invites Louie to come back when he has a serious bacterial or viral infection.'

'Yes, but is that really true?' Gabi asked, concerned.

'I think that your story fits beautifully with mine,' Urša intervened. 'Human beings aren't natural because they only walk on two legs.'

'What if we walked on all fours, would we be then?' Liza asked.

'It would be more natural, by all means,' said Urša, convinced.

'Yes but *Louie* is just fiction!' Gabi said loudly.

'Which still doesn't mean it's not true,' Urša said smartly.

'But whoever believes this theory presents a nice little market niche for those selling it,' Liza announced wearily. Urša looked at her angrily and fiercely protested that she had seen a very convincing diagram. Liza was ready to say something sarcastic about these little sketches, but Matjaž interrupted her; he felt obliged to interfere in the debate, which was becoming increasingly tense. 'You put it nicely, though, when you said there's sometimes more truth in fiction.'

Not too much liquor had flowed when the enterprising Urša organized the music situation with Ksenja's permission, and was let loose on YouTube. Matjaž and Ronja were now the only pair left at the table watching the dancing couples. 'Look at that happy group of colleagues – what a beautiful image of the working collective,' Ronja began.

'And so why are we both here?'

'Maybe we're just not into dancing,' she smiled charmingly.

'Maybe somebody is just pretending that they're not into dancing any more so that others don't feel guilty about not being into that kind of group enthusiasm,' Matjaž looked at her questioningly.

'Nah, but she is a young mum and there are some things that are no longer becoming,' she remarked sarcastically.

'I never knew that you took societally designated roles so seriously,' he retorted.

'I don't. My husband does, though,' she replied ironically.

'Lucky husband, having such an obedient little wife.'

Meanwhile, Tadej had got very close to Sandra, and only with a great deal of leniency could their swaying be considered dancing.

'I was never into dancing in pairs, anyway,' Ronja said honestly.

'Me neither,' agreed Matjaž. He noticed that in Andrej's arms the loud-mouthed Liza had stopped talking altogether, although his head was drooping suspiciously on her shoulder.

'I think our troubadour's had a bit too much to drink,' Matjaž said, expertly judging the scene.

'The poor guy's earned it,' Ronja said kindly.

Meanwhile Kristjan was gallantly leading his boss around the dance floor, while she tenderly placed her head on his shoulder during some of the slower songs. As she did this, Ronja's watchful eye failed to see that Kristjan was also softly stroking her back. At first Urša and Gabi jumped around next to one another, until Roko ensnared the hot-tempered Catholic and led her into a whirl of quick-footed polka, carried out to the unconventional accompaniment of Nirvana.

'You see, now there's a couple in the making,' Ronja said.

'You reckon?' Matjaž was surprised.

'Where'd you get that idea from?'

'Roko was rather obviously selective in his decision,' Ronja explained.

'How can you say that, when you've not been at work for God knows how long?' Matjaž protested.

'It's an observation, my dear Watson, an observation. Tiny details – to whom did he first offer the sweetmeats? Whose side did he take during the debate about humans not being natural? Gabi.'

'And what about her?'

'She still hasn't quite noticed his affections, but I doubt she'll resist too much when she does. It's clear she wants a boyfriend.'

'I shan't ask where you got that idea from.'

'Oh, it's simple – because every, well, practically every, girl her age wants a boyfriend. Unless she's a lesbian, but Gabi definitely isn't.' Matjaž nodded at Ronja's clearly superior detective skills.

'Urša does not like it in the slightest,' she added. 'Although right now what she wants more than anything is someone to dance with, whoever shows up first.' And it was true – the sight of Urša, who carried on pretending to enjoy dancing by herself, revealed that she wasn't really happy about it. In the next few moments she confirmed this herself, when she came over to beg Matjaž to join her.

'Sorry, I've hurt my foot,' he apologized.

'Have you really?' Urša was dismayed, like any loyal colleague would be, but the expression on Ronja's face made her realize that he was joking. 'Honestly!' she said, trying to protest seductively.

'OK, fine, but I really do have a problem with my foot: I've got two left ones,' Matjaž continued. Urša just shook her head, showing that his argument was not convincing.

'How about if I tell you that both of my feet have gone to sleep?' he looked at her, pleadingly.

With a wrinkled forehead she looked him over, then let it go. 'Have it your way, but you owe me,' she smiled. Her desperation was such that she then even asked Ronja, who also gently declined the offer. And so, obviously keen for a party, she found her own rhythm on the dance floor. And no sooner had Liza gone to the bathroom, Urša seized Andrej, who was by this point in need of a strong, supportive dance partner. When she returned, a disgruntled Liza found her chosen one in the arms of the other woman. She sat down near them for a while, eventually abandoning all hope. Then Andrej lowered his head towards the lawn and gave back something that nature had given to him. Liza stood up and calmly concluded, 'I think I know when the party's over.' And she left.

'You see, she also had illicit intentions, but now she's realized that it's not going to happen – at least not tonight,' Ronja said, schooling Matjaž.

'Are you kidding me? With Andrej?'

'Of course! Beneath that cynical façade there are some fairly strong feelings smouldering for our Andrej the Liberal. Urša had gone to put Andrej to bed, but she promptly returned and continued her fight for the party.

'What about Tadej and Sandra?' Matjaž asked.

'Hm,' said Ronja, starting to study them closely. 'There's potential there, definitely. Look at how relaxed Sandra is, how she loves smiling at him even though we know he's not all that – how to put it – he's not very sharp.'

'But they hardly say a word to each other at work!' Matjaž protested.

'And this, my dear Watson, is why we have office parties, where people can get a little bit closer to one another.'

'But doesn't Sandra have a long-term boyfriend?' asked Matjaž.

'Oh dear Watson, of course she does, but luckily she also has a very poor memory. Believe me, tomorrow she and Tadej will have forgotten about today's adventure, no problem.'

To Matjaž's surprise, Ronja's detailed predictions started to come true. Urša was leaping around to the legendary eighties hit 'Bolje biti pijan nego star' while sipping her liqueur, with a clearer conscience than the other dancers. The remaining couple, Sandra and Tadej, weren't paying any attention to their surroundings. Matjaž and Ronja watched Kristjan and Ksenja. 'So, by your reckoning, will today be a pivotal step in our colleague's career?' asked Matjaž.

'Very possibly. Undoubtedly, in fact,' confirmed Ronja, giving her expert opinion. 'Our dear hostess isn't in the happiest of marriages, and she needs to be close to someone.'

'But how do you know that?' Matjaž asked, becoming irritated that one person could be so insightful about relationships.

'Well, I listened. That's what people are saying. Her mum is friends with my aunt.' Matjaž gave a faint nod, and Ronja continued, 'And then there's the extremely visible evidence – how quickly she gave in to Kristjan's barely disguised intentions, the fleeting touch, the flattery, how she forgot about the other guests.'

'And how will this all turn out? Also with a poor memory?' enquired Matjaž.

'Exactly, dear Watson,' Ronja praised him, 'only in this case there'll be a price to pay for the amnesia. But they're aware of that already,' she added smartly.

'Are you suggesting that Kristjan will get preferential treatment at work?'

'Exactly, but she's also very cunning, because Kristjan already gets preferential treatment. And because he's a careerist, in the strongest sense of the word, because he wants to make a name for himself, because he really wants to be someone, there's no worry that he'll become lazy or not do his job properly. One night of passion and they both gain something; or at least, neither really loses anything . . .'

'Sherlock, I'm impressed!'

'Thank you, my dear Watson, thank you very much,' laughed Ronja.

The dancing had clearly taken it out of Urša, and after the end of her song she sat down, exhausted, and poured herself some beer. She downed it in one. 'Dehydration,' she said, as she quenched her thirst and hiccupped loudly. Then she couldn't stop hiccupping, and tried to get rid of the nuisance by pouring more beer down her gullet, which in the end only resulted in her calling out a farewell of 'You lot are all so miserable! Hic!' Matjaž and Ronja returned a polite smile in her direction, followed by a burst of laughter once the drunkard was out of sight.

They sat for a while watching the last remaining dancing couple. 'Well, any more thoughts?' Matjaž probed her.

'I think we've had all there is to be gained from this spectacle,' she replied.

'You're not ready for bed are you?' he worried.

'You clearly aren't,' she said, giving him a roguish look.

'No, I can't sleep when there's still so much blood in my alcohol,' he said, shrugging his shoulders.

'Fine, I'd quite like to dilute my blood a bit, too, let's go for a walk. The young couple deserve a bit of privacy.'

Matjaž grabbed the bottle of liqueur, or whatever was left of it, and the two of them left. Obviously the walk was just an excuse to get away from the terrace dance floor and for them to take refuge under the enormous cypress tree on the other side of the house. There they set themselves up, just drinking and smoking for a while.

'So tell me honestly now,' Matjaž began, 'are you happy with that brat?'

'Honestly? Is a young mother even allowed to say anything against her child these days?' She drank a little more, and said thoughtfully, 'I'd be lying if I said that I'm happy. Ever since he was born, I've been too tired to be happy. But I was never such big fan of happiness anyway. Happiness is for simpletons and people with no creative spirit.'

'OK, so do you ever think about returning him to the state, or depositing him somewhere and picking him again when he knows how to talk and wipe his own arse?'

'It crosses my mind now and again. But I'd do that with my husband first,' she added jokingly.

'He doesn't hit you, does he?'

'No, it's not that.'

'He doesn't hit you enough?'

Ronja smiled, and with a bitterness in her voice she went on, 'Do you know what he said to me the other day? It's a bit wrong me telling you this, given that I've not seen you in over a year . . .'

'And because I haven't always been the best of listeners,' he added.

'Well, I was trying to be diplomatic.'

'Today, Ronja, I'm all yours. Go on!'

'OK, so when I asked my husband half-jokingly if we were going to have sex any time soon, because since Ivor was born we just haven't, he said I'd have to take up running before that happened . . .' With that, her voice lost its spark.

'What the! Outrageous!' Matjaž blurted out, being funny. 'As if you'd become one of those types that runs around relentlessly in public spaces at all hours of the day!'

Ronja joined in with this frank dislike of healthy living, 'And now they do it in swarms, they chase down every street like mosquitoes, even the busiest ones, while respectable people are in the pub having a beer and smoking cigarettes.'

'I agree, it should be banned!'

'They ought to go back to the parks, their natural, healthy environment, they ought to do it at night when no one can see them,' Ronja continued militantly.

They sipped their drinks and sat quietly for a while.

Matjaž had a brainwave.

'I'd send them all off to an alcohol familiarization clinic,' he avowed.

Ronja looked at him with interest. 'I'm all ears . . .'

'Well, you know how we have these esteemed institutions where they help alcoholics, druggies and pillheads find the meaning of life after substances?'

Ronja nodded encouragingly, and Matjaž continued, 'Well, on the other hand there is a whole range of repressed people who don't even dare go outside because they're so scared of interaction. And who could blame them! Being sociable is a real effort. Few people realize that our ancestors invented alcohol precisely because of that repression; it abates all the awkwardness and tension, and allows something resembling a public sphere to even exist. So I'd just send people like that to a clinic, where they could slowly get used to alcohol.'

'Under medical supervision, obviously,' Ronja joined in.

'Of course. Under very strict medical supervision. And the clinics could provide a basic alcohol education, too – for example, the basics of drinking beer, wine, spirits.'

'The pros and cons of each?'

'That's it, so that people know exactly what they're dealing with. There'd be sociologists who would also explain to them that, let's say, beers go well with football matches; top chefs would add that red wine goes with red meat; cultural historians would inform them that spirits are a key feature of old Hollywood films, perfect for stressful situations like crime or formal dinners.'

'Excellent idea!' said Ronja, enjoying herself. 'I imagine that the supply of alcohol would take place behind closed doors at first, i.e. inside the hospital, and then at some point the patients would be sent outside.'

Matjaž burst out laughing, and when he'd calmed down slightly he added, 'Exactly, to begin with the patients would be sent out in a group for a Saturday night visit, supervised by a doctor. They'd try to identify the correct drink by themselves and administer the right amount, with the doctors and other people keeping an eye on them.'

'They could take notes', Ronja interjected, 'then they could tell each one what they did right and wrong, and advise them accordingly.'

'And if someone gets a good enough mark on, let's say, three of these supervised nights out, then the next Friday they could go out by themselves, without supervision. When they returned to the hospital they'd be examined thoroughly again, they'd speak to the doctor and the psychiatrist. Then they'd get new instructions afterwards', said Matjaž, elaborating on his project.

'They'd resit until the experts deemed them able to go out into the world by themselves and be independent enough to drink without supervision.' With that they both burst out laughing. 'Ha ha, yes, the aim of this clinic would be to make sure you know how to drink by yourself, unsupervised.'

When they'd exhausted themselves laughing they sat silently for a while, sipping their drinks.

'But that hurts', said Ronja eventually, her sentence confusing Matjaž slightly and causing him to look slightly surprised.

She explained, 'I mean, for a woman, who after childbirth is in one way or another only half the woman she was, a total slave to her baby, that kind of cold and detached attitude from a partner almost kills you.'

Matjaž didn't say anything, but then asked, 'And what will you do?'

'I won't be running, that's for sure!' she said decisively.

They laughed and raised their glasses to toast this grand idea.

'What about you?' she eventually asked.

'I'm not going to run either!' he said, and again they laughed and again they drank.

'No seriously, what are you going to do with yourself, with work, with women?'

'I have no idea. I'm just going to keep on having a good time.'

'Quiet desperation, then,' Ronja remarked wryly.

'It's better than loud desperation,' Matjaž smiled.

'There's no point trying to have a serious conversation with you,' she sighed.

'Why do we have to have a serious conversation?' Matjaž asked, raising his voice slightly. 'I know myself. I know what I'm capable of and what I'm not. I don't see why I have to dedicate too much time to myself, and even less so why others should dedicate themselves to me.'

Ronja smiled at this self-reflexivity. 'I get it, I just wanted to make you feel better.'

Matjaž looked at her seriously. 'You have done Ronja, really.' He took hold of her hand. Then his hand led itself away, and stroked her beautiful dark hair. 'You've no idea how long it's been since I felt this good around a woman, even if I've been attracted to them.'

'On no account must you say things like that, my dear Watson, because I'm going to believe you,' she said softly.

'You're just going to have to accept that men still like you, even though you don't run,' he persisted.

That sentence was painful for Ronja and she lowered her head, which Matjaž was gently stroking. Then she looked at him with a clear, open expression, almost free of pain. He stroked her face with the same openness and warmth, and so the kiss that followed seemed as natural to them as a summer breeze comforting warm bodies on a beach. Without saying a word they held hands and headed to bed. Indoors, Ksenja had already designated them her husband's small study, where two inflatable yoga mats were laid out proudly on the floor, along with the sleeping bags they'd brought themselves. Matjaž and Ronja lay down next to one another and carried on kissing. Together they slowly undressed and carried on sharing kisses, those fleeting but fundamental signs of intimacy. Then she started giggling.

'Ronja, if you're not sure . . .' said Matjaž sincerely.

'No, it's not that,' she laughed. 'I was just thinking to myself that I feel like a virgin. I don't know how this goes any more . . .'

Matjaž slowly stroked her naked body and said, 'When I was first in this situation, when it was my first time, I thought to myself while it was all happening, "This is it. I am having sex." And I swear I felt more satisfaction upon that realization than I did with the act itself.'

Ronja laughed, wholeheartedly and passionately, like her laughter had now acclimatized to the evening. She stroked his hair and snuggled up close to him, kissing his neck.

'Happy the man who loves Ronja,' said Matjaž, softened by her gentle touch.

'Careful what you wish for, maybe Ronja's love comes with urine.' She laughed uncontrollably again.

'Sorry, what?' Matjaž laughed back.

Ronja thought for a moment and then burst out laughing again. Her laugh reverberated so perfectly that he automatically kissed her on the lips, while her palm calmly and commandingly travelled around his body. 'It happened ten years ago, when I met my then-future husband. I went on a date with him, not expecting anything; I was indifferent, even. I liked feeling desired, but I resisted being in a relationship. I'd just moved into a rented flat at the time, and I felt so good on my own; I was content, maybe for the first time in my life, and I wasn't looking for a man. So the feeling that he stirred in me was almost too much. I went on a date to break it off with him, to basically convince myself that it wasn't worth changing everything again just for one stupid guy. Anyhow, we had such a good time on the date, we really clicked. He was good fun and really handsome. When he took me home he went to kiss me, but I just hugged him even though I wanted that kiss more than anything. I was still convinced that I wasn't going to let him get close. So I went to bed. During the night I got up to go to the toilet. But I must've still been dreaming, because I mistook my wicker chair for the toilet seat, sat down and, well, it happened. I woke up right in the middle of it, totally confused and in a mild state of panic, not knowing what was going on, where I was, what was happening to me.'

Matjaž looked at her confused. She quickly rolled her eyes – there was no point mincing her words over the situation, which to this day she still found embarrassing. 'I wet myself in the chair!' she shrieked.

'And so . . . what does that mean?' he asked her calmly, like an experienced psychoanalyst.

'Well, at the time, of course, it wasn't clear to me what it meant, at least not consciously, but then as things developed it became apparent what it was all about.'

'Well, obviously you got together, but what does that have to do with you weeing on a chair?' asked Matjaž.

'Is it not obvious? At first I fiercely resisted a new relationship, but then I literally let go.' Matjaž burst out laughing and gave her an even bigger kiss on the cheek, caressing her shoulders.

'There was nothing as dramatic as that with Sara,' Matjaž said, recalling his story frankly and continuing to stroke Ronja. 'There wasn't any drama between us in general. The most important thing for me was the domestic calm, which I felt from the moment I met her. I remember on our first holiday to Hvar, we had little need to talk about banalities such as how the food was, or about swimming or love-making. We were already in unspoken agreement. Those were good times. Maybe the best times; calm, and so gentle . . . That doesn't mean I didn't want to talk to her, though. Over dinner we'd speak for hours, deep in discussion about politics, about our parents, our friends, past loves and adventures. We spoke about school and university, anecdotes and aspirations.' He stopped for a moment, and then continued, not releasing Ronja from his affectionate hold. 'That's what I'd call being completely at ease. I wasn't used to that feeling around women, around anyone, at least not so . . . I think that's because I never really liked myself all that much. Maybe it sounds clichéd if I say that my ability to be sociable is tied to the fact that I'm not all that good on my own. But with her, being by myself was no longer too much for me. With her I felt good, safe, although that probably sounds incredibly lame.' He paused again briefly, and said thoughtfully, 'Being at ease, Ronja, that's the key. And it's so rare. Don't you think? Don't you think, Ronja, that's what you and I have, that we know how to do that? Be at ease, I mean?'

He didn't get a reply. He looked at the naked Ronja, who to the soft rhythm of his palms and words had fallen asleep. He kissed her on the cheek and, relaxed and contented himself, fell asleep beside her.

*

When he woke up, Ronja's smiling face was looking at him, while her hand stroked his head.

He smiled. 'What time is it?'

'Eleven.'

'And, what's the situation?'

'Some of the girls have gone, others are waiting for their taxi service. I think it's time to slowly get going.'

'God, you're right, I've got the burden of those hungover hens,' he said, clutching his head.

'You'll cope yet, dear Watson. With that charm, with those eyes.' She looked at him melancholically.

'Sherlock, my dear, are we going to have to succumb to amnesia as well?' His own sentence pained him.

'No, we're not.' Ronja hugged him tightly.

'What are we going to do, then? It's going to be hard to forget about last night,' Matjaž said, looking into her eyes.

She returned a sad gaze. 'You mean me falling asleep while you were talking.'

'Which was just the most beautiful thing.' He looked at her with affection, and leaned in to kiss her.

'Don't, dear Watson.' She pulled back and he was sure that she was on the brink of tears.

'What is it, Sherlock?' Do you not see a future for us?' He looked at her melancholically.

Ronja's lips stretched out into a wide smile. 'Of course I see one, that's the problem.' She hung her head, swallowed and looked at him again. In her eyes he saw all of her openness, peppered with anguish. 'I see it all too well! And that's why we mustn't repeat this, otherwise there really will be no going back . . .'

He could see restraint in her expression, even courage; now her eyes reflected only that kind of sadness that usually accompanies the parting of lovers.

Now Matjaž sensed tears, but he understood why. He offered her his hand. They shook hands as friends and smiled at each other, just about managing to hide the bitterness.

'Well, stay wise, my dear Watson!' she said, giving him a melancholy smile towards which two tears were now travelling.

'I think we all know who has the wisdom in this relationship, my dear Sherlock.' He looked at her encouragingly.

'OK, well, good luck then!' she said, pulling herself together somewhat.

'You too,' he said, raising his hand to signal goodbye.

Then Ronja left, and Matjaž burst into tears.

That Saturday evening, Matjaž didn't want to talk to Aleksander, but he had got in touch anyway, under the pretence of Karla having left her copy of *Global* in Matjaž's flat. His curiosity was torturing him.

'And what's that Urša like?' his friend asked, looking at him with inquisitive eyes.

'Crazy enough. You'd like her . . .' Matjaž said sarcastically.

'So nothing happened, then?' asked Aleksander, still probing.

'Many things happened: drugs, alcohol, orgies . . .' Matjaž said, purposely exaggerating.

'What?' Aleksander's eyes lit up. 'Tell me everything. I've waited all year for this! Is Sandra as much of a pest as I expected? No, actually, Liza is worse – those know-it-alls usually are.' He didn't wait for his friend's reply, but tried to interpret his stony look. 'No, no . . . Don't tell me . . . Ksenja, your boss! Of course, mature women, that's it, that's it. It's what I'm always telling you! And? Were the girls up for it? I bet Gabi was the driving force behind the worst behaviour. Or that Andrej – still waters run deep, right? Or maybe I'm wrong, maybe Ronja was the ringleader. I told you – young mothers, they're full of oestrogen. It was her, admit it, admit it!' he shrieked, not realizing that the mention of Ronja's name caused Matjaž to flinch.

Aleksander left his fantasy there and went on. 'That Kristjan is suspicious, though, I agree. A man's ambitions can go too far. I bet that Tadej was all over everyone. He's probably not that wild, though. It must have been an assortment – some kind of homosexual activity – oof! A big house with a pool – oh God, did you all do it in the pool? Oh my God, oh my God, what a party! That's it, first in the pool, then outside. Ah, the youth of today, capable of anything. Admit it! Admit it, that's what happened!'

And so Aleksander went on, letting his imagination run wild, not at all bothered by the fact that his friend only looked at him blankly. When he'd finished his monologue, he left – without taking the magazine – and repeated one more time, 'What a party, why can't I have colleagues like that, man oh man!'

SARA

Summer had burst into all its elements: the remote azure of the sky, the light breeze that chased along the scorching, neglected concrete. He had always loved Ljubljana when it was deserted; perfect for a simple, lazy life in the shade. He loved the cafés and bars, which now came alive in the evening thanks to the tourists, the increasingly frequent inhabitants of this quaint city, so big and so small in every way.

There was sweet tranquillity within him. It had been a long time since he'd felt so at peace, sitting with his three colleagues in the air-conditioned office, looking out at the hot, clear summer sky. He was a staunch advocate of a cloudless sky. True, clouds could sometimes intensify photographs, improve the light, but to him personally, photography aside, a clear sky that precisely framed the view of the city seemed much more meaningful, natural, purifying even. Never had the colonnades of Plečnik's market been so appealing to him as they were now. Never had the Triple Bridge seemed so truly wonderful as it did in this heat, as its rather deserted whiteness crossed the Ljubljanica river, linking the beautifully restored buildings on each river bank, which looked down with proud indifference on their inhabitants. Never had he wanted so much to go for a walk through Trnovo along the embankment as he did now, when the outline of the bank appeared to have yielded to the river's tranquil flow, seemingly reconciled to the occasional passer-by. As if the river had only just now made contact with the willows that bowed despondently towards its surface. They reminded him of old ladies at the seaside, hesitating before stepping into the generous waves on their first dip of the year.

Actually, he thought, it was only during summer that he looked upon his city as a space that extended elsewhere; with its footpaths, river banks, streets and squares, a city that led you somewhere or beckoned you to hide away from the sun in its various sanctuaries. Republic Square seemed magnificent in this sort of weather, patiently framed by the buildings that set the tempo for a mixture of lifestyles that the city-dwellers enjoyed throughout the year: educational, financial, political and, of course, commercial. Now they stood there like magnificent monuments to summer – a time when the only thing that matters is the expanse of space and sky. Even Čopova, the most promiscuous street in the capital, which greedily devoured everything and everybody all year long, was now able to show how it extended and stretched, linking places as well as people; how it was here as part of the city's network and would also benefit from a little less self-indulgent commerce.

Only in summer was he aware of the façades, the entrances and the decorative features on the buildings: the National Library, Nebotičnik, the Triglav Insurance building; façades that otherwise usually merged into what he intuitively took in from the city and so always remained like barely noticed backdrop scenery in a theatre of various destinies. But not now. Now he sensed that all these had fates of their own, that they could be beautiful in their own right to those rare eyes that looked upon them in the right way and for whom they were a consolation. They caressed such admirers gently but maintained their distance. There is nothing more beautiful than when buildings appear to be entities in themselves and passers-by merely their more-or-less-attentive observers. Countless corners of the city took on meaning only in summer; the area surrounding the Križanke Theatre and Rimska Street, finally free of students, now offered tranquillity for a quiet and contemplative coffee somewhere – maybe even at Žmavc, now that it was free from the wearying noise of all those young try-hards.

Summer! Summer at last. With all of its appurtenances, which declare a truce between people and nature and finally allow the stupid humans a sense of a gentler pace of life. For the first time in a long while he felt, without bitterness, that he was single and that at the same time he didn't need anyone, that the world was entirely bearable and he was happy with his own solitary entity, indifferent to everything, even to itself.

In such a frame of mind, maybe he ought to call Sara and just ask to take her out for a coffee, some tea or even orange juice, although he didn't really want any of that. For a moment he was tempted by the thought of two bodies silently, modestly losing themselves amid the grandeur of the city in summertime. Mainly it was because he knew that right now she was also alone in Ljubljana, because her darling Jaka was somewhere on a business trip. He'd been able to gather this from Aleksander and Karla, through passing remarks made in company or the odd phone call that had interrupted their socializing, always taken slightly more quietly than usual out of respect for him. But now the idea of calling her seemed a surreal and, in his current state, senseless act.

'Why are you smiling like that?' said Gabi, trying to be funny.

'What's it to you?' he shot back at her.

'Well excuse me for living!'

'Never mind "excuse me". Apologize to me,' he said, using that old, dumb joke that earned a laugh from his colleagues, and prompted a more conciliatory look even from Gabi. Such was summer; people smiled at each other to confirm that they were not alone.

Women are OK, he thought, they're very much OK, as long as they're kept at a safe distance. And he was convinced that he was also OK with that safe distance. Until now, he'd always believed that OK entities were only rarely in tune with each other. Evidently, it often boils down to there being two types of 'being OK', which just don't sit well together. Of course, she and he were in tune; they were sort of in tune in everything, and in some things very much so. It was a nice, rhythmic life when, now and again, the two of them locked into that joint rhythm.

It wasn't that he felt he was missing anything now; it just bothered him that things, such as life as a couple, were once a possibility – in fact, they were the only possibility. Now, in contrast, he lived a life of duality. He sometimes felt like he was two people: happy in the morning, difficult in the evening; or optimistic in the morning and moderately suicidal in the evening . . . But life as a couple? What's the point in that, he wondered. Where's the happiness in that? Whenever he tried to remind himself of the appealing side of life as a twosome he found himself staring into a void. He didn't understand what it was exactly; only fleetingly he recalled the feeling of comfort, occasional enthusiasm and, most of all, the feeling of happiness that he used to have in his routine life as part of a pair.

He became slightly angry with himself – damned summer, inviting all of these thoughts, confronting him with these reminiscences. He didn't want to confront himself; he didn't want to be the protagonist in his own story when, after all, it was obvious that the only reason he was there was to spice up the agonizing mundanity of life with a few jokes. People – quite a few people, his friends included – had children. A few – quite a few – of his acquaintances had well-paid jobs. Others – quite a few others – in his circle of drinking buddies had the luxury of not caring about anything, about family or about work. And what did he have? He was stuck in a rut in every respect. He wasn't at home anywhere. Apart from during the summer, he remembered, apart from here, in this cycle of thoughts that absolutely refused to end. Even though he never intended to reflect on anything, least of all himself. He was convinced that the less you knew about yourself, the better – regardless of what the ancient Greeks claimed.

He had already left the office and was striding towards a popular nearby pub called Izložba – had he even said goodbye to his colleagues, he wondered? But nobody really notices greetings in summer anyway, let alone misses them when they're not there.

When he arrived at the bar, he was pleased to discover that, apart from one other person whose face was hidden behind a newspaper, this place was empty. After a few minutes of silence he began to wonder if anyone actually worked there, or if the owners had all left for the seaside and forgotten to lock up their property. But that thought didn't last long.

There is nothing finer than a cigarette in summertime. A drag on a Gauloise settles the score imposed by the heat, and already the sky is brighter and your thoughts have cleared. How he wished that he had a newspaper as well – thinking your own thoughts seemed like such hard work. He was aware of them constantly, and he wasn't used to that. He was used to having every thought interrupted by a phone call or a work email, some obligation or another, by Ksenja's ruminations or instructions in a text message about every-thing that still needed to be done. He was used to the odd bad joke from Katja on Twitter, or one of Suzana's invitations for coffee – although she was actually in Istria now, with Saša of all people. It turned out that her Šeki, if they were still even together any more, just wasn't the holiday type. Aleksander was sunning himself with Karla on the island of Krk and only got in touch every other day, and then only in the evenings. Jernej was waiting tables all summer by the coast – some people really do have it all.

Gašper, Marko and Andraž were currently on their rich-kid weekends in Pula or with relatives on the Kvarner Riviera, having the most wonderful time of their life – admiring their still-beautiful women and their even more promising children, and thinking to themselves that life wasn't so bad – as long as their mum or dad or brother or sister with kids didn't knock at the door with a load of bright ideas about how they could spend the day together, what they could cook and, most importantly, what would be good for the kids.

It was possible that he missed the hustle and bustle of company – any Mini or Stela, Nada or Melita could at least have dropped him some kind of tasteless text. He'd like that, the offer of some kind of crazy night with no obligations. As it was, Stela was probably happily in the arms of an obscene mogul – at least for a day or two – and mother and daughter were probably off trying to flaunt their charms in the Caribbean or Cuba. Mini was no doubt tied up with the situation in Gaza or the Congo or suffering over the burning of forbidden books in Singapore.

Where did people get their money? Where did this money come from that allowed them not to report back to base, to him, Matjaž, who, after all, remained a magnet for every type of stupidity? Was he going to have to call someone himself one of these days; someone who knew how to pour their wages back into drink? Was he desperate enough to call his mum? She was probably at this moment lounging around with colleagues on some training course in Karlovy Vary that was just an excuse for bathing in the springs there, and that existed only so the relatively well-cared-for retired legal experts from the Republic of Slovenia's Ministry of Higher Education could enjoy their holidays and attempt to rescue what was left of their bodies and long-lost youth. Was he so close to the edge that he'd exchange a few dull remarks about the weather with his father, who was employed at the Republic of Slovenia's Environment Agency? To Matjaž, his dad's job had always been something just to do with the weather, although his father would be enraged by the idea since he was employed at the agency as a physicist who calculated God-knows-what for the good of us all. When he was little – and probably encouraged by his mum's wicked suggestions – he had always blamed his dad for the rain or for the winter that stopped him going out to play.

A game, he figured, that's what was missing. Maybe poker or billiards

– crazy people can probably be found in summertime, too, those who are prepared to waste their money and their lives on their passion for gambling. He started searching for names in his contacts, when a familiar voice from not too far away interrupted him.

'Mat!'

Was he dreaming? No one but her had ever dared use that name, that stupid, ridiculous name invented for him by his equally silly, completely shameless and now deceased grandma – the woman he had perhaps loved most in his life. It was his grandma who always said that children put their parents in checkmate by the very fact of being born. That's why she always liked names where she could see the beginnings of a 'mate': Matej, Matjaž, Matko, Matic, Matija, Matilda, Mateja, Matahari and so on. But Grandma is dead, he said to himself, he was convinced of it – she had a headstone at Žale cemetery, along with dried flowers, burned-out candles and all of that. Then maybe he was just imagining it; maybe the heat was messing with his head. Finally he looked up – and he saw her. Sara.

She was coming towards him with a crumpled newspaper and her distinctive smile, which struck him right in the stomach.

'Your newspaper's crumpled,' he said upon greeting her, slightly embarrassed. He hadn't seen her for more than a year.

'They say people with tidy newspapers are not to be trusted,' she replied, once again relaxing into that captivating smile.

'Hitler always had a tidy newspaper.' She winked.

'Probably because he never read it,' he added quickly, still feeling uncomfortable.

She started laughing, a lovely heartfelt laughter, almost as lovely and heartfelt as when they had still been a couple, and he knew that this laughter was a part of him and his sense of humour. Already he'd forgotten how her head tilted when she laughed, making her fair curls flutter, and how they magnificently complemented her light complexion, which not a single sunbeam had managed to compromise. He'd forgotten just how fair her complexion was; he'd forgotten how much they had avoided the sun when they were on holiday; he'd forgotten about her hats and her long tunics.

'Others say that it's only old people who read newspapers now, and that's only because they're checking that their obituary isn't inside,' she added. He remembered now how much he loved her wit.

'Then it's possible that you're not real and that I'm talking to a ghost,' he said, laughing.

'Quite possible. Maybe you can pinch me so we can check I'm alive.' It seemed to him as if her eyes twinkled at this point.

'Why, have you found your obituary?' he asked.

'No, but that doesn't mean anything.'

'How about you pinch yourself, and you let me know if you're alive.'

She did so and nodded. 'It appears I still exist.'

'Well, that's encouraging.' He could feel how hard he was trying to speak in a normal voice.

'I have to say, I didn't expect someone who doesn't believe in God or the afterlife to allow the possibility that I may be a ghost quite so quickly,' she said, still smiling.

'God is spelled with a capital G.'

'What?'

'Our Catholic readers are always giving us grief about that – especially if there's a full moon. If you're writing about a personal god, a god of religion, like Christianity or whatever else, you have to spell it with a capital letter.'

'So you do believe, then?'

'In what?'

'In capital G for God.' She looked at him playfully, making him shake with laughter once more.

'A man's got to believe in something.' He smiled and gestured with his hand, inviting her to sit down.

As she sat she remarked, in passing, naturally but flirtatiously as only she knew how, 'You're looking good.'

'Objection!' he let out, as if the situation was strange and familiar at the same time.

'So?' she went on.

'What?'

'How are you?'

'Are you really interested, or are you just being polite?' Matjaž was slightly confused.

'If you're asking me that you already know the answer,' she replied.

'What was the question again?' he said, now feigning confusion.

'How are you?' she repeated.

'Don't even go there.' He sighed dramatically.

'That bad?' She smiled.

'Nah, it's not bad at all,' he reassured her.

'Good, then?'

'Come on, do we have to elaborate on every nuance of "not bad" now? I'd rather you told me how you are. Either way, I'm convinced you only asked me so I'd return the question.'

'You're mistaken, my intentions were pure, so I'll also answer calmly and succinctly. I'm all right, thanks.'

'Oof, well that can't be good,' Matjaž answered in concern.

She laughed, saying, 'You still know me.'

'No, I don't. I thought that you really were fine, and obviously I don't begrudge you that,' he said with a hint of anger.

'No, nothing's wrong,' she said, as if trying to convince herself, but he detected that legendary 'but' lingering at the back of her throat.

The waitress sensed a point in the unease where she could take their order. When they'd amicably established all the things that weren't on the menu during the summer, they ordered the only two remaining dishes and agreed to share them, just like old times.

Matjaž hadn't felt this good around someone of the female sex since he'd been with Ronja, and he got the feeling that Sara felt similarly. They revisited old stories: the disgusting mussels on the island of Rab; the cheap but high-quality rakia on Korčula that led to night-swimming in the port; the ski slopes at Vogel where she tried to show him the joys of skiing, which he in no way wished to embrace; the goulash that kept cooking away, forgotten, while they made love on their weekend away in Piran (and was still not at all bad) . . .

They only spoke about current affairs long enough for them to change the subject. They gossiped a bit about Karla and Aleksander, about Suzana and Katja, about Gašper's kid and about Jure's new offspring, and counted up all the remaining children that had been recently born to people they knew. They established that we wouldn't be dying out any time soon.

When he'd settled the bill and silence settled in, he said seriously, 'Well, I'd best get back to work.' He stood up, while she remained seated and looked at him – strangely, actually. 'What is it?' he asked her.

'Mat, could we not – just for today – could we not have coffee together?'
It was her tone of voice, and her slightly bewildered – perhaps even disappointed – expression, rather than the meaning of the words, which moved him. He wasn't used to that. He thought about it for a second, and then said, 'Fine, it's nothing urgent anyway!' He worried that the cynic in him hadn't come up with a better reaction, something more decisive – it wasn't like he owed her anything, damn it! He was frightened of himself, frightened that he was starting to feel desire for her again. Then he quickly called work and made arrangements to put off his unimportant duties.

The coffee at Nebotičnik quickly, miraculously quickly, turned into a beer; in the more than ample sunshine Matjaž and Sara were still chatting away like old friends. Over the first beer they bitched about all the Asian tourists in Ljubljana, making cheap jibes about their umbrellas, or rather parasols, which defended them against the ozone hole. Together they also criticized the band that was spending the evening going around the various bars on Petkovšek Embankment; it consisted of some not overly talented Romanians.

'Do you still pay them to stop playing?' she asked him as she lit a cigarette carefully, elegantly and passionately, as only she knew how.

'I try, but they still don't understand. They don't even understand when I ask them if they think it's appropriate to start collecting money after the first song. They don't understand when I ask them to play something I haven't heard before. Nope, in this battle they are the victors,' he complained. It pleased him to see that his scornful storytelling brought a smile to her face again and again.

'And how are you getting on with the scroungers these days?' she pushed him, and he knew that she was hoping for his latest tales.

'Well, what can I say. We've agreed a truce, but one of them threw me a bit the other day; the one who operates all the way from the Ethnographic Museum to Petkovšek and who clearly doesn't know who's given her what and when and for which story – she really is a bit unprofessional like that. She could at least be a bit more prepared for work. So one day she got two euros from me with the excuse that she didn't have money to buy milk for her small child. The next day I bumped into her on Petkovšek and she claimed that she didn't have any money to pay the rent. And that's when I finally stood up for myself. I said to her, "If you didn't buy so much milk for your child then you'd have enough money for rent."' He managed to get another laugh from Sara. So he continued, 'Of course, coming up to summer she'd forgotten all about it and approached me again by the museum with a new problem. She said that she'd had to have an operation on her heart valves and that while she was in hospital she lost her job, was kicked out of her flat and was now left with nothing. I looked at her and decided that, if nothing else, her imagination had earned her a euro.'

Their conspiratorial closeness was interrupted by some loud English football fans and so they decided to change location. Sara suggested that they try another bar somewhere. 'Where would you like to go?' he asked her.

'Somewhere nice.'

'Everywhere is nice right now.'

'Let's go somewhere that's only bearable then.'

'Žmavc?'

She nodded and they left. It felt funny walking next to her, next to her short but decisive steps, next to her animated hips that were not afraid to show themselves to the world. She seemed taller than before, but Matjaž thought it was probably just her confidence that lent her the aura that a tall girl has; always decisive, elegant, superior.

'I'd forgotten, you know, how tall you look compared to how tall you actually are,' he smiled.

'I know.' She looked back at him, slightly nostalgic, then she smirked, 'It's my magnificent personality.'

They chatted casually most of the way. As they walked past Maximarket he asked, 'How's your fashion police force coming along?'

'Ah, we're still in the ideas phase; we've got a list of offences, and every day we see huge numbers of people who need locking up, but somehow we don't have the authority yet.'

'I'll give you all the authority. I hope you've put a few fashion designers on the list of offenders, too.'

'Sometimes I'd just like to lock up fashion itself. What shorts have done to the appearance of public spaces is unforgivable – but then shorts still reign supreme in every who-knows-which season in every H&M and Zara.'

'But I have to confess, they wouldn't be the first trend I'd send the fashion police after. Those raggy-rag things seem much more offensive to me.'

'Raggy rag things? Nicely put,' she teased.

'You know the ones I mean – those pieces of clothing that pretend to have an edgy design, but they're actually just raggy rags.'

'I'll remember that one and add it to our list.'

Slowly they wandered up towards Žmavc, which at six in the evening actually looked tidy and calm. Just a few people with their Aperol spritzers, their wine and sodas, and their obligatory iPads or smartphones. They knew that no one was going to bother them here.

Over the second beer they asked after each other's families. They were pleased to hear that everyone was well. Matjaž expressed his particular pleasure that his parents still kept a fair distance and didn't expect an excessive amount of attention – although he did acknowledge that things had taken a turn for the worst with Uncle Miha, who had been fairly insane even in his reasonably youthful fifties. Miha's decline was taking its toll mainly on his wife, whom the family felt had already been dealt her fair share just by marrying him in the first place.

Sara was restrained when she started talking about her niece and nephew. She still got on quite well with little Anton, but hanging out with little Marta now left her feeling uneasy. 'I don't know, more and more I see this cold callousness in her; I worry it's what you'd find in some kind of serial killer.'

'My Marta has degenerated like that?' Matjaž said, shaking his head. 'And you can already tell at the age of nine, or however old she is.'

'Ten. Yeah, sorry to have to tell you, Mat, but that child is not normal, to put it mildly.'

'I was an unusual kid, too, but just look at how I turned out,' he grinned.

'Well, exactly, that's what worries me,' she smiled back.

'What does the proud father Izidor have to say about it?'

'Well, I'm not exactly close to my brother, as you know, and the kids are his weak spot. I think he's completely blind to them, and especially to Marta.'

'I can sympathize with him, though. It can't be easy with those little people,' replied Matjaž in a pacifying tone.

'It's really not easy, no, but I think Lara brings up the little humans a lot more sensibly than my brother does. Maybe because he's still a child himself,' said Sara critically.

'Poor Lara – all alone with three children,' Matjaž joked again.

She looked at him, smiling. 'I thought of you, actually, when I was staying in this hotel in Vienna. People under the age of eighteen were banned there.'

'Oh, the most civilized place on this earth!' Matjaž sighed in reverie.

By eight-thirty Žmavc had become too loud. It was time to leave. They decided to go for a walk along the river and take a seat at whichever place took their fancy. The place that happened to call out to them was Le Petit Café. 'Ah, days of studying at NUK, so many days, so many coffees!' sighed Sara.

'You make it sound as if decades have gone by since then!'

'Well they have! More than decades! It won't be long until I'm an old crone!'

'Old, young, you're still a crone!' Matjaž said, winding her up, for which she clipped him round the head.

By the third beer they were talking about holidays. 'This year we went to Hvar. Hvar is still beautiful, you know. You can let go of all cynicism and irony over there,' Sara explained.

'Ah, I always knew there was a completely ordinary romantic beneath all that political incorrectness and dark humour,' Matjaž said, trying to sting her again.

'Don't insult me. Would you still be saying the same if I told you that I committed my first Hvar-crime while I was there?'

'What, did you go swimming at midday?'

'No, not that. You know I'd rather die than be in the sun at that time.'

'So what then?'

'I trod on a snail and destroyed his little house, and well, him, too,' she admitted remorsefully.

'You clearly did it because you were jealous that he had a house on Hvar and you didn't.'

Sara's face cheered up again. 'How about you? When are you going, where are you going, and, well, who are you going with?'

'Somebody's curious! I'm not exactly sure yet. Some guy's asked me if I'll take photos of his big Croatian wedding. I've been thinking that I'll go there in September, get the horror out of the way and then merge work into a holiday.'

'Hvar is at its most beautiful in September,' she sighed softly.

They sat quietly for a moment. Both were thinking the same thing: that it was September when they first went to Hvar together. They'd already set off on this topic now, and the temperature had cooled somewhat.

'Will you go on your own?' she enquired cautiously.

'It's looking that way . . .' he replied, without any discernible emotion.

'Maybe you'll meet the woman of your dreams there,' she said.

Matjaž thought he could sense bitterness in her voice. He wanted to say that he'd already met the woman of his dreams and that she left him over a year ago, but he held back. He just said, 'Without a doubt. I'll probably fall in love with the bridesmaid.'

'You never know,' she smiled again melancholically. 'I reckon weddings only exist so that the single guests get the chance to meet their future lovers.'

'I'll let you know how that goes when I get back. Based on current experiences I'd say that weddings are there to make you appreciate by comparison queues at the post office, the filling out of official forms and recycling.'

When they finished their drink they decided to persevere with finding a different bar. They drank their fourth beer at Bar Dvor on the end of Židovska Street, agreeing that at this time, Bikofe was too lively for the intimacy that they had recovered and reshaped that day.

'You know, I still remember when the City Library was on this spot,' she said.

'I know what you're trying to say. You've inhabited this planet for so long that you, too, have become one of the city's artefacts!' he remarked sarcastically.

'That wasn't my point. My point was that I love libraries, and I once swore to myself that I'd never sit around in this place because, to me, it will always be a sacred place of books.'

'Fine, well then we'll just pretend that we're in the reading room,' said Matjaž, trying to be resourceful. She raised her eyebrows, so he went on, 'In Mark Zuckerberg's library perhaps.'

'Mark Zuckerberg?' she raised her voice. 'Do you seriously think that guy reads, that he has books, that he has a library?'

'He probably has a library as some sort of antique shop.'

'Where they drink hundred-year-old whisky,' she remarked, scowling.

'Nah, he doesn't drink whisky. He drinks Coca-Cola Zero.'

This clearly put her in better spirits, as they then ordered a whisky from the waiter. Not exactly a hundred years old, but not bad.

Now the conversation slipped more easily towards intimate details. Matjaž mentioned a few of his triumphs from his season of love. He thought it important to pick out Stela, and Brigita too, but Sara was most amused by the fact that Suzana managed to fall asleep during sex.

'Some of us are just masters,' Matjaž remarked sourly, while her eyes sparkled with mischief.

'But do you see a future for you two?' she asked, seriously.

'No,' Matjaž replied, seriously. 'I think Suzana has absolutely no recollection of that episode and I'm very thankful. She has a brand new boyfriend, actually.'

'Does she?'

'No, I'm just guessing. She's at the seaside now and she always finds some exotic chap there.'

Over the next whisky Sara admitted that Jaka was getting on her nerves and she didn't know if she could stay with him. Matjaž didn't want to pore over the details; at the end of the day, if someone gets on your nerves, they get on your nerves, and there's nothing you can do – sort it out yourself. He had to admit, though, that this information left him feeling smug. He decided to quash that feeling. Sara also quickly wrapped up the topic of her beloved with the clichéd statement that only time would tell. Matjaž protested, saying that time was a very slippery concept that immediately passed by before a new time could begin. She had to agree, but in this state, she said, pointing at the whisky, she was not capable of thinking about her relationship. She didn't feel like it, either, she added. Matjaž knew the smile that followed that sentence was forced, which was why he gently stroked her on the shoulder.

She took hold of his hand and said that she'd like to go home with him. They downed the last of their drinks, left the money on the table and on the walk back to Matjaž's flat only exchanged the briefest of observations. The bridge that Sara and God-knows-which-friend had named as their favourite was no longer there – another sign of getting old. He offered up the fact that a bridge in Lyon had collapsed under the weight of so many lovers' padlocks, something that surely wouldn't have happened if they only counted the pad-locks of those who had stayed together. She liked Wolfova Street because it still had a bookshop. He noticed that there was a patisserie at the top of Petkovšek Embankment and that people were eating ice cream there. He'd never been one for ice cream – ice cream was one of life's great mysteries to him. Having lifted the veil on this secret, she didn't know how to help him; she only ate sweet things from time to time, and ordered chocolate soufflé on special occasions.

When they arrived at his, they kissed for a long time. After the kiss their bodies converged into the familiar grip of lovemaking; familiar as it was, it also felt like the conquering of completely new territory. The words and voices felt like home, the scents were known and alluring, but the two bodies cautiously uncovered contours once so known and inhabited, now surprisingly unknown and almost foreign.

When it was over, Matjaž lit a cigarette, lost in his thoughts, and poured them both a whisky. Like familiar lovers they sat side by side on the balcony, where things were already used to the impression of their bodies.

'It's really nice here, Mat,' she said softly.

'Thanks,' he replied.

'It's as if I'd decorated it,' she smiled.

'Seriously, thanks,' he replied, this time with cynical undertones.

'Well, I would never have put those pictures on that wall, of course,' she said, pointing towards his black-and-white photography above the sofa. She meant it as a joke, but nevertheless it hurt a little. They sat silently and sipped their whisky. It was a quiet night; no voices on the street, no noise coming from the neighbours, the odd light in the distance. It was as if even the night was nervously eavesdropping to see what was happening on the second floor of the block of flats on Poljanski Embankment.

'Mat?' she eventually said beseechingly, almost in distress. She confused him, and he didn't know how to show what she wanted.

'What is it, Sara?' he asked in the same patient voice that he'd always had.

'Mat, doesn't this seem so right, so natural to you?' she began. Her words stung him somewhere deep inside. He had dreamed of those words, longed for them thousands of times, but now when they were finally spoken, when she placed them so directly in front of him and they reverberated into the silence of that summer's night, they seemed utterly foreign, utterly misplaced. And so, unconvincingly, he managed to squeeze out, 'Mmm.'

'Don't you think?' she asked with a tenderness in her voice, and she didn't wait for him to reply. 'Maybe we had to be apart in order to arrive here once more. You know, like Hollywood – a Comedy of Remarriage, as Stanley Cavell calls it. Only the second time is love a true love and a comedy,' she laughed somewhat forcibly.

He looked at her seriously. Everything about her was so familiar and loveable to him, but he couldn't shake off the alienating effect that was clouding her image as a result of all this talk.

'Maybe we did exactly what was right,' he said seriously.

'You're joking?' She looked at him fearfully.

'A joke is exactly what I need right now. But that aside, I don't think I am,' he replied again, almost coldly.

'But isn't this what you wanted?' she pursued, and only a very attentive listener could have recognized the panic in her controlled tone of voice. Immediately afterwards she lit herself a cigarette, a little more hastily than usual.

'For so long this was the only thing I wanted!' he said decidedly, as he could be certain about that; the rest, not so much.

'And not any more?' She looked at him searchingly. Yet again, only an accomplished connoisseur of Sara could have uncovered the carefully concealed fear and pain.

'No, I think it's more complicated now,' he replied, searching through feelings that were still shrouded in mystery even for him.

'What does that mean?'

'That's just it, I don't know what it means. I admit, this is what I wanted, I wanted it like crazy, and now that it's happening I no longer see myself in this situation, as a recipient of your words, or as a part of you and I.'

'Do you not love me any more?' she began again, this time her voice showing signs of shaking. He looked at her but she turned her head to one side to hide the tears that were gathering in the corners of her bright eyes.

'Sara, you stupid cow! I can't *not* love you. I've never been able to stop loving you, and I probably never will. But where's all this coming from? Where's your desperation come from? Why do you want to make feel guilty by confronting me with some fact that has totally thrown me – and all this after it was you who ended everything a long, long time ago!' He raised his voice slightly, but realized just in time to calm down.

Without looking at him she said, 'I don't want you to feel guilty at all. It's not that. I don't know . . . For a while now I've been . . . So unstable and with Jaka I feel like, well, like everything's dying a death. And when we bumped into each other today it all just seemed as natural and normal as ever between us, like it always was.'

'Well, not exactly always, if memory serves,' Matjaž said, being firm again.

'Fine, call it a moment of confusion, of madness, whatever you like. But now it seems like it was all a mistake. And that you and I were, and always have been, the best possible match.' It erupted from her, tears streaming down her cheeks. Matjaž fell silent and smoked his cigarette. He looked to the sky, which was dark, and thought to himself that if he were by the sea he'd be able to see the stars right now, countless stars that hinted at an infinity, an openness up there, at other worlds about which we know so little and which make us all so small, stupid and . . .

'What I'm trying to say', she interrupted his escape into his thoughts, 'is that I'm sorry. What I'm trying to say is that you were right. You were always right and for that reason I love you even more.'

Matjaž was shocked to hear those words, and now the only thing he felt was unease and his racing heart, for which he could find neither cause nor remedy. They sat in silence for a long time. He began, holding himself back, 'Sara, I really wasn't expecting this, and if I'd know that you were going to –'

She interrupted him, 'Mat, now I know that you're the best man in the world!'

'And you're going to be content with the best?' His barb made her smile sourly.

This was Sara in desperation, like he'd never seen her before. He could remember her being sad, in a dilemma, in a quandary, worn out, overtired, gloomy, melancholic, even depressive. He'd seen her cry and sit up all night, he'd seen her angry, euphoric and he'd seen her being mean, and sometimes bitter. But such a fragile, such an entirely broken Sara, such an entirely lost Sara at his mercy, who surrendered unreservedly, he had never seen in his life. He felt sorry for her. But not enough, he thought, as he hugged her.

She then gathered herself, moving her sprightly curls away from her face. 'And you really don't know what's changed? With you, I mean? A year isn't that long, and like you said yourself, you haven't met anyone serious . . .' She said this in the voice of someone who no longer had any hope, but who was pretending that the slightest explanation could be of comfort and preserve a degree of the dignity slipping through their fingers.

'I don't think anything really has changed, Sara. Not you, not me, not the world . . . I've just learned how to live without you,' he said, mustering all the honesty he could bear.

'And you couldn't be without me, with me?' she said, with a desperate smile and tears in her eyes once more.

'No, it's just me now,' he said softly, but decisively.

She hugged him tightly. They promised each other that they'd go for a beer together some time. Then she left. When the door had closed behind her, with an ambiguous smile Matjaž sighed, 'There's none like her!'

*

'I don't believe it!' Aleksander said furiously, after his friend had recounted the story of the previous evening to him several times. 'You said no to the love of your life? Jesus, you are not normal!' They were talking on the phone; Aleksander had called him on the way to his nearby seaside shop.

'Maybe she's not the love of my life,' Matjaž said defiantly.

'As if! You were together for like a hundred years, you spent one year mourning her absence and now what? You've decided against it?'

'I can't explain it,' Matjaž said coldly.

'Oh fuck a duck!' Aleksander was fuming.

'I don't know, there was one point when we were there on the balcony and she was saying nice things, like we should get back together, and it occurred to me that I'm not that person any more,' he tried to explain.

'How are you not the same person any more when you're both exactly the same as before, Sara probably more beautiful than ever,' his friend protested.

'It's not about that, and it's not that I couldn't love her either. Something just wasn't there . . . or there was too much of something, I don't know! I didn't feel that unbearable need for her to be close to me,' Matjaž sighed simply.

'So now you're going to carry on looking for someone who's got that something, who'll be close to you?' retorted Aleksander, still fuming as he paced up and down in front of the shop.

'No, I'm going to stop looking! None of this has got me anywhere, clearly. I'm just going to stop looking,' he said cockily.

Aleksander still wasn't entirely able to calm down. 'And you think this strategy will work?'

'Not really. You know how it is . . .' Matjaž smiled.

Aleksander could see how a huge weight had lifted off his friend's shoulders, and he was happy for him despite his frustration. So he simply said resignedly, 'Yeah, I know. If there's none like her, there's just none like her!'

GABI AND THE PRIEST

Going out on location with Gabi wasn't exactly his idea of fun, but a man just has to do as he's told – even if that means photographing some church and the pastor who tended to his flock there. When he picked her up outside her block, at some ungodly hour, the car door had barely closed before she looked towards him and began to recite, 'The density of time, stone / rock, musical deafness / eternity in our blood / the sheer face, monument / of silence, / I am listening to you / now, now the wind will gather, three times it will strike / its good hand upon you, / faithful stone, / duly open yourself, / sepulchral stone, / north face split yourself in two / and allow me / to leave through you / for the other side.'

Then silence reigned inside the car. Matjaž focused ahead of him and swallowed his saliva, fearing what was coming next. 'Do you know who wrote that poem?' asked Gabi, somewhat smugly.

'You?' Matjaž quipped.

'Thank you very much, but no. Edvard Kocbek.'

'Mhm,' Matjaž yawned discreetly.

'It's nice, isn't it?'

'Mhm.'

'Stone . . .' – she paused momentarily – 'rock.'

'Sorry?' Matjaž was confused.

'That's the title,' she said in a ceremonial tone, looking at him pointedly.

'Mhm.'

'Stone Rock,' she repeated, as if the repetition would arouse in Matjaž a sense of appreciation for the poem's greatness.

But he didn't comply. He simply said, 'Mhm.'

'You have to open your heart to poetry, and then it will speak to you,' she instructed him prudently.

'Nothing can speak to me before my first coffee,' he said, apologetically but firmly.

'OK, well then let's stop somewhere for coffee,' Gabi suggested accommodatingly.

'Aren't we running late? We've got a meeting scheduled in half an hour, and there's still a good hour's drive ahead of us.'

'Oh no, it's all fine. I arranged with Father Simon that we'd meet at midday,' his colleague reassured him.

'Sorry, what?' Matjaž raised his voice. 'So why on earth are we leaving at nine?'

'Firstly, we left at half-past nine because you were late, and secondly, I thought we could turn our work duties into a nice little outing,' she smiled, quietly clapping her hands. She reminded Matjaž of a cocker spaniel puppy.

'For me the best outings are those that lead to bed!' he said bitterly.

'Well, I think we at least ought to get to know each other a little bit better before that,' she said sternly. Matjaž couldn't tell if she was joking or not.

'To bed to sleep, Gabi,' he clarified slowly and plainly.

'Where's your *carpe diem*!' she exclaimed.

'In bed, when I sleep,' he replied, determined not to give in to the unexpected, saccharine nature of this adventure.

'Oh, don't be like that. It's a glorious day, we're going to have a glorious time together!' said Gabi determinedly.

'You, me and the Slovene poets,' he muttered reluctantly.

'Not just Slovene; foreign poets can soothe the soul as well, you know,' Gabi laughed proudly.

'What are you on about? You sound like Hiperbola,' Matjaž replied, becoming irritated.

'Oh, thanks. I love *Ne cakaj na maj*, and *Vesna* as well!' She turned to look out of the window dreamily and started to hum, 'Don't wait for spring, don't wait for May . . .'

Matjaž decided that he wasn't going to say anything until he'd had a coffee – at the end of the day it was disrespectful to his brain, his heart and his circulatory system. He pulled over at the first sight of a bar and sat down at the first table. The coffee was pointless, though; he was too exhausted by Gabi, who still looked up at him, blinking and smiling, like a puppy.

'So, go on then!' Her intense gaze was wearing him down.

With a deep, hushed tone she recited, 'I travel your body as I travel the world, / your stomach a sunny plaza, / your breasts two churches, in which blood performs parallel rites . . .'

'Not that, you twit!'

'Call me a twit if you like, but you will not lose your temper over Octavio Paz!' Gabi said, becoming flustered.

To console her, Matjaž said, 'Sorry, Gabi. Let's leave Paz in peace for a moment. Tell me why it is we're going to see this pastor . . .'

'Parish priest,' she corrected him.

'Parish priest . . .' he corrected himself.

'Simon,' she said.

'So why are we going to see Simon the parish priest?'

'Why do you want to know?' Gabi was surprised.

'I'm going to photograph him, and I'd like to know what the context of the conversation is.'

'It's a good context,' she quickly replied.

'I'm pleased to hear it. Could you be a little more specific as to how and why it's good?' he said carefully.

'It's good because, well, Father Simon is cool, and because what he's done for the parish in Hajdina is crazy!'

'And what's he done?' Matjaž asked, slightly impatiently.

'Thanks to his ingenuity the parish has become, um, how to put it, a social space too . . .'

'Isn't every parish like that, in the sense that it creates an environment for the gathering of the Christian community, or whatever you politically correct lot call yourselves?'

'Of course, but here things are so friendly and home-grown that everyone feels good.' She stared at Matjaž dreamily.

'Hm, I wouldn't count on it,' he muttered quietly, thinking of himself and the task ahead of him. But Gabi heard him; the sentence was not to her liking, and she pulled a face and groaned.

'Yes?' Matjaž enquired.

'Nothing,' Gabi replied defiantly.

'No no, I recognize a female grunt when I hear one,' he insisted.

'Grunt!' she repeated angrily.

'That's exactly what I'm talking about!'

'It's nothing, I'm just increasingly doubting whether you're the right person for the job today. Sin has a hold on you and most of the women you associate with are surely . . . fallen,' she said, looking him in the eye defiantly.

'Fallen women? Because they have sex before marriage?' asked Matjaž, intrigued.

'Well, you and I know we're not in the nineteenth century, but that reckless sexual activity really never leads anywhere!' Her cheeks reddened with agitation.

'May I console you by saying that such reckless activity doesn't occur anywhere near as frequently as I would like?'

'They're fallen women all the same,' Gabi replied stubbornly.

'Well, there aren't as many fallen women as I'd like,' he tried to explain.

'Sin is sin,' she concluded, and looked away defiantly.

After that enlightening conversation Matjaž paid for the coffee and signalled to Gabi that they ought to be on their way. In the car they sat in silence for quite some time, for which Matjaž thanked the capital G for God, or any letter in the universe that had inspired his co-passenger to be silent.

'Roko's not like that,' she said at last.

'Like what?'

'Like you,' she hissed, still defiant.

'I'm very pleased to hear it. I wouldn't envy anyone for being like me.'

'You see, this is where I don't believe you. If you were a man of God and you really did feel guilty about the way you were, you'd accept the light of God and you would convert.'

'Hang on, why do I have to convert? And upon whom would you unleash your self-righteous indignation if all guys were like Roko?'

'Don't bring him into this. He's a great guy! He buys me flowers, takes me out for hot chocolate, we go to the cinema in the evenings and then –'

'Please, stop right there, I'm not interested in what happens after that,' he implored her.

'The two of us usually just go to church and light a candle!'

'Well, quite – you can't control yourself! Now I'm going to have to live with that image for the rest of my life,' he complained.

'Pft, there's no point in talking to you.'

Matjaž did not protest. While Gabi thought dialogue was impossible, he had the opportunity to drive in peace. Here and there he let a thought escape to Sara, although he never doubted how had he handled that evening. Well, even if he had doubts he knew that now he must persevere with his commitment to the life he had chosen by rejecting Sara. Even if it meant life without her was sometimes desperately frightening because the outline of the future was so hazy. Before, it had seemed that his existence progressed in accordance with a certain idea of the world, the organization of the everyday – connected to Sara, of course – but now that model had collapsed, along with the abstract vision of what love should be and what kind of woman ought to fit with it. He was without vision, without routine, without focus, without a framework. Now he drifted across the earth, light as a feather, but at the same time he had a feeling that he didn't belong, that all the coordinates were jumbled and he was going to be sucked into a black hole. Only now did he – for the first time after breaking up with Sara – feel free. And however much the drifting and wandering was welcome in its own, unfamiliar way, it was at the same time a source of anguish more than anything else.

Father Simon, a bloke of around fifty years old in seriously good shape, was waiting for them in front of the doors of the attractive church. Smiling, he greeted them, 'Praised be Jesus!'

'Praised be Jesus,' Gabi blushed.

Matjaž merely mumbled, 'Hello.'

After a brief handshake, Father Simon led the two of them into the church and showed them where all the noble activities took place in the name of God. Gabi helped him by positing obvious and obviously flattering questions, which the priest answered in a matter-of-fact and rather reasonable manner – as far as Matjaž could tell. When they had finished looking around and talking, the man of God said, 'Well, I think we've earned some refreshment, don't you?'

Matjaž nodded enthusiastically, as of course he hadn't eaten breakfast. The parish table was full of bounty – the dedicated parishioners brought it, the priest explained – and Matjaž barely held himself back from getting stuck in immediately. When everyone had sat down, he rushed to say 'Bon appétit!' so that he could set upon the prepared food, when a stern look from the priest interrupted him. Father Simon lowered his head, placed his hands together in prayer and began to thank the Creator for the food that they were about to eat.

'No, no, no!' Matjaž cried out in his thoughts. He was convinced that it was the parishioners, the dedicated men and women – maybe even a Mercator and some of its producers – who were actually responsible for supplying him with food; the Almighty didn't have much to do with it. Luckily the grace was short, and the food also proved delicious. 'That Creator of yours is a really a good cook!' Matjaž joked.

'Don't take the Lord's name in vain!' exclaimed Gabi, flustered.

The priest looked at her seriously, and said, 'Gabi, I'll stick up for the Almighty if I think it's necessary.' Matjaž gathered that Father Simon did not exactly serve the stereotype that he'd previously held about priests. And when the priest opened the wine, Matjaž was convinced that a sort of G must exist, one who jumped to his rescue at such moments.

It turned out that there were perhaps even more Gs, or neighbouring letters, than he'd believed; the priest had quite a few similar bottles in store and he didn't appear to want to keep them to himself. For a while Gabi restrained herself, but then even she succumbed to the effects of the priest and his offerings. At first Gabi and the priest kept to the planned journalistic agenda, while Matjaž added a few unofficial portraits of the priest to a series of photos of the church, but after a few hours they were covering slightly merrier topics – which became all the merrier as they became merry themselves.

In the glow of all the delights that the priest bestowed upon them, Matjaž managed to listen to Gabi's poetry recitals, her singing along to the priest's guitar, and her lamentations over the sickening and sinful world that was running off the rails. She spoke of a crisis of values, and about the power of Christian doctrine; the priest interrupted her several times to ask her to calm down. He had to remind her that a Christian's main duty on this earth was to love, and not to constantly complain, even though the world may seem so misguided to them. As soon as the priest mentioned the word 'love', Gabi took it as an invitation to start talking about Roko. At that point Matjaž noticed that the priest's eyes darkened slightly; it was clear that he was already very much up-to-date with her relationship, with all of Roko's gentlemanly traits and all of his hidden talents. When she sang praises of Roko's unbelievable culinary abilities, which were not formed by some Jamie Oliver or – heaven forbid – Nigella Lawson, but by the good Sister Vendelina, he simply said resignedly, 'So I heard, yeah' or, later on, 'I know, yes.'

But Gabi didn't let that bother her. She thought it important to inform the priest about her love of Jesus, which hadn't suffered any damage because of

Roko; Christ was still the only true light in her life. The majority of songs that she wrote were in fact dedicated to Him and His endless benevolence, and she explained how she was convinced that He would also shine light upon her darling Roko. Before this point Matjaž had been happily lost in his own thoughts, but the words 'endless benevolence of our Saviour' were not ones that he could ignore.

'Where was His endless benevolence when the Twin Towers collapsed?' he erupted. 'Why didn't this endless benevolence take notice of the hungry in Africa, or the crisis in the Middle East? Why did it tolerate the accumulation of wealth and the growing poverty of the masses, or rape, or paedophilia . . .'

'What is wrong with you, my son? Why are you so angry?' The priest looked at him, surprised.

'How can you begin to believe in Him after having taken one look at the state of the world?' he asked, at least lowering his voice a little.

'Therein lies the trick of faith. When everything seems against His existence, faith endures,' the priest said, remaining calm.

Matjaž lost his temper again. 'But that seems completely crazy to me! You see everything that's going on around you, but faith somehow excuses it all.'

'Blasphemous!' Gabi cried out, but the priest only looked daggers at her.

'True faith grants strength, hope, love, freedom, if you want it,' Father Simon said, still quite persistent. 'You presumably won't deny that it provides a comfort that people need.'

'Faith,' Gabi sighed heavily, at which point it became clear that she was not used to alcohol. She stared longingly towards the cross on the wall.

Matjaž just shook his head slightly. 'Well, if we accept that faith is immune to all logical reasoning, which – by the way – is really reductive, you're not going to claim that we have to accept all the traits of the Church entirely without criticism, too?' he asked in a considered manner.

'No, of course not – but why did you go straight for the Church when it doesn't mean anything to you and clearly doesn't have any influence in your life?' the priest challenged.

'Because it presents itself publicly as a place of unquestionable truth – and don't get me started on taxpayers' money!' said Matjaž, carrying on while Gabi hung her head in despair.

'Well, I think things are nevertheless a little more complex, and that you're simplifying them intentionally,' the priest said, reasonably peacefully.

'I would say that it's the Church that grossly simplifies things, when it prohibits marriages, persecutes the gays, prohibits abortions,' Matjaž persisted. 'I would say that you don't actually want to talk about the Church, you want conflict. There's something else in your soul, something that isn't quite connected to faith. Maybe it would be better if we started talking about that.' The priest took Matjaž by surprise, but he looked at him doubtfully from beneath his eyebrows all the same. 'Seriously, Father? I think you're cool and all that, a really pleasant surprise, and you've got a great organization going on here. But as you have ascertained, I simply don't have that faith and neither do I miss it.'

'That's why you're so lost!' Gabi shot at him loudly.

'Sshh!' the priest started to calm her. 'Being overly found is not always good, either. I know what will open our young friend's heart,' he smiled.

Matjaž was already guessing how he'd be participating in the recital of some carefully chosen psalms, but the priest took him by surprise once again. This time he placed a bottle on the table that Matjaž could have sworn contained 'the water of life', as the French so dramatically call it.

'Is it homemade?'

'Of course, Franci makes it and Franci makes it well,' the priest laughed, while Gabi's eyes bulged at the sight.

Matjaž quickly emptied the glass that was offered to him and nodded. 'Make that Franci a saint!'

Over spirits, debates concerning the holy realm were abandoned and they descended into more human and carnal matters, as they are sometimes called.

'What about you, Father, don't you ever think about sex?' Matjaž enquired, smiling.

Gabi let out an almost entirely silent scream. Without looking at her, the priest replied, 'What's it to you? The only relevant question is whether I carry out my work well, whether I'm at the height of my spiritual and parochial calling.'

'Right at the top, Father, you are fantastic . . .' Gabi could not praise her priest enough.

He, on the other hand, looked at her angrily and blurted, 'Silence!'

Matjaž bowed his head remorsefully, and for a few seconds they sat in silence. 'Well, at least in your mission you're spared the scramble for love,' he threw in cautiously.

'Well, tell us then, how has love got one over on you?' The priest looked at him sympathetically.

'Oh, you don't want to know. It's a long, long story . . .' Matjaž sighed.

The priest looked at him indifferently, shrugged his shoulders and said, 'As you wish!' This encouraged Matjaž to start talking. At first he recounted at length and in great detail everything about Sara: her curls, her smile, how she appeared taller than she actually was, and how she playfully ascribed this to her grand personality. Then he progressed on to their relationship: all the years of love that had been cosy and exciting at the same time, and how the two of them had constructed their own world. Then he had to recount how everything had ended, how it had completely broken him and for a long time he had not known how to go on.

'And how did you move forwards in the end?' the priest enquired.

'Through other women,' Matjaž said pointedly. He noticed the priest's face, which remained unchanged. 'Interesting. And how did that idea work out?'

'Well, this is where the devil comes into it,' Matjaž said, almost adopting the priest's diction and making himself comfortable in the chair. 'First I met Saša, who was pretty and rather stupid. We were only capable of talking about the weather. She left me immediately, probably because I asked her to marry me.'

'How long had you been together?'

'One night,' he explained.

'You didn't waste any time,' the priest smiled.

'No, I didn't,' Matjaž shrugged his shoulders.

'And how long did it last?' asked the priest with a slightly cynical undertone.

'Until the morning.'

'Just a few hours?' The answer had rather surprised God's unconventional messenger.

'Things always look different in the morning,' Matjaž explained.

The priest nodded, as if he understood. 'What happened next?'

'I called off the wedding and she left.'

'And the matter ended there?' the priest asked.

'Mostly, yes. We saw each other at a New Year's Eve party and we talked about love.' The priest remained patiently silent, and Matjaž went on. 'Yeah, we just talked. She was actually tied up with some guy who didn't know how to appreciate her. It didn't seem right to me.'

'Of course it's not right, she's a human being!' Gabi piped up. The priest merely glanced seriously in her direction, making her bow her head submissively.

'So I comforted Saša a bit and did something to make that moron of a boyfriend take notice of her again,' Matjaž concluded. 'But after that came the second and third and fourth . . .'

The priest sighed inaudibly, while his guest carried on openly, 'Then I found Brigita in Žale Cemetery – she was utterly refreshing. A pretty redhead, covered in piercings and full of obscenities. Oops!' he said, looking at the priest warily, as if the word 'obscenity' was obscene in itself. But the priest's calm expression consoled him and he went on. 'So, she was an attractive goth, and a Marxist to boot. Maybe you're, well, relaxed enough now to find this amusing: she went to study economics in order to gain an inside perspective on the problems of the system.'

Matjaž laughed and looked at the priest searchingly, but the priest only sighed wearily. 'Oh dear, have you never heard about liberation theology, the movement within the Church that was based on Marx's writings?' The guest became awkward and nodded at Father Simon, who fell silent again.

'I invested quite a lot in Brigita,' Matjaž continued. 'Maybe most of all. It took quite a few dates, a lot of words, many romantic destinations and a lot of alcohol – not to mention my wounded feelings – for her to eventually come home with me.'

'And?'

'When I started to undress her, she said that it tickled.'

'How?' the priest expressed surprise.

'I don't know how. It was the first time I'd heard that, too, that my touch made somebody ticklish. Then she said it was because she was a lesbian.'

'Obviously,' the priest remarked, as if this happened every day.

'Hang on a minute – what do you mean by "obviously?"'

'Nothing.'

'Are you suggesting that you'd ascribe to me the power of turning women into lesbians? Because this is the only instance of the sort, I can assure you,' Matjaž said, slightly irritated.

'I suggested nothing; you suggested it. Let's leave it there.'

Matjaž looked at him suspiciously and decided there was some truth in his words. Once again he resumed his story. 'Then there was New Year's Eve – the same New Year's celebration that I was telling you about, when I ran into

Saša, the blonde. So, there I had an intimate meeting of the third degree with Katja, my friend of many years, who was planning our wedding in the event that we both remain single.'

'Aha, but you don't have feelings for her?'

'No, gross!' Matjaž winced.

'But that wasn't all?'

'No. At first she wanted to change me; she said that my rudeness, my sarcasm, was problematic.'

'Is it not?' the priest asked.

'Maybe it is, but no one is forced to hang around in my vicinity. And that time I tried, Father, I really did. At some points she actually cried, because she felt alone and ugly and completely useless. I tried to comfort her and then I danced with her to make her smile again.'

Matjaž was checking the priest's expression to see whether he had grasped how good-hearted he had been, and when he didn't feel any particular approval he proceeded cautiously, 'There was also some girl, Maria, there, too, a really good-looking, alluring girl – ginger hair, if you can picture it – who pretended that I was a guy called Zoki. I think that was her way trying to seduce me, but it didn't work.'

'Her neither?'

'No, she was far too . . . I really don't want to waste words on her, her arrogant stories were exhausting.'

The priest simply nodded patiently.

'So, at the end of the evening I almost got some,' said Matjaž, skipping through events a little.

'Got what?'

'Well, sex.'

'With whom?'

'With Suzana.'

'And who's Suzana?'

'A long-term friend, whose house we were partying at.'

'And?'

'Everything was going smoothly, a bit of dancing, some touching and kissing – you can imagine, or maybe you can't – and then she . . .' Matjaž stopped himself.

'What?'

'Ha, well there's no nice way of saying this,' Matjaž hesitated.

This roused the priest's curiosity. 'Go on, be brave and spit it out! God is merciful.'

'Then she fell asleep during sex,' he admitted repentantly.

The priest burst out laughing at the top of his voice and said, still laughing, 'She's one of ours!'

Matjaž looked at him reproachfully and concluded seriously, 'Thankfully she doesn't remember it.'

'That she fell asleep during sex?' The priest calmed down slightly and wiped away the tears that the laughter had brought to his eyes.

'No, that anything happened between us at all.'

'Or she's just being polite,' the priest said, still grinning.

'Thank you, Father. I would expect a little more understanding from you,' Matjaž said, pretending to be disappointed.

The priest didn't pay any heed to that remark, and so the unlucky lover began once again, 'Then followed Stela . . . or, however I ought to put it . . .'

'I don't follow; speak more clearly,' the priest demanded, becoming serious.

'Ah, I once went astray after a rather intensive evening, if you know what I mean,' he said, pointing to the shot glass of herbal liquor. 'At Tiffany in Metelkova, you know, where the gays and transvestites hang out – although not exclusively those types. There are also normal people like you and me there, too.'

The priest smirked. 'And?'

'I was fairly inebriated and I hadn't exactly realized where I was. A girl with heavenly legs and a beaming smile caught my eye. We started chatting and she was, well, very flirtatious, but gentle, understanding . . . At some point, when the kisses became rather too hot, I invited her back to mine. That's how it usually goes, or at least on those kind of nights,' Matjaž continued.

'And?' The priest was all the more curious.

'Well, while we were – you know . . .'

'Something was missing once again?' asked the somewhat impatient priest, stepping in.

'Not exactly. I'd say it was more that there was too much of something.' Matjaž cleared his throat. 'I made an unexpected discovery.'

'What kind of discovery?' Matjaž had succeeded in intriguing the priest.

'Yeah, the *Crying Game* kind' Matjaž confirmed.

'No!' the priest exclaimed, while Gabi didn't entirely understand what Matjaž was saying, and looked between the two of them, bewildered. The priest was not going to let himself be disturbed by explaining anything to that nuisance, and he continued, 'Well, how did it all end?'

'Very well, I venture to say,' Matjaž continued. As he saw the priest's questioning expression he quickly answered, 'No, nothing like that, nothing kinky, no hanky-panky . . .'

Gabi was becoming increasingly pale during this conversation. The priest merely nodded understandingly, and Matjaž went on. 'After the awkward discovery and all the embarrassment that followed – because all along she obviously thought that I knew what kind of woman she was – we watched an episode of *Seinfeld*. Do you know it? It's that sitcom about nothing . . .'

'It doesn't matter,' the priest said, gesturing with his hand.

'Of course,' said Matjaž, reigning himself in. 'So after that we fell asleep – but that's all – and in the morning she gave me a lovely surprise.'

'With what?' the priest asked, preparing himself for another shock.

'While I was still asleep she went to the shop, prepared breakfast, bought the Saturday papers and everything. We had breakfast together and read the papers, then we said a friendly goodbye and that was it.'

'It doesn't get better than that!' the priest concluded.

'Sorry?' Matjaž was confused.

'Nothing, it just seems that of all the women you've listed so far Stela seems like one of the nicest,' the priest remarked wisely.

'It's true, maybe the nicest I've ever met,' Matjaž agreed pensively. Upon hearing this, Gabi appeared rather upset.

'But the story doesn't end there, I imagine,' the priest said, not showing any sign of tiring. He poured himself another dose of the strong stuff; he had a feeling he was going to need it.

'Where does it end?' exclaimed Matjaž. Laughing, he continued, 'Back in spring I met a girl by the name of Mini at Metelkova. I disliked her right from the start, even though I thought she was attractive. And of course everything went wrong. I offended her immediately; I don't remember exactly how or why. I just know that she got right on my nerves because she was so self-righteous, so politically correct, so by-the-book – like this one here,' he said, nodding towards Gabi, who at this point hadn't twigged that this was not the most Christian of observations.

The priest calmly overlooked the insult.

'I thought that would be enough', Matjaž said, 'but it wasn't. She really liked me and wanted to go out with me.'

'In that sense, women are always surprising,' the priest commented.

'What!' Gabi lost her temper. 'That is just . . .'

'Calm down, my child, and listen – you might learn something,' the priest said, patting her on the shoulder without turning to look at her.

'So, my motto is that it's not all about personality and intelligence, but that sometimes you have to give appearances a chance. Which is why I took her out for lunch.'

'And how was that?'

'Really good, we went to a Spanish restaurant where they do fantastic meat . . .'

'Not the food. How did the date go?' the priest interrupted, a little impatient once again.

'A good question. Awful, obviously. She was talking about horoscopes and the Jolie-Pitt wedding and recycling, and it ruined everything. She seemed even more stupid than the first time I met her, and I couldn't go through with it.'

'So, go on . . .' the priest said, wanting details.

'I don't know any more than that, really. To be very brief – I pretended to be straight with her, saying it was me and not her, that women who put off marriage and children into their thirties because of their endeavours for peace just don't do it for me.'

'And you didn't see her again?'

Matjaž shook his head.

'So, onwards we go,' the priest encouraged him.

'Let me think, spring, spring. Yes, of course, then I went to Jajce for Tito's birthday.' He paused long enough to light a cigarette and then returned to Jajce. 'Ah, how to put this? There were around thirty of us on the bus, half of whom were middle-aged married couples, and the rest of us were unburdened single men or women. So it was quite an interesting dynamic, but there were two in particular who received almost all the male attention: Melita, a stunning sixteen-year-old with a lively nature and her mum, Nada, a very well-maintained and tenacious woman in her forties who was – even more importantly – recently divorced. One evening, while we were singing and dancing, Melita and I ended up alone. We got chatting and had a bit to drink, which brought us close enough together for us to, well, you know . . .'

'With a sixteen-year-old? That's not even . . .' Gabi was alarmed.

Once again the priest gave her a scolding look. 'Oh, don't be such a purist. Anyone could say – and this observation would not be entirely negligible – that priests pick them even younger!' Gabi bit her tongue and could barely catch her breath, but neither of the men took too much notice of her.

'It was bittersweet, as always,' Matjaž told the priest. 'As soon as she had me, she rejected me and started trying to win over another guy. She had us all, she put a spell on us all.'

'And how did you hang on until the end of the trip?'

'With her mum.'

'Excuse me?'

'Yeah, her mum, Nada, as I said, was very approachable following her divorce; extremely at ease, and very, very attractive to the male sex. Similar to her daughter, but in a slightly more mature way.'

'But?' the priest calmly asked.

'But what?'

'I feel there's a "but" here, too,' he replied.

'You know me so well, Father!' said Matjaž without irony. 'There really was a "but". She also forgot about me after she'd seduced me. It's true that we set off home the next day, so obviously circumstances immediately got in the way, but . . . that "but" still remains.' He fell silent for a while so that he could wet his lips with his stiff drink.

The priest made the most of this moment, going in for a slightly analytical question. 'Have you ever thought to yourself that you may not be the most talented lover?'

'Of course I have, but I'm afraid that's no excuse for their behaviour, either of them.'

'Well, I wasn't just thinking about those two,' the priest said, to himself more than anything, and exhaled.

Matjaž listened to him attentively and added delicately, 'With those two it was about attention, and that attention was never going to be enough; they had to be desired, they had to be loved by men, by all men . . . at least that's my interpretation.'

'Were there any others after that?'

Matjaž looked at him in disbelief from under his eyebrows. 'You ought to know by now how these things go.' The priest was starting to understand the true meaning of eternity. He leaned in to listen. 'One evening I arranged to meet my friends for a drink, but instead they set me up with this Kat.'

'A cat?'

'A girl called Kat.'

'Ah, I see,' the priest said apologetically.

'The evening started out like a dream, we got on so well, had a similar sense of humour, had similar tastes and attitudes towards the world. Everything was going great: her smile full of slightly crooked teeth; her long, delicate fingers; her matter-of-fact outlook on life – you wouldn't believe how rare the quality of worldliness is – all until my lawyer friends showed up. They were awful. Jure had just had a baby.'

'What?'

'Oh, Father, don't be so uptight. Jure's piece had just given birth, and he'd gone out with his mates to celebrate. And, of course – as is customary for these types of men – they overdid it, to put it mildly. When they sat down to join Kat and me they were already fairly wrecked; in fact, they were so wasted they were slurring and throwing up. Then Jure forgot that he'd just had a baby girl and not a boy, and then, when the rest of them wanted me to get them some cocaine so that they could carry on drinking . . .'

'The wretched things!' the priest moralized.

'Don't look at me like that. I'm not wretched and I'm certainly not a dealer,' Matjaž defended himself.

'I've heard far worse than that in the confession booth – you wouldn't believe, dear boy . . . but carry on!'

'Obviously I told them that I couldn't do anything for them. After that came the final blow, at least for Kat, who had had enough of them by this point.'

'What was that?' The priest looked at him with interest.

'When Jure said that his child was named Julija, these friends started to sing Mežek. You know, the song *Julija* by Aleksander Mežek?' he asked, and wrinkled his brow.

The priest just said, 'Holy mother!'

'Yeah, then Kat stood up and left.'

'Because of Mežek?'

'Mežek was the straw that broke the camel's back . . .'

'Alcohol, arrogance, disregard for women and children . . .' The wise priest supported him.

'Those were the words she used, too, although I do think she was exaggerating.'

The priest was quiet for a moment. A long sigh followed. 'Well, we've started so we may as well go on 'til the end.'

'Let me think,' said Matjaž, who was now beginning to enjoy his storytelling. 'The next one was Ro . . . Oops, I can't talk about this in front of Gabi.' He clutched at his mouth.

'Gabi, go to the toilet,' the priest gestured to her.

'What? I don't even need to,' she protested.

'Listen, Matjaž here wants to tell me something but he's not going to say it while you're around, which is why I'm asking you to respectfully remove yourself!' The priest was strict and to the point.

'Father, I'm not sure if it's good for you to listen to him too much,' Gabi said softly, frightened.

'That's enough now. Go to the toilet, quickly!'

'Fine, I'll go to the toilet, but there'll be absolutely nothing respectful about it,' Gabi protested.

'There's no doubting that,' Matjaž said quietly.

When Gabi had left, downcast, Matjaž continued. 'We had a work party at our boss Ksenja's house in Kras. You've no doubt already heard about this picnic, because that's where Gabi met her Roko.'

'Yes, it rings a bell.'

'Anyway,' Matjaž continued, 'there I met Ronja, a friend from secondary school who is also my colleague. But she hadn't been around for a year, even longer, because she'd had a baby. At the party we became close. Different from before, different to the others. She was so easy to talk to, and lovely and funny. She was the reason that I survived that evening at all. Together the two of us watched the others, and she remarked on what their gestures and actions said about them. It was really enlightening, and good fun. Oh, Ronja,' he paused briefly. 'She guessed it all! Who wanted what and who wanted whom. She was like Sherlock Holmes – do you know that detective?'

'Only by name,' the sarcastic priest replied. 'Anyway, we don't need to go into all of that. I'm already confused by all the names. So what happened with this Ksenja?'

'Ronja,' Matjaž corrected him.

'Ronja, then.'

'As I told you, nothing.'

'Oh, well, how is a man supposed to know in such drunken surroundings.' The priest was restless now.

'At the end you're going to say you don't believe any of it!'

'Alas, I've been in this business for an awful long time and I guarantee you'll be hard pressed to shock me.'

'So at some point Ronja and I were left just the two of us, beneath an enormous tree', said Matjaž, finally realizing that the priest was now tiring of his adventures, 'and then we stopped joking around. We became more affectionate. She was vulnerable, and I was also strangely moved by just this closest kind of closeness between us.'

'You fell in love with Ronja?'

'Very possibly. I hadn't felt as good as I did with her for a long time. And a man always falls in love with the feeling he has around another, right?'

'Maybe. We don't have time for definitions of love. Continue.'

'In short, it was very affectionate. By some miracle, God's grace as you would call it, we were sharing a room – or rather, an office. We went there to get to know each other – you know, in the biblical sense.'

'And did you?'

'Not really.'

'What the devil does that mean?' the priest asked crossly.

'We were naked and we were caressing each other a little. We really had good intentions of it being biblical, but we were chatting in between.'

'And that was it?'

'No, at some point she fell asleep, you know, because she's got a little kid and she's exhausted and all that', Matjaž explained.

'Another one you've managed to send to sleep!' the mischievous priest burst out laughing.

'You might laugh, but this time it was beautiful, really beautiful.' With those words Matjaž fell silent. He was thinking about Ronja again, her gentle presence.

'And you didn't repeat this?'

'No, some people are already spoken for, and put the well-being of their little ones first', Matjaž concluded bitterly.

'And here is where your odyssey ends?' the priest asked, interrupting Matjaž's trail of thought.

'No. There's summer, too.'

'Which isn't over yet . . . but go on, be brave,' the priest said encouragingly, more to himself than to Matjaž.

There was a knock at the door and they fell silent.

'Yes!' the priest called out.

'Can I come in now?' Gabi asked patiently. The priest felt a bit guilty, as he had completely forgotten about her.

'Of course, Gabi,' he called out kindly. 'Carry on, Matjaž.'

'Well, then the unimaginable happened!'

'What?' Matjaž's story unnerved him again.

'Sara, my ex!'

'Impossible!' the priest said, enraptured.

'What's impossible?' asked Gabi, as she sat down on her chair.

'Well, sit here quietly and listen to your elder and you might find out,' the priest replied, clearly used to bad-mannered children.

'But it is possible,' Matjaž asserted, and a trace of pride could be heard in his words. 'We bumped into each other by chance over lunch. It was one of those magnificent July days, when Ljubljana is so pleasingly deserted, the clear sky –'

'OK, I get it, get to the point,' The priest's patience was slowly coming to an end.

'So, we bumped into each other in some almost-empty restaurant. Everything between us was as it always had been. She was beyond beautiful, beyond fun, and I felt as if no time had passed, as if we were still connected as before. Then we set off elsewhere: for coffee, for a beer, for more beers, then for a whisky. We had a wonderful time; we told each other everything, passed comment on everything, just like our good old times.'

'And then?'

'Then she wanted to come back to mine.'

'And you went, and it happened,' the priest said matter-of-factly.

'Exactly, and it was . . . strange, actually. Pleasing and familiar, but at the same time totally foreign. I don't actually know how to explain it.'

'What about that Jaka of hers?'

'Jaka Shmacka,' Matjaž replied childishly.

'Ah, Jaka didn't quite make her happy,' the priest said, interpreting Matjaž's words, and signalling for him to go on.

'Then she just told me upfront that she wanted to us to try again.'

'Really?' The priest smiled proudly. 'That's splendid!' Congratulations! Sometimes it pays to be patient. You see, Gabi, like I'm always telling you, patience is . . .'

'I told her no.' The priest's enthusiasm was crushed by his interlocutor.

'Idiot!' Gabi shouted out. 'After you had fornicated, you at least ought to . . .'

'Gabi, enough!' The priest rolled his eyes. He looked somewhere out of the window, and slowly said, 'It's interesting that you rejected exactly what you wanted the most. Have you any explanation?'

Matjaž calmly replied, 'No, I don't know if I can explain.'

'Do you think you were maybe still thinking about Kat, or the other one?'

'Which other one?' Gabi enquired.

'The one we were talking about when you weren't here,' the priest replied, once again without looking at her.

'No, it wasn't that,' Matjaž reflected. He attempted to distil some thought from his inebriated head, and continued, 'I've thought about it a lot, and I still don't know for sure, but I think it's that when I was with others I was always thinking about her, at least a little bit, but then when I was with her I wasn't thinking about her any more. It was like the Marx Brothers said: "Everything about you reminds me of you; your eyes, your throat, your lips – everything reminds me of you except you,"' Matjaž tried to explain clumsily.

The priest nodded as if he understood. After a short silence he said, almost resignedly, 'Is that everything?'

'Yes.'

'Thank God!' he said, and crossed himself.

They sat silently for a while, and then Matjaž looked over tenderly at the priest.

'Thanks for listening, Father. I never thought I'd open up to a priest.'

'You see, after all the complaining you did when we set off –' Gabi began, but before she could finish her outburst a glance from the priest stopped her in her tracks.

'And what do you think about it all?' Matjaž looked to the priest. It seemed only right that he ask the man of God for advice after he'd bothered him with his life story for so long.

'I'm happy that I pledged myself to God,' he replied diplomatically.

'That's all you've got to say?' Matjaž was disappointed.

'Well, what did you expect? That I'd scold you, give you a penance for all of your sins? That I'd stroke you and say, "There, there"? Did you think I'd be full of good advice?' the priest asked, raising the tone of his voice slightly.

'Not exactly, no, but something, anything . . .' Matjaž said beseechingly.

'God be with you, then!' the priest replied.

'No, that doesn't do anything for me because I just don't believe in Him,' he protested.

'The Lord moves in mysterious ways, in that case.'

'So do I,' Matjaž laughed.

'On no account must you be so bloody self-satisfied,' the priest began gravely, and Gabi turned slightly pale once again. 'I have a good mind to say that you're just another young man gone astray. But now that you've lost Sara for the second time, you've maybe gained an opportunity to become a better man.'

'Yes, but what if I don't know how – or don't even want to?' Matjaž asked him.

'Don't start philosophizing. Why are you asking me for advice if you're already so pleased with yourself, in one way or another? What do you want to hear? That you're special? That your story is testimony to your charming misbehaviour? You won't hear that from me. You're nothing special and you probably never will be!'

'Ha!' Gabi shrieked mockingly.

'Neither will you, so don't you start laughing!' the priest said sharply.

'Thank you, Father.' Matjaž shook his hand sincerely. The priest's words hadn't bothered him. Quite the opposite; his conversation with the unconventional priest didn't seem like anything particularly special but it had nevertheless had a calming effect upon him. Maybe because just once he had had to condense all of last year's stories, turn them into a narrative, a timeline. Left unexamined they loomed over him in a vague formation with all kinds of apparent hidden meanings and potentials, which he now knew had passed already or never would have materialized anyway. He didn't understand himself any better than before, nor women for that matter, but it didn't seem important to him now. With the priest's help he had reconciled himself to his own stupidity and ignorance – and to other traits that had succeeded in throwing so many people off the track. That, to him, seemed like a job well done.

*

'I don't get why you're so offended,' Matjaž looked at Aleksander, who was nervously shaking geraniums from a plastic container and potting them up into ceramic ones. The idea was to give them a change of soil and add a bit of fertilizer. Karla obviously wanted a balcony in bloom.

'I don't get how you can confess to a priest,' Aleksander replied, alarmed.

'They're people, too,' his friend shrugged.

'Maybe, but you have me. What's wrong with me? Have I not been your confessor ever since we've known each other?' Aleksander continued, more downcast. He momentarily let the flowers drop from his hands.

'But it's not as if I've deceived you,' Matjaž said apologetically, sipping his spritzer.

'Well I'm not sure, it sounds to me as if you had just a bit too much fun with your storytelling,' the newfound gardener said somewhat obstinately.

'What am I supposed to say? You care about me too much, Aleksander, and you have too many feelings towards me. I liked that the priest didn't pretend to like me, nor was he disgusted with me. He was indifferent towards me, but at the same time he was strict. And that's how I was able to come out with everything, the whole story, the whole stupid, awful story,' Matjaž tried to explain.

'Your story isn't stupid at all,' his friend protested. 'And no priest should convince you of that!'

They sat silently for a moment, watching as one of the flowers rejected its new bed and lurched uneasily to one side. When Aleksander had reclaimed victory over it, he asked, now a little less offended, 'And what did you take away from this synopsis, this outpouring of your heart to a complete stranger?'

'I didn't take anything away, at least not any new discoveries. But his indifference towards both my suffering and my happiness put things in a new perspective for me, if you know what I mean,' Matjaž replied, blowing out his cigarette smoke.

'I've no idea. In relation to what?' He looked reproachfully at his friend again. 'Just don't tell me you're at peace with God!'

'Worry not. Even if I were at peace with Him, he probably wouldn't want to have any dealings with me,' Matjaž continued openly.

'So what now?'

'I'm calm. I'm not annoyed by anything any more. I don't need Sara, which means, in truth, that I don't need anyone else either.'

'Because they're all the same, or what? Fucking hell!' Aleksander sighed.

'This is Gabi's fault! I think you're still in shock at her poetry. Or are you going to say now that you know how to handle her?'

'It's not Gabi, not Sara, not anyone else. You're not getting it. I am completely content by myself. I think I've experienced all types of women . . . what else do I need? Do you remember Stela? I gave it my all throughout.'

'Ah, Stela, I still long for her and her particulars even now.' Aleksander looked to the sky, as if the fundamental error was that all good women were not men.

'Anyway, I think I'm destined for the single life. I have no desire to fall in love,' Matjaž concluded.

'You can't plan for that, though. It just happens,' his friend informed him. He removed his gloves and allowed himself a cigarette.

'I know, but I don't want it to happen. I actually don't want anything, apart from this feeling of calm, sitting with you on this nice summer's evening.' He looked fondly at his muddy friend.

'You'll want it when it comes!' Believe me, even the best people crack,' he said, almost disappointed, looking involuntarily at his wedding ring.

'To be honest, I don't know what all the fuss over love is about. It's just problems. The priest knows that well, and he chose the right profession.'

'Yes, but each and every human being is clearly designed to always complicate their life. That's just the way it is and I see no reason why you should be spared that worldly experience.'

'You know, every now and again someone is born who is fortunate enough to slip through the net,' Matjaž said encouragingly.

'But that won't be you,' Aleksander said decisively.

'Why not me, exactly?'

'Because you don't deserve it!'

ALL TOGETHER AGAIN

It was quite hot for a late August evening, but it didn't take a genius to notice how things had changed in the time since he and Sara had conquered the quietly scorched surface of the city. The dense treetops along Petkovšek Embankment were still green, but now somewhat haggard, as if they'd had enough of the evening noise – the clattering of beer glasses and the voices of the people below. The solitude and desertion of summertime was no more.

Matjaž didn't have himself down as the sentimental type, but he always felt a lump in his throat when the season began to turn towards autumn like this, with the eternal promise that summer would still one day return. But by that time he'd be another autumn, another winter and another spring older. It wasn't the fact of ageing in itself that he found particularly galling, as he was lucky enough to feel relatively well physically – or it would be more appropriate to say, perhaps, that as yet his body had not begun to hold his foolish behaviour against him. But nevertheless he realized that as time poured away, his life was pouring away in just the same way. Actually, what troubled him more than the passage of time was repetition; a thought that caught up with him on occasion, at times such as now, when he encountered the handshake between late summer and early autumn. The repetition of time, of working days in the office, of adventures with friends, with women, of numerous photographs piled inside an external hard drive with the promise that he would sort them at some point, but that remained there because it was easier to forget about them that way.

It scared him that this was all everything was – a multitude of repetitions, a multitude of the same faces, scenes and words that pretended, in a series of permutations and combinations, to be different to what he already knew but merely recycled the same boring formula for living. The melancholy of late summer, he smiled to himself, as he walked towards his friends. But when he caught sight of them again, he was happy, even if they were only repetitions in slightly different outfits. In this they were just like Matjaž, who had made sure while shopping the sales that he would continue to look like a new-age gentleman who artfully gave the impression that he was entirely indifferent towards his appearance.

They greeted him with a smile. Karla waved as soon as she caught sight of him, as soon as he turned off Butchers' Bridge.

'So you've finally shown yourself!' she exclaimed.

'What sort of a welcome is that?' asked Matjaž, sitting down. He looked around to see Jernej and Aleksander already giving him welcoming nods; only Suzana was preoccupied in explaining to Katja the magic of the United Left party. The expression on Katja's face clearly indicated that she'd rather be left to wind up Matjaž and the others, if only the political debate could be resolved. 'Come on Suzana, we haven't seen each other in over a month and you're already wasting your energy on political debate,' Matjaž said, leaping to his friend's rescue.

Suzana looked at him askance. 'Have you got something against the United Left?'

'Nothing, actually, unless they take away my Friday evening with friends,' he shot back at her, and lit himself a cigarette. Katja took advantage of the moment of silence to ask Matjaž, 'And where have you been this summer?'

'Nowhere, actually, my dear. While you were all lazily roaming around the world some of us were working,' he said cheerfully.

'You know what, you're not calling me lazy! I worked bloody hard for every minute of my holiday,' Katja protested.

Suzana rolled her eyes, turned to Matjaž and said, 'So, now do you see why I have to talk about politics?'

Matjaž picked up on her harsh tone and politely asked Katja where she had been. She'd been to Sicily with friends. No, not with Suzana; Suzana had gone to Istria. 'And how was it in Sicily?' It was wonderful, Katja explained. Such a beautiful place, and to think that there in Syracuse Plato was received by the ruler, who brought him over from Athens to explain his vision of the state in the hope of trying to realize it, and to think that Elizabeth Taylor visited Taormina, to think that they named the village Don Corleone after the film by Francis Ford Coppola – that's when you know it's a special island. The friends decided to leave Katja in blissful ignorance as far as *The Godfather* was concerned, while Matjaž turned to Suzana and asked, 'And how was Istria?'

'Istria is Istria, Matjaž. Nothing special at all. The campsites are campsites, the bars are bars, the beer is beer.'

'I see you're not going to waste words on the best holiday of all time –'

'For the best you have to go to Sicily!' Katja interrupted him.

Suzana overheard and said, 'I've discovered that the success of a holiday depends on who you go with.'

Katja's eyes lit up. 'I know exactly what you mean. Borut and Janez were such good travelling partners, so thoughtful . . . without those two –'

'Oh, please,' Suzana interrupted. 'Those two gays are the most boring people I've ever met.'

'What do you know! They're great gays!'

'Particularly when they're enquiring after every detail of every single flavour on offer in the ice-cream parlour,' Suzana replied vehemently.

'You know what, the locals are happy when people show interest in their ice-cream industry,' Katja retorted, not giving in.

Matjaž stepped in. 'Good, well, go on then Suzana, did you not get on with Saša or what?'

She wrested a heavy sigh from deep inside her, after which she had to light a cigarette. 'No, Saša's problem is that she's the best person in the world.'

'What a fine cynic you are,' he smiled.

'But it's true! She's not of this world. She's patient, kind, helpful, sweet and gentle as can be – she even gave me cold compresses when I burned myself on the beach.'

'And what's the issue there?' Matjaž asked with a smile.

The look on Suzana's face told him that he ought to have recognized the implication by now. 'You know what I'm like around people like that. A monster!'

'Well, you're always a monster!'

'Thanks, but you can imagine what that boundless kindness did to me. I had to challenge her, I had to test her.'

'But she didn't give in, right?' Matjaž was still laughing.

'No, she didn't,' Suzana said bitterly, and took a long drag on her cigarette.

'And how did it all end?' Matjaž enquired.

'Dishonourably,' Suzana said quietly.

'Dishonourably for whom?' Matjaž teased her, although he knew what the answer would be.

'One evening I'd had quite a bit to drink and I was quite, well, more than usually, insulting towards her. That time she stood up to me and said she could see that it'd be better if she left. That she hadn't wanted to tell me before because she felt sorry for me, because I was so alone and sunburned, but she wasn't going to put it off any longer. She had fallen for a guy at the campsite who was going to take her away from the awful Medulin to Dalmatia. She packed up and left. Along with the car, of course, as she drove me there; I had to hitch a lift back.'

'Do they not have buses in Medulin, or what?'

'Oh, of course, but on that drunken evening I had managed to lose my phone, my purse and all my documents, so the only way back was to beg.'

'Someone once told me that bad things happen to bad people, but I never believed them,' Matjaž quipped, after hearing her story. Suzana only nodded remorsefully.

Matjaž thought to himself for a moment and then turned towards Jernej, who up until then had been immersed in Aleksander and Karla's dispute over biodegradable carrier bags. In answer to Matjaž's question of whether he'd had a good time working as a waiter on the Slovene coast, Jernej just said, in his particular manner, 'It was crazy mate, crazy!' And he really did look quite tired.

So here they all were, together again, everyone apart from him nicely tanned and healthy – in principle, at least. Acting youthfully and trying to maintain the appearance that they had not yet come into contact with adulthood – just as if summer had not yet met autumn.

'Do you think any of you will ever grow up?' asked a smiling Jaka. He stood right next to Matjaž, with Sara on his arm. They said hello. They looked like a Hollywood couple: he with his slender, chiselled physique and thick fair hair pushed back behind his ears; she with her fairy-like presence, vital white smile and slightly tinted lips, flushed as if someone had woken her from sweet dreams. 'How are you guys, then? I haven't seen either of you all summer,' Aleksander greeted them, shaking Jaka's hand and giving Sara a hug. The two of them sat down and explained about their break in Mauritius.

'Were you inspired by our former prime minister and his wife, Urška?' Suzana asked sarcastically, but she was sitting far enough away that the recently returned guests didn't hear her. Matjaž didn't have Sara down as the type of girl who could have a good time in Mauritius. And given that it was only Jaka speaking about the island in superlatives, clearly impressed by the infinite opportunities that the resort offered to the budding golfer, he concluded that Sara must have had plenty of good books with her.

'We actually only went for the golf,' said Jaka self-deprecatingly.

'We actually went because of your boss, Sandi, who plays golf,' Sara corrected him with a smile that revealed her mischievous side. She then admitted to Karla in rather a mitigating tone that Sandi's wife, Sabina, was quite a handful. This conversation was of more interest to Matjaž than Suzana's resurrected tale of groundbreaking new politics. He gathered from Sara that Sandi and Sabina were two people of good standing – *nouveau riche* as Sara loathingly called them – who were nevertheless good-humoured and generous enough. 'Although you can afford to be with that sort of wealth,' she added.

Sabina had totally worn out Sara with her incessant schooling on where to find the best sales in Milan, or at which shops just over the border you could get a Fendi bag for a snip at 500 euros. Next was Pilates and her infallible instructor, who came to your house for a very reasonable price. She could list all of the truths and misgivings about vegan nutrition, and in particular specialized in which colours of foods must be eaten at certain times of the month. Her astrologer had revealed this to her. Sabina believed in science, of course, but obviously thought that we had to admit that in addition to science there was a little part of life that eluded us and that remained – thank God – unclear. 'How else could she put up with a banker, where there was no room for mystery?' Sara concluded sarcastically.

Of course, Karla still wanted more. She questioned Sara on how old the banking couple were, how many children they had, where they worked exactly, how much their holiday cost and if Sara had had a good time with Jaka. To that final part of the question, Sara answered in a way that only she knew how; she concealed every possible bit of tension between them with the truth. 'He was with Sandi all day; he left me with Sabina. There wasn't a single evening when we went out for dinner or even just a drink together. Yep, Jaka has ditched me for his boss!' she said, placing her head on his shoulder and casting a concealed glance over towards Matjaž. Jaka stroked her curls mechanically, and then explained to Aleksander about the toughest scenarios within the game of golf. Aleksander was doing very well at pretending to be interested, thought Matjaž, as he watched his friend's face. Once Jaka had finished his tale of happy golfers, golf courses and his fantastic boss, Aleksander eventually let slip, 'Did anyone actually ever have sex on Mauritius?'

While Matjaž waited in quiet anticipation for Jaka's answer, he noted that Aleksander's comment had caused a slight contortion on Jaka's face – mainly, Matjaž imagined, because he'd realized that his tales about golf had failed to impress his conversation partner. But then he caught sight of a familiar female character. It was moving along Pekovšek Embankment beside a male figure and a pushchair. 'Ronja!' he called out. She waved at him, left the pushchair with her husband, said something to him and came over to the group.

'Is this where all the interesting people hang out on Fridays?' She looked at him fondly.

'You come over here and you're insulting us already,' Matjaž smiled and immediately rushed to find her a seat.

'No, it's fine, I just came to say hi.' She and Sara looked at each other, and quickly asked how each other were.

'And how are you? Have you caught up on sleep?' he asked her seriously.

'After our party, you mean? Not yet,' she smiled at him, with an unusual glint in her eye.

'So you're not going to introduce us to all of your men, then?' he asked in embarrassment, gesturing towards her nearest and dearest. He was happy that the others were all occupied with one another, and it was only Sara who he noticed looking towards Ronja.

'No, one half of my men needs to eat and sleep, and the other half has to complain about the first half.' She smiled again, but with a slight bitterness. Her cheeks reddened slightly when Matjaž patted her on the shoulder, and with that same arm she waved goodbye to the others and left. Still embarrassed, Matjaž quickly looked at his phone as if exciting events were unfurling there.

'What about you, Mat?' he heard Sara ask.

'Sorry, what?' He looked up, confused.

'When are you going away?'

'Tomorrow. Well, today, in fact,' he replied, puzzled.

'Where are you off to?'

'To Hvar.'

She nodded with a faint smile, which once again concealed more than it revealed. 'Hvar is beautiful,' she said, filling the strange vacuum of their exchange. 'I'm don't know if it will be this time. I'll actually just be working – I think I told you, that wedding. So it could well be the ugliest Hvar of all Hvars.'

'Here's to Hvar, then!' Sara raised her beer, her chin raised proudly. The others joined her, abruptly wrenched from their own conversations and therefore with no sense of what Hvar might signify within her toast.

Before Matjaž was able to shake off the confusion that Sara's smile and eyes had caused him, the group was interrupted once more by a new female voice, 'It's Matjaž, right?'

'Depends who's asking,' he replied, and turned around to see who was bothering him. It was Mini, with some guy – or rather, some boy – at her side.

'Don't panic, I just came to say hi,' she said, smiling. She quickly asked how he was, and he confessed that he was most excellent and due to leave for Hvar shortly.

'We met some super Greek tourists in that restaurant over there – a really super, big Greek family with a sense of humour,' said Mini, and it became clear that she didn't just come over to say hello. She carried right on, her bored boyfriend meanwhile just watching people walk by. 'They gave us a gorgeous idea for a holiday. Mediterranean, Greek Mediterranean – I always say that. They recommended this gorgeous little island to us.' She turned to her boy. 'Bor, what was it called again? God, don't tell me you've forgotten already. I want to go there! That's where we must go, we absolutely must,' she said, looking at Matjaž.

'Sorry, you said you met some Greeks?' Matjaž asked suddenly.

'Some Greeks, yeah.'

'What are Greeks doing in Ljubljana?' he asked her with a completely straight face.

'What do you mean by that?' Mini asked, completely confused.

'Isn't there a crisis in Greece?' he asked, as if it were the most obvious thing in the world. 'It doesn't seem right that Greeks are travelling all over the place while they're in crisis,' he said decisively.

Mini suddenly lost her temper. 'And what about Slovenes travelling around, even though we're in the wors –'

Her boyfriend stopped her, then leaned towards her and whispered something. A great big smile appeared on her face. Then, with her anger barely concealed, she said, 'You haven't changed at all, Matjaž, and you never will!' She and the little guy turned and walked away.

The entire group, who until not long before had been engrossed in various conversations, had to laugh at this performance – even Jaka and Katja forced their facial muscles into a smile.

'What? I didn't know that saying anything about the Greeks was a no-go!' he said innocently.

'That's enough now!' Katja righteously intervened.

'It's true, that's a bit close to the line,' Suzana joined her.

'What have things come to? Next you'll both be saying that ugly people should be allowed on Petkovšek Embankment, too!' Matjaž protested.

Suzana and Katja exchanged glances. It was no longer clear to them whether or not Matjaž was joking.

Taking advantage of their confusion, Aleksander continued in a similar tone, 'As far as ugliness is concerned, you're right. Don't you two think,' he asked, looking towards the political correctness camp, 'that this part of Ljubljana is so beautiful, so tidy, that it's just not – how to put this – that ugly people just don't fit, walking around here?' Suzana and Katja could only stare at each other.

'It would make sense to divide the country into aesthetic zones.' Aleksander went on. 'The good-looking ones in the centre, that would be Zone A, and then we allocate the others in the same way, in alphabetical order up to somewhere around D.'

'And of course you'd be on the committee that decides who fits where?' Suzana looked at him, outraged.

'Of course, but I wouldn't be alone. There'd be a few other beautiful people in the select committee, too,' he quipped. The group laughed. Suzana and Katja were the only two who were unable to force a smile.

'And presumably ugly people would be barred from the centre?' asked Jernej ironically.

'Exactly,' Sara reiterated. 'There'd be special permits to allow the ugly ones who would like to bring food from the fields and supply other goods.'

'What about the good-looking ones, would they be allowed into zones B, C and D?' enquired Katja, whose temperature had now risen dramatically.

'Of course,' uttered Jernej seriously. 'They'd organize safaris around those zones. The most expensive one would naturally be around Zone D, where the most hideous specimens would be. They'd have guides to steer you around the extremely dangerous regions, which would obviously be heavily fortified for safari purposes, and to lead the beautiful tourists around.'

'And what happens to the beautiful ones if they, say, put on weight or – heaven forbid – get old?' Suzana asked, horrified by this vision of civilization's last stop on the road to Nazism.

'They'd have to gradually move out, too. Beauty knows no mercy,' Jernej replied.

'What are you lot getting so het up about?' Matjaž heard yet another familiar female voice.

'Kat!' Karla called out, and rushed over to hug her friend. That was the end of the debate on aesthetic zones, but Matjaž was certain that this idea had to be noted down somewhere.

Kat sat down next to Matjaž. 'What was that hot topic all about?' she asked interestedly.

'Nothing, we were just saying how the standard of sewing on trainers made by Asian kids is getting worse and worse,' said Matjaž, trying to sustain the tasteless conversation.

'I know what you mean, they're beginning to slacken,' Kat agreed with a wry smile.

'Yeah, they're not flogging them enough,' Matjaž declared solemnly.

Kat wasn't really OK with that sentence, so she tried to change the subject. 'I just found this page on Facebook that takes the piss out of healthy living.'

'And?' enquired Jernej. He liked to follow raw-food vegans on Facebook himself, for the purpose of mockery.

'They're organizing these, like, seminars on healthy lifestyles and then give them a caption: *Toxic Sugar, Toxic Soul or Albumens are Great. Between Two Slices of Spelt Sourdough.* And stuff like that.'

'I'm not sure. This all seems a bit much to me,' Katja spoke up.

'What's too much for you, Kati?' Matjaž looked at her sweetly.

'This piss-taking, picking on minorities, poor Asian children, vegans. It's not that many years since they gained certain rights, a certain standard of living . . . you can't just –'

'Yeah, but on the other hand political correctness isn't the answer, either,' Sara said, taking the others by surprise.

'But it's the right thing to do!' exclaimed Katja.

'Fuck the right thing!' flew out of Suzana's mouth, making everyone else laugh.

'It's patronizing,' Kat said, backing up.

Sara added further weight to the argument, 'And actually it just conceals the fact that problems and tensions, which are implicit within apparently neutral phrases, persist in real life. If equals can insult each other, and in this society people are as unforgiving towards one another as they can be, that just means that what we have to treat with political correctness isn't politically correct.'

'But hate speech only encourages that!' Katja protested.

'Of course, and that's always been the bind. But the alternative is even worse, as it presupposes that those offended are incapable of articulating what bothers them, in order to stand up to hateful insults,' Sara replied.

The seriousness of the argument began to bore Matjaž; he'd have preferred to stick to the jokes. 'But we're not politicians, we're not going to make sure that we don't offend each and every group in society – like women, for example – while we're having a beer on a Friday,' he eventually said.

'Well, maybe on Fridays we should make an exception, and only abuse and offend Matjaž,' Kat said.

'Agreed!' Suzana shouted. Katja and Karla clapped, too, while the guys just laughed.

'You may well laugh, but one of these days I'm going to leave for *Native American Summer* camp in the USA, and you can all offend whoever you like in Ljubljana,' he said, as if disappointed, and the mood in the group livened even more.

It was one of the most enjoyable evenings that a group of people could have manufactured, thought Matjaž to himself, as he left the others to chase the remainder of summer at Metelkova on his walk back home alone. The fact that people could be together for a long period of time without killing each other, or at least hating each other, was just another miracle of life on earth, he thought – especially for him, having become increasingly demanding of his surroundings. A sign of ageing, boredom, fatigue? Maybe he was becoming a grumpy old man? Maybe he already was a grumpy old man? He panicked for a moment.

When he arrived home he put on a *Midsomer Murders* DVD. How nice, how calm and civilized, he thought to himself, as the sombre opening credits came to an end. He was crazy about English television series. He particularly appreciated them for their British rhythm, which was so pleasantly soothing. That was the final thought that sent him off to sleep – even before the first murder.

BRIGITA ON HVAR

MONDAY

Matjaž could think of no greater pleasure than sitting on the island ferry while the rest of the world came into season: the cultural–artistic season, the football season, the educational season, the new fashion season, the season for picking apples and pears or whatever. To him there was no greater pleasure than travelling to a place where only one season existed, only summer time, where the main concerns were when lunch would be, what would be for lunch and which restaurant would prepare it; how best to position the sun-lounger on the beach so that you were able to read in just enough sun but not too much; and whether to drink your first beer on the beach, or maybe even have two.

Here there was no crisis with the coalition, or parliamentary sessions about retirement legislation, here they didn't know about the financial crisis let alone wars and unrest around the world. The crisis in the Middle East was no more, and people were no longer starving in Somalia. The world was free of tax havens, mega corporations didn't have a monopoly on the international economy and children in the Third World no longer went to sew in factories instead of going to school. No woman was raped, no child was beaten, all murderous impulses of man had been eliminated and evil of all kinds suspended.

The sea was all there was, strewn around the island where olive trees, vines and rocks thrived. There was sun in abundance, shade a little less so, and the nights were warm. The promise of the ancient coastline could be felt from the ferry; he saw it from the ferry back then, when he and Sara first sailed there. He found it interesting how the island had remained the same while his memories of their first time on Hvar had become so dusty; the image of him and her had faded. The only feeling he recognized was a slight melancholy, not because of her or them but because of time itself and the years that could not be halted; the years that carried on inexorably forwards, trampling over him, transforming him, making him look upon his first trip to the island as if he were looking at a postcard from a good but increasingly distant friend. His only connection to his former self was memory, and this alerted his attention to the fact that there were no consistencies in life, nothing permanent and stable. It may be sunny today, raining tomorrow, or it may be windy today with static cloud tomorrow. There was nothing permanent, nothing, other than the island, he thought. Then he also thought that Hvar had been called an island for a very long time, and only in being known as an island did it arrive at its true conception, as his former love would probably have said – in accordance with Hegel.

Matjaž was pleased that he was leaving everything behind him, that there would be no Aleksander or Karla, no other crazy friends, and – even better – no crazy girls, who through some strange cosmic system always found him and enticed him into their Friday night and weekend peripeteias. Only one tiny circumstantial detail was casting a shadow over that fine thought of peace and relaxation. The wedding. He had to go to a wedding. He didn't exactly hold these ceremonies in high esteem as a guest, and on top of that he had to work at this one. A wedding album. 'Gross!' he thought to himself. Those 700 euros would come in handy for the break he was giving himself a few days before the unhappy event, though, and a few days after it, too; to get over the trauma in his own time.

It still wasn't clear to him where the groom Lovro had found him of all people for this job, nor was it clear to him why he and his chosen one – what was her name again? – had decided on a big wedding on Hvar. But it wasn't important now. What was important was to take a holiday on the island.

So, to take a break from this laborious thinking, Matjaž took a sip of his drink and lost himself in the newspapers. In an hour or so he'd be arriving at the promised coast once again. He'd barely started reading when he heard that language from which he loved to flee so much: his mother tongue, Slovene. As if there weren't already enough Slovenes in Ljubljana, they had to follow him here, too. He couldn't understand why, of all the holiday destinations on earth, they had to choose the very same island as him and cause him so much stress. Unbelievable!

The conversation that unfurled between the Slovene women was far too close and far too Slovene for him to be able to ignore it.

'I can't believe you're nervous already. Everything will be fine,' said a soft female voice.

'Nothing will be fine. It will always be the same. Awful, unbearable and humiliating,' said another, a more sombre and resistant voice, whose wit reminded him of someone – but whom? There were so many of them, he thought to himself self-pityingly. And now he had to carry on listening. The complaining voice continued, 'But you know how awful they can be, and how they take every opportunity to torment me.'

'Hey, it's not so bad,' said the other voice, comforting the complaining one.

'But you don't know how it is, though, because you've always had boyfriends, you've always achieved everything you set out to, you have a job and your own flat, and you've just always been the ideal daughter in every way.'

'That's not true. You know very well how much good advice I have to swallow in spite of my own perfection. But anyway, I don't see what they've got to reproach you with. You're successful in whatever you do. And not just that, you're creative and your work is so prolific.'

'It doesn't mean anything to them if I write, if I publish anything. They see a woman as an incomplete being who only reaches a certain completeness if she starts keeping company with a man, and who only achieves her real goal when she gives birth. But you know how I can't stand men, let alone children.'

'I know, my dear; you despise those two species, even more than women. And whoever knows you, knows that you tolerate so few female specimens that it's not entirely clear how you hold out in human civilization. We're both quite similar in that way. I can't stand people either.'

'Your guest list seems to suggest otherwise,' smiled the complainer, and her sarcasm was even more familiar to him than her grumbling.

The softer voice also laughed and added, 'You're right. If it all goes ahead without any fatalities, I'll be rather pleased with myself.'

'You're more likely to be able to escape somehow, though; I, on the other hand, will have to survive an evening with the parents.'

'If it's any consolation, I won't hold you in any way responsible for the odd murder in moments of madness.'

Both of them started laughing and at that point Matjaž placed beyond doubt the laughter that belonged to the grumpy voice – he turned around with a jolt and blurted, 'Brigita!'

When he caught sight of her he stopped for a moment; both girls were looking at him bewildered and he was suddenly convinced that he'd made a mistake, for he didn't recognize his sweetheart that never was. Long hair, of a colour that complemented her skin tone, tumbled down past her shoulders; there was no make-up on her lightly tanned face, and no sign of the piercings either. Illuminated by the evening sunlight, her naturalness seemed to him divine. So beautiful that he didn't even notice the virtues of her travelling partner.

After a few seconds of shock, Brigita also recognized Matjaž and introduced him to her sister – not without a hint of irony, 'Sonja, this is my love that never was, Matjaž.'

'I think that "friend Matjaž" would have been enough, but I guess "love that never was" is also fine,' he said, offering his hand to Sonja.

'But he looks entirely civilized,' said Sonja, turning to her sister.

'Oh, thanks, I assume that was meant as a compliment. What exactly have you been saying about me?' he said, turning to Brigita.

'Oh, nothing she wouldn't say about every man,' replied Sonja, reassuring him.

'Well, that makes me feel so much better,' said Matjaž, pretending to be hurt.

'Enough of these niceties,' said Brigita severely, interrupting the introductory procedure. 'Instead, tell me: what are you doing here, and where are you going exactly?'

'It's nice to see you, too,' he said, feigning courtesy. He extended the polite exchange even further, taking on the task of questions and answers himself, 'Yeah, it's so nice to get away to the sea in September time. I think Hvar is beautiful, too. Oh, where am I going? To the town of Hvar itself. I booked an apartment. Where? On the Križni rat? No, of course that area doesn't have anything to do with the war; it's just the headland. Yeah, I've been there several times and come back several times. There's nowhere better, seriously –'

'Oh, stop pretending to be offended. You're fluent in shameless!' Brigita said, taking issue with Matjaž's passive-aggressive behaviour. Sonja was visibly enjoying their interaction.

'Still, you might have exercised a little more restraint after a year,' Matjaž said. 'Deep down inside I'm actually a very gentle and vulnerable soul.'

'Firstly, it's not yet a year since our fiasco; secondly, there is not a single gentle, let along vulnerable, cell within you. And thirdly, you're a man.'

'I suppose I should apologize for that, too,' said Matjaž.

'For starters you can try to explain your presence on this ferry – and even better, your future presence on the island – more convincingly,' Brigita said severely.

'Brigita!' Sonja exclaimed, a little taken aback.

'Thank you, Sonja, at least someone in this family possesses basic manners,' Matjaž said, pitying himself.

'Don't you dare talk to me about basic manners, we're both too old for these games,' Brigita retorted decisively, rather too pleased with herself.

'I am absolutely not too old, ha ha!' he said teasingly, and Sonja laughed at him.

Brigita snorted. It seemed to Matjaž that she was only pretending to pull a face, but her sister wasn't so sure so she started talking. 'But it really is an unusual coincidence that we should meet here.'

'I know, my basic aim was to escape my compatriots at whatever cost,' Matjaž said convincingly.

'I understand, but I'm still interested to know what you're doing here,' attempted Sonja in the same gentle voice that had calmed her sister earlier.

'I'm going on holiday. In between I'll have to take pictures at some wedding but that will only – fingers crossed – ruin one day on the island.'

'Wedding? Whose wedding?' Brigita burst out.

'Oh, I don't even know what the poor guy's surname is. His name's Lovro, and I've forgotten hers.'

The girls looked at each other, and let out, 'Sonja.'

'The bride's name is Sonja,' Brigita said.

Matjaž was slightly taken aback. 'You mean, that you, that you two, that we'll all be, that it's . . . I don't believe it!' He thought for a moment and turned to Sonja, saying, 'But you seem completely normal, what do you need this for? To ruin the island, and so many people for a whole day – why?'

Sonja laughed. 'I know, that's exactly what we were saying. But it is what it is, and we must see this tragedy through to the end.'

'And you, poor thing, how will you cope with these traditional conventions? Are you going to stand at the back, so it's easier to throw up?' Matjaž turned to Brigita.

'I'm afraid I'm going to have to throw up right at the front. I'm Sonja's bridesmaid,' she smiled sourly.

'Oh the poor thing,' he said to Sonja. 'Don't you have any other sisters, brothers, friends, strangers, homeless people who would cope with this role a bit better?'

All three of them had to laugh at this.

'I'm going to get beer. I won't survive these last few hours without alcohol,' Brigita eventually sighed, and set off in the direction of the bar.

'So you're Matjaž, then,' Sonja said, more rhetorically than anything, when her sister had disappeared from view.

'Unfortunately I am. Did she really speak so badly of me?' he asked, concerned.

'On the contrary. For a while I even thought that she was going to drop this whole lesbian thing. But who knows, maybe she really doesn't get on with men.'

'Well, I'd like to know who she does get on with.'

'But she doesn't seem that terrible to you?'

'No, not to me. I wouldn't be able to say so many terrible things to someone if I actually thought they were terrible.'

'I understand,' Sonja smiled. 'There's just one tiny detail that you should know.'

'What?' Matjaž acted frightened.

'No one actually knows about Brigita's, erm, orientation. I only gave a slight hint even to Lovro, so he took it as some kind of teenage phase. But our parents are – well, how should I put this – very conservative, well and truly Catholic, and that kind of news would probably destroy them. And then they'd destroy Brigita.'

'Brigita seems like a strong enough person to be able to stand up to them,' Matjaž said, now slightly more serious.

'No one is strong enough to stand up to our parents, believe me. Least of all Brigita. I think she'd rather move to the other side of the world than have to have that conversation with them.'

'And that's probably why she hasn't brought a girl along with her.'

'She doesn't have one. She's never had one, at least as far as I know.'

'So then how does she know she's a lesbian?'

'I really don't know, but I have to trust her on that. She's my sister and I love her,' Sonja said, concluding the debate simply. A moment later the accidental threesome enjoyed their well-deserved beer.

'Where's the unlucky groom, then, while we're on the subject of the wedding?' Matjaž enquired.

'He's already on Hvar with friends, and he's going to be waiting for us in Stari Grad to take us into town. As long as he doesn't forget, that is,' Sonja replied.

'Forget about the time, you mean?' Matjaž asked.

'Or the day,' Brigita remarked bitterly.

'Aha, our bridegroom is diligently making the most of his last few days of freedom. At this very moment he's lying down recovering after a night of debauchery with floozies and random women on the Pakleni Islands. He deserves it, poor guy . . .' Matjaž teased.

'You won't manage to unnerve Sonja, Matjaž,' Brigita replied with satisfaction. 'Lovro isn't like that. The most excess he's capable of is diving one centimetre deeper than usual. Or stargazing a bit later into the night, or staying up all night reading books and studying,' Brigita explained.

'So where'd you find this boy – Scouts?' Matjaž said, turning to Sonja.

She laughed good-humouredly. 'That's right, when I wanted a serious relationship I went to the priest in Zgornje Pirniče and asked him for a solid, honest scout. He said he'd only got one unmarried scout of a suitable age left, but he could also be a bit strange,' she fabricated ironically.

Brigita continued, 'Of course he acted normal for half a year, but then he started to stumble. More and more often he would go to bed at ten o'clock, get up early at six so that he could calmly do his morning twenty-kilometre run before cooking breakfast for Sonja and preparing for a new scientific experiment at CERN. Slowly he began tidying up around the flat, too, doing the washing and ironing and putting it back in the wardrobe.'

'Before we realized how serious the symptoms were, he'd started cooking lunch and dinner, too,' Sonja added.

'Until the plot thickened so much that he took it upon himself to wash all the dishes as well,' Brigita went on.

'And then after that he got a promotion at work, so he started going to bed even sooner and getting up even earlier, and he compensated for his longer afternoon absence by preparing some sort of soup or goulash for the week ahead during the evenings.'

'Beef soup on Sundays, obviously,' said Matjaž, bringing the musings to a close.

*

Once the trio had grown tired of characterizing Scout Lovro, Matjaž found out that the portrayal was only partly accurate and that Mr Groom ranked as one of the most exemplary members of human civilization. He genuinely did run every day, he actually liked cooking, he really was a successful lawyer, and he read a lot and studied various things – he was especially interested in space. He loved diving and hill walking, and he actually was loving and attentive towards Sonja and – perhaps more importantly – towards her relatives too. He patiently followed the musings of Sonja's father and the grumblings of her mother for hours on end. He helped Brigita where he could, including when it was necessary to stick up for her in front of her own parents, and also when she left home or when she needed to be subbed a bit of money. He also had a sense of humour, although you wouldn't call him a joker. He cooked beef soup and goulash on Sundays for lunches throughout the week, to make things a bit easier for Sonja, who as a landscape architect worked in an office every day into the evening.

'Seriously now, it sounds too perfect. Where's the problem? What's wrong? Is he addicted to amphetamines, sex, online chess?'

'No, it's not that,' Sonja replied.

'What, then? Does he have some sort of terminal illness that we don't know about?'

'No, nothing like that,' Brigita said.

'Well what then? No one can be that perfect. Seriously, people like that ought to know what a disservice they're doing to the remaining three billion men in the world.' Matjaž said, becoming impatient.

'He has one serious fault,' Sonja smirked.

'Just don't tell me that he doesn't know how to use some stupid iPhone app.'

'No, he masters his Samsung smartphone perfectly well and knows his way around a computer,' Brigita remarked.

'Come on, seriously now. What's the catch?'

'He can be a bit unreliable sometimes,' admitted Sonja.

'Unreliable in what sense?' Matjaž enquired.

'He forgets things a lot,' Brigita explained.

'If he's too engrossed in a book, study, whatever, he simply forgets about the rest of the world. Sometimes he can get stuck in a shop for more than an hour if the mechanism of a child's toy or something similar has intrigued him enough,' Sonja said, providing a more substantial explanation of the problem.

'I get it. Lovro is insane. That's why you two are worried about whether he'll come to get you or not . . . but that doesn't concern me as much as the question of whether he'll conveniently forget to turn up at his own wedding?'

The girls laughed. Then Brigita explained, not joking, 'He has fewer mishaps whenever Sonja's with him.'

'Well, at least you two don't have to worry about a lift – I'll take you into Hvar if crazy Lovro forgets about it.'

And that is what happened. Lovro knew what time the ferry got into the port, but since he'd arrived on the island with his friend Samo and been harpoon-fishing every day, he'd somehow lost track of the days. While the girls were looking around the port for his silver Volvo, Lovro was cooking freshly caught octopus for his friend – who, in terms of time and often places, too, was even less reliable than he was. He'd also handily lost his phone somewhere in the apartment. When the two girls turned up at his door, he could only clutch his head in his hands and then run to give Sonja a hug. 'Are you sure you really want to marry such a fool?'

Matjaž, who was watching the scene from his car, didn't wait for the answer. He set off to his apartment, only a few kilometres away from the soon-to-be-newlyweds' holiday home. Amid the euphoria of the freshly reunited lovers he hadn't exchanged any sort of grand farewell with the two girls; he was only thrown a casual 'See you later!' from Brigita, with a timid wave, as she dragged the heavy suitcases towards the door of her temporary residence.

When he left the funny family – aside from the apologetic Lovro he had caught sight of one other specky-four-eyes, who he'd swear had devoted his life to the world of computing, he wondered if he'd see them at all before the wedding. He then quickly tried to exchange that question for a new thought, as within it he recognized a desire to still be in their company. Sonja really was a lovely girl, quite pretty and good fun. But again he was aware that behind that thought there lay some strange kind of attraction towards the anti-social grump that went by the name of Brigita. He also acknowledged that the whole situation was attractive to him because everything was taking place within the realm of the impossible, and the impossible always stirred the human soul. Luckily he didn't have a very big soul, he thought to himself, so he was worrying over nothing.

TUESDAY

Relatively early, at least by his standards, Matjaž set himself up on his favourite bit of beach. It was one of those small, improvised rocky beaches, constructed at the bottom of quite a steep hill with small winding roads running down to it. Luckily there wasn't anyone here yet, or not any more, so he calmly stretched out in a more or less comfortable space between the cliffs. He then immediately jumped up again and dived in, his mouth open to consume the sea, which he had clearly missed more than he thought. His favourite activity was to float on the surface like a corpse, partly because it allowed him to shut himself off from everything and forget about all exterior sounds.

Before long, the solitary set-up – between the white of the cliffs and the calm of the sea, with an endless view of the Italian coast – began to appeal. He opened *None Like Those* and read. It made him think how long it had been since he'd read anything, how long since he'd even been completely alone, and how good it was to read in solitude – even if it was just a novel by some average female author.

By evening he'd grown tired of solitude already. Spending long seconds in the company of your own thoughts, as enticing as the surroundings may be, sooner or later stirs some sort of feeling of self-pity or melancholy. It was therefore time for a visit to town. He was pleased to note how little things had changed since he was last there. He bought newspapers at the kiosk and turned towards the little café in the nearby main square, the place where he'd felt most at home ever since the early days. On the way there he heard a familiar voice calling his name. It was Sonja. 'Matjaž! Matjaž!' It took him a few seconds to locate the owner's voice and her present company.

The future wife was sat in Archie's Bar with her Lovro, who at that point was trying or pretending to relax and was full of affection towards his love. They invited him to sit down, which he did rather fancy, even though he would have felt better if someone else was also sat with them. As if she read his mind, Sonja said, 'Brigita and maybe Samo are going to join us, too.' She looked questioningly at Lovro, who hadn't noticed her expression.

'Yeah, they've gone for an afternoon swim. Samo convinced Brigita that he knew the most beautiful rocky beach imaginable,' Lovro began to explain, although no one had really asked for an explanation. It nevertheless stung Matjaž a little now that it had been said; even more so when Lovro went on, 'I think Samo really likes Brigita.'

'Based on what?' Sonja asked him, slightly concerned.

'Nothing. He told me. And truth be told, my dear, your sister is a pretty little thing.'

'Darling, please, don't ever say "pretty little thing" in front of her. You know she kills people for saying such things. It's very likely one of the reasons she despises the male sex so much.'

'But I said something nice. That was a compliment, Sonja,' Lovro said, pulling a face almost like a child.

'I know it was, darling, but as you know Brigita has trouble accepting compliments.'

'Anyhow,' Lovro said, concluding there where his thought had ended, 'don't be surprised if the eccentric Samo tries to hot things up with Brigita a little bit.'

'Oh Jesus!' Sonja put her head in her hands.

'What's that reaction for now? I mean, I know you've never liked Samo, but you've got to admit that if you put two and two together – i.e. his figure and status – he's a thoroughly decent bloke. Brigita would be lucky to have anyone interested in her at all, considering how prickly and sarcastic she constantly is.'

'Brigita would be best off if that bloke, whatever you call him, left her in peace as much as possible.'

'Oh please!' Lovro was becoming ever so slightly angry. 'We all know that young girls like affection from the opposite sex – and while we're at it, any attention at all.'

'Darling, I don't know if our Brigita is that kind of young girl.'

'Well, then she's only got herself to blame if she's alone and unhappy!'

Before Sonja could come to the defence of her younger sister and her solitary, unfriendly nature, Brigita was already walking swiftly towards the table with Samo shuffling along behind her. Samo's head was bowed, something that secretly pleased Matjaž.

'What are you two doing here already?' Lovro laughed cheerfully, clearly not having noticed that Brigita was even more miserable than usual and that it was a huge effort for his friend to lift his head to say hello.

When Brigita started speaking, bolts of lightning flashed from her eyes. 'He took me to that part of the coastline where there are sea urchins and, obviously, because I had to climb out of the sea along the most awkward rocks, I stood on one.'

'Stepped isn't maybe the right word, Brigita, seeing as you landed on the urchin with your hand,' Samo corrected her.

Brigita looked at him, incensed, and then continued, 'Anyway, we spent most of the afternoon getting the spines out of my palm. And he's supposed to be a PE teacher! How many schoolchildren have to die outdoors before you learn what a quality beach is?' she said, turning towards her lover that was not to be.

He apologized bashfully, 'No one's died yet. And, in any case, I don't teach swimming. The school hires a special instructor for that.' So the poor computer expert Samo was actually a poor PE teacher, Matjaž thought to himself. Who'd have thought it?

'Someone else will probably be pulling urchin spines out of some poor child, too, then,' Brigita snorted. In reply, Samo merely explained that there weren't any urchins in Savudrija and Piran, where they take the children, and so they weren't in danger of needing anything pulling out of them – well, occasionally the odd thorn buries itself in a child's foot, but that kind of operation is very rare, maybe one or two per season.

'Typical' muttered Brigita, 'that you tested out the removal of spines for the first time on me.'

Matjaž, who by now honestly felt sorry for Samo, turned towards Brigita and said, 'At least you can console yourself with the fact that the poor urchin has already departed this world thanks to your careless paws!'

Brigita almost flew off the handle, but laughter got the better of her. Samo, who clearly had not only failed to tease a single smile from the stubborn young woman but had also only been on the receiving end of insults, let out a visible sigh of relief upon seeing her cheerful expression. Matjaž could have sworn that the poor bloke seriously feared for his life with the disagreeable Brigita on the island.

The evening progressed in a relaxed way. Lovro explained the ins and outs of underwater fishing to Matjaž and the girls, and his description of his few days on the island with Samo also included a list of the best fish, meat and vegetarian restaurants, and a list of decent watering holes on Hvar. Samo blushed slightly with the mention of the Bar Carpe Diem, and Lovro explained with a chuckle that a couple of days ago they had a few too many in there, which caused both of them to sleep in until nine o'clock the next morning. Brigita rolled her eyes, Matjaž shook his head in concern, while Sonja just smiled besottedly.

'This little animal here can take a lot more than I can, you know,' Lovro said, turning to Sonja. Matjaž checked whether the 'little animal' was at the very least quietly disgruntled by this phrase, and established that she wasn't. She clearly – for some unknown reason – really loved him. 'In general, my little animal has all the social skills and I don't have any.'

'That's why you have so many others,' Brigita said, patting him on the back. It wasn't clear to Matjaž whether this was her ironic side speaking up or just a genuine acceptance of her future brother-in-law.

The company parted at around twelve. Samo and Lovro had a long day ahead of them; they were going fishing again for tomorrow's dinner. 'Of course you're welcome to come, too, Matjaž!' Lovro invited him enthusiastically. But when Matjaž realized that the fishing expedition was leaving at five in the morning, he thanked him but politely declined his kind invitation.

'So what are you doing tomorrow morning?' Sonja asked him. 'We have a great beach practically to ourselves. Lovro and Samo won't be there tomorrow, either, and I promise that we'll leave you in peace.'

'Just not too much peace, please,' Matjaž said.

'You definitely won't be bored with those two chatty geese around,' Lovro giggled, tugging at Brigita's sleeve and receiving a fake smile in return.

Matjaž happily agreed to the offer. Before he said goodbye, Brigita took hold of his hand and said to him, 'Tomorrow's the last day of freedom, then hell is let loose.' Matjaž couldn't make out if she was forewarning him or looking to him for consolation.

'Why? What's happening?'

'Our parents arrive,' explained Brigita, with an expression of grave concern.

'It can't be that bad, surely.'

'It'll be even worse, you'll see!' she persisted.

Her companions started to make a move towards their place. She looked over towards them and then to him, with a slightly pleading look. 'See you tomorrow!'

'Deal,' he said. He watched as the girl, who had for a moment become vulnerable right in front of him, hurried towards her family. Before she caught up with them, she looked back one more time and waved at him, smiling genuinely. Then she raised her middle finger and smiled from ear to ear. The gesture resonated with him as the sweetest and most playful thing. 'See you tomorrow,' he thought with considerable happiness in his heart; at that moment he didn't feel any need to try to understand her.

WEDNESDAY

When Matjaž showed up in the late afternoon at Podstine Bay, where the bride-and groom-to-be had rented an apartment, he found the sisters on the beach stretched out like two seals, each one engrossed in what they were reading. He gave a friendly hello, making both of them jump, then they smiled and invited him to put down his towel wherever he wanted. He did so and politely enquired, 'Have the two fishermen set off?'

'Of course, hours ago now,' Sonja replied.

'We were both still sleeping when the mission for dinner began,' Brigita explained, and smiled playfully at Matjaž.

'And when can we expect them back?' he asked, returning the smile.

'Not before dark, I'd say,' Sonja replied calmly.

'I'm going to have to nibble on something before then; I'll die otherwise,' Matjaž said concernedly.

'Worry not, Lovro has made a fish stew, so that will keep us alive for at least a week,' Brigita spoke up from beneath her straw hat, which suited her very well.

He surrendered himself to the sun, then surrendered himself to the sea, and then he began to read.

'What are you reading?' Brigita asked him. She looked a little bored from lazing around.

'Mark Twain.'

'Which one? *A Tramp Abroad*?'

'How did you know?'

'I saw the front cover,' she laughed. 'Good, isn't it?'

'Have you read it?'

'Of course, many times. A few stories at least – have you got to the ones where he writes in German and Italian?'

'Yeah, I have. I'm a bit concerned that you gave over your communist mind to such a fanciful text as this, though.'

'Believe me, you don't want to get into a debate with me about the political role of Mark Twain,' she replied seriously.

'Of course I don't. I don't want any seriousness, that's why I'm reading this book, and I'm surprised that such a serious girl lets herself be seduced by laughter and enjoyment,' he said, goading her.

'What do you even know about me?' Brigita snapped, not at all nicely, which stung Matjaž a little.

'Brigita!' Sonja chimed in, as if she'd recognized him wincing slightly.

'Well at least one sister has some feeling for fellow humanity,' Matjaž said, still trying to be funny.

But Brigita just snorted, then concluded seriously, 'You see why me and you can't get on? Because you turn everything into a gag. You only listen to me so you can twist my words into a joke.'

'And you want to twist every joke into a political row, or a serious debate at the very least,' he answered back.

'Well excuse me for thinking about things,' Brigita complained.

'Try thinking a little less and living a little more,' Matjaž flung at her fiercely.

'And you try interfering a little less, and the world will be a better place for both of us!' Brigita replied angrily.

'Quiet, children!' Sonja said, laughing. 'This place is way too beautiful for bickering.'

'It's your sister creating a row out of every single innocent remark!' Matjaž complained, almost like a child.

Brigita was ready to cut him down again, but Sonja said, 'If you two want to squabble, go and do it somewhere far away from me. I think fate has punished me enough already, what with our parents arriving tomorrow – and Leon, too, as it seems . . .'

'That, that . . . creep!' her sister shuddered.

'Who is "that creep"?' Matjaž enquired.

'Lovro's brother, Leon,' Sonja explained. 'He's the same age as Brigita and acts as if he's really good-looking, really popular with girls. He tried to lead our Brigita astray, as well.' A mischievous smile escaped from her mouth.

'Seriously? So I should be wary of him, should I?' Matjaž asked, looking at Brigita.

'As you well know, I am a committed lesbian, so there's no need to be wary of any man in my vicinity – least of all him.'

'But you did have a little more patience for Leon, my dear,' Sonja said, without looking up from her magazine.

'That was a year ago!'

'And what happened?' Matjaž asked.

'Oh, the classic washout. I don't want to talk about it,' Brigita said, turning away.

Her sister enjoyed repeating the story. 'Lovro and I had been together for about two years, and we once invited those two, Leon and Brigita, over for dinner. Leon very clearly fell for Brigita over one of Lovro's lasagnes. He was amiable and entertaining –'

'Definitely not entertaining, just amiable,' Brigita corrected her.

'Anyway, he fawned over Brigita a lot and the evening resulted in him inviting her out on a date. And Brigita agreed. Their first date was amazing.'

'Not so amazing the second time,' her sister butted in.

Sonja continued as if she hadn't heard. 'He took her out for dinner at Špajza, brought her daisies and they then went for a walk around the old town. Anyway, after that first date, on which Leon stole a kiss, there followed a few other charming evenings.'

'I wouldn't exactly say charming,' Brigita interrupted again.

'How come he got a kiss on the first date, then? You didn't even give me your phone number!' Matjaž accused petulantly.

'Ahem.' Sonja looked at him in a teacher-like manner. 'Just as our little girl started to warm towards Leon, he cooled off.'

'He didn't cool off at all, he remained very much on fire, just obviously for a new victim!' once more getting angry over the inaccuracies in her sister's story.

'As I was saying,' Sonja continued, 'since then Brigita can't stand the sight of Leon, even though he's tried to renew his pursuit several times.'

'Ah! How Jane Austen of you, Sonja – "tried to renew his pursuit". He wanted to fuck me!' she said coarsely.

'If I may continue . . .' Sonja looked at her sister a little crossly. 'But of course our Brigita didn't give in to that sleazeball!' she concluded.

'Your Brigita remained indifferent towards that moron,' protested the protagonist fiercely.

'Yes, and she is still clearly indifferent towards "that moron",' Matjaž said ironically.

'Quiet, you!' Brigita rebuked him.

'That's enough!' Sonja gave her a dirty look. 'This is my story!'

The disobedient pair fell silent, as did the bride-to-be.

'I'm waiting,' Matjaž said expectantly.

'That's everything,' Sonja said mischievously.

*

Afterwards, the need to talk subsided for a while and the three bodies surrendered themselves to the hardships of the seaside, such as swimming, sunbathing and now and then sifting through magazines. Sonja was reading *Cosmopolitan* and other similar magazines. When Matjaž asked her, somewhat mockingly, if she was enjoying her reading, she replied with a short lecture on the beneficial effects of these kinds of magazines. She explained that the nice photographs of new collections, examples of the latest fashion trends, advice on which eye shadow to use in summertime, smatterings of gossip about the rich and famous, are a great relief to a woman. Brigita's raised eyebrows didn't stop her from elaborating further on how all these trivialities were ways of people not thinking too much about themselves, and instead relinquishing themselves to a world that of course didn't really exist. And, anyway, it wasn't good to think about yourself too much, especially not three days before your wedding.

Matjaž was convinced that Brigita was going to respond to her sister's declaration with a long left-wing protest about consumer culture, about all of its lies and connections with various forms of exploitation, but she agreed with Sonja. She went on, admittedly with the help of her first beer, to recall an inspiring story that she had read in one of these magazines. It spoke of a regular British woman, a working woman, a mother, who once got the irrepressible urge to take off her shoes. At first she was just at home barefoot, but then she began to take off her shoes at work, and then she started constantly walking around all over the place in bare feet. This emancipation of her feet caused her to lose her job, her marriage collapsed, she lost both her children, but she persisted – and remained barefoot.

At this point Matjaž raised his eyebrows and already had a comment at the ready, but Brigita intercepted it. 'If you say that story isn't beautiful then you really are the most soulless person I've ever met.'

'Fine, I won't say anything, but if you're going to be barefooted too often I won't be able to resist provocative comments!'

Sonja grinned, to herself more than anything. Brigita was disappointed, mainly because Matjaž assumed that she, a passionate activist, could be blackmailed like that.

When they had forgotten about the bare-footed British woman, Brigita offered to go and heat up the fish stew and, for a change of scenery, Matjaž decided to go with her. The joint preparation of lunch eventually led to

Brigita debating the pitfalls of the global market with all her might, namely the paradox of buying vegetables from the Netherlands in a shop on Hvar, while Matjaž diligently chopped those imported tomatoes, heated the stew, tasted it, duly seasoned it, sliced the bread, set the table in the shade of the pine trees and chilled the homemade Malvasia. Finally, as Brigita was complaining about the lack of self-sufficiency with regards to food in Slovenia, he invited the by now visibly tanned, or rather reddened, Sonja to join them. After lunch, while Brigita recalled the Haitian revolution at the end of the eighteenth century, Matjaž saw to the dishes and cleaned up all traces of their ample meal.

Brigita, who was a little tipsy after the Hvar-grown Malvasia – 'at least something's local', as she put it – took Matjaž by the hand and led him back towards the beach, humming the *Marseillaise*. He laughed uncontrollably, something to which the revolutionary didn't take offence. Sonja, despite being a little better at handling her alcohol, accompanied her sister in her Malvasia-induced revolutionary zeal with the thinly veiled excuse, 'That's how it goes on the last day of freedom!' Matjaž parked Brigita in the shade to relax in peace, which was of course an excuse for the fact that she had fallen asleep.

Sonja and Matjaž lay similarly and comfortably installed on sun loungers in the shade.

'Don't take the question the wrong way, but Lovro seems so different to you. I find it hard to imagine that he's the man you'd most like to marry. And you don't seem like a girl who would have to compromise in that field.'

Sonja smiled. 'Every girl has to accept compromise. Zala and Špela think similarly to you, too, though.'

'Who are they?'

'Friends from secondary school. You'll meet them at the wedding . . .'

'And what's your excuse?'

'I don't need excuses. I love Lovro.'

'But he's not the love of your life . . .' He looked at her curiously.

'Oh,' she smiled with a hint of melancholy, 'with so many loves, who can ever really know who the one for life is? Was Ožbej, who I had a short and explosive relationship with, the love of my life? Was it that pathological liar and exceptional lover, Davor? Was it one of the others: Tadej, Edi or Aljaž?

The first was completely engrossed in his own work and only rarely found time for me, even though I was supposedly the most beautiful, the most intelligent woman, and he was the luckiest man alive to have met me. Edi was the complete opposite in terms of work: unemployed, highly sociable and with friends every evening, extremely entertaining, no responsibilities, but likewise found it hard to make time for me. Aljaž on the other hand was overly attentive, overly dedicated, overly possessive – and my parents adored him. And as for Damjan, Luka and Matjaž – not you, obviously – let's not even go there.'

'You got tired of searching,' Matjaž concluded.

'No, it's not that. It's about how good it is to be around someone. My criterion became that it in order for it to be worth being in a couple, it had to be nicer than being alone. And with Lovro, it is. He loves me as I am and he's just interested in different things. He's protective enough without being possessive. He's a good cook and doesn't expect any domestic talents from me, although he can sometimes behave like a complete chauvinist. But I find that funny, too. I find it funny when he wonders about silly things and spends hours and hours on them. I even like it when he researches his symptoms like a hypochondriac, and I like it that he doesn't judge me when I drink and smoke a lot. And as well as all that I like how he is with my family, especially with Brigita. In truth it's not about how Lovro is or what he does at all, but that everything that he is and does is precious to me because he does it. I'm not sure if I'm making sense . . .' She brushed her fingers through her hair, searching for the words.

'I completely understand,' smiled Matjaž. 'That's what they call the miracle of love.'

'I hope you're not being cynical, because I'm being damned serious. And if you haven't noticed, Brigita is also fond of him and she's a litmus paper for people. Obviously she's an unpleasant misanthrope herself, but she's really sensible and can smell a bore three kilometres away – a Tadej, or a selfish *bon vivant* like Edi, likewise an evil obsessive like Aljaž, and as for Damjan, Luka and Matjaž . . .'

'Which wasn't me!' the real Matjaž jumped in. 'Let's not even go there.'

Sonja smiled at him. 'Something like that. When I saw how she was protective towards Lovro, how she noticed when I spoke about him rudely, even scornfully sometimes – at the start, when I didn't think it was serious – she made me realize that maybe Lovro wasn't like that. And she was right.'

'Where does poor Samo stand with our human detective, then?' Matjaž asked cautiously.

'No, that's nothing, Samo just gets on her nerves.'

'Oh, well that's reassuring . . .' Matjaž said. After a couple of seconds' break he asked her, 'How do you get on with his parents?'

'A little better than with mine, but I still prefer them from a distance. Well, you'll meet them. They're mostly harmless, of course, but parents don't know how annoying they can be, especially when they're being so bloody well-meaning. Fortunately Lovro's dad, Borut, likes his peace and quiet and interferes as little as possible, in anything. He avoids any kind of unnecessary interruption in his way of life, so he never quarrels with Zofija, Lovro's mum. Now that takes skill. I think a part of Lovro's craziness is down to her. You'll never meet a louder, crazier, stupider woman. My father's the only one who can stand up to her. My theory is that faced with her overbearing presence and, more than anything, the noise, Lovro started to retreat to parallel worlds of space, mathematical equations, studies and whatever else.'

'Leon is obviously another story.'

'Leon is a mummy's boy, and he knows it.'

'Are Leon and Lovro not exactly the best of friends?'

'Oh, no way!' Sonja avowed. 'I'm not sure you'd find two brothers further apart, or two people – who supposedly have the same parents – more different from one another than they are. On top of that there's a quiet resentment between them that Lovro has repressed, but it means he's always distanced himself from his brother. Have you got any brothers or sisters?'

'Luckily, no.'

'Why luckily?'

'I think one genetic cocktail like me is quite enough for this world.'

'I think you're too hard on yourself.'

'Not as hard as your sister,' he said, almost with a touch of bitterness.

'I wouldn't count on that,' Sonja smiled.

Just as the bride-to-be had predicted, the two fisherman returned to the dock at around eight in the evening. Firstly the two of them gave a speech on the fish they'd caught. There were five smaller ones and four bigger ones – Matjaž forgot their names immediately – that made the mouths of the domestic trio start to water even before the (very detailed) explanation was over and the preparations began.

As Lovro was chief fisherman, the work of gutting these creatures fell to his loyal sidekick, Samo. He hinted to Brigita that they could share the task between them, but she replied that she had enough on her plate preparing vegetables of problematic ecological origin. And so Matjaž offered to help Samo. While they were preparing the fish, Matjaž gathered that Samo was a very mild-mannered being with many moral principles. He was a loyal friend, was passionate about fishing and – this surprised him – was a shrewd online poker player. He was aware of how unattractive this last hobby might be to young ladies who like attention, but on the other hand he didn't actually have a young lady and so he wasn't hurting anyone if he gave into debauchery every now and again.

Matjaž agreed with him and added that young ladies could cause an awful lot of grief. He himself still hadn't recovered from the twelve – or however many it was – that he had met over the past year: some young, some not so much, some ladies, some not so much.

When they went back over to 'Lovro the Great's' barbecue, it became clear that the two young women were hard at work sampling the Malvasia while the future bridegroom was seeing to all the necessary domestic duties himself. Pretty soon the other two joined in with the sampling themselves, while Lovro started to cook and fired off the odd order every now and again, 'I need a plate! Charcoal! A pot! I need . . .' Samo and Matjaž were happy to oblige him, while the sisters preferred to carry on smoking and drinking. At around eleven they eventually sat down for the feast, and thanked the fisherman, cook and organizer-in-chief for a job well done.

A game of tarocchi followed. Lovro was against the idea, especially when combined with alcohol. If he wanted to catch enough fish for the parents tomorrow, he and Samo ought to be on their way. Sonja's idea, that they could all go into town for dinner, had seemingly fallen on deaf ears. In any case, Lovro wanted to get out and do his usual run in the morning; he'd got out of his usual routine far too many times already on this holiday. The remaining four were already far too rowdy and drunk to sympathize with his problems, but Lovro decided that this didn't make him love them any less and even he reached for the homemade *digestif.*

The consequences of the seaside merry-making were catastrophic, at least as far as Lovro was concerned. By the time morning had broken he had just about managed to put Sonja to bed, but with Brigita they gave up and left her to sleep outside on the beach, while Matjaž collapsed not too far away. And at five in the morning, Samo and Lovro didn't have to strength to gather anything other than a blanket for those collapsed outside. Likewise they decided to leave the clearing up until the morning, even though now it was technically already morning; given the circumstances, an operation of that sort was just not doable.

THURSDAY

None of this would have been so bad, had Stojan and Anka not decided to surprise the wedding party by boarding the first morning ferry from Split. Luckily, they weren't too familiar with the island or the town of Hvar and – after several missed calls – only found their daughters' apartment in Podstine at around eleven. Their furious knocking was answered by a dishevelled Lovro in his underwear, who at the sight of them standing on the doorstep thought he must still be hallucinating from the potent herbal rakia.

Stojan's scathing question 'So when do people on Hvar actually get up, then?' convinced him that his future in-laws weren't just a mirage caused by his guilty conscience but were, in fact, fairly actual versions of the people in question. He sat them down in the kitchen and told them he would go and get Sonja. The father of the bride grumbled, 'What about Brigita, where is that girl? Stuck in a corner, reading that filth of hers again!'

'Karl Marx is a renowned theoretician, though, Stojan,' Lovro said, trying to calm his almost-father-in-law as he walked towards the bedroom.

'And the rest!' Stojan shouted, pulling a face and looking over to his wife. 'Go on, go and get Brigita, I'll see if I can make something of that girl!'

Samo, who had been woken by Stojan's booming voice, realized the dangers of a full disclosure of yesterday's revelry and offered to fetch Brigita instead. 'I think she went for a morning dip. No one expected you quite so early,' he apologized, and ran off to the shore.

'Eleven is early now, he says! Good one!' Stojan roared, now already visibly riled. Meanwhile Lovro had somehow managed to convince Sonja that this was not a nightmare, but that the worst had really happened. He dragged her, in a somewhat unkempt state, before her parents.

'What on earth happened to you?' her father asked, horrified. 'Who's going to want you if you lie around like that all day?'

'Me,' Lovro piped up with a smile.

'You just wait a couple of years, you'll soon change your mind,' Stojan remarked sarcastically, while Anka meanwhile spent most of the time staring at the floor.

'Thanks, Dad!' Sonja said smiling, and started to make some coffee.

'Where's that darned Brigita?' the father roared, looking around.

'She's on her way now,' Lovro replied, casting a reassuring glance at Sonja. 'Samo went to find her at the beach.'

Sonja tried to calm the situation. 'So how are you two? How come you're here already? We weren't expecting you until early afternoon.'

'Well, it's practically afternoon already,' Stojan said stubbornly.

'Would you like anything to eat?' Lovro asked politely.

'Of course. Not inside, though, it's so stuffy in here. Where's that terrace of yours?'

'You're right, the terrace is nicer. Just give me a minute to spruce it up. Samo was pickling cucumbers yesterday and he didn't manage to clear it all up afterwards,' Sonja said apologetically.

'Cucumbers? Samo? Is there a single real man in this house?' Stojan raged.

'Dad, please . . .' Sonja said, trying again to calm her parents down.

'Never mind "please". This house is a pigsty and that's because you and Brigita are spoiled brats . . . And these two wet blankets aren't man enough to keep you in check.'

A similarly awkward scene was unfolding on the beach. Brigita yelped at the sight of Samo, and was even more horrified to hear of her parents' arrival. 'Matjaž!' she cried out. Samo looked at her in confusion. 'We have to somehow get rid of Matjaž, you know what my dad will think if he sees him here.' Samo grasped the severity of the situation, located Matjaž's body and tried to bring him back to life. It was not going to happen. In a panic, Brigita looked around and caught sight of a lifeboat – actually a little old fishing boat moored up on their little beach. With great difficulty she and Samo dragged Matjaž over to it, covered him with the ropes and towels, and decided that they'd come back to rescue him at a more suitable time.

At that point Brigita could already hear her parents' voices, especially that of her father. 'Well, where is that girl? Has she completely lost her mind?'

'Hello, Dad, I've just been doing a bit of exercise,' said the intimidated Brigita, offering them a seat at the not-exactly-clean table.

'You've done far too much, judging by the state of you!'

Brigita bowed her head and sat down next to her parents, feeling deflated.

Her father then focused his attention on his coffee. The local Dalmatian prosciutto did nothing to impress his taste buds. He looked around, over at the islands imprinted on the crystal clear Mediterranean Sea, and said, 'I'm not sure this is worth all this circus.' Sonja smiled at her father obligingly, while Brigita rolled her eyes when he wasn't looking.

Lovro turned to Anka and addressed her formally, 'Lovely, though, don't you think?' But Anka only dared give a gentle nod.

'Lovely? Lovely!' Stojan raised his voice again. 'You young people today have no idea what real life is about. And this kind of frolicking and raving around on Hvar, or whatever you call it, is completely unacceptable to us, the older and wiser generation.'

'But Daddy, we're getting married. Don't you think that Lovro and I have earned a little break? At the end of the day we've really slaved for this.'

'Slaved, slaved – as if you young people know what slavery is! You've got no idea, and then you go fooling around like this.'

'Well, Stojan . . .' the mother finally joined in, 'you and I did spend our honeymoon in Dubrovnik.'

'But only after the wedding!' Stojan blurted, as if he was offering a particularly convincing argument.

'But these two wanted to share this beautiful scenery, this wonder of nature, with everyone. Isn't that nice?' Samo spoke up, and Brigita rolled her eyes more markedly than before.

Trying to steer the conversation away from this hurtful topic, Sonja asked her father about the weather back home in Slovenia, although it turned out that even there something was wrong: there were conspirators, uncles, The Octopus (an undercover political organization), who were all, especially in September, making sure that nothing was right. When it was supposed to be sunny it rained, and when the sun shone it was too hot, when it grew cooler you couldn't go on picnics outside the house any more, and the house would be at its most beautiful right now, at the start of September. The conspiracy, masterminded by meteorologists, was of course connected to the political crisis and the internal political conflict, wherein old communists were gnawing away at the healthy core of the Slovene Catholic right. Stojan kept on complaining, getting even louder and showing no sign of stopping. At first Matjaž's sweet dreams were spoiled by words such as 'UDBA', 'champagne socialists', 'conspiracy', 'traitors' and a rendition of the patriotic 'Slovenia, Whence Thy Beauty' before they eventually woke him completely. But all that seemed like a lullaby compared to the ropes and towels under which he found himself buried. He let out a short yelp, but luckily the parents were sitting with their backs to him and therefore didn't see the monster trying to escape from the ropes. Brigita and Sonja, who saw the entire scene, could barely hold it together. 'What was that?' Stojan flinched.

'I've got hiccups, I'm sorry,' Brigita said quickly, while Samo tried to signal to Matjaž that he was to stay down at all costs. Lovro, a man of action, was now trying to divert the parents' attention; he stood up and shouted, 'It's so, so, so, so NICE to finally have Sonja's parents here!' The others were confused by his euphoria, and then by his next sentence, 'I think I remember where I left my harpoon!'

'Harpoon? What do you need a harpoon for now?' Stojan asked, agitated. Sonja explained to him that yesterday Lovro was really upset because he couldn't find the harpoon that he uses when he goes fishing, and he would not rest until it was found. Stojan turned around to see if this harpoon was going to turn up, but Sonja asked if he would instead tell everyone about the difficult times under communism, like some gory detail from his time serving in the Yugoslav People's Army. Samo and Brigita were so enthusiastic about this that Stojan finally forgot about the harpoon.

In the meantime, Lovro had cautiously approached the boat and whispered, 'Listen . . . their parents have arrived. If they find you, it'll be a disaster, especially seeing as those guys hid you in a boat. We're already on the brink of a total meltdown as it is. Hang on a bit longer. We'll come and get you as soon as we can!' Lovro did not account for the fact that, with all the noise and being buried under ropes, Matjaž only caught the odd word of this.

Lovro then returned to the table and explained that he hadn't found his harpoon, but that he wouldn't get upset over it. When it was time for lunch, Sonja dragged Lovro into the kitchen, asking, 'What are we going to do with Matjaž?'

'I said that we'd go and rescue him at the first opportunity . . .'

'And when will that be?'

'How should I know? They're your parents. Ask your mum to help you with your wedding dress, or ask your dad for some advice.'

Brigita ran in behind them in a panic and said, 'What are we going to do? The guy can't even go for a wee, he hasn't had anything to eat, and the sun has just started to beat down on him . . .' Neither Sonja nor Lovro had thus far considered that poor Matjaž could be shrivelling up in the little boat.

When the three conspirators returned to the table, they were met by a horrifying scene. At that very moment Stojan was heading towards the boat. 'I thought I heard a voice coming from in here. I'm just checking you haven't been infested by a family of cats,' he said, nodding in the direction of the boat.

'Help!' Brigita cried out, pretending to collapse.

'What is it now?' Stojan asked, turning towards his daughter.

'I think she's got something stuck in her throat. Goodness me!' cried Anka.

Everyone gathered around Brigita, but her father said nonchalantly, 'It's probably one of those chewing gums she's always got in her mouth.' He continued towards the boat.

Now Lovro jumped up and shouted, 'Stop!'

'Oh, for the last time, what?' Stojan snapped, losing his temper.

'I think there's a spider on you!'

'What are you on about, a spider?'

'A dangerous spider,' Lovro replied.

'What do you mean?'

'It's a tarantula, sir,' Lovro fabricated.

'Nonsense! I've never heard of tarantulas on Hvar.'

'Please, sir, just wait there a moment. Samo, Samo, come and help me.' The two of them steered Stojan away from the boat and towards the table, and carefully patted him on the back, increasing his agitation.

Meanwhile Brigita had miraculously recovered and she immediately leaped up to hug her father; now saved from the alleged spider and trapped in his daughter's tightening grip, he was more disgruntled than ever. Samo took advantage of the hugging and went over to Matjaž, helping him to disentangle himself from the ropes and the towels, carefully vacate the boat and hide in a nearby bush. It didn't cover him completely, but sufficiently to conceal him from Stojan's careless and by now furious eyes.

Sonja diverted her mother's attention to the flowers that were growing near by, and involved her in a conversation about whether they might actually make a good wedding bouquet. Stojan began to walk towards the boat, accompanied by Lovro, Samo and Brigita so they could shield the bush from view as best they could. While the father ranted about how people ought to be fined for leaving their boats to be infested by cats like this, Matjaž crept past them like a weasel, almost managing to evade Anka's distracted eyeline, too. Yet she caught sight of a man's behind climbing up the stairs. 'Who's that?' she asked her daughter.

Sonja's cheeks turned a strong shade of pink and she slowly replied, 'That's Stipe, the neighbour . . .'

'But how did he end up here?'

'He probably went on one of his swimming expeditions and landed here. All the locals are like that here,' Sonja explained.

'But he wasn't even wet.'

'Oh, Stipe's renowned for his ability to dry off immediately, because he's so bald,' Sonja babbled. She quickly continued their conversation about the flowers, which it transpired were actually cacti. It was difficult enough to make them look nice as it was, let alone use them for a wedding bouquet, her somewhat confused mother explained.

Not long afterwards, Matjaž's phone rang. It was Brigita. She apologized to him profusely, half-laughing at herself as she did so because she was currently pretending to be in the shower. She told him that her mother had summed up events rather well, 'What an afternoon! My daughter almost went and choked on her own saliva, they rescued my husband from a deadly tarantula that then mysteriously disappeared, and Stipe the neighbour dried off in record-shattering time after his swim. But the craziest thing of all was that my other daughter wants a wedding bouquet of cacti . . .'

She also told him that after their afternoon siesta they were going out for dinner in Hvar with their parents, and that she'd really like it if he could rescue her afterwards from the ongoing torment and take her somewhere for a drink. She'd already made up an excuse that she'd have to dash off to meet a friend who might be able to help her find a job. Lovro was thrilled, her father sceptical of course, and it was only Sonja who realized that the potential employer was Matjaž. When he heard all this, he couldn't say no. Nor was he ever going to say no.

As he walked towards the centre of town, he ran into the large, happy family with a loud Stojan at the head. He walked past and greeted them politely, and the younger generation politely greeted him in return. Brigita also gave a knowing look, which seemed to him as if it could be fairly accurately translated as 'Sorry, I'll be there as soon as I can.' Right behind him he heard Stojan enquiring as to who he was and why the others had greeted him. Anka was still looking at him with obvious interest, when she suddenly realized that it was the secret swimmer, Stipe, their neighbour. Matjaž only hoped that the night was dark enough to avoid yet another catastrophe as a result of this whole charade.

An hour later, at the agreed location, it transpired that the young woman behind the knowing look had not let him down. He listened to Brigita's account, 'And then a proper inquisition followed. Who was Ana, what was I going to do with her, how did I know her and why hadn't I introduced her to my parents...'

'And who is Ana?'

'My made-up friend. Surely you didn't think I'd tell them I was meeting up with Stipe?'

'Why not?' Matjaž jibed. 'I'd say that your old man's getting a little bit anxious by now, seeing as his youngest daughter hasn't shown any interest in becoming an honourable wife and mother.'

'Oh, stop it. You can't imagine how damaging all of that is for me. Even today he was interrogating me about my life – he's even more suspicious now that I don't live with them any more – and after all that questioning he was in an unusually bad mood. He's hurt because I left the Catholic faith. He's worried because after a promising decision to study economics I've turned towards theory – and worse, towards Marxism. He sees that as an attack on him, which of course is partly true. He's even more unhappy because never during my twenty-three years have I brought a man home. He and Mum have spoken about it many times, about whether there's anything wrong with me, and they want to send me to a psychiatrist. But what eats away at him the most is whether I'm going to attend the wedding on my own, as if that would bring shame on the family.

Sonja then stupidly blurted out that actually my boyfriend would be attending the wedding – I just didn't want to talk about him because it was still early days and I didn't know what was going to become of it all. On the one hand it cheered up Dad a bit, but the phantom boyfriend – I have no idea how Sonja is going to manufacture him – unfurled a whole new list of fears: that I might get pregnant, that I might mess everything up because I'm such a handful, whether this phantom son-of-a-bitch deserved me in the first place, etc., etc. I don't know if I can survive until Saturday . . . Sonja has such an accomplished way of ignoring them, whether it's Mum or Dad, but I can't. I don't know how to react. I don't know how to stick up for myself. You can imagine how painful that is to someone who has such a specific standpoint.'

'I know, yeah.'

'What is that supposed to mean?'

'It's as if for every second that you're not trying to confront your father, you constantly have to seek out confrontation with the world and with everyone around you. You're always arguing over every lousy little thing,' Matjaž said, being very straight with her.

'Not over every lousy detail!' Brigita scolded him.

'Like now, for example!'

Brigita screwed up her face, and Matjaž laughed. 'Don't despair, you're really hot when you're constantly arguing and getting into disputes.'

'That chauvinist discourse again!'

'That's exactly what I'm talking about. But you can't fool me any more. I mean, I don't think it's a bad thing if you're vulnerable sometimes, if you don't always feel like fighting. That's what being human is.'

'But I don't want to be human!' She looked at him desperately.

'And that's what most makes you human . . .'

'I don't get it, why do you have to have such a way with words all of a sudden? I think I preferred you with your bad sense of humour.'

'Don't worry, there's still plenty where that came from!'

A few hours, a few drops of alcohol and one half-stolen kiss later, a satisfied Matjaž walked back towards his apartment. The clip on the ear he'd received after tasting her lips was still resounding in his thoughts, but he would have sworn that she reacted ever so slightly too late for it to be considered a genuine objection. He also bore witness to a tiny smile that she gave while scolding him for only wanting her for one thing, and she then let herself be invited for a swim at his private beach the next day without a single comment. He imagined the two of them lazing in the sunshine, saying very little to one another, just as it should be between two close people. He imagined how it would become too hot for them and how they'd hide from the violent rays in the sea, swimming together. Maybe he'd dunk her, maybe he'd toss her under-water. Maybe this time it would be her that glided in for a kiss, wet and salty

. . . Maybe she would finally loosen up around him, maybe they'd become a couple that surrendered to the welcoming cloak of a retreating summer. 'How are the wedding preparations going?' flashed up a text from Aleksander. There was obviously some joke at his expense there, but Matjaž replied to himself, 'Not bad at all, not bad at all.' He decided on a provocative message: 'This will be the wedding of my life!'

FRIDAY

Alas, the next day things were no longer quite so clear. It was cloudy in the morning, quite wet towards the south, and to him it was unheard of that such meteorological negligence was affecting the island. Brigita came regardless and suggested that the two of them go to the nearby bay for a coffee. In quite a humorous tone, which was not really in keeping with her usual nature, she immediately started talking at great length. Lovro's parents had now arrived on Hvar and of course the chaos was unrivalled. Brigita's story made Matjaž laugh; now he was looking forward to the wedding purely on the basis of being able to witness a social explosion.

'Zofija, i.e. Lovro's mum, entered like a hurricane. She started bitching about Croats even before she'd found time to say hello to Lovro, Sonja or our parents, because someone had nicked her purse on the ferry. Borut just sat down on the terrace and calmly started reading. Sonja asked Zofija if she was sure she hadn't merely misplaced it somewhere. "Nonsense!" she cried. "Those Croatian pirates stole it from me, they probably saw my new watch!" At this point she lifted her fat left arm so everyone could admire her fortieth wedding anniversary present from Borut. Then she carried on: "I've searched through everything, I've checked and I can't find it. Isn't that right, Borut? That's why we've just come to say hello, we're heading off to the police station now – isn't that right, Borut? – so at least it will be reported. I don't hold out much hope that any sort of barbarian from around here would return foreign property." The rest of us tried to persuade her that it would be more practical for her to first cancel her cards, if she was certain that the purse really was gone for good, but Zofija just cast a feeble glance back at Borut, beseeching him to support her plan. Naturally, she didn't get anything from him. He just sighed "Uhuh" and "That's right!" every now and again. So she stuck to her plan of going straight to the police station, with or without Borut. Nothing we did helped; not our offer of coffee, nor charcuterie, nor a fantastic chocolate torte that Sonja had made for her specially. That was when we knew that it was serious.'

'And?' Matjaž enquired.

'She got mad at her husband just like in a movie, and decided to take matters into her own hands. She gave Lovro an accusatory look, which of course he skilfully avoided until Sonja dropped him in it, saying, "Lovro, maybe you could leap to your mum's aid!"

'"At least there's someone who understands a woman in need!" Zofija complained, and turned towards the car.

'"I'm just getting the keys," Lovro said.

'"Take your dad's car," insisted his mother. "I'm not going in any other. You know how bad my back is and how sensitive I am to the air conditioning. It's all set to my levels and I'm not going in any other car!"'

'Lovro nodded submissively, turned towards his father and said, "Dad, please could I have the keys so that I can carry out this charade with Mum?"

'"They're in that bag!" said Borut, without taking his head out of the newspaper. Lovro looked around, spotted three bags in addition to the two enormous suitcases and started rifling through them.

'"Dad", he said, "I can't find these bloody keys anywhere . . . Hang on, what is that? Mum!" He turned quickly towards Zofija, who was at this point already waiting by the car and puffing in the apparently unbearable heat of Hvar.

'"What is it?" she shouted back.

'"Is your purse big and red?"

'"Yes. Made of crocodile skin, a present from your dad for our thirty-ninth wedding anniversary," she yelled.

'"Dad, is this her purse?" asked Lovro, showing him the great big red thing, which he'd found while searching unsuccessfully for the keys. Borut passed a fleeting glance over the thing and mumbled that it looked like her purse, and quickly diverted his attention back to his newspaper again.

'"Lovro, what are you waiting for now?" He heard the vocal Zofija once again.

'"Mum, I've found your bloody purse!"

'"What are you talking about, have you no shame?" she shouted at him, and slowly started to return towards the apartment, while loudly asking where damned thing had been and who found it and why didn't they find it before.

When she got back, she had to immediately consume some cake as her nerves had been so shot since Zagreb onwards, and nothing helps as much as a high-calorie Nutella cake. So the three couples, two of which are probably the most unbearable on the entire island, sat down at the table.'

'And then they all had a civilized chat about the weather and world hunger?' Matjaž joked.

'Yeah, right. I don't know if I told you this but, in contrast to my parents, Lovro's are passionate atheists and quite left-wing in their beliefs. So the debate soon led down precisely the path that my Mum and Sonja wanted to avoid, and Zofija and Stojan were just waiting for a chance to come to blows with one another. Zofija praised Kučan and the Left, who never squeezed Slovenia dry like Janez Janša and his lot did. My Dad, a passionate Janša man, of course replied that the Left had been in power an awful lot longer and it was therefore logical that they were responsible for the shit Slovenia was in now.

'Sonja intervened, saying that we were by the sea, she was about to get married and there was no need for us to involve ourselves with daily politics. Lovro added that the problems were systemic anyway, and that Slovenia was part of a larger and equally complicated system. My mum said it wasn't very Christian to have political debates on such a beautiful island. Zofija and Stojan got even angrier at all this, and Borut took himself and his newspaper off to the sea to find some shade.

'Zofija insisted that if you looked at it from a purely practical perspective, Slovenia had no better alternative than the Left, but Stojan said such talk was typical of the apathetic Communist Party generation that slept on a bed of roses and did nothing to fulfil its civic duties. Then at this point Zofija really flew off the handle, referring to the socialist labour brigades and insisting that even though she didn't take part in them they should remind us of that generation's effort, which enabled these two young people to get married in the first place – and, what's more, here on this beautiful island.

'The only thing the two of them could agree on was the wedding cake, which was "satisfactory", and after that they delighted in continuing their argument, obviously choosing not to hear Lovro's remark that it was he who had made the wedding on this island possible, with his wages. This rather annoyed Sonja, who likewise had contributed a share of the money. Then the row was going on at both ends, so it wasn't difficult for Samo and I to get away from that mad lot. I mentioned to Mum that we still had a whole host of things to do before the wedding, but she was too het up by all the arguing to really register that we were leaving.'

'And where's poor Samo now?'

'He's not poor at all, he went to pick up Zala and Špela from the ferry.'

'And what's the big deal with that?'

'Our Samo has sordid intentions with those two,' said Brigita conspiratorially.

'Really? Like what? Is he going to take them out for an ice cream?'

'No, maybe even for a glass of red – at least until the situation calms down, he confided in me.'

'But is that it, then, in terms of guests?' Matjaž asked.

'As if! Tomorrow we've still got Lovro's brother, Leon, and his grandma coming, then a few cousins, aunts and uncles should be invading as well. And Sonja's also invited quite a few more relatives – it's going to be a rather large wedding, I fear . . . Luckily, though, the majority of them will be left to their own devices when it comes to sleeping arrangements. Sonja just ordered two or three boats to take everyone to the neighbouring island.'

'Ugh, that's quite a handful, though.'

'Tell me about it, and I'm the bridesmaid, too. I'm going to be under constant fire from all directions.'

'What are you wearing?' asked Matjaž.

'You're just saying that to wind me up, aren't you?' she replied, looking at him from underneath her eyebrows.

'No, honestly, I'm interested.'

'What will you wear?'

'I'll have a suit on, obviously.'

'I didn't expect such professionalism from a photographer like you.'

'And what is that supposed to mean? Next you'll be saying you didn't notice I was a man of style.' Brigita laughed and confessed to him what she'd be wearing. Matjaž noticed that while she was telling him about her simple dress with a few tasteful details, she wasn't doing a very good job of hiding her enthusiasm about it, and maybe even about the ceremony itself.

Her eyes sparkled while she talked, and Matjaž remarked, 'You do realize that your eyes are sparkling while you're talking about all this bourgeois excess?'

'Why do you have to ruin everything?' said Brigita, getting annoyed. 'Why does everything have to be a joke or a piss-take, why can't you just listen to me?' She bowed her head and pulled that pretty, frowning face like a child.

Matjaž stroked her hair and apologized, 'Even I don't really know why I said that. I'm probably just jealous that you're going to look better than me.' Brigita's face brightened up a little, and she stroked his hand.

Afternoon turned into evening and the two of them, walking towards the centre of town, stopped off at various places and conversed about all the important things in life. They went to the outskirts of the other bay for something to eat and had an involved discussion about films, which chiefly meant that they ranked famous actresses – by their looks, sex appeal and any interesting trivia. After that instalment they agreed that the night was young and that the fish dinner deserved to swim around in a little more red wine. They found a suitable bar on a little side street, so as to avoid potentially bumping into any wedding guests, who were probably already swarming around the place. The main question for Matjaž and Brigita here was the role of poetry and other literary forms, in terms of how much they could really impact the wider population. They established that, unfortunately, there were too few decent comedies these days, but the most endangered type of poetry – just as Marx had once claimed – was the extinct form of the epic. Then, feeling a certain pressure to maintain a sense of good humour in their lives, they both had to agree that popular music was the great exception, a place where poetry remained very much alive, for instance in the opus of Justin Bieber or One Direction.

On the way to the bar next door they were already listing their favourite lyricists. Brigita tended towards the side of the Beatles, Seattle grunge and David Bowie, while Matjaž preferred the Stones and the jazz artists, with Louis Armstrong at the top of the pile – 'So what if I like old jazz and somehow just can't relate to the contemporary stuff?' he said to Brigita, excusing himself. Aside from that, he was seriously into Bach.

'Which Bach?'

'Johann Sebastian, duh! What were you thinking of?'

'That catastrophe, Richard Bach.'

'But we're talking about poetry,' Matjaž said.

'I know, yes, strange are the ways of the subconscious.'

At the fourth successive bar, Brigita looked at her phone. Matjaž noticed the look of surprise on her face and asked, 'What is it?'

'Fifteen missed calls.' She turned white in an instant.

'Jesus, what is going on?'

It turned out that one of those calls was from Sonja. Brigita called her back immediately, but she didn't pick up. Then she called Lovro, to try and get some idea of what was going on, but his phone went unanswered, too. Samo's phone was turned off.

'He clearly doesn't want to be disturbed while he's keeping Špela and Zala company,' Brigita grumbled. Next she called the person who had called her the most. It wasn't her mother with six calls, but Zofija with eight. Matjaž could only make sense of the phone call through Brigita's replies.

'Hello! I'm sorry, I didn't hear . . . Never mind where I am, what's the crisis? Seriously?' Brigita's face dropped. 'No, I can't get hold of her . . . nor him.' She started running her fingers through her hair with her free hand. 'Yeah, it's best if you do . . . No, I'll take care of that. With Samo, yes, or whoever else,' she said, looking at Matjaž. 'Of course, drink it all!' She smiled, and then became serious again when she had to relay instructions. 'There's a bottle of whisky in Sonja's car, and another in the cupboard. Beers are in the fridge . . . I think so, that should be enough.' Her forehead wrinkled again slightly from the tense deliberation. 'Wine? I understand, just in case . . . True, my Dad could drive Gandhi to alcoholism . . . I think there's a few litres in the same cupboard . . . Sure, just give me call if you can't find it.' She raised her eyebrows, and in a calm voice said, 'Mum? Yes, put her on the phone . . . Hi Mum! . . . Nothing much, I went for a bit of a wander, I just felt like it . . . I heard, yes. No, I don't think it's anything to worry about,' she said unconvincingly. 'Of course I will.' Then she went a bit red. 'No, I haven't had anything to drink. Why do you ask? . . . No, maybe I'm a bit tired after swimming . . . .' The wrinkles gathered on her forehead again; these were from lying, Matjaž decided.

'I went swimming all the same. I'm with Ana now, yeah, having dinner, yeah, we're getting on really well . . .' She raised her eyebrows, while Matjaž felt a pleasant shudder all over his body, as he took that as a personal compliment. Then she added rudely, 'Of course I'll go! I've been calling her constantly! I know Lovro's unreachable! . . . And Samo, yes!' She rolled her eyes. 'No, I think it'll all be fine . . . Of course I'll ring if I hear anything.' Now she firmly gritted her teeth. 'I know it's hard being a parent, especially at times like this. Mum, don't worry . . . or rather, have a drink, your conscience will be clear.' She planted her palm on her forehead, growing weary of the conversation. 'I'm sorry, I know you don't drink, you just have the odd tipple. I just wanted to say that today of all days you can enjoy a tipple in peace, and I'll call you if I find out anything.' The hand on her head became restless, and squeezed her whole face. 'I love you, too, yes. Yes Mum, yes, yes, I know that you sacrificed everything for us, now just pass the phone back to Zofija. Yes, mwah to you too, bye.'

Brigita put the phone down and hiccupped. 'It appears our lovebirds have had a row and in the maelstrom of war have disappeared into the unknown. The wedding's off,' she said, summing up several minutes of phone call.

'What?'

'Oops, sorry, yeah, it's over. Hic,' she hiccupped.

'Yes, but what happened?'

'Clearly that stuff about work, money, earnings caused a slightly more serious conflict. Hic,' said Brigita.

'Stop hiccupping, pull yourself together. You promised to look for them, and that's what we have to do!' He looked at her severely.

'Hic, but how should I know where to look for them, hic?' She was being rather hesitant.

'We'll do it systematically, from bar to bar, pier to pier,' Matjaž encouraged her.

He took her by the hand and together the two of them wound their way around Hvar. At first things looked utterly hopeless; they'd visited everywhere possible, even the more hidden bars and restaurants, and had even asked after two people looking lost, but no luck. Not only that, but Brigita's hiccups were still clinging on. At one point Samo called, as he'd also received a stack of missed calls and text messages. Brigita brought him up to date with the situation.

Samo, along with the two beauties, as he now called them, met up with Matjaž and Brigita in front of Bar Sidro and formulated a search plan. Samo and the beauties were to go around the bars in which he and Lovro had disgraced themselves over the past few days, while Matjaž and Brigita would try to track down Sonja. They would call one another if they found either party. Just like Brigita, Samo and the girls did not appear to be too concerned at all; what's more, Zala was hiccupping, too. And Samo and Špela already seemed entirely at ease in each other's company.

'What the hell is wrong with you all? We need action, not flirtation!' said Matjaž. The others laughed, and then immediately assured him that they were entirely on board. The search therefore began. The trio went in their direction, the other two in theirs.

'Why did they decide to get married on Hvar?' Matjaž asked Brigita, now concerned for the future bride and groom. He'd never have expected that such a couple could mean anything to him.

'How should I know, hic?'

'Just try, will you!'

'Now is not the time for questions of romance, now is the time for action, hic,' Brigita said decisively.

'And that's why I'm asking. What sort of stuff like that is there on Hvar?'

'I don't get you, hic,' Brigita said, taking hold of his hand. Matjaž gently stroked hers.

'Why is the wedding on Hvar?'

'Their first romantic break together was on Hvar.'

'Aha.'

'And then many times after that, hic, whenever they had the chance.'

'Do you maybe know where they liked to hang out, where they had their best times together?'

'Yes, where he proposed to her.'

'Where?'

'On the Pakleni Islands, in some place called Paganini or something like that. Where the wedding's going to be tomorrow,' she replied.

'But they can't be there, because as far as we know they haven't taken the boats,' Matjaž said, being methodical.

'We don't know that.'

'Would either of them go there if they were angry?'

'Lovro might, not Sonja. But I doubt it. He wouldn't go there now, hic, now he's angry at her. He'd go there when he loves her.'

'Fine, do you know anything else? Anything at all?' he asked, trying to rally her.

'Hic, let me think . . . hic, I think that last time they pointed out where they went dancing and had a lovely time . . .'

'Where?' Matjaž leaped on this information.

She crumpled her forehead and thought long and hard. 'I can't remember, hic . . .' She looked at the floor.

Meanwhile they'd arrived at the marketplace. Matjaž started to shake Brigita. 'Listen! I'm being serious now. You have to find your sister – now think, where is it? Where would we find her at this time?'

Brigita seemed to be sobering up a bit to think, when from the darkness of the empty market stalls a voice sounded, 'Right here.'

'Sonja!' cried Brigita, running to hug her.

'I thought he'd come here,' said Sonja, visibly under the influence. 'This is the place where we've fallen out the most, over chard, potatoes and tomatoes, obviously. And then we'd make up again right here, on this very spot. But this time he's not coming, this time I've gone too far.' She wept and tipped back her whisky.

'But what did you say?' Matjaž asked her, while her sister was still holding her tight.

'I said that he was socially inept and didn't understand what went on around him,' Sonja said, crying.

'But that's not so harsh,' he comforted her.

'Besides, it's fairly accurate,' added Brigita, clearly relieved of the hiccups after the fortunate encounter and the hugs.

'It's the worst thing you could say to Lovro. Once, when we had a similar argument, he said he wouldn't stand for that accusation – for the words "socially inept" and the claim that he didn't understand anything, especially not in the presence of others.'

'Well, in any case he'll understand that you're struggling and under pressure with both sets of parents around, and it just slipped off your tongue,' Brigita said.

'No, he won't,' Sonja burst into tears, 'because I said it spitefully, with the intention of hurting him. He told me that he wasn't going to put up with me being spiteful. I promised him that I'd never be spiteful . . . and now I've been spiteful.' She cried helplessly. Brigita had to embrace her again and stroke her hair.

Matjaž, standing to one side, said that being spiteful was an extension of being a woman, and all men knew that and were prepared for it. This only made Sonja cry even more, until Brigita got cross. 'Enough wailing now. You love this guy and I'm not going to let your spiteful behaviour ruin a perfectly beautiful love affair!' she said decisively.

'Especially as Brigita has to ruin those for everyone else around as it is,' added Matjaž.

Brigita gave him a furious look and said, 'Why don't you go and see if you can find Lovro. These two aren't usually very far apart!'

That sentence set Sonja off crying again, and prompted her to take another swig of whisky. Matjaž obeyed his order and walked a little further on, past the nearby supermarket and towards the pharmacy. As he passed the police station, he thought he saw someone sitting by the side entrance. Discreetly, he drew closer and tried to work out who it was.

'Who's there?' a stern voice startled him. For a moment Matjaž panicked, before he remembered that any Croatian policeman would probably be speaking Croatian. Then he knew whose voice it was.

'Lovro! Thank God!' Matjaž cried out.

'Some God,' said Lovro bluntly, holding his bottle of cognac. Matjaž sat down uninvited and helped himself to a glug of the strong stuff.

'Well, that was quite a fallout!' Matjaž said. 'You had us all really worried.'

'And so you should be – there won't be any wedding! I've had enough. I can't take any more! As if it's not already enough that she's got parents like that, and, well, a difficult sister who's probably going to be living with us her whole life, and then she goes and calls me socially inept!'

'I know,' said Matjaž. 'Unbelievable! Is there anything I can say to make you change your mind and take back that beauty?'

'No chance!' Lovro snapped back, taking a swig.

'Well, I guess you're right. Who gets married these days anyway? And to a woman like that. She doesn't even know how to cook!'

'That's true, but she makes really good coffee,' Lovro corrected him passionately.

'Fine, but she gets up really late when she's on holiday,' Matjaž prompted him.

'On holiday that's fine, because normally she's always up before me – to make me coffee.'

'She drinks a shameful amount of alcohol,' said Matjaž, provoking him further.

'Always within normal limits,' the groom-to-be replied, defending her again.

'And she smokes even more to make up for it.'

'But she's so hot when she does,' Lovro smiled softly.

'Don't forget about her parents, though!' Matjaž was slowly running out of counter-arguments.

'I know, but she's normal. We're really similar in our political beliefs, you know,' Lovro explained to him.

'Fine, well, then there's also, as you said yourself, that insufferable sister of hers!'

'Who you've fallen in love with!' Lovro retorted, getting cross.

'OK, I like her, but she's hard work for you,' said Matjaž, calming him.

'She's no trouble at all. If it weren't for her, Sonja would never have realized that I'm actually socially inept and that I don't understand anything.'

'You mean that you're not socially inept and that you understand everything!' Matjaž corrected him.

'That's what I said . . .'

'Of course you did,' said Matjaž, and took a swig from the bottle. 'So, what's the problem, then?'

'You're the problem,' yelled Lovro, somewhat inebriated.

'True. Shall we go and console your future wife, then? The one who hasn't been able to stop crying since you fell out?'

Lovro looked at him anxiously. 'What, why didn't you tell me? The poor thing. I thought she'd be hanging out with those girls, slagging me off. If I'd known she was crying . . .'

'She's in a real state, and completely regrets saying what she did,' Matjaž told him.

'And so she should!' Lovro insisted. He stood up suddenly and started to waver, so that Matjaž had to hold him up.

'Anyway,' concluded Matjaž, shifting Lovro towards the direction of Sonja. When husband- and wife-to-be caught sight of one another, they rushed into each other's arms; a torrent of words, incomprehensible to normal mortals, poured out from the two of them.

'Where did you find him?' Brigita asked Matjaž, smiling.

'At the police station.'

'What?' Brigita asked, worried.

'Don't worry,' Matjaž smiled. 'He wasn't locked up, although he seemed like he was heading for it. He was sat drinking outside.'

Brigita smiled at him and Matjaž drew her gently into his arms. 'I think we'll remember this as one of the good days by the sea.'

'Definitely', said Brigita, shirking away from the hug, 'but it's already morning and we have to go home if we're going to get these two jackasses married.'

'I know,' said Matjaž, 'and call those older jackasses to make sure they haven't already drunk everything today unnecessarily.'

'Ah, it's probably already too late . . .' Brigita said. 'Samo's got his own adventure, though.'

Sonja and Lovro walked up to Brigita with their arms around each other, as if to say that – at two in the morning – they really ought to be getting home, if they were planning on getting any sleep at all.

'See you tomorrow!' Brigita said, and stretched out her hand to Matjaž.

'Paganini at eleven, right?' Matjaž asked. Lovro stopped in his tracks and turned around like one of the Furies. 'What do you mean, Paganini? It's Laganini, you have to be at Laganini at ten!' Sonja burst out laughing at the bridegroom's discipline. Turning towards Matjaž, she mouthed him a 'thank you'. Matjaž gave a slight bow and waved to Brigita, who was walking behind the two lovebirds and looking back with an expression that was probably a concoction of melancholy, intoxicating substances and tiredness. She raised her hand to wave goodbye.

'Don't worry!' he called after her. 'I'll find it.' He could still hear her chuckle as she slowly disappeared into the dark.

SATURDAY

He arrived at the Palmižana resort a minute or two before ten. There weren't many people on the small boat – probably because it was September, he thought. During his walk through the forest on the other side of the island, where the main event was due to take place, the familiar scent of this island's pines had momentarily catapulted him to some other point in time. One when some young guy was here, searching for shelter from the scorching heat for his girl, whose salty curls were peeping out at him from beneath her covered head. He sensed himself becoming nostalgic, and so he tried again to redirect his thoughts. But to where?

A solution presented itself in the form of a small café in the middle of the island. There sat Brigita, alone and reading something. She seemed utterly calm and relaxed, immersed in her book. Her hair tumbled over her shoulders, and got on her nerves every now and again by getting in her eyes. With a calm gesture she drew it back, only for the game to be repeated a few minutes later. The sight of this caused a friendly smile to appear on his face – something that he wasn't in the habit of doing ordinarily. He sat down next to her and lit a cigarette without saying a word. Brigita caught sight of him, but she pretended as if she hadn't, and Matjaž acted as if he hadn't seen her pretending.

He fiddled with his camera, preparing it for action, and without looking at her eventually asked, 'And where is everyone?'

Without lifting her eyes from her crime fiction, Brigita replied, 'Around here somewhere.'

'The bride and groom?'

'They're getting ready.'

'Everything under control?'

'Absolutely,' Brigita replied in a manner of complete calm, although it wasn't clear if there was an ironic undertone hiding in her response. By the time she'd finished telling the tale, it was clear to Matjaž that she had been extremely restrained in her response.

'Yes, everything's under control, leaving a few details to one side.' She looked up at him. 'At eight o'clock the florists delivered the bouquets, but they looked nothing like wedding bouquets and an awful lot like funeral wreaths. Sonja's Croatian clearly isn't as advanced as she thought it was.' Brigita fell silent again for a while, and then summed up the morning's events. 'When our dad heard about the flower situation, he started elaborating on his infamous theory of the backward Croats and how incompetent they were. He said we should call off the wedding, as the wreath was a clear sign that the day would be a catastrophe with a capital C. The Croats didn't deserve our money for the ceremony. The beauty of Hvar had nothing on the beauty of Slovenia, and it would therefore make sense to invest in our own beautiful homeland.'

She coughed, and calmly continued, 'As you can imagine, Zofija did not agree with this. She was of the opinion that the Balkans were home to a civilized people, who at the time of the Enlightenment were just as progressive as the Slovenes. She felt that it all clearly came down to misunderstanding, and that matters were by no means as grave as people tended to make out. She added that she, personally, was highly predisposed to the idea of the ceremony on Hvar, as the best place to be in September was by the sea and consequently Croatia was fully entitled to all the funds they were going to invest in it. And as soon as my father got the chance to point out, according to his misleading logic, that the wedding funds were mainly coming from one single source – i.e. the bride, or rather, her family – my mum jumped in and asked Zofija if she'd help rearrange the miserable wreath into something that resembled a wedding bouquet.

'It seemed like all of this was of little comfort to the bride. She ran back to her room, the groom running after her, too, trying to rescue her from the floral torment. What he said to her exactly I don't know, but it sounded like a few thoughts on the insignificance of the bouquet, which even though it might seem like a crucial wedding artefact would not make the wedding any less valid if the bride were without it. Judging by the cry of desperation that followed, Sonja had not appreciated the groom's conciliatory efforts.

'Anyway, a good half-hour later I was summoned to the bride's room. She was half-dressed in her normal clothes, and the expression on her face indicated that we had found ourselves faced with a new challenge. Clearly, our Sonja had let herself go a bit on holiday, probably even before that too, making her dress rather too tight on her; so tight, I'm afraid to say, that we lost a button while squeezing her into it. Mum jumped to the rescue once again, and it turned out – perhaps for the first time in our lives – that her thirty-year "career" as a housewife, an opportunity afforded to her by her conservative husband, was not entirely for nothing after all. She had clearly developed her sewing skills over the years, and she showed that wedding dress and its troublesome button what for.

'However, this rather elegant fashion rescue effort did not satisfy my dear sister's latest attack of hysteria. She even started questioning what it was all for, what all the effort was for, what was the point in life, love, etc. The groom, who had forgotten that according to popular culture he was not allowed to see his bride in her wedding dress before the event itself, didn't have any luck in easing the hysteria either. His declarations of unconditional love, even if she were fat, somehow didn't go down so well. So Zofija also had to intervene, reminding the bride that many men prefer their wives on the slightly rounder side. God knows what effect that was supposed to have on Sonja, but it didn't work either; in fact I'd go as far as to say it made the situation even worse. It was a fairly desperate state of affairs, as our bride was now convinced that she wasn't worthy of her wedding vows.

'Luckily (or perhaps unluckily) new guests knocked at the door at this point. Our cousin Eva, Sonja's competitor ever since they were tiny, had clearly overheard the clothing debacle and took full delight in it. Just as Sonja had finished declaring the end of everything, Eva remarked that it really wasn't worth rushing things when it came to weddings and that, anyway, Sonja wasn't really the marrying type. Everyone there was staggered by Eva's comments, but somehow it helped to focus the bride, who chased everyone out of the room except me, and started to do her make-up. "I'm not going to let myself be ruined by that jealous, boring conservative!" she said, looking into the mirror, to which I could only nod my head.

'Eva was just the first casualty to hamper our morning. Her parents, my aunt and uncle, hadn't managed to make it to Hvar in the end, so we had the pleasure of the company of some other guests instead. Out of our relatives the relatively normal Uncle Drago and Aunt Dragica arrived; both of them are very reserved, and probably not too clever either, not that it shows too much. My Grandma Evridika arrived, too – when you know she brought my father up it's no surprise to learn that she isn't exactly the most progressive liberal of all time. It has to be said that she possesses a few more emotions than my father, though.

'Out of Lovro's lot, Leon the seducer appeared at the least convenient moment possible, and his and Lovro's uncle – so that's Borut's brother Edvard, and his much younger and – how should I put this – not exactly quick-witted wife Linda. She has such a cute name, doesn't she? To complete the joyful occasion they brought their five-year-old son Anže to the wedding with them. Zofija's mother also arrived: Grandma Katarina, as they call her, and it quickly became clear that she was just like Zofija in every way possible. Full of opinions and convictions, the only difference being that she was a little skinnier and with slightly more direct, colourful language.

'Anyhow, shortly after the arrival of this mass of people, it took the youngest member of the family a relatively short period of time to remind us that children can also be an inconvenience sometimes. I don't know how that little ray of sunshine managed within a mere ten minutes to find chocolate, scoff it, get it all over his hands and mouth, and then in that filthy state leap into the arms of his cousin Lovro. What had seemed delightful to his parents brought about a look of sheer horror on the groom's face, as his light-coloured suit was now adorned with brown stains. At this point I ought to point out that nothing that I've just said – well, apart from the bouquet and the tight wedding dress – would have happened if all relatives had followed the original instructions and met on the boat, just as Sonja had planned.

'But my Grandma Evridika had clearly made up her own rules. As early on as the ferry to Hvar, where all the aforementioned guests had met, she had started to persuade everyone that they ought to surprise the newlyweds and their parents – because what in the world would make the bride and groom happier than old traditions, specifically the one that dictates the bride's family must accompany her to the altar? And so, on the spur of the moment, we had to redirect boats to the Pakleni Islands on which one family clan and the other were of course going to travel separately. Granny Evridika was very obviously unimpressed when Sonja pointed out that she and Lovro had already seen each other in their wedding outfits several times by this point, and therefore it made no difference whatsoever if they travelled in the same boat.'

'Where were Samo and Sonja's friends while all this was going on?'

'Thanks for bringing that up, I was just about to broach that problem.'

Matjaž leaned in attentively and waited for an answer. 'We couldn't locate Samo or the girls anywhere,' Brigita said dryly, and just carried on looking at a page in her book.

'You lost the best man?'

'That's right.'

'And where did you find him?'

'It's a long story.'

'Please,' said Matjaž, gesturing elegantly and giving the floor to Brigita.

'I have to go back a bit in order to explain it to you. As you probably remember, we left off at how we'd freshened up the bouquet situation and fixed the wedding dress; the groom's outfit was beyond salvation so he'd changed into some perfectly reasonable chinos. So, just as Granny Evridka had changed the plan, Lovro said, "Fine, we'll do it that way. But we really ought to start making a move now, otherwise there won't even be a wedding today. Samo! Samo!" he called but received no reply. "Where is that Samo?"

'"Who's Samo?" I heard Evo and Edvard enquiring.

'"Samo is Lovro's best man," my mum explained.

'Meanwhile Lovro started chasing all over the house, disappearing off somewhere and returning in an even greater state of panic. Again and again he ran in and out. Within a few moments we realized we had a problem.'

'Samo wasn't there,' Matjaž said, offering the answer up himself.

'Exactly, he couldn't find him. But that wasn't the only problem. Lovro wanted to call him, but he couldn't find his phone,' Brigita replied.

'Then all of us, well, almost all of us, started running around all over the place trying to find the damned phone. Utter mayhem set in: people running back and forwards, Granny Evridika asking for updates every five minutes, my Dad raging against the entire world, Grandma Katarina and Zofija taking it out on Lovro by saying that he'd always been too much of a dreamer, Eva philosophizing about how much energy people would save if only they were tidier. Then some genius, I think it was Leon, had the thought of calling Lovro's phone and tracing the ringtone. "Why didn't we think of that earlier?" asked Edvard, who actually had participated in the search as much as Borut had, by simply retreating into a corner of the room and surfing the internet. Then something weird happened. All of a sudden nobody could find their phones. I heard someone, I think it was Eva or Linda, say that it was all a bit like being in the Bermuda Triangle.

'Anyway, there we were, about ten or eleven of us, none of whom could find our phones, all feeling like we were approaching the end of life as we knew it. It took an incredibly large and reasoned intellect come up with an idea. Dragica whispered something to Drago – that woman doesn't like speaking publicly, even if that public is family – and her husband voiced her thoughts out loud for her: "Dragica has noticed that Anže hasn't been seen for a suspiciously long time."

' "Oh of course, blame it on the child!" Linda said, adopting a defensive motherly stance. But barely five minutes had gone by when Anže came running into the room with a mischievous look and a devious smile on his face. Zofija bent down to him and asked, "Where've you been darling? Tell Aunty Zofka, where did you potter off to?" Anže only grinned and fidgeted. Linda lost her temper, shouting, "How dare you blame my child like that!" and hugging the little villain. Then she stopped for a second and reached into his trouser pocket. "And what is this?" "Nothing," replied the child innocently. Obviously it was a phone, Edvard's phone. "You . . . you . . . you!" his father threatened him, laughing. My dad, on the other hand, was not capable of such levels of patience. "Listen, you cheeky little brat, give us our phones back right now! Where are the phones? Where are our phones?" he screamed, completely crimson. Linda did not stand for that, and started throwing rude insults at him, during which time Katarina approached Anže. To cut a long story short, it turned out that at home, hiding mobile phones was his favourite game and was one that he always won.'

'And? Where had he hidden all the phones?' asked Matjaž.

'He'd put most of them in flowerpots outside, he had two more in his pockets and he'd flung some of them into the sea. Lovro's, too, of course, among others.'

'Have you got your phone?'

'Yeah, but my battery's dead after, you know, yesterday evening when we, well, got slightly off our heads.'

'Sonja's got her phone.'

'Yes, but that doesn't make a difference to this story, because the key figure in all of this was Samo.'

'I don't understand, everyone got their phones back. Well, almost everyone.'

'Yeah, but Samo still couldn't be reached. I probably don't need to spell out how in this situation the accusations started flying from all sides. Grandma

Evridika was disgusted with Samo's behaviour as best man, and Zofija was still screeching at Linda about Anže. Borut and Edvard ignored the quarrel and sat down on the terrace; one with his paper, the other engrossed in his smartphone. My dad had a go at Lovro for not being more careful with his phone and his friends.

'Amid all this, Eva had started flirting with Leon and it was obvious that he wasn't putting up much resistance. Sonja shouted at me to do something and find Samo, until Dragica started to calm her down. Drago and Katarina started debating about ships and boats on the Atlantic; Drago loves sailing and actually knows a lot about these things, while Katarina's maritime qualifications are based on the fact that she once went on a cruise around the Atlantic. Meanwhile, Anže had already found himself a new project and had, as far as I could tell, already stolen other items – mainly from the ladies' handbags that were lying around. It was all rather stressful, basically.

'So, in all the chaos my mum ever-so-quietly sidled up to me and said, "Brigita, I've just remembered something." "What, Mum?" I asked, a little fed up. "Stipe!" she said. "Stipe?" I repeated, confused. "Your neighbour here. Stipe, the one who came back from his swim last time." It still wasn't entirely clear to me what she meant. "Him, you know, the one who walked past, the one with the nice bottom who dries out quickly in the sun." "Oh, Stipe," I said, a little downbeat, as I didn't immediately grasp that she was on to something.'

'Now even I'm lost,' said a confused Matjaž.

'I realized that Mum had remembered about the neighbour Stipe (which at the time was you), but there was a totally real neighbour Stipe – whose name probably wasn't Stipe, but Ante or something like that – who could maybe come and help us. So I set off next door, but then Mum grabbed hold of me and offered to come with me. You can imagine the dread I felt; all the possible situations whirling around in my head for when Mum was confronted with the fact that Stipe was not Stipe. Obviously I insisted that she let me do this job, but she said it wouldn't do any harm for someone with very good Croatian to join me. I gave in, because if I put her off any more it probably would have been suspicious.

'So the two of us approached the next-door-neighbour's house and knocked. Nothing. We knocked a bit more – nothing. Then we knocked even more aggressively and finally our Stipe came to the door – well, a man of around forty, with a rather well-maintained figure, wearing nothing but his underwear.

I'd obviously just woken him up and I apologized for that, but he didn't look too annoyed and invited us inside. Just as I started explaining our wedding story, my mum jumped in. "How are you, Stipe?" He replied in Croatian, "Who's Stipe?" while I went red and said, "Mum, that's not –" Mum interrupted me and muttered, "Don't, I'd recognize that . . . that face, anywhere." She turned to "Stipe" and started again: "I've heard you dry out very quickly in the sunshine." Not a single trace of any sort of Croatian. The confused neighbour replied, in Croatian, "Sorry?" "Sun, the sun – you dry out very quickly!" Mum said hurriedly. "The sun, the sun, yes, I adore the sun!" he replied. "I can see that – the sun loves you," mum remarked poetically, and blushed. "What?" said the neighbour, not understanding that time either. I took the initiative. "My mum says that the sun loves you." He smiled in embarrassment and said, "And I love the sun."

'At that point I heard some sort of murmuring in the background and looked into the reception room, where I saw people in sleeping bags on the sofa and on the floor. Two of them had their faces covered, but the third one seemed familiar somehow. I was sure that I'd seen that hair, that nose, and those eyebrows somewhere before. "Samo!" I heard myself cry out.'

'Samo? Our Samo?' Matjaž likewise cried out.

'Correct. It was our Samo. Stipe quickly explained to me how they danced and drank, and drank and danced, and in the end everyone apart from him was flagging. He took them back to his place because none of them could find their keys to the apartment anywhere. They had a few more drinks and did a bit more dancing at his, and went to sleep as the sun was rising. "Oh, the sun!" sighed Mum, but this time Stipe and I ignored her. Anyhow, I quickly explained to our good-hearted neighbour that we'd come about a wedding emergency, and then I immediately set to work on Samo. I couldn't wake him up for love nor money. Stipe helped me poke him, beat him, everything, but he just wasn't shifting.'

'And what did you do then?'

'I resorted to my most reliable weapon.'

'You didn't!' Matjaž looked at her severely.

'I did. I screamed in his ear at the top of my voice that if he didn't get up that instant, I would stick all of the spines from every single sea urchin on this island in his eyes.'

'And?'

'Well, the story continued in a slightly calmer manner than it had done up to that point. I managed to wake Samo up, quickly get him washed and dressed, sorted his phone out and took care of the rings, as our Samo still wasn't quite on top form. And here we are!'

'It didn't all go smoothly from then on, surely.'

'Of course not,' Brigita replied with a pained voice. She took another deep sigh. 'When we were all ready, Zala and Špela included, we went back to our place and came across a chilling scene. Two groups of people yelling at each other, with the bride and groom stood in the middle cowering and holding each other's hands as if they were waiting for an impending execution.'

'What was the problem?' Matjaž asked curiously.

'It turned out that the families had separated into two groups. On one side was my dad, mum, uncle, aunt, Grandma Evridika and Eva. On the other was Borut, Zofija, Leon, Edvard and his family and Grandma Katarina. Admittedly not all of them were going wild; the parents were the main culprits, or at least some of them were, and the grandmas, too. Granny Evridika's fury, which she took turns to direct at Sonja and Lovro's parents, said it all.'

'What was the problem?'

'I'm getting to that now. Don't be so impatient. Granny Evridika was fuming, saying that the whole thing was one big fraud and that she wouldn't have come to Hvar if she'd have known that it wasn't going to be a church wedding.'

'Ah, of course that upset her. And how did it get sorted out?'

'Steady on, Matjaž. My dad then turned to Sonja and said that she had disgraced him, his family and his homeland. Zofija's remark, that Croats were also Catholics, fell on deaf ears. Dad was saying that he wasn't going to be part of this atheist conspiracy, that he was going to disown his daughter, that the whole thing was one great big fiasco and that he was going home at once.'

'Then Granny Katarina spoke up calmly, explaining that it wasn't a conspiracy and that they just had to listen to the young couple's wishes. Dad kicked off, saying that it was all Lovro's bad influence on Sonja, that she used to go to mass regularly and respect the teachings of the Church before she met him. None of this could have been further from the truth, but we'll leave that to one side.'

'This then infuriated Zofija, who said that atheism was not a disease and she wasn't going to listen to insults from anyone, and that she had no qualms about leaving the island immediately. Things got serious. Meanwhile, the boats had arrived and the boatmen were nervously watching the scene. My dad and Zofija were on the brink of beating each other up; the two grandmas got involved in the altercation over why a commitment made in front of God was more binding, or rather, why it even mattered who confirmed the marriage just as long as the couple made their vows to each other in public.

'By this time Zofija was shoving my dad, and Eva had jumped in to defend Grandma Evridika with her hypothesis on how God was just security, that God helps couples during difficult times and watches over them. Grandma Katarina went ballistic and reminded Eva that Catholic couples were also divorcing on a mass scale and asking where was their God to save them then. That's not to mention, as Edvard said, getting involved in matters, the amount of suffering that couples go through when they stay together for the sake of God. Evridka then got personal and shot back at Edvard, saying that he obviously only thought that way as a means of excusing his own sinful existence. Of course, this angered Linda, who furiously explained how Edvard's first wife had ruined everyone's life. "Isn't that right, Granny Katarina?" she added, hoping to confirm how Edvard's first marriage exemplified that it doesn't pay to stake too much on a wedding. Granny Katarina was far too caught up in bickering with Eva to even react to Linda, even though her criticism had just unintentionally discredited the institution of marriage.

'Leon had meanwhile started seducing Zala and Špela. Zala wasn't showing any real sign of interest, so Špela began to flirt with him rather intensely. Samo was constantly trying to calm one squabbling pair or another, but they didn't let him get a word in. My mum took on a similar role, which in her case involved leading an interesting non-verbal conversation with Dragica and Drago, signalling with her head and raised eyebrows while the other two replied with shrugged shoulders and glances at the clock. This bloody situation, with no end in sight, was eventually brought to a halt by the one person to whom you would not, in your wildest dreams, attribute such social talents.'

Matjaž was all ears, and so Brigita quickly continued. 'For what was probably the first time in his life, Borut put down his newspaper and stood up, which astonished everyone to such a degree that they fell silent. The atmosphere was tense, because it seemed to everyone as if they were going to hear this man speak for the first time in their lives. Borut looked around at everyone present, straightened his suit and said, "Well. Now we've all vented our feelings and so nicely called each other names and insulted one another, perhaps we can head off to the wedding location and help these two poor lovers finally ruin their lives before the eyes of family members who do not deserve them."'

'Wow!' Matjaž said, impressed. 'And? Did they listen to him?'

'Granny Evridika wanted to start up again, she was already in battle mode, but my mum intervened diplomatically. The only measure my father took against the newly installed authority was that he decided he wasn't going to travel to the island with his daughter, but with Lovro's family instead. That meant that we had to put some of Lovro's family in our boat, but compared to everything else that it was still the least of our worries.'

'And that's how it was sorted out!'

'Yeah, for the first time in my life I might be proud of myself.'

'And how come you're here, reading?'

'I needed a little bit of downtime away from it all. Things will start in about an hour. Oh yeah, you ought to be there to start taking photographs.'

'And you've got to get ready, presumably.'

'Sorry?'

'Well, that's not the dress you described to me . . .'

The shriek of terror that came from Brigita resounded across the entire island. In all the commotion she had obviously forgotten about herself. The fact that all of the others were yet to arrive at the Palmižana resort was of little consolation at the present time. Matjaž, seeing perhaps for the first time a forlorn look in her eyes, tried to galvanize her. 'No, don't listen to me! You're beautiful as you are. Maybe it's even better this way, so you don't outshine the bride.'

Brigita laughed bitterly and said, 'Thanks but please don't, being nice doesn't suit you.'

Her statement upset Matjaž. So he suggested that perhaps she ought to shift herself to the site of the event, where *deus ex machina* might solve her problem.

'I don't believe in God' was Brigita's response.

When the two of them emerged from the dense stretch of pine trees, a ceremonious view was laid out before them. Matjaž still remembered the Hvar landscape well. The venue stood on a section of the bay that was chiefly covered by olive trees. There were carved wooden tables among the trees, as if they had grown there with them. The view of the rest of the bay opened up to the right, with the stony beach below and the walled restaurant above. A view of the sea spread out to the left, the type of sea that Matjaž loved the most – boundless and infinite, and above all without people.

He looked at Brigita, who was enraptured by the entire scene and was all the calmer for it. But as they continued walking, their calm was shattered by the noisy relatives and wedding guests relaxing in the marvellously designed venue. The first to run into them were the bride and groom, now smiling – perhaps because they'd had something to drink by this point, or maybe because they'd succeeded in the superhuman feat of bringing two such families here together.

'At last!' said Sonja, hugging first her sister and then Matjaž. Lovro was also emotional on the day; he gave Brigita a kiss on the cheek and Matjaž a manly slap on the back.

'Sonja!' sobbed Brigita.

'What is it, my love?'

'Look, look at me!'

'What do you mean?' replied Sonja in high spirits, and looked at her attentively.

'This isn't the right dress!' Her sister looked her up and down one more time, as did Lovro.

'Of course it's the right one, the best one,' Sonja replied, reassuring her. In light of all the morning's disasters, she thought Brigita looked regal.

Lovro jumped in, too, as he did so well. 'Just look at me in these smart-casual chinos – things basically never turn out as people expect. I mean, I should have anticipated it, really. What with your family, my relatives and our friends, it's impossible to imagine anything other than a wedding catastrophe. Oh look, there's Samo!' He pointed to a table to his right, where the sleepy best man was propping up his head, sipping coffee and Red Bull and seriously struggling. Beside him sat Zala and Špela in a similarly wrecked state; before the trip to Hvar they would have almost certainly have imagined that they'd make a better impression on the local boys on the day of the wedding. Pallid, they sipped lemonade and espresso and hid the black rings under their eyes behind enormous sunglasses. Dialogue was not exactly lively on that table. Every so often one of them could be heard sighing 'Eugh!' or 'Hanging!' or 'Oww!'

The surroundings had clearly somewhat calmed Brigita, who decided that she would no longer worry about the unjust structure of the universe, or anything else at all.

'How are things looking now?' she asked her sister.

Lovro looked at his watch and said, 'It's eleven o'clock now, so get something to drink and to eat. Matjaž, you're welcome to take a few photos of our entourage here. They're quite nice, really. That's Leon and Eva over there by the sea – they've clearly taken a fancy to one another.' Sonja snorted loudly. 'And Linda and Anže are sitting on those rocks over there,' Lovro continued, as if he hadn't noticed Sonja's sounds of disapproval. Matjaž spotted the intriguing sight of the mother and son scuffling with one another; he couldn't tell if this dispute was a loving one or if it would end in injury for one side or the other. The more he observed the scene, the more he was convinced that the duel would not end without a considerable number of scratches. It was only a few seconds before poor Linda started to shout, 'Edvard! Edvard!'

'What is it?' her husband replied reluctantly, still playing with his phone not too far away.

'Help me!' exclaimed Linda, who clearly didn't know how to restrain her son.

'With what?' Edvard protested, frowning and preferring to lie down among the olive trees rather than restore family harmony.

Before Linda had even answered him, Grandma Katarina ran to her rescue. 'Anže! Anže!' she called, and started sticking her tongue out at the little boy. Why she made these gestures remained to be seen, but at least she succeeded in making the child let go of his mum and set himself upon his grandma.

Once again it wasn't clear to Matjaž whether he was pulling her hair with an unrefined affection or whether it was merely excitement over the fact that he was hurting his grandma. 'Gosh boy, you're so strong!' chuckled Katarina helplessly. 'Wow, you're so strong. OK, stop it now. You're hurting grandma. Listen, listen!' she pleaded with the boy, who was setting upon all the unprotected parts of his grandmother, from her hair and her ears to her nose. So much so that she soon started shouting, 'Edvard, Edvard, come here, come here. This one clearly needs a male hand.' Then she turned back to Anže saying, 'Stop darling, that's enough, darling, listen, darling, you're hurting me, darling!'

'Edvard, are you even listening? Your child is beating your mother!' yelled Linda nervously. Edvard finally got up and, looking rather irritated, started rushing towards Anže. As soon as the boy saw him he let go of his grandma and ran off. This obviously angered his father even more, as now he sprinted after the boy into the woods. Only the pine trees would know how much of a hiding Anže's backside received.

*

The gathered company of wedding guests only cast a glance at Brigita and Matjaž before quickly returning to their conversations. Evridika, however, took notice of Brigita – and the handsome young man beside her.

'Brigita! Come over here, won't you, and introduce us to your companion?'

'He's not my –' Brigita began, but Matjaž immediately silenced her by stepping towards Evridika and politely saying, 'You must be Grandma Evridika – I've heard so much about you!'

'Really? I've heard absolutely nothing about you, young sir,' she replied.

'Please, there's no need to address me so formally, it makes me very uneasy,' he said, bowing ever so slightly.

'Brigita,' Granny Evridika said sternly. 'How could you keep quiet about such a handsome and respectful young man? Stojan! Stojan!' She roared across her table to the neighbouring one and interrupted her son, who had just started to unfurl his global-conspiracy theory. Brigita had turned slightly pale.

'Not now, mum, I'm just explaining to Zofija and Katarina about how the Jews are still draining everything in this world and beyond. Same with black people, obviously, but that's another story!'

'You won't mind then if I keep this young man to myself? A very sturdy boy, just right for our Brigita,' Evridika giggled.

This obviously caught Stojan's attention. 'Which young man?' he asked, and looked suspiciously at Matjaž. 'Aaahh, there he is. Come right here, come right here, boy, let me take a look at you,' said the father with an inspecting look on his face. 'I didn't think it was true. No, really I didn't. Right here!'

Brigita, shuddering with horror, ran up to her father and said, 'Dad, Dad, this is all just one –'

Matjaž interrupted her again. 'Sir, I've heard all good things about you from Brigita,' he said, offering his hand.

'Well, that's hard to believe,' grinned Stojan. 'Why don't you just come and sit yourself down here and tell me how you two met each other.'

Again Brigita opened her mouth, but Matjaž intercepted her words. 'Ah, in a graveyard.'

'A graveyard?' Stojan asked, confused.

'Yes, a few months ago she was sitting in there and I was taking photographs, because I'm a photographer,' Matjaž said. He pointed at his camera, as if to convince her father that he knew what he was talking about.

'And then?' Stojan was curious.

'Yes, so of course your daughter didn't want me to take photos of her, but I thought she looked so beautiful next to this grave, with a book in her hand.' He only just managed to refrain from mentioning the author.

'And then?' asked Brigita's father, becoming impatient, while his daughter meanwhile looked around for someone or something to save her.

'Then we fell out, because she didn't want to be in the photographs.'

'Of course you fell out, that's our Brigita,' Stojan said, with good intentions. He lovingly patted his daughter, who was standing beside him, on the arm. 'Well, anyway. What happened then?' he asked with interest.

'Well, sir, for a long time there was nothing – only, how should I put this, the odd bit of friendly contact here and there.'

'More there,' Matjaž heard Brigita's barely audible remark, which made him slightly stumble over his words. Sonja, who had in the meantime sat down with Lovro at her father's table, came to his rescue.

'Come on, Dad, you can imagine how it went. Don't embarrass poor Matjaž. Besides, he promised to take a few pictures of us before the ceremony, so release him from your clutches!'

'Release him from my clutches? Are you mad? Anka, Anka have you heard this? Our youngest daughter brings a young man to a wedding, I've barely been introduced to him and now I'm supposed to leave him be! Honestly!' Stojan said, getting worked up.

'But Daddy, this is my wedding and I'd like to have some pictures.'

'Pft, wedding! As if this is anything of the sort. People get married every day.' Stojan said dismissively. In a slightly more affectionate tone he added, 'Now, the fact that a man loves Brigita – now that is an event!'

'Thanks, Daddy,' Brigita remarked sarcastically under her breath.

'That's enough, Stojan,' Anka finally intervened. 'Leave Matjaž to go with the bride and groom for a while. We have to go and take our seats for the ceremony anyway.' She knew her daughters well enough – and her husband even better – to understand how quickly things could escalate.

Brigita led Matjaž away by the arm and pulled him to one side. Whispering angrily, she demanded, 'What is wrong with you? What do you think you're doing?'

Matjaž didn't understand her reaction. 'What are you getting angry for? I was trying to make things easier for you. After that you can think what you like!'

'Make it easier, seriously? You have no idea how many months of nagging await me because of what you've just done. And what is going to happen when after you not a single man steps foot in his house ever again?'

'At least they'll all know who was to blame for your complete transformation,' Matjaž smiled in embarrassment. Then Sonja and Lovro approached them, and Matjaž went with them towards the woods while Brigita, clearly dissatisfied, went to join her family.

If anyone were to judge the wedding and festivities by the photographs that Matjaž took in the woods and during the ceremony, they'd likely conclude that it was a magical day full of happy people who loved one another. As much as that held true for the bride and groom, who at some point just stopped concerning themselves with difficult friends and relatives, the true picture of the event was altogether very different.

The adults held it together reasonably well during the ceremony; the women cried fairly intensely while the men – with the exception of Drago, who enjoyed a good procession – found it all a bit much. Sonja's girlfriends were still hiding behind their sunglasses and Eva kept looking at Leon while the registrar was speaking, as if trying to sense whether he was moved by the words. Leon was meanwhile looking at her admiringly, which the annoying bridesmaid took as confirmation of her suspicions. Brigita was unusually unsettled, and she didn't know where those feelings were coming from. She had never really had any particular feelings towards the institution of marriage, perhaps other than critical ones, but now she was affected by every single element.

The two grandmas sat together and provided a commentary on proceedings to one another. Katarina commended Lovro and praised Sonja's dress; the other commended Sonja and complimented Lovro on his good posture. Samo, meanwhile, was barely managing to stand up, and on a couple of occasions it seemed to Brigita as if he had to really try to stop himself from being sick. That'd be an appropriate response, she smiled to herself.

The first few moments of the ceremony were precious, as not long afterwards Anže became restless and decided that the stunning location for this ritual was actually his playground. Everyone apart from Sonja and Lovro found it difficult to concentrate on the wedding ceremony, as they tried to ignore the troublesome child who could not be restrained by his mother. Anže's father just looked on at the situation angrily and shouted alternately at his wife and son in whispers, 'Learn how to restrain that monster, will you?'

'Why don't you restrain him, he's your son, too,' Linda snapped back at him. 'Shhh!' could be heard from the assembled crowd; that is, until Eva shrieked loudly – this time Anže had crept up behind her and pinched her bottom. 'That's enough now!' roared Edvard. He tried discreetly to hunt Anže down within the crowd of wedding guests without bothering anyone, but he didn't exactly succeed.

In the meantime Anže began terrorizing the remaining targets. He pinched Špela and Zala too, stole Samo's hanky from his trouser pocket, tugged at Brigita's dress, pulled rude faces at Dragica and Drago and stuck out his tongue at his grandma. He even tried to start on the bride and groom, but the fierce stares of the registrar and the approaching figure of his father deterred him from making further mischief.

Most people heard the lovers' fateful 'I do' and the registrar's conclusion that they were now husband and wife before Edvard grabbed Anže and carried him out – something that was, of course, impossible to do without the child screeching wildly. No, none of the background or foreground activity was picked up by the camera, nor did it catch the sound of Matjaž's phone vibrating in his pocket during the culminating moment, signalling a call from Aleksander and then a subsequent curious and mildly obscene text message.

Nor did the photos capture the essence of the event after the official part of the wedding. Matjaž made a record with his camera of all the family members and friends coming to congratulate the newlyweds. The first to approach them were both pairs of parents. 'Congratulations, truly, from the heart. May fortune favour both of you!' said Anka.

'Well, fortune, or may you both know how to be patient and loving and build the best possible future for yourselves!' Zofija asserted wisely.

Stojan squeezed Lovro's hand and said, 'If God is gracious and the two of you are gracious to him, you will tread a good path, full of descendants of mine.' Then he turned to Sonja piously. 'And don't you forget about God, so he doesn't forget about you.'

'This man of yours is perhaps a sign that he's already forgotten about you,' Borut said cynically, squeezing Sonja's hand. Zofija protested furiously.

Leon hugged his brother. 'Nice one, mate! That's how it's done.' While he hugged Sonja he whispered, 'Be patient with him, he's a good guy, you know.'

'What about our gift?' his new sister-in-law mischievously asked him.

'Hm.' Leon felt awkward. 'I said to Lovro that we'd sort that out in Ljubljana. I've just had so much on recently . . .'

'It's fine, it's fine,' said Sonja. 'I'm only saying it to embarrass you.'

'Yeah right it's fine!' Brigita could be heard saying, as she came to congratulate her sister and her new husband. 'Had so much on that you didn't have time to buy a gift, did you?' she yapped.

Leon had just started smirking when Sonja jumped in. 'Brigita, it's fine. Have you never heard that it's good to be surrounded by friends and family with guilty consciences? We're going to make the most of that with Leon.'

The next moment she was hugging her sister, then bringing Lovro in, too. 'You two are, you two are . . .' she managed to say, and then could barely hide her tears.

'For you!' Brigita said, and handed them an envelope.

'What's this?' Sonja was moved.

'A weekend by the sea – I thought you'd both need a rest after this holiday,' she explained. 'What did the parents get you, by the way?' Brigita asked.

'Nothing,' said Lovro. 'I think amid today's confusion they forgot about presents.'

'Strange, very strange. I'll remind them how these things work,' Brigita muttered to herself.

Samo came over to give them a hug, squeezing Sonja first and then Lovro. The only thing he could say was, 'I'm sorry, I'm sorry!' Lovro gave him a friendly pat and then sent him to rest on a nearby bench.

The girls were next in line. 'You look so beautiful!' said Zala, trying to squeeze some life out of herself.

'Congratulations, guys!' said Špela, unable to find anything profound to say.

'What on earth happened to you two last night? You don't look yourselves at all,' Sonja asked them, half jokingly. 'Did you get on well with Samo?'

The two girls started fidgeting and making excuses about how everything was always a bit different by the sea. In the end Zala admitted that a large part of the evening was lost to them both, so they didn't actually know what they did or who they did it with. However, Špela did seem to think that their neighbour, who Brigita's mum kept calling Stipe for some unknown reason, had phoned her quite a few times.

'Yeah, what's his real name then?' Sonja asked.

'Stipe?' Zala said, giving a surly smile. A few words were also spent explaining how they'd left their gift in the apartment amid all the confusion, and expressing their deepest apologies. Sonja understood, of course, but it seemed to Brigita as if no one had taken this wedding seriously enough. She didn't get the opportunity to yell at them, though, as Drago and Dragica had already crept up to the chief couple. They'd waited very patiently to shake hands with them and give them an envelope, obviously crammed with money. 'Treat yourselves to something nice!' they said. Sonja and Lovro thanked them, and at the same time Sonja whispered in their ears that she was happy to have some normal relatives, too.

As if she'd overheard, Eva sidled up beside them, gushing, 'Oh you look so beautiful, you can't see that button at all. God, it really has been concealed well. And Lovro, such a handsome man. You can be happy you've found each other. Congratulations, really. From the heart. I'm so happy that you made up yesterday. I mean so what if Sonja's lazy, and so what if Lovro's a bit weird. If you love each other, everything works itself out, everything puts itself right. Congratulations, really.'

'And what about a gift?' Sonja smiled spitefully, with a similar agenda as she'd had with Leon.

'I thought my Dad had already sent you our family present,' said Eva, playing dumb.

'No, I haven't received it yet,' Sonja answered coldly.

'Hm, it's probably waiting for you at home,' her cousin blushed.

'What is it?' Sonja enquired.

'Hm, something wooden.'

'I hope it's not utensils,' said the bride.

'Why not – maybe it's time you learned to cook,' Eva smiled vindictively.

'Or beat things,' Sonja added, but her cousin was already heading over towards the other guests. 'That one's already getting on my nerves,' the new bride remarked.

Standing beside her sister, Brigita was also caught in the shower of all the relatives' possible wise and congratulatory remarks. She huffed rather loudly and rolled her eyes at Eva.

Grandma Evridika also got on Brigita's nerves with her speech on God's prudence and generosity, on the miracle of birth and the roles of mother and wife. No one was surprised when Sonja received as a wedding gift from this grandmother a very special lacy apron that had been passed down between women in the family for generations. However, along with the teachings according to Grandma Evridika, Lovro received a five-year subscription to *Family* magazine. 'You understand, Lovro, don't you? You know – family, you know,' the grandma winked.

Granny Katarina didn't do much better. She was full of good advice from her wedded love life, explaining that she had experimented with her sexuality quite a lot, which had come in handy because her husband was similarly open-minded and there was nothing like marriage to preserve a rich and provocative sexuality. She looked at Sonja, as if wanting her to know what her principal role as a woman was. With this in mind, she had bought Sonja a Thai sex manual, which helped a woman to satisfy her man. 'Because we also know that things can cool off sometimes,' she winked. She then placed a small bottle in Lovro's hand, which later transpired to be some sort of aphrodisiac. Sonja and Lovro could only smile sourly, and Brigita rolled her eyes with a particular fervour.

Linda, Edvard and Anže were the last to present their gifts to the newlyweds, and the most reticent of the guests. The gift was a year's gym membership – you know, health and all that – while Anže had created a doodle for the wedded couple, which his parents presented as the definitive manifestation of modern art. 'Good luck, yeah!' Edvard smirked. Linda made an ambiguous remark about children, and just before Sonja and Lovro were able to reply Anže had started pulling both parents away. This was an extremely welcome break, for which Brigita rewarded Anže by secretly pressing a Ferrero Rocher into his hand.

The giving of gifts had clearly come to an end, and the wedding guests sat down at the tables and sipped their champagne. While Matjaž skipped between the spontaneously formed groups of guests, who were now waiting for further signs of celebration, Sonja led Brigita away to a picturesque rocky inlet on the shore. 'Listen, you need to pay more attention to Matjaž, otherwise no one is going to believe you're a couple.'

'But I don't want them to believe it!' her sister said stubbornly.

'Don't be stupid!' The bride looked at her seriously.

'I'm not. He had no right to say that. No one has the right to say that, especially if it's not true,' Brigita insisted.

'I don't understand why you're so mad at him,' Sonja said, struggling to keep her temper. 'Remember how he's stood by you, by all of us, during these past few days.'

'No, he's made life more difficult. Now Dad is going to be nagging me constantly, asking why I don't bring him home. Grandma Evridika is going to start ringing me again, just like the last time she remembered I existed, when I had my appendix out. Cousin Eva is going to be keeping tabs on me and my relationship – don't you see, I'm not the kind of person that has relationships in order to please the family. I hate family and I hate relationships.'

'Yes, but this family is never going to release you from its clutches, not in any event,' Sonja smiled sympathetically. 'What I'm trying to say is, there'll never be a situation where Dad doesn't question you and humiliate you because you don't live in accordance with his standards and outlook. It's not like he's going to stop that now, it probably will get even worse, but whichever way you look at it what Matjaž did was sweet, noble even. What kind of nutter would let themselves be dragged into that kind of situation without any kind of reward or expectation?'

'Well, I don't know,' Brigita replied, still resisting.

'Be honest with me, did you get angry at Matjaž because that's what you were secretly hoping he'd do?' Her sister looked at her seriously.

'As if!' Brigita burst out. 'Even you'd like me to conform to your silly standards!'

'Don't be such a fool. If nothing else, you could at least feel a little gratitude towards Matjaž,' Sonja said, calming her down.

'Oh really? Why's that?' her sister retorted.

'How many more times! Because of how he hid in a boat, because of how he searched for me and Lovro?'

The bridesmaid thought about it quickly and said, more acceptingly, 'I know, he's not as bad as he seems.'

'No, he's not bad, and I fear he is actually very good. And if it's for no reason other than that, you have to behave more nicely towards him. For tonight at least.'

At this point, their mum appeared. 'There you are, girls! Sonja, the guests are waiting. Brigita, you mustn't leave Matjaž on his own – or even worse, with your father. He's got him cornered at this very moment.' The girls immediately jumped up and went to rescue the unfortunate photographer.

'Here you are,' Brigita said, patting Matjaž clumsily on the shoulder. He put his arm around her while he patiently listened to her father's teachings. From a conversation about the global economy, which was governed conspiratorially by the Jews, they arrived at Norway's oil reserves and then at a review of Nordic civilization, of which the only drawback was the renunciation of Catholicism. Stojan then took the topic off on a tangent and started to ruminate on love. 'Don't waste any time, get married straight away – that's my motto. Then you don't run the risk of committing any sins!' he said, and it was only then that Matjaž realized the champagne had rather gone to the father's head.

'We're going to move over to the restaurant upstairs now, Dad,' Sonja said.

'It's about time, too!' bellowed Stojan. Then, a little more quietly, he continued, 'As long as you don't sit me down next to that awful woman, what's her name, the mother, Lovro's mother, Zofija.'

'Of course, Daddy.' Sonja smiled at him.

There were photographs from the evening that were misleading in every sense, not least because judging by them you'd think it was all a rather relaxed and entertaining affair. But perhaps it was only right that the lens overlooked the wedding dramas, both minor and major.

PICTURE 1

'Eugh, breeding is a hellish thing. If anyone knows that, it's me. I had too many of them,' sighed Granny Evridika, as she munched on some tomatoes and mozzarella.

'But Granny, you only had two!' Eva interjected, obviously personally offended by her grandma's remarks.

'Two too many,' said Granny Evridika, without looking up from her food.

'I'm going to be a much more loving mother. How can you even say something like that?' Eva asked angrily.

'Because she knows what they're like,' Linda replied drily.

'It's a question of upbringing, in my opinion. Of how much time and effort you invest in the baby. Then you reap the rewards,' Eva mused.

'Are you trying to say that my, our, way of bringing children up isn't good? Have you any idea how much time, how much suffering, how many sleepless nights I've invested in this boy?' Linda erupted. 'For you to then go and spout some drivel about how I don't know how to raise a child! How about I let you have him? One, two, three, four of them! Then I'd like to hear about how lovely children are. And I can't wait for you to reap the rewards.' She smiled spitefully.

'I take it that neither of you are planning on having another one, then?' Granny Evridika asked politely.

Edvard frowned and shook his head, as if to say what a stupid question that was.

'Not in this life,' Linda replied.

'You're all exaggerating,' Eva persisted. 'Where there's a will, there's a way!'

'My dear, keep those catchphrases to yourself. You'll need them one day,' Granny Evridika said, patting her patronizingly on the shoulders. 'While we're on the topic of offspring,' she continued, addressing the embittered couple, 'where is that scoundrel of yours?'

Edvard and Linda looked at each other, looked around, looked under the table and – just in case – looked up at the sky. 'Oh my God! Oh my God! Anže!' Linda shrieked.

'Anže!' could be heard echoing across the bay. Linda stood up, as did Granny Evridika immediately after her. 'Come on, girl, I'll help you look for him.'

Linda looked at Edvard. 'I'll wait here, just in case he comes back in the meantime,' he replied. Before she could lose her temper, Granny Evridika was already dragging her away to start the search. Edvard sighed, raised his glass and looked at Eva, who smiled at him suggestively.

'And what do you do, when you're not surrounded by your lively family?'

PICTURE 2

'Sit, Matjaž, sit for a minute so I can look at the two of you together,' said Stojan, directing the photographer to his chair next to Brigita, face to face with Anka and himself. The never-to-be son-in-law forced a smile.

'Goodness me, Stojan, you're such a nuisance!' giggled Anka.

Matjaž obeyed, sat down and had something to eat. Brigita remained rather sour-faced, and observed her father to see how he was looking at her and her apparent boyfriend. 'Not bad, not bad at all,' he burst out laughing, and looked into his glass. 'It must be said: these Croats know how to make wine, ha ha!' He laughed, raising his glass and bursting out into laughter once again. Brigita rolled her eyes and looked over forlornly at Matjaž, who stroked her thigh to console her.

PICTURE 3

'Samo, Samo, Samo, such a handsome man with so little talent for the art of seduction.' Granny Katarina shook her head at her conversation partner and lit herself a cigarette.

'Granny, Samo's not actually here to seduce you,' Lovro looked at his grandma warily.

'A real seducer isn't able to help it, if you know what I mean.' Katarina winked at Samo. 'According to what he's told me, he couldn't even seduce Eva.'

'Psst!' Sonja hissed, nodding in the direction of her cousin as if to say that she might pick up on such a comment. Luckily her competitor was far too occupied with Edvard. It wasn't entirely clear to Sonja why Eva was having to look so carefully at his palm, but she had enough mysteries to unravel herself.

'Well, in any case a certain confidence, charm, lust for life is needed. When I look at you in that way, Samo, I don't see any passion, any life,' Granny Katarina went on.

'Granny, you know very well that he was running wild until the early hours of the morning, with those two ladies at least,' Lovro responded.

'Perhaps he did run wild until the early hours, as you put it, but one thing is clear: those two girls have never been ladies,' she giggled. Sonja employed her classic 'Pssst!' and nodded towards her left, where her two best friends were standing.

'Matjaž, Matjaž!' Stojan yelled from the top of the table. 'I need to ask you something!'

Matjaž, who had been walking around on the lookout for human subjects, sat down again. He looked adoringly at Brigita, then dutifully turned to Stojan. 'Yes, sir?'

'What faith do your parents belong to?' he asked.

'I'm not sure I understand the question,' said Matjaž, feigning stupidity.

'What do your mother and father believe in?'

'My mum believes in the free market, and my dad believes in destroying it,' he replied openly.

'So you're an atheist?' Stojan asked him.

'No sir, I believe in good times.'

'In what, sorry?'

'You must know Dickens, his famous introduction to A *Tale of Two Cities*: "It was the best of times, it was the worst of times . . ." I personally believe in the best. Especially now, since I've met Brigita.'

'Well, you see, that's where I'm an atheist!' Stojan burst out laughing. Anka angrily elbowed him in the ribs, making him blush slightly.

PICTURE 4

'According to what I heard, you don't have a chance!' Granny Katarina said in reply to Špela. 'You made it too obvious that you liked him.'

'I don't see what's wrong with that,' said the guest defensively. She was now feeling a little more sprightly.

'Aah, men love games, and part of the game is that they have to sense that the girl doesn't want to be conquered. They have to charm her again and again, if that's what it takes,' said the experienced grandma.

'But I don't play those games!' Špela was cross.

'No, darling, you're just not mastering them,' the granny said, vehemently brandishing her fist.

'Don't tell me that you always kept your husband in suspense!'

'Of course. May he rest in peace, poor Dani, but that one never knew where he stood with me,' the granny smiled charmingly.

'Don't exaggerate, Mum,' Zofija interrupted firmly. 'My father was a real charmer, who was rarely at home and who knew how to play the game as well as she did. If not better.'

'And what do you know? You weren't in our bed!'

'Thank God!' her daughter remarked, chewing on an enormous piece of meat.

'Don't answer me back, you know very well there's no God!' said Katarina, becoming agitated.

PICTURE 5

'God, I adore the sea! I could live here,' Zala said, glancing dreamily at Leon.

'Why don't you?' he asked provocatively.

'But how?' She looked up from her daydream to face Leon.

'A little bit of ingenuity, a little bit of courage,' replied Leon, sipping on his Malvasia.

'Since when have you been so clever?' smiled Zala alluringly.

'For a long time,' Leon smiled back at her flirtatiously.

'I don't believe you. You're a fraud,' she challenged him. Drago and Dragica, who were sitting opposite, could only look at each other in astonishment.

'Where did you get that idea from! Ask whoever you want here. I'm younger than Lovro but I live better than he does,' he boasted.

'Really? That's not what I heard about you. How could you be living the high life? What do you even do with your life?' she provoked him, while the palm of her hand rested, as if involuntarily, on her décolletage.

'Import–export,' he let out.

'Sorry?'

'Import–export.' Face of a charmer.

Her provocation, 'And what do you export?'

'Pumpkins, of course,' he looked at her seductively.

'Of course!' Zala tilted her head backwards.

'I can see you don't believe me.' Leon smoothed his hair.

'You're right, but that doesn't mean I like you any less,' she replied, and chinked glasses with him. Drago and Dragica cowered awkwardly over the table and shook their heads.

PICTURE 6

'Has anyone seen Edvard?' a desperate Linda asked Brigita and Stojan.

'No. Where could he have got to?' Anka shrugged her shoulders.

'He's probably gone looking for Anže,' the unhappy mum muttered to herself.

'And Eva clearly rushed to help him,' Brigita remarked, as she realized that her favourite cousin wasn't at the table.

'Oh I don't doubt that,' Linda snapped bitterly.

Granny Evridika turned to Borut and Zofija and said, 'Listen, the little one has gone. We've looked everywhere . . .'

'Jesus, what if he's drowned!' Zofija blurted out.

'Don't be stupid,' her mother replied, now already well acquainted with the Croatian Malvasia. 'That kid is so loud we'd sure as hell hear him if he threw himself into the sea.'

This did nothing to reassure Linda, who at this point burst into tears and had to be promptly hugged and comforted by Granny Evridika.

'Fine, then I'll go and look for that bloody rascal as well!' said Granny Katarina, getting up.

'Granny, please!' Lovro cried, despairing over the loose vocabulary of the older citizens. Anka was next to follow the grandmother's good example, and they went to search for the little terror.

Stojan clearly thought this mass departure gave him permission to increase his influence over the table. 'So then, Matjaž, sit down for a bit, you don't have to take photographs all evening – we're not that famous, you know!' His own joke sent him grinning from ear to ear.

'Stop bothering Matjaž now, Dad. Let him have a bit of a rest,' Sonja said, calming him down.

'Why have we got to look after Matjaž so much? Why is he so special? Just because he's chosen to be with our Brigita doesn't mean he's untouchable,' he bellowed.

Matjaž and Brigita were both on the verge of saying something when Lovro's cry drowned them out: 'Time to dance!' The wedding guests looked at one another, as up until this point they hadn't even realized that the venue was employing some sort of DJ, who – as if having heard the request for dancing – finally turned up the volume.

Naturally, the young newlyweds occupied the dance floor first, and then shortly afterwards began to encourage the others to join them. Drago took Dragica by the hand and led her over, and Eva and Edvard appeared in among the dancers. Leon turned to Zala to ask her to dance, and she didn't need any encouragement; Špela looked invitingly in Samo's direction, signalling that she too would like to go for a twirl, but Samo wasn't sure how to interpret her persistent gaze. Zofija intervened, telling the young man – with all the indiscretion of which she was capable – that he had to take this movement-hungry girl to the dance floor. And then, as if she'd only just realized that she was now talking to herself, she turned to her husband. She didn't have to say anything – he immediately recognized her intentions and shook his head definitively. But she remained determined. 'Well fine then. I shall find someone else to dance with.'

She looked at Stojan, who besides Borut was the only man left on her side of the table. 'Listen, Stojan. I'm not going to sit here like a pudding. Let alone stay to watch you torment your son-in-law, as he almost is. Come and spin me around!'

Stojan stared at her for a moment, as if mulling over her words, then he got up, looked at Matjaž and Brigita and said, 'Fortune favours the brave!' He walked towards Zofija, looking over at Borut. 'You don't mind, do you, if I take this young lass for a dance?'

'You spin away!' Borut remarked, and Stojan led her into the crowd of dancers.

If Matjaž and Brigita hadn't been so eager to tell each other what they thought of all this madness, they would have noticed that Cousin Eva had no rhythm. Not that this mattered to Edvard, as long as he was able to touch her behind in a fairly obvious manner. They would have seen that Samo's and Špela's awkward steps, which they were trying to pluck from memories of school dance lessons, were only surpassed in their lack of coordination by those of Drago and Dragica.

Stojan and Zofija were reasonably in step with each other, although they did have to stop every now and again to decide who was leading. Leon was a fantastic dancer and spun his dancer around in the most skilful way; as he did so, he whispered lewd remarks in Zala's ear, making her blush – not that anyone noticed. Just as no one noticed when, after three songs, they crept off to some unknown place. The newlyweds mixed dancing with caresses, and it was clear that none of what was going on around them was going to bother them any more.

At that point the grandmas, the unhappy mother and the child all returned. 'He was at the bar,' Anka explained to Borut, as if he'd ever been truly concerned about the child.

'What a waste of time,' exhaled Katarina, and she looked around confusedly at where her companions had disappeared to. She caught sight of Špela in Samo's arms and was mildly enraged. 'Oh it's like that, is it? I spend all evening with him, only for him to dance with another woman!' She had already set off towards the dancing pair when a worn-out Anka put a stop to the intervention on her way back from the dance floor. Granny Evridika calmly sat down in her previous place next to Brigita and Matjaž. 'Are you two not dancing?'

'We don't know how to,' Brigita replied, looking at her grandma innocently.

'Nonsense – that's why you've got each other,' the grandmother observed wisely.

As if she'd said something incredibly convincing, Matjaž took Brigita by the hand and they joined the others on the dance floor. When Stojan returned to the table he didn't even notice his wife; he only signalled to his mother in a childlike way, pointing at the young pair and smiling like a lunatic, so much so that Anka had to tell him to calm down again.

The young couple didn't exactly know their way around the dance floor, nor could they rival Leon and Zala – nor Špela and Samo, who had somehow found their feet. They were even less of a match for the newly-weds, and in terms of the execution of the steps they were almost, almost, a match for Drago and Dragica. But neither of them noticed. They were launching themselves around the dance floor and laughing at their lack of skill, clinging on to each other in between and affectionately poking fun at each other's dancing slip-ups. And they would likely have remained on the dance floor until morning, had it not been for the arrival of the main course.

PICTURE 7

The food reunited all those present around one table again, certain ends of which were dominated by tension. Linda was looking over at Edvard and Eva furiously, and couldn't stop herself uttering a cynical 'Thanks for helping me to find our son!' Granny Katarina was also pretending to be upset, having decided to ignore Samo. Unfortunately he didn't notice her displeasure, not even when he asked her to swap seats with him so that he could sit next to Špela. But the main family bombshell was just around the corner, and threatened to ruin the excellent grilled fish and potatoes.

It started with an innocent question put to Matjaž by Stojan, which the majority of guests didn't even hear. 'Matjaž, ever since I met you, and we all know it's not been very long, I've been trying to figure something out ... It's obvious that you're a good guy, you've clearly found your place in society, earning a living from photography. You're not ugly, I'd even say that girls find you attractive ... Basically, what I can't get my head around is how you've hooked up with a girl like our Brigita.'

'Stojan!' Anka shouted, horrified, while this hit Brigita so hard that Matjaž started to rub her back. Sonja and Lovro froze.

'Well, what do you say to that?' Stojan persisted, and neither Anka's jabs in his ribs nor Sonja's glaring could do anything to help that time.

'It's difficult to say anything to that, sir, other than that I'm honoured that she chose me,' he said seriously, looking at him straight in the eyes and then calmly carrying on chewing.

'Don't play games with me. We all know what our little Brigita is like. She might somehow look as if she knows how to behave, but as a person she's very unstable – without wishing to say hysterical – and what with all her education and her so-called progressive ideas, she hasn't got anything to show for it. Or anybody, as it were. And if she's not going to have children, as she has assured us many a time that she won't, then we might as well say that her existence on this earth was for nothing!'

Those potent words astonished the entire table. The colour drained from Brigita and Sonja's faces, and Anka stood up and left the table. Matjaž looked at Stojan coldly, put down his knife and fork and said, 'Sir, I can't begin to think what possesses a father to say such awful things about his own child ... I can, however, guarantee you that we are not going to get on well if you speak that way about the woman whom I believe is not only the most beautiful but also one of the most intelligent, principled and quick-witted women I've ever met. If you were smart, you'd do well to learn a thing or two from her!' He picked up his fork and continued eating.

Matjaž's words were followed by a bustle around the table, and at one end even clapping could be heard – no doubt coming from Zofija. Sonja's eyes filled with tears and Brigita's could not be seen, as she'd already hidden her face behind her hands during her father's outburst. Lovro commended Matjaž with a knowing look. A moment later, an avalanche of protests poured upon Stojan. Sonja chastised him, Granny Evridika scolded him, Lovro and

Samo objected, even Drago and Dragica shook their heads more intensely than usual.

'But what are you all starting on me for? I was testing him, to see if he's the right one, if he's one of us . . .' Stojan defended himself, but his words were to no avail; the sound of indignation only increased even more.

Matjaž took advantage of the confusion, putting his napkin on the table and calmly, almost solemnly, saying, 'And now, if you don't mind, I'd like to go for a walk with Brigita.' He took his sweetheart by the hand and led her away. Sonja and Lovro leaped after them and started to check if they were OK.

Likewise Anka went over to them and apologized on behalf of the family, and then hugged her daughter. 'I know it's not easy to love your parents. But don't despair!' she smiled.

Gradually the tension at the wedding table died down and with time the controversy faded into oblivion. Some remembered the evening as a night full of passion; some remembered having lost a few hours led astray by the devilish island. Others had fond memories thanks to the good fish, or the excellent wedding cake, while others still cursed the dangerously drinkable red wine or the smooth brandy. Many would remember the wild dancing long into the night, some children would recall how they drank some three or so glasses of wine when no one was paying attention and then became rowdy and boisterous and – in one case – staggered into the wedding cake. For some the evening was the beginning of love, for others the end; for some it was the continuation of a beautiful friendship, for others the end of an acquaintance. Some remembered their patience, others forgot about their impatience. Some were sad that it was all over, others were happy to put it all behind them. Some marriages were consolidated that evening, others came undone, while some remained the same as they always were. The waiters didn't see the group as anything special at all, other than the odd pretty girl – some of whom were far too debauched – and a few fathers who really couldn't handle their champagne.

But none of that mattered to Matjaž and Brigita any more, as they stumbled along the shoreline of the beautiful coast. At first they walked in silence, holding hands. Every now and again Brigita looked at him searchingly, and eventually said, 'Thank you for that. People so rarely stand up to my dad like that.'

'I wouldn't have had it any other way,' Matjaž said, at ease.

'Well, that's why I wanted to say thank you.'

'Honestly, there's no need!'

They were still holding hands in silence when Brigita said something else. There was sadness in her voice. 'And you really did play that role very well!'

'What are you talking about?' He looked at her inquisitively.

'Well, it looked as if you really meant everything you said about me,' she said, looking up dreamily at the stars.

'That's because I did, and don't you dare pretend you don't know that,' he said firmly.

Her voice was even firmer. 'Stop messing with me! We've known each other for too long, my friend!'

Matjaž instantly stood still. 'That's enough now! You can say that you don't feel anything towards me, that you don't like me and that you'll never love me, but if all the things that I've done – if the way I've behaved, if all the effort I've made – suggests that I love you, no one is going to try and tell me that I don't. Is that clear?' He had now lost his temper.

'Clear,' whispered Brigita, slowly looking up at him as he placed a long and tender kiss on her lips.

THE FINAL PICTURE

When they awoke the next day in one of the nearby rooms that they'd booked for wedding guests, the sun was shining outside – or it was as far as they could tell from the scarce but powerful rays of sunlight pushing themselves through the Venetian blinds. They had barely slept, but were somehow full of energy. Brigita, carefully concealing her nakedness with a thin sheet, was looking at him with a particular charge in her eyes. Before he had completely come round, she stroked his curls and immediately he had to put his arms around her and kiss her. The calls and texts from Aleksander would have to wait until their recipient remembered that there was a world outside that room, beyond Brigita's beautiful neck, beyond her silk-like skin, beyond her bashful smile and her eyelashes that lifted like veils to reveal the glow of her cheeks.

Communication with everyone that connected him to life before Hvar with Brigita was postponed until further notice. Now he had to let his hands loose over her shoulders, arms and hands, and to impress a stack of kisses upon her neck. She kissed him passionately, only for him to return an ardent kiss and an intense embrace. And so it was that they celebrated a new day with an unequivocal act of love, inadvertently conceived on Sonja and Lovro's wedding night on the island of Hvar.

'So, that's that then,' she said, as they sat drinking coffee and smoking on the charming terrace over a late breakfast – or an early lunch.

'I suppose it is rather,' Matjaž replied with a feigned indifference. They spent a while sitting in idle silence.

Eventually she said, 'You do know that there's a minor obstacle for you and me, right?' A smile began to tease away at the corners of her mouth.

'Really, what's that?' Matjaž enquired with ease, looking at her directly.

'Well, you do know I'm a lesbian,' Brigita replied in a serious tone, although the corners of her mouth were still rather lively.

'I know, but I'm not overly concerned about that,' he replied, unruffled.

'Seriously?' She looked at him defiantly.

'Seriously.' He looked back at her, barely managing to conceal his mischief with a neutral expression. 'No, not what you're thinking! I have gone through a year with all sorts of encounters with all kinds of women, and I have had to become the most humble slave to the fact that there are no rules for a good relationship. Every love has its own rules, which establish themselves through the fantasies or the various transgressions of every lover – both male and female, just so you don't accuse me of chauvinism again!' He fell silent for a second and then quietly added, 'And if two people find their own rules, in the end they arrive at the same point as everyone else.'

Brigita beamed, but she was still not without her critical observational zeal. 'Is that right. Where's that, then?'

Tiny laughter lines gathered at the corners of his eyes. He threw his hands vehemently in the air and affirmed, 'At the point where there's just nothing else like it!'